NORTHWEST COLLECTION

THE UNDAUNTED

ALAN HART (1890-1962), assigned female at birth, was born in Hall's Summit, Kansas, the only child of Albert and Edna Hart. After his father died when Hart was two, Hart and his mother moved to Albany, Oregon, where his mother remarried. As a child, Hart dressed and regarded himself as a boy. He attended Albany College (now Lewis & Clark), transferred to Stanford, then returned to Albany and graduated in 1912. He graduated from the University of Oregon Medical School (now Oregon Health & Science University) in 1917 with the highest honors. In medical school, Hart wore the required skirts for women but masculinized his appearance by wearing men's coats and collars. After graduating, he persuaded a doctor to perform a full hysterectomy on him, making Hart the first trans person in the United States to receive gender-affirmative surgery. Afterward, Hart cut his hair short, wore only men's clothing, and changed his name to Alan L. Hart. While living in Washington state during the Depression, Hart published four socially-conscious novels (*Doctor Mallory*, *The Undaunted*, *In The Lives of Men*, and *Dr. Finlay Sees It Through*), all medical dramas set in the Pacific Northwest. In 1948, he and his wife, Edna Ruddick, moved to Hartford, Connecticut, where Hart earned a master's degree in public health from Yale. Hart dedicated the rest of his professional life to tuberculosis research and was one of the first doctors to document how tuberculosis was transmitted and how it could be slowed by detection. Hart and his wife lived together in Connecticut until Hart's death from heart failure in 1962.

CARTER SICKELS is the author of the novel *The Prettiest Star*, published by Hub City Press, and winner of the 2021 Southern Book Prize and the Weatherford Award. *The Prettiest Star* was also selected as a Kirkus Best Book of 2020 and a Best LGBT Book of 2020 by *O Magazine*. His debut novel *The Evening Hour* (Bloomsbury 2012), an Oregon Book Award finalist and a Lambda Literary Award finalist, was adapted into a feature film that premiered at the 2020 Sundance Film Festival.

THE UNDAUNTED

ALAN HART

Foreword by
CARTER SICKELS

Portland, Oregon

ABOUT THE RESTORATION
An existing pdf of *The Undaunted* was photographed and scanned to create a new digital manuscript. Errors created in the scanning process, as well as flaws in the original pdf (missing, damaged, or blurred passages) were checked against an archival copy of *The Undaunted* held in the Watzek Library at Lewis & Clark College. The restoration is the original published version of the novel except for typographical errors in the original (which have been corrected) and minor instances of punctuation inserted for clarity.

Restoration supervisor: Dan DeWeese
Rights and permissions coordinator: Madison Rogers
Digitization process: Madeline DeWeese

SPECIAL THANKS
Hannah Crummé, Head of Special Collections, Aubrey R. Watzek Library, Lewis & Clark College; Steve Duckworth, University Archivist, Oregon Health & Science University; Aurora San Miguel, Museum of History and Industry, Seattle, Washington; Tuck Woodstock, Sylveon Consulting; Rachel Greben, Lewis & Clark College

THIS IS A NORTHWEST COLLECTION TITLE
PUBLISHED BY PROPELLER BOOKS
4325 NORTHEAST DAVIS STREET, PORTLAND, OR 97213
www.propellerbooks.com

Copyright © 1936 by Alan Hart
Foreword copyright © 2022 by Carter Sickels
All rights reserved.

Photo of Harborview Hospital courtesy Museum of History and Industry, Seattle.
Elliott Bay [ID 174275] and Third Avenue [ID 4060] photos courtesy Seattle Municipal Archives.
Photo of Alan Hart courtesy Oregon Cultural Heritage Commission.

Cover and interior design by Dan DeWeese

ISBN 978-1-95559-303-8

THE NORTHWEST COLLECTION is a series of titles that represent the rich literary history of the Pacific Northwest, published in editions featuring introductions and insights from contemporary writers.

FOREWORD

In the opening scene of *The Undaunted*, handsome, heroic Richard Cameron flirts with a young woman on a train, who guesses correctly that he is a doctor. "What gives you away is your hands," she says slyly. Cameron playfully calls her a "detective," and she cautions, "Is it ever wise to think you are safe, doctor?" Eventually, she implies, a person's secret will be exposed. The truth will be detected.

The Undaunted, published in 1936, is not directly about transgender lives or experiences, but, as the first novel published by a trans man in the United States, it's an important documentation of trans existence. The novel follows a doctor's search for a cure for pernicious anemia, a life-threatening disease in the early 1920s, and explores power struggles, hierarchies, and jealousy among doctors and medical researchers in research hospitals in Seattle and on the East Coast. It's a novel about the growing importance of medicine and medical research in the early twentieth century, but it's also a novel about masculinity and, through a potent secondary storyline, about a closeted gay man. Hart's novel asks essential questions still relevant to trans experiences today in America: How does one live fully as oneself in a hostile environment? What toll does fear, secrecy, and shame take on a person's life? What does it mean to be regarded as an outsider, to experience America from a liminal space?

I'm a trans man and novelist living in the twenty-first century in America, and I didn't know who Alan Hart was when I was invited to write this introduction. For many decades, Hart's work and documentation of his life vanished into obscurity—not a surprise, as trans and queer histories are routinely rendered invisible, distorted, or forgotten. Conservatives routinely try to depict transgender people as a recent phenomenon, but the truth is that transgender, nonbinary, and gender nonconforming people have existed across centuries and continents.

A doctor and medical researcher, Alan Hart made important contributions to X-ray detection of tuberculosis and, in the years following the Great Depression, published four socially-conscious novels, all medical dramas set in the Pacific Northwest. He was married twice, lived in the Pacific Northwest and on the East Coast, and was the first transmasculine person in the United States to receive gender-affirmative surgery.

Alan L. Hart, assigned female at birth, was born October 4, 1890, in Hall's Summit, Kansas, the only child of Albert and Edna Hart. After his father died of typhoid fever when Hart was two, Hart and his mother moved to Albany, Oregon, where his mother remarried. Hart attended Albany College (now Lewis & Clark College), transferred to Stanford, then returned to Albany and graduated in 1912. He graduated from the University of Oregon Medical School (now Oregon Health & Science University School of Medicine) in 1917 with the highest honors. Hart did well in school—he was creative, ambitious, intelligent, and active in student groups. He led the debate team in high school and college, wrote for student papers, played sports, and published editorials in defense of women's liberation and dress reform. Possessing the privileges granted to a white, educated, middle-class person, he seemed to be headed toward a successful career—to join the other female physicians who were starting to find work in the medical field.

Then, in 1917, twenty-six-year old Hart approached Doctor J. Allen Gilbert, seeking psychiatric treatment for his "phobia." At this time, the U.S. medical community overwhelmingly regarded homosexuality to be a malady, a perversion that needed to be cured, and there was little understanding about gender identity or expression. Gilbert attempted to "treat" Hart's sexuality, not his gender identity, through analysis and hypnosis, and three years later published his psychoanalytic sessions with Hart as the case study "Homosexuality and Its Treatment" in the *Journal of Mental and Nervous Disease* (1920).

As was typical for sexologists during this time, Gilbert is most interested in documenting Hart's sexual fantasies and experiences, and his romantic relationships with women—Hart had several sexual and long-term romantic relationships with women in high school and college. But what I find most interesting in the report is the revelation of Hart's proactive role in constructing his own autobiography and gender history. Hart reveals to Gilbert a long history of rejecting traditional gender roles and expectations. As a child, he was allowed to dress as a boy and play with boy's toys, and his parents seemed to be supportive. Are we surprised that parents in the late nineteenth century supported their child's gender expression? Hart performed "boys' work" around the farm, longed to cut his hair short, and from an early age "regarded [himself] as a boy" (302). As an adult in medical school, Hart followed the rules and wore the required skirts for women, but he masculinized his appearance by wearing men's coats, collars, and ties, and was often "mistaken as a man," Gilbert writes. As Hart discussed his years of unhappiness in trying to live as female, including suicide ideation, he resisted any treatment that would "ruin any chances of losing [his] general masculine psychological characteristics in exchange for any benefit that might be derived from a proper orientation… as a female sociological unit in the world of sex" (319). One day, after "long consideration," Hart came into the office and told Gilbert that he had made up his mind "to adopt male attire in conformity with [his] true nature and try to face life under conditions that might make life bearable." He asked Gilbert to perform a full hysterectomy, and Gilbert agreed.

Not all or even most trans people choose surgery or take hormones, and, despite the common linear portrayals of transitioning, for many trans people, transitioning often doesn't have a single start or end point. But for Hart and his doctor, the surgery symbolized a door: once Hart walked through it, he could live his life as a man. What did Hart—or Gilbert, for that matter—know about trans people? At the time, there would have been very little research, but both Gilbert and Hart would have put their faith in science and medical advances. Was it possible either had heard about Magnus Hirschfeld, a doctor and medical researcher in Berlin who studied gender and sexuality, advocated for trans and queer people, and educated other doctors on gender and sexuality diversity? Hirschfeld founded the Institute for Sexual Science in Berlin in 1919, a library, lecture hall, and medical clinic, but that was two years after Hart approached Gilbert.

According to Gilbert, Hart reasoned that having a hysterectomy would also benefit society, because persons with "abnormal inversions" should be sterilized. What are we to make of Hart's alleged eugenics rationale? In the early 1900s and continuing into the 1940s, the racist eugenics movement, a pseudo-scientific argument designed to uphold white supremacy and patriarchy, grew as a force in the U.S., both in academia and in mainstream popularity. Perhaps Hart actually believed this reasoning, or maybe he used this line on Gilbert because, like generations of trans people, he possessed the acumen to know how he needed to narrate his gender in order to access healthcare. I have also simplified my story to appease medical gatekeepers, and I'm not alone. Especially in the early 2000s, trans masc people knew they needed to recite medical-ready narratives, that they "felt trapped in the wrong body" or "felt like a boy since he was a child," in order to obtain a prescription for testosterone, regardless of whether this narrative actually characterized their experiences. Because of decades of hard work by trans people and activists, more available trans-affirming healthcare exists, but gatekeeping still prevents trans people from accessing affordable and comprehensive healthcare. Doctors can still withhold treatment from trans patients or require hoop-jumping in order to obtain hormones or trans-affirmative surgeries. Maybe Hart was covering all his bases. His primary point, and the one Gilbert accepted, was that this medical procedure would help him live his life as a man. Providing his medical stamp of approval, Gilbert wrote in his report, "In fact, from a sociological and psychological standpoint [Hart] is a man" (332).

After his hysterectomy, Hart cut his hair short, wore only men's clothing, and changed his name to Alan L. Hart. Although Gilbert seemed to be uncomfortable with Hart's eloping with his girlfriend Inez Stark, the doctor held Hart in high regard and approved of his decision to live his authentic life, attesting that if society would "leave [Hart] alone," he could fill his "niche" and "leave [the world] better for [his] bravery." Gilbert treated Hart with surprising empathy and respect, and did not try to commit or "cure" him.

Hart married Inez Stark, a schoolteacher from Independence, Oregon, in 1918. After he received his Oregon medical license, Hart and Stark moved to Gardiner, Oregon, a remote village on the coast where Hart planned to open a practice. However, the couple only stayed about six months. Over the next five years, Hart and Inez moved frequently, across Oregon, Washington, and rural Montana, Hart leaving jobs out of fear that he would be outed, which happened at least once. According to scholar Peter Boag, a woman Hart had gone to medical school with recognized him and told their peers and colleagues; the story even made the local newspapers under a variety of tantalizing headlines, including: "Woman Doctor Parades as Man."

Perhaps the hiding and running became too stressful. In 1923, Inez left Hart, and two years later, the couple divorced. After his divorce, Hart returned to Oregon, where he met Edna Ruddick. The couple married in New York, and Hart received a master's degree in radiology from the University of Pennsylvania in 1930. From 1922 through the 1930s, Hart held various hospital positions in Washington, Illinois, Idaho, and New Mexico. While living in Washington during the Depression years, Hart had trouble finding steady work, and turned to creative writing. Over the span of seven years, Hart published four novels: *Doctor Mallory* (1935), *The Undaunted* (1936), *In The Lives of Men* (1937), and *Dr. Finlay Sees It Through* (1942).

Hart's four novels take place in the Pacific Northwest and focus on medical research and health care, two characteristics which set his work apart from other socially-conscious fiction of the 1930s and 40s. Hart writes about idealist protagonists searching for cures or justice, evokes sympathy for outcasts, and exposes greed, arrogance, and prejudice in the medical world. The novels were reviewed positively in the *New York Times*, the *New York Herald-Tribune*, and the *Saturday Review of Literature*, among other outlets, and appealed to a mainstream audience. His fiction gave readers a look at medical and scientific advancements that would have been exciting at the time, and he was also one of the few pre-WWII authors writing about the Pacific Northwest, a region still unfamiliar and intriguing to the majority of Americans.

Hart is no prose stylist, and often draws the reader into the weeds of medical research, which can be challenging for the modern reader (at least it was for this reader). As with the majority of novels published in the early twentieth century, *The Undaunted* centers on white experiences and relies on stereotypes to describe minor Black characters. Hart's focus is not nuanced character development but heroic protagonists, plot, setting, and ideas around medicine. As medical drama and love story, *The Undaunted* caught the attention of the New York Times: "for any one interested in the development of medical science… Alan Hart's new novel will prove little less than fascinating." The critic praised both the adventurous plot and the humanity of the characters.

The novel begins with Richard Cameron taking a new job

at Safe Harbor Hospital in Seaforth, Hart's fictional name for Seattle. Hart describes Seaforth as a beautiful city overlooking the Puget Sound and doused in continuous rain and fog; Cameron jokes that he'll be "mildewed" by the rain. In addition to the descriptions of the weather and geography, Hart gives historical insight into Seattle as a developing city in the 1920s, as well as how it was regarded in the medical field, especially when compared to the established research hospitals of the East; another researcher describes Seaforth as a "raw city in a raw young state" and urges Cameron to get out, warning him that professionally it's "like dropping into a scientific vacuum" (46-47). After facing resistance from the irascible and jealous Dr. Ascot, Cameron heads east for a job at a research hospital in Northdevon, Connecticut (Hartford), where the last two thirds of the novel takes place.

Hart details the characters' physicality and clothing, especially tall, manly Cameron: "He was older, there was something bold about his nose and chin, his red hair seemed to crinkle with energy. The movements of his lean body and freckled hands were quick and deft and casual" (67). Cameron is a WWI veteran, bachelor, doctor, and all-American hero: white, masculine, heroic, and, obviously, handsome. Hart frequently describes Cameron as an adventurer and explorer who looks out for the underdog. He is alluring to women, and in one disturbing scene nearly assaults his date, "ripe for masculine domination" (66). Women are mostly dismissed as naïve or ignored until Cameron meets Judith Emerson, a librarian at the research hospital described as an intelligent woman who "had more than the average woman's intelligence and tact" (136). Hart's portrayal of Cameron reinforces and idealizes traditional masculinity, and essentialist views on gender and sexuality.

But the novel includes another storyline, one that may reveal—like the X-ray technology Hart studied—a truer story beneath the surface. That storyline belongs to Sandy Farquhar, an X-ray technician who carries a secret. In contrast to Cameron, Farquhar, a "small Scotsman" (51), is fearful and anxious, and his "existence had been a mosaic of fear and inner conflicts and outer bravado" (75?). (His last name is derived from the Scottish Gaelic fearchar, from *fear* ("man") and *car* ("beloved"). Like Hart, Farquhar moves from job to job, frequently resigning before his secret is exposed: "he had been driven from place to place, from job to job, for fifteen years because of something he could not alter any more than he could change the color of his eyes" (257). The last third of the novel—when Hart reveals Farquhar is gay—is the most riveting. Though it may be tempting to dismiss Farquhar as a stereotypically tragic queer character, writing a gay character with empathy during the early twentieth century was groundbreaking. It's likely many of Hart's readers had never encountered a queer character in a novel before, and certainly not one written about with sympathy.

Throughout the novel, Cameron is protective of Farquhar. He convinces Farquhar to leave his toxic work environment and travel east with him, and proudly watches as Farquhar goes for his doctorate in radiology and advances in his career. Hart contrasts their masculinity and blurs this with sexuality—Cameron is the straight, heroic, masculine hero, while Farquhar is the tragic queer man in a small "half a man" body. But their friendships is one of the enduring relationships in the novel, Cameron remaining sympathetic and protective of Farquhar even after he learns he is gay. Cameron cares for Farquhar and describes him as "always an outcast," but also a man who was "kind and honest and brave, he was a good doctor, he loved beautiful things, and in, spite of all that happened to him, he loved people" (263).

It would be a mistake to read Farquhar simply as a stand-in for Hart, however—not the least because Hart settled into a different kind of life. After marrying Edna and publishing four novels, Hart and Edna moved to Hartford, Connecticut in 1948, the same year Hart earned a master's degree in public health from Yale University and dedicated his professional life to tuberculosis research. Tuberculosis had no available tests or known treatment at the time, and Hart was one of the first to document how the disease was transmitted and how it could be slowed by detection. He headed mass X-ray programs in Connecticut and published several articles and a nonfiction book, *These Mysterious Rays* (1943) on X-ray technology. The cover included a black and white author photo of Hart in a tweed suit jacket, wearing thick wire-rimmed round glasses and holding a pipe. His hair is cut short and slicked to the right. He looks pensive, serious, and intelligent.

Hart and Edna lived together in Connecticut until Hart's death from heart failure in 1962. Nothing was revealed in Hart's obituary about his gender history. His ashes were scattered in Port Angeles, Washington, and in his will and testament he instructed that certain letters and photographs locked in a safety deposit box be destroyed. Even in death, Hart still asserted control and agency over his biography—perhaps trying to protect himself, and his wife, from sensationalism or misreading.

There is only one record of Hart speaking publicly about his life and transition. After Hart was outed by his classmate in 1918, reporters from the local *Albany Democrat* confronted him about his "sex change." Hart said, "I had to do it...For years I had been unhappy. With all the inclinations and desires of the boy I had to restrain myself to the more conventional ways of the other sex. I have been happier since I made this change than I ever have in my life, and will continue this way as long as I live...I have long suspected my condition, and now I know" (from Boag, p. 481). It's an incredible, affirming quote about identity and autonomy: since he began to transition, he's never been "happier," and chooses to live as a man for the rest of his life. Instead of reading Hart's story as one of manipulation or betrayal, I choose to read it as one of self-acceptance and truth. Over a hundred years ago, Hart imagined another way of living for himself. In his fiction, too, Hart argued for a kinder, more compassionate world, and as a transgender man, he lived a life of authenticity and courage.

—Carter Sickels

BIBLIOGRAPHY

Boag, Peter. "Go West Young Man, Go East Young Woman: Searching for the Trans in Western Gender History." *Western Historical Quarterly*, Winter 2005, vol. 36, no. 4, pp. 477-497

Gilbert, J. Allen. "Homo-sexuality and its Treatment," *Journal of Nervous and Mental Disease*.

Skidmore, Emily. *True Sex: The Lives of Trans Men at the Turn of the 20th Century*. New York: New York University Press, 2017.

Manion, Jen. *Female Husbands: A Trans History*. Cambridge: Cambridge University Press, 2020.

Stryker, Susan. *Transgender History*. New York: Seal Press, 2017.

Note: Biographical information on Alan Hart comes from J. Allen Gilbert's published case study *Homo-sexuality and its Treatment,* and Brian Booth's *The Life and Career of Alberta Lucille/Dr. Alan Hart with Collected Early Writings.*

THE UNDAUNTED

To E.R.H.

cui
obligatio mea maior est
quam pensare possum.

CONTENTS

BOOK I   SEAFORTH   1
BOOK II   NORTHDEVON   97
BOOK III   THE VALE OF ELAH   269

BOOK I
SEAFORTH

CHAPTER I

Quite unperturbed the girl with greenish-blue eyes looked across the table at the tall red-haired man who had followed her into the dining car and was settling his long body into the chair opposite her.

"Good morning, doctor."

As she spoke she watched the man's tapering freckled face for signs of surprise, but Richard Cameron's gray eyes did not flicker for an instant.

"So you are a . . . sleuth. I wouldn't have suspected it. So young and yet so wise!"

"Do you expect a woman to be what she seems?"

Cameron grinned. "Oh, no. Not at all. I am not that simple-minded."

While the waiter spread a fresh cloth and laid the silverware, Richard studied the girl. He had noticed her the previous morning as soon as she installed herself in the section across the aisle from his berth and, if a suddenly perverse sense of humor had not prompted him to leave the first advance to her, he would have spoken to her as soon as the train pulled west out of Minneapolis. But, although he knew that she was as conscious of him as he was of her, he did not say a word to her all day. It was only just now, when he found her ahead of him in the vestibule of the diner, that he decided to have lunch with her. His dark gray eyes lingered appreciatively on her face: instead of the coolness one might have expected from a dead-white skin and green-blue eyes and honey-colored hair, there was about her a warm sensuousness that attracted him.

"May I put your order down with mine?" he asked. "What would you like?"

"I loathe selecting food," answered the blonde young woman. "Won't you do it for me, doctor?"

Richard looked at the menu. "How about a cold lunch? It's warm today. Suppose we have cold meats and salad and iced tea—for two." He wrote busily for a moment, then put down the pencil. "And, now, will you tell me why you are calling me doctor?"

The girl laughed.

"You are obviously not a business man, and you aren't smug enough to be a lawyer. I thought perhaps you might be a teacher, but they always have an air of having been badgered half to death. The thing that really gives you away is your hands."

"My hands?" Cameron looked down at his thin, blunt-ended, freckled fingers.

"Yes. Quick and sure in their movements. A professional man who does things well with his hands—a doctor."

"I see. But how do you know I'm not an engineer? They do things with their hands too."

A faint color crept into the girl's cheek.

"Last night you took a book out of your case to bring into the diner. No engineer would read about diseases of the blood while he ate dinner."

It was Cameron's turn to laugh. "I salute you! You really are a detective. And here I thought I was safe because I'm not carrying a pill-bag."

The young woman smiled and turned to look out of the window.

"Is it ever wise to think you are safe, doctor?"

The Pacific Limited was hurling itself west through the irrigated fields of alfalfa and sugar beets that filled the valley of the Yellowstone, and now it flashed past a forlorn gray hamlet on whose small red-and-green station the word "Custer" was painted in tall white letters. The village seemed to writhe in dusty heat. As the little depot receded swiftly from sight, Cameron's mouth twitched and his long hands smoothed the napkin on his knees.

"Green meadows are a relief after the desolate country we've come through," he heard the girl saying.

"My dear young lady, these are not meadows. They are alfalfa fields. And, as you are evidently a city dweller, I will add for your information that—however nice alfalfa may be to look at—it makes poor eating, unless you're a cow."

The girl turned a startled face toward him.

"Oh, I know about alfalfa. I ought to. Believe it or not, I used to live here. I practiced in Custer, that little town we just passed."

Into the young woman's face there came a trace of amusement.

"How could you ever tear yourself away, doctor?"

"Well"—the tartness that had come into Cameron's voice died out and he grinned at the girl—"the farmers couldn't pay their doctor bills and I couldn't live on alfalfa and sugar beets. I tried it for three years but I couldn't make it work."

"You surprise me. I should have thought you more resourceful."

"It wasn't resourcefulness I lacked," retorted Richard. "It was a stomach that could digest hay.... I came out here, eight years ago, in 1914—a brand-new, fresh-laid medic—from Chicago. And when I got off the train in Custer I was thrilled. I could see in that dirty little hole a bit of the old romantic West I'd read about when I was a kid. Why, the very name of the place seemed like a memorial to hopeless gallantry."

The man's gray eyes darkened thoughtfully. Those years behind him—three in Montana, two in France, three in Northdevon University—lengthened like the glistening rails behind the

Pacific Limited. Only eight years, and yet it was as though 1914 belonged to a dead era. It was a long while since he had come to Custer to begin his first practice, it was a long while since he had left, to help make the world safe for . . . what?

Across the table the greenish-blue eyes were growing more and more interested. The girl was at the stage where men of her own early twenties seemed to her mere boys and she preferred on all counts those in their thirties.

"But you didn't stay long in Custer, surely?"

Cameron laughed shortly. "No, I went to war in 1917. Being shot is a more attractive prospect than slow starvation. And besides, there is an impression that wars are nicer, more respectable, if both sides have doctors and chaplains."

"And you were in France?"

Richard nodded. "Nearly two years."

"And after that ?"

"I've been studying, doing post-graduate work in Northdevon. So now, you see, I'm a mixture of midlander, westerner, and easterner."

"Once people have lived in the West they're never content with the East again."

"Aren't they?" Cameron smiled slightly. This young woman was more than feminine; she was female and perhaps predatory. It was time to be cautious. "But I might be the exception . . . Miss Brooks."

The chagrin he saw in her green-blue eyes he knew was genuine.

"If you wish to conceal your identity from inquisitive males, don't have your name on your luggage tags. Unless you've run off with some other woman's bags, you are Miriam Brooks and you live on Ninth Avenue in Spokane."

When he rose to follow Miriam from the dining car Richard reflected how nearly impossible it was for him to be frank with an attractive young woman. He simply couldn't say to this girl, "See here, I can't pay for your meals and my own too. It's the middle of August and I'm going to a new job where I won't get any salary before the first of next month, and I've got exactly ten dollars to my name. So I won't be seeing you tonight at dinner time."

Increasingly discontent, he excused himself and left her in her section. At every step he took toward the observation car he became more annoyed. It was time he began breaking himself of the penurious habits the last three years had instilled in him. His new job in Seaforth would pay three hundred a month. Once he got started out there, he wouldn't need to live in a back room on the top floor of some third-rate boarding house or eat in dirty restaurants on side streets or press his trousers under the mattress and wash his socks and underwear in the lavatory and festoon them to dry on a labyrinth of cords in his bedroom. Before 1919 he had never squeezed nickels, he had always spent what he had and when it was gone had done without. He scowled to himself. It was coming out of the army with a half-healed bone infection and just enough money for one year's tuition in the Graduate School of Medicine at Northdevon that had thrust economy upon him, and here he was worrying because he had a fortnight to wait for a salary check.

At the door of the little barber shop in the parlor car he paused. Damn that ten dollars! He was sick of going a month between hair-cuts. He would begin now to act as though he had plenty of money: he would have a shave and a hair-cut and he would ask Miriam Brooks to eat dinner with him tonight. After all, she was getting off the train at Spokane early in the morning and he could eat a frugal breakfast and go without lunch. Tomorrow evening he would be in Seaforth and very likely Dr. Ascot would meet him at the station and take him home for dinner and over Sunday. And there were always pawnshops in every city.

"Clippers all around, sir?" asked the barber, looking with professional interest at the thick wiry red hair that covered his customer's head like a close-fitting cap.

"No, just in the back. And I want a good close shave, too."

Richard slid down into the chair and swung one long, brown tweed-clad leg across the other. It was good to have a job again, to know there would be three hundred dollars coming in the first of every month. If he had had to go another year or two as he had the last three, he might easily have become a parsimonious creature incapable of appreciating a pretty girl when he saw one.

Idly he wondered what Miriam would think of his experiences in Custer. Should he tell her how he had turned kitchens and dining tables into surgeries and operating tables and called in neighbor women from down the road to give ether for him? Did she know how a gasoline lantern worked, and how mud froze into ruts ten inches deep in winter, and how miserably cold and wretchedly hot tar-paper shacks could be? No, he thought, a girl like this would probably find his stories of country practice revolting. She wouldn't understand that it was high adventure to get a baby safely into the world even when it wasn't wanted or to save human lives even when they weren't worth saving. Only a doctor could understand that.

Cameron's mind went back to a bitter cold night when he had done his first Caesarian operation in one of those two-room shanties that dotted the floor of the valley. There had been only the light of a gasoline lamp and no one to help him except the woman's husband and a neighbor. As the barber's fingers explored his cheeks ahead of the razor, Richard could feel spreading through him again the glowing pride in which he had stood the next morning on the tiny porch of that tar paper shack with a living mother and a living child to his credit. Tired, disheveled, spattered with blood, he had faced the reddening eastern sky as a man ought who has fought for two lives and won them both.

He wondered who was sitting in Custer today in the squat, three-room cottage that had been his office. Did his successor like driving over the gaunt benchlands and up and down the valley, sweltering in summer and stiff with cold in winter? Did he, perhaps, have better luck collecting? Did he ever stop on the crest of the ridge on his way home from Billings to look down on the great wind-made billows in the green wheat fields on the benches along the valley, and feel on his face the damp coolness of the air that swept up from the irrigated land below?

That evening Cameron could not keep his attention centered on Miriam. They talked and laughed gaily enough at dinner and later, when they strolled on the station platform at Butte, he found a dark corner where he kissed the girl with a degree of enthusiasm which she seemed to find satisfactory, but at intervals his thoughts strayed to other things. This job he was going to in Seaforth might be the first step in a new career. In it he might have a chance to show what he could do, he might even go a little way along that tempting avenue of research he had glimpsed last spring in Northdevon. But eventually he must go east again—or to Europe—to study, and get into a research institute somewhere. He had always had a lust for exploration, always felt that there were things waiting for him to discover. Hadn't Kipling once written something about men like that?

"Something hidden. Go and find it. Go and look behind the Ranges.
Something lost behind the Ranges. Lost and waiting for you. Go!"

It was after two o'clock when Richard went to sleep, and before he woke next morning the section across the aisle had been vacated.

CHAPTER II

I

In spite of the fact that one might have expected a woman to have that sixth sense called intuition which would have told her the cause of her husband's perpetual ill temper, Mrs. Ascot would have been astounded had anyone said to her that the real reason for Dr. Ascot's chronic disgruntlement was that he was disappointed. But this was the truth. Samuel Ascot was angry much of the time and sullen whenever he was not angry because he could think of nothing that had ever happened to him that was exactly what it should have been.

Although he was an only child his parents were unable to give him an expensive education. From a grubby little boy whose nose was in constant need of wiping he grew into a short tubby young man with pale brown hair and pale blue eyes and then into a short, thick-bodied man of fifty-odd who had grayish hair and a red face and a petulant, turned-down mouth. All this was entirely contrary to his imaginative picture of himself as a flat-stomached, muscular individual with piercing eyes and an aquiline nose.

But these were only a few of Fate's cruelties. When he was barely twenty-one he was driven by biological urges to marry a plump, sweet-faced, brown-eyed girl of eighteen who—perversely, it seemed to Samuel Ascot—had turned during the next thirty years into a deep-bosomed, middle-aged woman who was still sweet-faced but who walked, pitched forward by high heels, on feet too small for her weight. Dr. Ascot sometimes felt that it would have been better if he had never married at all, or—failing that—if he had chosen a woman who would have still been slim and graceful in her late forties and a better advertisement for him. Now and then he took his wife to a dinner-dance at the University Club and usually he told her afterward in their bedroom at home that his idea of a good time was not to spend an evening pushing fat women who had forgotten how to dance around over the floor. It was, he observed, too much like shoving a wheelbarrow.

Neither did Ascot approve of his children. To begin with, it was the advent of the twins, Ronald and Roberta, twelve months after his marriage, that drove him to seek a location with greater financial possibilities than the small up-state town in New York where he had grown up, and he never forgave the infants for the difficulties that attended that removal to the west. Then they grew up very independent young persons and left home before they were nineteen. Ronald refused point blank to consider studying medicine and practicing with his father; instead he had gone into advertising. Roberta had studied painting, an occupation which her father considered both silly and immoral. Neither of them had yet married and neither ever came home for more than a day or two, but they managed to get their mother down to visit them in southern California almost every winter at a season when her husband was too busy to go with her.

There was, however, a younger son who was still at home. Kenneth, a stocky, long-armed lad of sixteen, took little interest in anything except golf and the perpetual guerilla warfare he waged with his father. Vexed by the knowledge that the boy played a much better game than he, Dr. Ascot took pleasure in making his son's golf the butt of many of the excoriating tirades at which he was an expert.

Nor was it only his family that irritated him. Ascot felt that life had treated him shabbily in other ways as well. Financially, for example, he had not had his just deserts. He had come to the Puget Sound country late in 1893 after a visit to the Chicago Exposition and, with some hesitancy, located in Seaforth. Although he failed to establish a large following because, as he put it, "people haven't got sense enough to appreciate a man who tells them the truth without trying to kid them along," he made some money in real estate at the turn of the century. With part of the proceeds he went to Boston, took a few months' training, and returned to Seaforth to open a medical laboratory. Here, since he had less direct contact with patients, he was quite successful, and within a few years he secured the appointment as pathologist to the Safe Harbor Hospital. After that he made more than a good living, but he was always dissatisfied. He drove a Buick while many of the other physicians in town had Packards. He lived in a simple seven-room house and could not afford a gardener. He could take but one vacation a year while many of the men he knew went in summer to the sea or the mountains and again in winter to Arizona or southern California.

Indeed it seemed to Dr. Ascot that he could never do as he wanted. Conciliatory though she was in most things, his wife was leagued with the tailor to keep him from buying the checked suits he admired. And, although he longed above all to be a sportsman, he had got too fat to play tennis, his shooting was so poor that he had been forbidden the gun club and could get no one to hunt with him, he had a chronic sinus infection and consequently dared not swim, and his golf compared so badly with Kenneth's that he took no pleasure in it.

Next perhaps to his desire for sports, he craved male companionship. Before he came west he had had two or three boyhood chums, but after he settled in Seaforth he made no real friends among the men he knew. None of the doctors made a habit of dropping into his office late in the afternoons to exchange professional gossip, few of them called him "Sam" to his face, no one insisted on his making up a foursome at golf on his free afternoons. He was not invited to join Rotary or Kiwanis, and he was seldom put on the program at hospital staff meetings and had never been elected to office in the medical society.

Sometimes he wondered a little at the sense of isolation he felt creeping over him. He was now in his fifties and it would not be long until he and his wife would be left alone in their home. Now and then, when he allowed himself to think of it, this prospect appalled him. Not that Eleanor wasn't a fine woman, of course, but that she seemed almost a stranger. All the years he had been going to the office she had led her own separate life at home and he knew nothing, really, about her. It was not so much that he craved feminine attention, although he dreamed at times of being angled for by women who were still slender and youthful, but that he could see himself confined by age and ill health to a small house and the company of a woman for whom he had come to care very little. When he considered that there would be no one to carry on the laboratories, he was even more dismayed. For not only had Ronald declined to follow his father's profession and Kenneth announced that he intended to be a golf professional, but it seemed impossible to keep a good assistant.

Dr. Ascot had two women technicians who had been in his laboratories for six and seven years respectively and who, he felt, were thoroughly broken into his ways. So confident was he on this point that he never suspected how well these young women understood him or how skillfully they managed him. But none of the male assistants who came in a steady succession had ever stayed more than a year or two with him.

The usual thing was, first, an interchange of letters with a medical school or hospital in which Ascot detailed his needs, described himself as "a plain, blunt man with no nonsense about him" and the opening in his laboratory as "an exceptional one for a man who can deliver the goods." When the new doctor arrived, Ascot would take the man in hand, tell him where to live, show him over Safe Harbor Hospital, introduce him to the staff, tell everyone how well-trained he was, and advise him to have cards made up and to go about and call on all the doctors in person.

But sooner or later Ascot always had a change of heart. The instant any physician who sent work into the laboratories showed a disposition to accept the assistant's reports without question he became uneasy, and the moment anyone betrayed a preference for the assistant's opinion he became indignant. After that he would never lose an opportunity to berate his subordinate or to tell the other doctors that all assistants were lazy and unreliable.

Now and then, after he had discharged one of these men, he would have an uncomfortable half-hour in the night when he could see before him in the darkness the surprise and resentful fear in the assistant's eyes at hearing his own dismissal, and once or twice Ascot had a fleeting impulse to rescind his action. But he never actually did so, for he knew that he could not tolerate in his office a man who knew more than he did or was more highly thought of by the local profession.

So Featherstone, who had come to Seaforth from Boston in 1920, was obliged to leave in the spring of 1922. He was a short thick man no handsomer than Ascot himself, but so genial and kindly that everyone liked him. Although he lived in a modest boarding house he was soon riding horseback on Sunday mornings with certain of the local plutocrats who had never taken any notice of Dr. Ascot. What was worse, he played excellent golf and was promptly taken into the Seaforth Golf Club to which his employer had aspired in vain for several years. Nor did the undisguised admiration rendered him by Kenneth help his case.

At first Samuel Ascot simply envied the man, but in a few months he came to hate him, and from then on Featherstone could do nothing that was not questioned or criticized. The climax came when a local banker urged Featherstone to play for the Seaforth club in the coming Northwest tournament;

it would mean, he explained, only a few days away from the laboratory. When Ascot found this out, he called his assistant into his private office and gave him thirty days' notice of discharge. Then, upset by the recollection of Featherstone's ruddy face suddenly gone white, he went home to dinner and badgered his wife with caustic comments on a drawing of Roberta's which had appeared in a current magazine, until she burst into tears and locked herself in one of the smaller bedrooms.

A little later, when Ascot came to think more coolly of what he had done, he was sorry not that he had discharged Feather stone, but that he had not waited until fall. This hasty action was going to interfere with his vacation: even though he were able to get a new assistant by early summer, he could hardly go away on a long trip until the newcomer was broken in. Besides, he might not get a man as reliable as Featherstone or one the technicians would like so well.

With his fears realized as it came on toward midsummer with no assistant, Ascot's temper grew more and more brittle. He was not accustomed to the double burden of the work in the hospital and that in the downtown laboratory as well, and fatigue made him increasingly irritable. Overwork, he felt, was now added to the other indignities which life heaped upon his head. The technicians tactfully slid in and out of his presence like drifting shadows and Kenneth retreated to a boys' camp two weeks sooner than usual. Even after arrangements had been completed for Richard to come to Seaforth, Ascot was aggrieved because he had not found Cameron earlier and stormed about complaining of the four days it would take him to travel from Pennsylvania to the Pacific coast.

Just how she came to make such a blunder Mrs. Ascot never was sure but, looking out the window at her husband digging in the garden, she was moved to go out and suggest that they meet Dr. Cameron's train. Now Ascot had actually had it in his own mind to go and meet the man; after all, he realized, it wasn't Richard's fault that Featherstone had become impossible at an inconvenient time of the year. But the instant he heard his wife suggesting this, he changed his mind. Not only that, his whole emotional state changed as well.

From being an irascible man who had temporarily forgotten his troubles, he turned instantly into a peevish disagreeable one who had no intention of following any advice. This abrupt transformation disturbed Ascot himself not a little. Only a moment before he had been almost contented, almost happy, kneeling there on the ground with his hands in the loose soil of a flower bed. He had noticed before that he felt quieter alone in the garden than anywhere else, and that afternoon he had been quite tranquil there.

But no sooner did he hear his wife say, "Wouldn't it be nice to drive down and meet Dr. Cameron?" than he raised himself from his knees and bellowed that he had not the slightest intention of meeting the man. He was not a baby and he ought to be able to look after himself. If he couldn't, it was just too bad. What was the big idea—to run after the fellow and put notions into his head? She ought to know by this time what assistants were like, always thinking they knew more and were more important than anyone else, always wanting more money, always doing just as little work as they could get by with. He had made up his mind to do differently with this man, Cameron. There'd be no foolishness at the start, none of this bringing the fellow out to the house for dinner and all that sort of thing. He could damned well go to a hotel and look out for himself. Monday was soon enough to have another green assistant hanging around.

II

Although he was surprised that no one met him at the station Saturday evening when he arrived in Seaforth, Cameron was not at all upset. The Ascots, he supposed, had a week-end engagement they couldn't break, and that was that. But some personal planning was necessary: there were only six silver dollars in his pocket left over from the dinner with the yellow-haired girl on the train, and no salary could be expected until the first of the month. Furthermore, Saturday night was a poor time to be hunting pawnshops in a strange city.

His eyes fell upon a neatly dressed, middle-aged woman who wore a Travelers' Aid badge and he grinned to himself. There was no reason why she should not help a man; she would certainly know the cheap hotels in town and she looked a sensible, human sort of person. So, when she turned away from a flashily dressed girl who had declined assistance, Richard accosted her.

"Is it against the rules for you to help a man? I don't need protection, you understand. The only woman I talked to west of Chicago got off the train this morning at Spokane and left me flat. But I'm darn near broke and I want a cheap hotel."

Miss Baer looked up at him. She liked the frankness of his tapering freckled face and the twinkle in his gray eyes; evidently this man did not take a thin pocketbook too seriously. But he didn't look as though he'd take to the hangouts on First Avenue either. She began running over in her mind the inexpensive hotels.

"I have one stipulation," went on Cameron, still smiling. "No bugs. I met enough cooties in France to last me a lifetime."

Miss Baer realized that, according to the rules, such a speech might be considered impertinent, but fifteen years in railroad stations had taught her a great deal and she saw no impudence in the lean red-headed man standing in front of her. She smiled back at him and went on checking off Seaforth's cheaper hostelries.

"The Occidental—won't do. The Decker's no better. The Holland . . . The Gontier . . . The Primrose. That might do, I think. Its grandeur departed with the A-Y-P Exposition in 1909, but the beds are clean."

"How do I get there? . . . Thank you very much. I'll put the Travelers' Aid in my will."

Having inspected the room to which he was shown at the Primrose and found no insects, Cameron unpacked and hung up his clothes to shake out their wrinkles, then reconnoitered down the hall for a bathroom and speedily got himself into a hot tub. In clean pajamas he stretched his legs comfortably between cool sheets long enough to tuck in solidly at the foot of the bed, and had only time to reflect that he must one day advise Miss Baer to add to the list of the Primrose advantages its nine-foot sheets before he fell asleep.

When he woke in the morning, he sat up and peered through the single window in the end of his room. The Primrose Hotel, built during the Klondike gold rush, was just far enough above the waterfront to give a good outlook over the harbor, and this morning Richard looked out upon a half-moon of sparkling blue water dotted over with anchored vessels and riffled into whitecaps by a northwest wind. Like many people born and brought up inland, Cameron found open water fascinating, and although he had crossed the Atlantic twice since 1917 and had lived for three years on the eastern seaboard he scented romance in the fresh breeze that swept into his room from Hancock Bay.

Without waiting to eat, he dressed and hurried off toward the waterfront down steep sidewalks cross-ridged to prevent pedestrians skidding down at too stiff a pace. In a vague fashion he had known that Seaforth was an important port in the Alaskan and trans-Pacific trade, but he was surprised to find Puget Sound so much like the ocean. Hancock Bay, which spread before him like a huge crescent, was full of life and movement. Like a giant's fingers dock after dock stretched out from shore, and between them, edging in and out, were many blunt-ended white ferries. Here and there big freighters were tied up beside wharfs and launches dashed recklessly among these larger boats like snapping terriers among English sheep dogs. Although the piers he went into were merely noisy crowded places devoted to loading vessels with freight and passengers as rapidly as possible, Richard invested all he saw with glamor. He lingered looking at a Japanese liner with the word "Maru" in its name and then at a shorter, thicker-bodied boat loading for Alaska, until hunger drove him in search of food.

Over his hot cakes and ham and coffee he found himself half wishing he could go on north to Skagway or Nome or Juneau.

THE UNDAUNTED 17

Magic names, of magic northern towns! But after breakfast he turned instead to more immediately practical affairs. The meal he had just eaten had cost him fifty cents—"four bits," the waiter called it—and that left him five dollars and a half until his first pay-day two weeks hence. It was time to start looking for loan offices. He possessed a good gold watch of his father's, a ring or two of considerable value, and a scarf pin with a small diamond, all of which he had pawned in other crises.

Up the steep streets he climbed, hunting among shooting galleries, girl-shows, ten cent movies, and "For Men Only" establishments until he found a pawnshop that seemed promising. He wrote down the number of the place and of a restaurant nearby that looked clean and had a sign in its window—"Home Cooked Meals—35 cents"—, then bought two chocolate bars for his lunch and strolled on along a street of locked offices and stores until he came to an open grassy plot beside a large public building.

Here he sat down on a bench in the sunshine and watched pigeons pecking at the tidbits tossed to them by loafers, and listened to the idle talk around him. When he became restless he walked back down to the waterfront, where he chanced upon a sharp-bowed, two-decked passenger ferry that plied between Seaforth and Battenridge Island, five miles due west of Hancock Bay. This island he found when he arrived at its rolling shore to be much larger than he had thought when he noticed it from the city; accordingly he gave up the notion of exploring it on foot and contented himself with tramping along the beach.

Above him on the tall bluffs that lined the shore were a few neat country homes and many vacation shacks with bright flower beds about them. Five miles away across the Sound he could see Seaforth lying in the hollow of its harbor, rising tier by tier as though it were built on shelves over the hills back of the waterfront. Presently he lay down in a sheltered cove and ate his chocolate bars and loitered there with the warm sunshine on his face and the breeze ruffling his red hair.

There was something about this city with its harbor and its steep hills that he liked. It seemed more stimulating than

Chicago or Custer or Northdevon. It was the gateway to the North and to the Orient, it must be a gateway for him too.

When he was eight years old Richard had decided to be an explorer, and it was one of his boyhood's major disappointments to find that exploration was not for a lad without money or influence. Driven by an impulse he could not then understand, he studied medicine, but not until he had finished his medical course did he find out what he really wanted to do with himself. It was in the laboratory of the hospital where he interned that he found Geoffrey Kendall. For fifteen years Kendall had been trying to discover a practical way of making tissue extracts, particularly a pancreatic extract for the treatment of diabetes, and although he had not succeeded in doing this he had accomplished many other things and had made a great name for himself in his profession.

When Richard finished his internship he went to Dr. Kendall and begged for a post with him.

"I want this more than I ever wanted anything else. When I first saw what you're doing down here, I knew I had to get into research. I don't mind sleeping in that dog-house they have for the internes or wearing shrunken white duck pants or living on twenty-five dollars a month. I'll do anything to get into your laboratory."

But Kendall objected.

"You haven't got the background yet that you need for research, Cameron. You don't know enough about things outside the laboratory. I'd have been a better research man if I'd practiced medicine longer. That's the only way to learn how disease works in the human body, and it is just as important to know that as to understand how germs behave in a test tube in the incubator. There's an art to medicine as well as a science; you need to know both.

"The thing for you to do, Cameron, is to get out and learn to stand on your own feet, in the country where you can't get help whenever you get into a tough spot. Do that for five years and I'll make a place for you in the laboratory, because I think you've got the itch to find out things that makes a research man."

It was this advice that sent Richard west in 1914 to the hamlet of Custer. There, in a yellow three-room cottage, he waited for patients.

Richard B. Cameron, M.D.
Physician & Surgeon.

Each morning he polished his sign until it shone and every day he scrupulously kept office hours, but it was not until winter made the roads to the county seat impassable that more than an occasional person dropped into his office. When collections began to trickle in, he bought new books and more instruments and started to pay up his debts; by 1917 he was not only square with his creditors but had a few hundred dollars in the bank. But, more important, he still found it an adventure to set out into the country to struggle in some isolated ranch house for a human life.

To such a man America's entry into the World War seemed to offer an opportunity for adventure too great to miss. At a week's notice he left his practice and joined the base hospital being organized by his medical school, and by a stroke of what he was pleased to consider good luck he was sent to Europe that summer. In 1919 he came back—having had a good deal of experience treating the defenders of democracy for infected wounds, influenza, and venereal disease—with a chronic osteomyelitis in one ankle and just enough money for a year's tuition in the Graduate School of Medicine in Northdevon.

By a variety of expedients he stretched one year into two and two into three. Hard going and lean living made small imprint on Cameron and poverty did not dampen his ambition. Six months before, Geoffrey Kendall had written him that as soon as he finished his post-graduate training there would be a place for him in Chicago, but only a few weeks later Kendall fell dead of heart disease and his successor canceled all recent appointments in order to take assistants of his own training with him to his new position.

At the Damon Fifer Research Institute in Northdevon Richard found a temporary post as substitute for one of the younger assistants who had suddenly developed a gangrenous appendix. There he one day heard Dr. Thornton, who was head of the Laboratory of Physiology, speak regretfully of Geoffrey Kendall's death, and a little later Cameron ventured to tell him of his own earlier plan to work with Kendall. After this Thornton regarded Richard with more interest and when he heard of an opening in Seaforth he gave the younger man some sound advice.

"You'd better grab this job, Cameron. It isn't time for you to be particular yet. Any experience you get is just that much to the good. Take whatever you can find for the present. But watch for a chance to get into a teaching hospital or a big clinic or a medical school. And keep in touch with me. Even in Northdevon men do occasionally get fired or move on to bigger jobs, and now and then someone dies. Something might turn up here one day. You can't ever tell."

To Richard it had seemed a good omen that his new position was on the west coast. And now that he had reached Seaforth, he found something stirring about the place, with boats sailing out and coming back again, from everywhere. Behind the harbor rose the bluffs on which the city stood, and behind them rose the blue foothills of the Cascade Mountains. It made a man feel that he could do things.

Conscious of vigor and high hopes and a physical joy in being alive, Cameron stretched himself luxuriously in the warm sunshine and fumbled for his pipe and tobacco pouch.

III

At ten minutes to nine o'clock Monday morning Cameron walked up a long curving driveway toward a huge eight-story building of cold gray concrete on Detmar Hill. The brass name plates on either side of the entrance said "Safe Harbor Hospital."

"It may be safe enough," thought Richard as he stepped inside, "but it's a damned chilly looking place. I wonder why hospitals are built so that they look like garages, anyhow?"

The pert young woman at the information window directed him to take the elevator to the top floor and turn down the corridor to his left. The elevator operator informed him that the top floor was occupied by three departments: the surgery at one end, and the laboratory and Xray rooms at the other.

In the long central hallway Cameron paused for a moment to watch surgeons and internes in undershirts and baggy white trousers going in and out of the doctors' washroom; they were scrubbing up for operations and probably telling one another what they had just done when a patient went bad on the table. Close-capped nurses wheeled rubber-tired carts with patients covered with blankets into the operating theaters. The sharp odor of ether drifted into Richard's nostrils and recalled the day when he too had played with the idea of being a surgeon. But the muffled note of a clock somewhere striking nine jerked him back to the present, and he turned away from the surgical wing.

Down the corridor to his left he could see two brass signs swinging on opposite sides of the hallway: "Clinical Laboratory" and "Xray Department." Under the first of these Cameron turned into a small room with a white tiled floor and walls lined with narrow white shelves filled with bottles. At one end, under the windows, there was a broad black counter and at it sat a rabbit-faced nurse who looked up from her microscope when she heard the door open.

"Did you want something?" she inquired timidly.

But before Richard could answer her, pandemonium burst out in an inner room. A hoarse male voice bawled out a stream of broken words in Italian and English, a woman shrieked "I can't hold him," and a broad swarthy man in a short hospital nightshirt dashed into the room where Cameron was waiting, with a long, thin, red-rubber tube clutched in one hairy paw. Behind him ran a young woman in white who paused uncertainty at sight of Richard.

The nurse at the work bench gave a startled exclamation and let the dropping bottle of red stain which she held fall to the floor where it broke into a little pool of crimson. The man in the short nightshirt flung his stomach tube on the floor beside the puddle of dye and plunged toward the door into the corridor, but Cameron grabbed him by the arm.

"Wait a minute, big boy!" said Richard in the inaccurate Italian he had picked up in the army abroad. "What's your rush?"

Part of what he said seemed to penetrate the patient's brain: he stopped and looked up into the cool gray eyes above him. Then he pointed dramatically to the tube on the floor and spilled out another flood of rapid words.

Cameron kept his hand on the man's arm and tried to explain the situation as well as he could in a language of which he, at best, had an inadequate command.

"Listen here. You're all mixed up. The lady wasn't trying to poison you. The doctor told her to pump up what you ate this morning so he can find out if there's anything wrong with your stomach. See? She does this to lots of people. She didn't want to poison you. Nobody does. This is a hospital, Joe. Your name is Joe, isn't it?"

At these words, even though they were spoken with a queer accent, the patient ceased struggling.

"You know Italian, mister!" he cried joyfully. "You speak my name, all right. How you know?"

Richard grinned.

"Oh, I know lots of things, Joe. You'll find that out when we're better acquainted." Then he reiterated once more in the man's native tongue the reason for the stomach tube. "The lady wasn't going to poison you, Joe. She wants to help get you well again. Now you go back in there with her and do as she tells you."

At this moment Joe realized that he had on no bathrobe and, clutching the tails of the hopelessly inadequate hospital night shirt in one hand, he looked wildly about for cover.

"Where is this man's bathrobe or whatever he had on when he came down here?" demanded Cameron sharply of the rabbit-faced nurse who was staring at the two men from her stool at the laboratory bench. But before she could answer, the young woman who had followed Joe from the inner room darted back and reappeared with a gray woolen dressing gown in her hands. She helped the excited Italian put it on and then looked up inquiringly with alert, intelligent hazel eyes.

"He'll be all right now," Richard assured her. "He simply misunderstood your intentions. I expect he forgets much of his English when he gets excited, and what you told him probably didn't register.... Go along, Joe, and do what the lady tells you."

Reluctantly the man followed the young woman away, and when they had disappeared Cameron turned back to the rabbit-faced nurse.

"I'm looking for Dr. Ascot. I had word from him to be here at nine o'clock. My name is Cameron."

"Oh!" The girl's eyes became round and expectant. "Then you're the new doctor.... Well, Dr. Ascot stepped out but he'll be back in a minute or two, I guess."

She did not suggest that he sit down to wait, so Richard stood, holding his hat behind him, looking at the rows of bottles on the shelves. From the reagents he saw he decided that they probably did the simpler examinations here. He wondered whether this timid nurse was as uncertain of her work as she was of her employer's whereabouts.

Then his eyes wandered to the windows above the work bench. About the foot of Detmar Hill on which the hospital was built looped one of the long lakes that distinguish Seaforth from other cities. Beyond the lake were still other hills terraced with houses whose windows glistened in the morning sun, and over all arched the soft gray-blue sky of the Pacific coast. Even the mid-summer sunshine seemed soft and mild.

Cameron did not hear anyone come into the room but presently, seeing the nurse start and drop a pipette, he turned around and found a short, red-faced man standing behind him, glaring at him with pale blue, angry eyes.

"Dr. Ascot?" he inquired, holding out a freckled hand with long blunt fingers. "I'm Dr. Cameron. Glad to see you, sir."

But Ascot would not shake hands. "You're late," he said hotly. "The first morning! I distinctly told you in my note to be here at nine o'clock, and when I say nine I don't mean five minutes past nine. I need a man who can get to work on time, and if you don't want that kind of a job you'd better go on back to Northdevon where you came from."

The nurse cleared her throat uneasily.

"Please, doctor," she said apologetically, "he was here. But you'd gone out, so he had to wait."

"That will be enough from you," retorted Ascot. "When I need your help, young lady, I'll let you know."

Unable to take all this too seriously, Richard spoke again.

"The clock struck nine just as I walked up the hall, Dr. Ascot. So I couldn't have been more than a few seconds behind."

"Well, I want everybody here ready to go to work at nine—not walking up the hall." Ascot's face had turned purple by this time and his voice had risen to a ranting shout that reminded Richard of certain itinerant evangelists he had heard as a boy. "Now that you're here at last, get your coat off and let's see if you know anything. Lily, you give him that microscope and let him do the blood counts and sputums and you go on out and help Mary in the back room."

Having given these orders, Dr. Ascot turned his short wide back and marched away. For a minute or two Cameron stood staring after him. He was not accustomed to being spoken to in such fashion and his impulse was to put his hat on his head and walk out without a word. But the thought of the four dollars and forty-five cents remaining in his pocket kept him where he was. Even if he pawned all his personal belongings he wouldn't have enough to pay his fare back to Northdevon, and there would be nothing to live on during the weeks or months he was hunting another job.

So, straightening his mouth until it was a grim gash across his freckled face, he threw his hat on a chair and did as he was told. With swift, skillful fingers he made smears and stained slides, picked up pipettes of diluted blood and counted the red and white cells. While he worked he could hear sounds of people coming and going in the other rooms of the suite, and once or twice Ascot's voice shrilling out irate orders. But no one came into the room in which Richard was working except one man who stuck his head in the door and said, "I was just looking for Ascot, but I guess he's busy" and went on without waiting.

At eleven-thirty the young woman who had taken away the Italian reappeared.

"I want to thank you for quieting down that patient," she said. "He was so wild I couldn't do a thing with him. If it hadn't been for you he'd never have kept that tube down for an hour."

Cameron, who had been thinking that it was hardly fair to expect a girl who weighed at the most a hundred and fifteen to hold down an excited Italian weighing fifty or sixty pounds more, asked with interest whether fractionals were routine in the hospital.

The young woman shook her head. "No. But, you see, there was no free acid in the first sample I got from this man and in those cases I go ahead and do fractionals whether they've been requested or not. And it was a good thing I did this time, for there was no free acid at all any of the time."

Richard's gray eyes lit up with suppressed eagerness.

"Has he had a blood count? I wonder what his reds are like."

The girl was curious. "What's the idea ? Has acid in the stomach something to do with the blood?"

"I don't know—it may be just a coincidence. But lots of people with no gastric acid are anemic."

The young woman had been turning the pages of a large record book that lay on the work bench and now she pointed to an entry.

"Yes, here it is. Joe DiPallo. Blood count, done last Friday. Four million reds and normal hemoglobin. . . . That means a color index of . . ."

"We must get a count every week," interrupted Cameron, "and follow the man after he leaves the hospital. It takes a long time to get cases enough to prove anything. I wonder if I can persuade him to come in once a week."

The girl looked up at Richard with hazel eyes as level and straightforward as his own.

"That sort of thing you'll have to do on the quiet. Dr. Ascot wouldn't like it." Then she paused a moment. "I suppose we'll have to introduce ourselves since there's no one to do it for us. My name is Mary Compton and I'm the technician here at the hospital."

"And I'm Dr. Cameron. I'm afraid I made a mess of things my first morning, too."

"Nonsense! The beginning doesn't count. I know. I've worked here for seven years." She spoke in a soft voice which somehow seemed to reassure Richard. He began to feel that the situation might not be so bad as it seemed.

"Thanks, Miss Compton. If you've stuck it out, maybe I can too."

"But you'll remember what I told you about those blood counts, won't you?"

Cameron nodded and the girl slipped out of the room as silently and unobtrusively as she had come in the first place.

IV

At exactly ten minutes before twelve Dr. Ascot came out of his private office and entered the room where Richard was still working. It was at once apparent that he felt no need to apologize for his earlier outburst.

"I expect you think this is pretty elementary stuff you're doing," he said as genially as it was possible for him to speak, "but you'd be surprised how many men can't do a good sputum or blood count. Most of these examinations are a waste of time, of course, but the doctors order them because there's a blanket laboratory fee for every patient that comes into the house and they're afraid they won't get their money's worth if they don't ask for everything they can think of."

Ascot paused to check over the slips on which Richard had set down the results of his work, and Cameron watched him and thought about Joe DiPallo. Only three days before he had but four of the five million red blood cells to which he was entitled. Was there some connection between this mild anemia and the absence of free acid from his stomach? Was this the beginning of a more serious anemia? What would Ascot say about following the man up and making more examinations? Eying his employer's red face Richard felt that complications might readily arise in relation to the first patient he had seen in Seaforth.

For the time being Ascot's temper had blown itself out, and he was as pleasant as it was in him to be; presently he even condescended to say that he was glad to see that Cameron had found tubercle bacilli in one instance where the girls had both been searching for them unsuccessfully for two weeks.

"Afternoons you and I will spend in the downtown laboratory," he went on. "That is, unless business up here increases a lot. Mary is at the hospital all the time except when we get into a jam and have to have her help in town. Of course we could do all the work up here in the forenoon if things were managed right, but the doctors are always ordering things done in the afternoons that might just as well wait until morning.... Well, Cameron, let's go on over to the surgery. Some of the men may still be hanging around and I want you to meet as many of them as you can right away."

"Telephone, Dr. Ascot," called the timid voice of the rabbit-faced nurse from the inner office.

"Now, who the hell is calling up at noon?" exclaimed Ascot. "Some fellows seem to think a laboratory man never has any hours."

Sputtering noisily, Ascot bustled off and Richard, left alone, teetered up and down on his heels and toes and looked about him. This, come to think of it, was really a very pleasant workroom. From where he stood in the middle of the floor he could catch a glimpse of the lake at the foot of the hill and see across the water a cliff dotted as thickly with houses as a seaside rock with gulls. Never before had Cameron seen a city that leaped gulches and lakes and sprawled carelessly over bluffs, and his instinctive liking for Seaforth strengthened within him.

He could hear Ascot talking in the private office: apparently this was an important call which would consume some time.

Not wishing to invade the inner rooms of the laboratory suite, Richard opened the door into the corridor; perhaps if he knew the layout of the floor he could orient himself a little better. But when he looked out into the hall he was confronted by a surprising spectacle.

About six feet away, with his back to Cameron, stood a bulky man on thick legs spraddled truculently apart and, facing him from the doorway of the Xray department, was a short slight figure in a white coat.

"I'm sorry you feel this way, Dr. Steinberg," said the little man in a reedy voice in which Richard caught a note of fear. "I didn't mean to criticize your methods. But I can't change the report on the patient's chart."

"Well, what the hell did you write it for, in the first place?" demanded Steinberg. "Damn it all, Farquhar, who do you think you are anyhow? You can't do this to me and get away with it. I'll make you sweat for it. You'll see!"

The small man looked nervously at his burly antagonist. In his muddy brown eyes Cameron saw apprehension mixed with a queer, desperate determination.

"I wrote the report, Dr. Steinberg, because the position of that bone *is* unsatisfactory. Unless you do something about it, your patient is going to have enough shortening to leave him with a good deal of deformity and a permanent limp."

"Say, I don't need any Xray man telling me how to set broken bones. So hold your jaw, Farquhar. All you've done for the last two weeks is sit up here like a monkey and make pictures of this guy's leg and say 'The position is unsatisfactory.' Why, if he took a notion to sue me for malpractice, he couldn't ask for anything much better than these cockeyed Xray reports of yours."

"There is nothing in any of my reports that isn't true."

"True!" snorted Steinberg. "What's that got to do with it? Say, you little, shriveled-up, Scotch snipe, if you were only half a man, I'd . . ."

Over Farquhar's white face surged a tide of scarlet, he put a small thin hand to one cheek, then suddenly threw back his head and looked up at the big man.

"Don't let my size keep you from hitting me again, Dr. Steinberg. I can't very well stop you.... But I won't change that report until you've got that man's leg straight, like it ought to be."

Ready to go to Farquhar's aid if the big man should attack him, Richard watched the back of Steinberg's fat neck turn crimson, saw that the little Scotsman, despite the fear betrayed by his eyes, stood his ground without flinching. Then Cameron heard Ascot calling and quickly closed the door lest he should see what was going on in the corridor.

"Come along, now. If we don't hurry we won't catch any. body in the surgery. Besides"—self-satisfaction flooded Dr. Ascot's voice—"I have an autopsy at one o'clock, and I want to have my lunch before I go to the undertaker's. It makes me laugh when these fellows who think I'm not good enough to do their regular work come to me for special things like this. It's a case with a lot of insurance involved if we can only prove that death was due to an accident. Well, I'll go over the man with a fine tooth comb and I bet you I'll find something they can collect double indemnity for."

"I'll bet you will, too," thought Richard, observing the craftiness in Ascot's face.

"Get your hat and come out this way. It's shorter." Talking volubly and with evident pleasure of the post-mortem that awaited him within the hour, Ascot marshaled his assistant into the hall and started toward the surgical wing.

Over one shoulder Cameron stole a glance back along the corridor, and then grinned a little. Greatly to his relief, Farquhar was nowhere to be seen and Steinberg was waddling off with an air of discomfiture.

"I suppose I ought to've taken you over to meet our Xray man this morning," Ascot was saying. "He's right across the hall. But that can wait. Farquhar's a light-weight. I wouldn't give him house-room myself. No more guts than a rabbit except now and then when he loses his head entirely. A lot of the men here in town haven't any use for him either. He thinks he knows so damned much."

Richard looked down with an expressionless face at his choleric employer. He was sure that he already knew more about Farquhar than Ascot did, and he was equally sure that in the Scotsman's slight body there lived a man bigger than Steinberg.

V

There were many elements in the dislike Samuel Ascot soon conceived for Richard Cameron. One of them was really a rudimentary jealousy. Before her marriage his wife had once kept company with a young man who had auburn hair, and when Ascot caught sight of Richard's thick red hair, that just missed being curly as well, he experienced a sort of emotional upheaval.

Then, in his dreams, he had always made himself a lean, muscular individual with an aquiline nose, and when he saw that his new assistant was but an inch short of six feet and had a jutting nose and a narrow head with small, close-set ears he was envious.

Most annoying of all, perhaps, was the fact that Richard wore the sort of clothes Ascot longed to wear but was forbidden by wife and tailor. His first morning Cameron had gone to the hospital in a suit of brown homespun flecked with threads of orange and red, and a tie of the plaid to which his Scottish forebears entitled him, and a soft brown hat stuck carelessly on one side of his head. In him Ascot saw at once a man built after the physical pattern he most admired and dressed as he would never be allowed to dress.

Vaguely realizing that this dislike was irrational, he made feeble efforts to conceal it and even to banish it from his own mind. He took Richard to call on the doctors who sent him the most work; he presented him with a reprint of the only scientific article that had ever appeared under the name of Samuel Ascot, M.D.; he told his wife that he thought they ought to take Cameron out in the car and help him find a good place to live.

"He's a bright fellow, Eleanor. It'll be perfectly safe to leave him in charge by the first of September. I need a good vacation and I'm going to have one. I don't think we'll even start back before October."

From this announcement Mrs. Ascot recognized that, for the time being, her husband's whole existence was centered on his long-anticipated trip into the Jackson Hole country. Patients, laboratories, collections, and new assistants were temporarily banished from his consciousness. Until the moment when they drove out of Seaforth with their car packed full of camping and hunting gear, bound for a certain widely advertised dude ranch in Wyoming, he would think of nothing else. It was at times like this that she realized how far her Sam—thick body, gray hair, and loud voice notwithstanding—was from ever growing up into anything more than a spoiled, irascible child.

CHAPTER III

I

On a rainy Saturday forenoon the next winter Richard Cameron was striding across the campus of the State University toward the imposing new Gothic building that housed the biological sciences. Sometimes he wondered whether he would ever get used to Pacific coast winters, but today despite the gray sky and the water that dripped steadily off the downturned brim of his hat, he felt his spirits rising; the friendly note he had had from Professor Carey of the Bacteriological Department seemed to promise better prospects for the future.

Autumn in Seaforth had been beautiful—cool, with bright skies and soft, smoke-scented air—but in November rain and fog and wind had appeared and in February they were still here. Fog, moisture-laden winds from the sea, and rain—endless rain, it seemed to him. Once there had been a skiff of snow but it lasted only a day or two and was damp and sloppy all the while. Up in the mountains, of course—at Snoqualmie Pass and Mt. Baker and in Rainier Park—there was snow, eight to twenty feet of it, but Cameron had no time for pleasure trips to the mountains.

All fall Dr. Ascot had gone to a football game every Saturday afternoon, and on Sundays unless the course was too muddy he played golf on the municipal links. After snow fell in the uplands he spent almost every week-end at some of the resorts devoted to winter sports. And now he had gone to Detroit for the annual meeting of the American Association of Pathologists, expecting to be away from Seaforth for almost a month. This made it necessary for Richard to be on emergency call Sundays and weekdays alike; when he went to a movie he left his name at the box office and if he drove out into the country in the roadster he had bought he stopped every few miles and phoned to the hospital to see if he was needed.

This concentration on what was after all mostly routine work, combined with cloudy weather and constant rain, had made him edgy. He said one morning to Mary Compton that he expected any day to find himself mildewed. "I don't mind any reasonable amount of rain, you understand, but I would be glad to see the sun once or twice between October and April!"

But Mary had laughed and looked at him with understanding hazel eyes.

"Now, Dr. Cameron, don't let the climate get you down. I hated Seaforth too, the first winter I was here, and now I love it. I wouldn't go back to Minnesota for anything. That is, unless..."

She did not finish the sentence but Richard knew what she meant. Unless Ascot fired her. That possibility stared everyone who worked for him in the face, no matter how long they might have been in the laboratory, for there was no predicting the man's moods. Sometimes he was genial and even Mary, who had worked for him for seven years and ought to have known better, thought his disposition might have changed. And then some trifling thing—a phone call, perhaps, or something someone said about Kenneth's golf or an insignificant error in a calculation—would set him off and he would scold and shout at everyone all day. As a result an air of tense expectancy pervaded both the hospital laboratory and the downtown office.

In midwinter a wave of respiratory infections filled the hospital and made so much extra work that Cameron had to spend most of his time there. He enjoyed working with Mary Compton. She was a cheerful young woman of twenty-eight with dark hair, red lips, and hazel eyes, small-boned and finely built, and very good at her job. She had trained in Minneapolis and come to Seaforth in answer to a want ad in the Journal of the American Medical Association.

"I hadn't enough money to pay my way home," she confessed to Richard one day. "So I stuck it out. And now I've been here almost seven years; I'm sort of a fixture, like the laboratory sink."

She laughed when she said this and Cameron knew that she meant to convey to him that if he could only manage the first few months things might be better later on. He still doubted whether this was true but nevertheless he hurried on toward Jackson Hall.

At the entrance to the building he paused to let the rush of students sweep by; boys and girls in sodden cloth hats and dripping slickers swarmed in and somewhat drier ones came out. Richard looked at them with more interest than they at him. The memory that it was nearly fourteen years since he had been graduated from college made him feel much older than when he came up the steps an instant before. Most of the faces he saw seemed thoughtless and immature, but now and then there was one with harder lines and cynical eyes: some fellow who had been in the service, probably, and come back to take his degree.

When Cameron made his way to the Department of Bacteriology on the fourth floor, he was shown into a cubbyhole of an office crowded with bookcases where he found Professor Carey, the head of the department. Carey was a kind-faced, soft-voiced man of fifty-five or six, with thinning hair and short-sighted eyes behind thick spectacles. He shook hands with his caller cordially and asked him to sit down.

The interview was interrupted more than once. Richard had hardly finished telling Carey how thought-provoking had been his paper presented the previous week to the Prince County Medical Society, when the telephone rang. After that, at intervals Carey was obliged to excuse himself to speak to an assistant, to give instructions to a typist, to sign papers brought in by his secretary. Between interruptions Cameron attempted to say that he had come to ask advice and help with a scientific problem.

"I have a hunch about something, but so far it's just a hunch, with very little to back it up. But after I heard your paper I began to wonder whether we couldn't collaborate on some experiments and clear the thing up."

Dr. Carey smiled a little wearily.

"I try to keep a little research going here. What did you have in mind?"

"Well, last spring I worked in Fifer Institute in Northdevon for a while, and in the library there I came upon some translations of papers written about ten years ago by two Italians, Pirera and Castellino. They had used meat—liver particularly—in experimental anemia in animals with great success. After that I went through the literature on anemia as well as I could in my spare time and found that some men in this country had treated pernicious anemia with a diet of eggs, meat, and milk. Mosenthal and one or two others reported encouraging results from forced over-feeding in this disease.

"Then I ran into an article about the blood chemistry in anemia: all the patients seem to have low blood protein. And I found a paper in the Journal of Physiology by some men who'd been studying experimental anemia in dogs: they said that a meat diet did more to bring these animals' blood back to normal than anything else they tried."

Carey was interested at once and made a note of the references Richard gave him so that he might read these articles for himself.

"Then a funny thing happened here, Dr. Carey. The first day I was at Safe Harbor Hospital, I ran into a big fellow, the picture of health, who proved to have a mild anemia and no free hydrochloric acid in his stomach contents. I've been following him ever since. I won't bore you with details, but the fact is that this man has developed pernicious anemia. Couldn't you and I do some experimental work that would either confirm or disprove the effect of a meat diet on anemia in animals? Then, if it worked in the laboratory, I'd try it on this man and see what happened."

"Will you come with me, please?" asked Carey. His face, it seemed to Richard, had lost all its animation.

Cameron followed the older man down a long corridor that ran the full length of the floor, into students' laboratories with work benches and Bunsen burners, into lecture rooms with demonstration tables and blackboards, and into small seminar rooms.

"If appropriations are increased next year," said Carey wistfully, "I hope we can fit up separate quarters for the staff and our graduate students. As it is, the undergraduates have access to everything and many valuable cultures are spoiled or lost."

Last of all, he took Cameron through a door marked "Animals" into a room crowded with cages of white rats. Opening from it on one side was a similar room for rabbits and on the other side one for guinea pigs. All were warm and dry and well-lighted, but all were so crowded that there was barely room to walk between the rows of cages.

"This is all the space we have for animals, Dr. Cameron. It is hardly enough for the routine teaching. What little research I do has to be done at home, for the most part. I have a small place just outside the city limits and I keep some animals of my own out there."

"You mean that you have nothing more than this to work with?"

To Cameron's astonished question Carey nodded sadly. "I know how it must look to you, coming from Fifer Institute. But for us this represents a substantial advance in the last four or five years. Until then we were crowded into half of a single floor in one of the oldest buildings on the campus, and we had to keep our animals in the students' laboratory. If some boy brought in a stray cat we thought we were in luck. Now, you see, we have the whole floor here in this new building. Oh, things are distinctly better than they were."

When they returned to the private office, Carey motioned Richard to sit down again.

"I wish I could offer you space and equipment, doctor. I think there may be something valuable in this idea of yours. But I simply haven't the room or the facilities for the sort of work you'd have to do."

"But," exclaimed Cameron, "why do they starve research this way? This is a big school and a rich one—at least it's supposed to be. They have a big campus and fine buildings, much better, many of them, than the ones at Northdevon. Then, why don't they give you a decent laboratory?"

Carey smiled a little. He had seen other energetic young men, newcomers, similarly perplexed.

"Seaforth, Dr. Cameron, is a raw city in a raw young state. There is as yet little cultural background out here in the far Northwest. That takes many years of living and dying to accumulate. Our buildings which visitors always admire are paid for by the income the University gets from certain valuable city property it owns. By law that fund must be used for building purposes.

"But maintenance and operating expenses are met out of appropriations made by the state legislature. Who was it said 'Democracy is the best form of bad government'? I think he must have had in mind the way our president must go to the state capital every two years and fish out of the muddy waters of politics whatever he can get for the University. Once we had a president who worked out an honest budget, and the legislature cut it down so that all departments were on short rations. A wise president takes a padded budget, several influential bankers, and plenty of whiskey with him to the capital. Then, if he's lucky, he brings back enough for us to muddle through with."

Carey's voice, which had gradually risen while he spoke, fell again to its original soft pitch; there was something in it that seemed even sadder to Richard than the man's brown eyes.

"I'm lucky, Dr. Cameron, to have this much space and equipment. It's taken me ten years, more than ten years, to get them. And I resent having to concentrate on things of this sort. One of our graduate students—a brilliant chap of Swedish descent—went to Stockholm to study last fall. At Christmas he wrote me that, although he was homesick, it was good to be where books and men got more emphasis than buildings."

Suddenly Carey leaned forward and looked sharply at Richard.

"May I ask you a personal question? . . . Are you married?"

"No. Not even about to be."

"Then don't stay here. If you want to do research, get away from here before you're paralyzed by having a family. Believe me, I'm giving you good advice. Coming out here from the East is like dropping into a scientific vacuum. There are none of the stimulating contacts with great men and coming men that one gets in Chicago or Boston or Northdevon or the other centers of research. There's nothing to prod a man on, keep his curiosity alive."

Carey stared at Richard, his brown eyes opaque with feeling.

"I've watched other young men who came here ambitious and full of energy. At first they try to keep up with things, but after a while they marry and build homes. Then children come and they settle down to support and educate a family. They read one journal or none at all; they stay in their offices in order not to miss a patient instead of reading in the library. If they listen to a paper on a basic science, like the one I gave last week, they complain that it isn't practical, or go to sleep. They don't study, they don't think, they're slaves to their practices. Whether they once had it in them to be scholars or not, they turn into drudges who never add anything to the world's store of knowledge."

While he said these things Professor Carey talked in a tense hurried torrent of words, but now he seemed to feel suddenly that he had said too much.

"Perhaps I'm getting garrulous, Dr. Cameron, and addicted to giving unnecessary advice. Forgive my outburst. Things probably aren't nearly as bad as they seem to me."

Then with the old gentleness in his voice he assured Richard that he was welcome in the department and its library at any time. "I have a good many files of foreign journals at home, too. You must feel free to use them whenever you like. I wish I could take you in, give you space and animals to work with, but . . ."

Presently Cameron took himself off. Thoughtfully he made his way through the throng of students streaming off the campus, bound for home, for boarding houses, for fraternity row, for the movies, anywhere, to escape what they were pleased to regard as the tedium of their daily lives. When he reached the avenue and climbed into his roadster and buttoned the storm curtains after him, he sat there for some time thinking.

He had just been talking with a man who considered his own life a failure, who felt he had accomplished none of the things he had once dreamed of doing, who saw in the future only the emptiness of half-achievement. The sincerity of Carey's attitude Richard found disquieting, but this outlook was incompatible with his own adventurous spirit. He could not help feeling that a man need not allow his environment to stifle him, that a strong enough man could wring out of life what he wanted.

Shaking off the depression brought upon him by Carey's portrait of the scientist as a failure, Richard filled and lighted his pipe and started his engine. "That sort of thing," he muttered to himself as he shifted his gears, "is not going to happen to me. I'll do what I set out to do, in spite of Seaforth and Sam Ascot and anything else that gets in my way."

II

Cameron went straight to the laboratory at the hospital. It did not weigh upon his conscience that he had stolen time to call on Carey while he was in charge during Ascot's absence, but something was brewing in his mind. Since it was Saturday he feared that Mary Compton might have gone before he returned, but when he went into the back room he found her still there.

"Oh, hello!" he said, relieved at sight of her. "I thought you might have gone before this. Would you mind taking another blood count on Joe before you leave?"

"Dr. Steinberg's Joe?"

"Yes. . . . If you're not in too much of a hurry."

Mary went at once to a drawer from which she took a small tray with little bottles of solution and tiny pipettes.

"I'm not in a hurry and I don't mind doing the count. But—I wonder if it's wise to make so many with Steinberg knowing nothing about it."

Cameron laughed. "I'm not afraid of Steinberg, if that's what you mean," he said.

Mary Compton shrugged her small shoulders. "Well, that's all right then. Only I'm glad it's you—not I—he'll be getting after."

Left behind, Cameron sat down on a high stool and stared out of the windows at the lake circling the foot of the hill on which the hospital stood. It had once been a beautiful body of water with densely wooded banks, but now there were gas plants and lumber yards and littered docks and marine filling stations strung along the near shore, and in the middle of the lake lay row after row of wooden Shipping Board vessels built in war time and abandoned to rot or be sold to the highest bidder. Beyond the fringe of dingy frame houses that bordered the farther shore he could see the University campus with its maples and clumps of hazel brush and buildings of many sizes, styles, and colors. He eyed the institution with distaste—a university that starved science departments!—and frowned. If he must, he could work out his problem alone. Perhaps that would be the best way, after all.

At the sound of a door opening he turned around. Farquhar, the Xray man from across the hall, put his head into the room.

"Hello, Sandy. I thought all good roentgenologists quit work promptly at noon on Saturday and went out to play in the sunshine and take care of their bone marrow."

Farquhar had on hat and raincoat but he came across to stand beside Richard and look down through the rain at the lake.

"And where would you suggest I go this Saturday to find

sunshine? California or Florida? For all the ultraviolet we get here between October and May we might as well be north of the Arctic circle. And what are you doing for your health? Admiring the fountainhead of learning in the middle distance or the works of the cost-plus ship-building industry in the foreground?"

The caustic comments Farquhar had begun to make as their acquaintance progressed were one of the reasons Cameron had grown to like him more and more.

"No, Sandy. As a matter of fact I wasn't thinking about either. Let me ask you a question. How would you go about getting some dogs and finding the money to feed them and get a place to keep them?"

"I wouldn't," replied Farquhar drily. "I won't want any dogs." He paused a moment and then said, "Are you still fussing around about that research business? If you are, you might as well forget it. Ascot wouldn't stand for it. He'd hit the ceiling if he found you trying to do something on the side."

"Then he'll just have to hit it, Sandy. I've got a hunch so strong that I've got to run it down and find out whether it's right or wrong. It's just a question of finding a way to do it without much money or time."

Farquhar lifted his eyebrows in a gesture of resignation. "Yes, that's all. When you find the answer I hope you'll pass it on to me. It might come in handy some time. . . . But why should I worry about you? It's no skin off my back what you do. Only, if it's not too much to ask, precisely where do dogs come in?"

"I want to confirm or disprove the findings of some fellows in California and two Italians back in 1911, about meat feeding in anemia. I told you something about it once before, don't you remember? We weren't as busy as usual this morning and so I ran out to the University to see Professor Carey, but . . ."

Farquhar held up a thin hand after the fashion of a traffic cop.

"I know the rest. Don't bother telling me. I had a brother who attended that institution of so-called learning back in 1905 or thereabouts. The boys all called Carey 'Pop' then, though he couldn't have been over forty. The trouble with him has always been that he's a gentleman. That's fatal for the head of a department in the State University. Carey could never get anything on anyone who was close to the purse strings, and he wore himself out trying to get what he needed some other way. Of course, he couldn't do it, and he's been tired and discouraged ever since. There's no money, there's no room, there are no animals, and what can he do about it?"

The small Scotsman took out a cigarette and lighted it, then stared thoughtfully at the burned match between his fingers.

"But why should that surprise us, Cameron? Why should a board of regents care about research? Why should they care about anything except buildings? Look at that barn of a library on the campus! And there aren't enough books to go around the classes. Would the regents give Millikan or Frederick Soddy a job? Not they—unless brothers Millikan and Soddy could guarantee to develop something practical, something like a new building material that could be made for next to nothing and sold for more than anything else on the market. Don't you know that the president of the regents is the head of the most prosperous contracting firm in the state? I wouldn't be surprised if he makes filling for the heads of new faculty men before he hires them. But no matter. You found out you can't get anything at the University. So what?"

Cameron laughed; Farquhar's biting comments always amused him. "That's exactly where I was when you came busting in here just now. What do I use for money? How do I conceal my nefarious activities from my employer? Where can I keep my dogs?"

"And if you hold down this job too—when do you sleep?"

Richard flipped a hand impatiently.

"Oh, hell! I don't care whether I sleep or not if I can settle this thing."

Rapid footsteps came to the inner door and paused there.

"Dr. Cameron, I just saw Dr. Steinberg. He says he's coming up here to tell you what he thinks of you, and he's very angry."

"Then you didn't get the count on Joe this afternoon?"

"Oh, yes, I did." Mary Compton's voice was as demure as

her face but both seemed to ripple with suppressed laughter. "I heard him talking in the next room and I hurried. But I thought I ought to warn you. He'll be here before long."

"Thanks for the tip, Miss Compton. And now if you'll just run the reds and the hemoglobin, that'll be all I need."

When Mary had gone back to her count, Cameron turned to Farquhar, who was looking at him with worried, apprehensive eyes.

"Here's a case that 'gets' me, Sandy. Joe is a patient of Steinberg's. He was in for stomach analysis the day I came. It turned out that he had a mild anemia and no free acid in his stomach. Well, I got a hunch that he might be developing pernicious anemia, and so I got him to come and see me once in a while, just to keep tab on him. You see, Joe's an Italian and he feels friendly to me because I talk Italian a little. And last month he showed up with a sore tongue."

"Ah!" exclaimed Farquhar.

"So you see daylight through the ladder, too? Well, I hardly knew what to do then, but finally I made Joe promise to go back to Steinberg. And the next thing I knew he was back in the hospital to have his teeth out, on account of the sore tongue. Of course I had to tip him off not to let them pull his teeth, and Steinberg got sore at Joe for being stubborn. He still didn't realize what made the sore mouth, so last night I put a note on Joe's chart suggesting that the blood counts done here might have some significance and that the man might have pernicious anemia. That's why he jumped on Miss Compton just now. He doesn't relish having a man tell him what's wrong with his patient."

Farquhar's face twitched: Steinberg had roared at him more than once and the recollection was unpleasant.

"I don't mean to butt in," he said hesitantly. "But Steinberg's a bad man to have a fuss with." It was on the tip of his tongue to tell Richard about the scene he had had with the bully a few months before over a poorly set fracture, but he thought better of it. "Can't you be more careful?" he concluded lamely.

"Until today I haven't said a word about any of this except to

Joe himself, and I swore him to secrecy. But I had to follow the fellow up; he might be the case that will prove the connection between the stomach anacidity and the anemia. Those two things are hooked up somehow, I'm sure. And I'm going to find out how."

Mary Compton, dressed for the street and ready to leave the laboratory, came into the room quietly and handed Richard a piece of paper. He glanced at it eagerly and then thrust it at Farquhar.

"Look here, Sandy. The man's count is steadily going down. Lower today than ever, color index crawling up, and the red cells gone haywire. Yesterday Joe told me his hands and feet felt tingly and numb. I tell you he's developed pernicious anemia right under my eyes."

Farquhar looked uneasily at Cameron; he had a feeling that something unpleasant was about to happen and he wanted to get away. But there seemed no way to leave while Richard was striding up and down the floor, running his fingers through his stiff red hair and talking.

"Now, you see, Sandy, if I could only figure out a way to ..."

"You won't need to figure out anything," interrupted a bull voice from the door into the main corridor, "not when I get through with you."

Farquhar started and looked around with quick frightened brown eyes. More slowly Cameron turned toward the burly figure that seemed to fill the whole doorway.

"Come in, Dr. Steinberg," he said civilly enough. "I was just telling Sandy about an idea of mine."

"Yeah, I heard you." Steinberg was breathing hard and the air whistled in his nose. He was more than six feet tall, broad in the beam and thick through the middle. Over his collar, which was slightly wilted, his neck lay in folds and his eyes were almost lost between fat cheeks and puffy eyelids. He looked angrily at Farquhar, who seemed to shrivel before his glance, and then took a step or two toward Cameron.

"What the hell do you mean, monkeying around my patients? I know what I want done to them and what I don't want, and

I don't need any help from you. Of all the whipper-snappers Sam Ascot has ever had out here, I'll be damned if you're not the worst! I wouldn't be surprised if it was you told Joe not to have his teeth out. I'd like to know what business it is of yours, anyhow, damn you!"

The fat man stopped, puffing, and glared first at Cameron and then at Farquhar. Richard had drawn himself up very straight and now he strolled slowly across the floor and leaned against the workbench at the end of the room. His hands deep in his jacket pockets, he stood there silhouetted against the windows behind him.

"Perhaps, Dr. Steinberg, you don't know that I am a physician too. M.D. in 1912, eleven years ago this spring. Two years in Cook County. Worked there when Geoffrey Kendall had the laboratory. Then I practiced in Montana for three years, spent two years in the service, and studied three more in Northdevon before I came out here."

Steinberg's face seemed to swell almost to bursting. His cheeks turned dark purplish-red and his lips quivered in rage.

"I don't give a damn where you've been or what you've done, you impudent cub!" he shouted. "You keep your snotty nose out of my affairs and let my patients alone! You're not practicing medicine now and you're not supposed to be telling men who are how to do it. You're not a real doctor. You're just a laboratory man, a piss boiler! You're working for Ascot for a salary, and I could have you kicked out of here tomorrow if he was at home."

Richard's face turned a shade paler so that the freckles stood out more boldly. He knew that what Steinberg said was true: his job did hang by a thread and he had no other resources than his small salary. But the Scotch-Irish blood in him would not be balked of independence. He took his hands out of his pockets and looked straight into the scarlet face now but a foot or two from his. Then he cast a quick glance at Farquhar who was standing near the door, not knowing whether to go or stay.

"Sandy, will you close the door? There's no need to broadcast Dr. Steinberg's opinion of me over the whole hospital, especially when he'll be changing it before long. . . . And will you please stay here, Sandy? I'd like to have a witness to what I'm about to tell this ... gentleman."

The deliberate slight hesitation before the last word was not lost on Steinberg. He let out a roar and reached two huge hands toward Richard.

"If you touch me, Steinberg, I give you my word I'll break your head open. This microscope is heavy and it's hard." Cameron's hand was resting on the upright section of the instrument. "You weigh eighty pounds more than I do. That's reason enough not to fight you. Fighting isn't my business anyhow. And I'm afraid I haven't got Dr. Farquhar's moral courage to face you down empty-handed. . . . No, Steinberg, if you touch me, in thirty seconds afterwards you'll be on the floor with your head split open. I mean it."

At these words Sandy's blood almost curdled. That anyone should threaten Oscar Steinberg with physical violence seemed to him so incredible that he hardly noticed what Richard said about his own encounter with the fat man. But obviously Cameron meant exactly what he said; he stood there, leaning against the work-bench, tall and thin, with eyes as hard as gray steel and his hand on the microscope. To Farquhar's amazement Steinberg drew back a pace or two and let his fists drop.

"That's better." Cameron kept his cold eyes on the big man while he took his hand from the microscope and wiped his fingers with his handkerchief. "Better for your head and for your blood pressure too. One of these days, if you're not careful, you'll burst an artery in the internal capsule while you're in one of these rages and your wife will be collecting your insurance. A man like you, whose neck is bigger than his head, should learn to control himself."

This audacity so astounded Steinberg that he stood perfectly still, staring at Richard with puzzled pig eyes.

"I've got a few more things to tell you, Steinberg. One is that I've forgotten more about medicine than you ever knew. And the same thing goes for Farquhar too. Another is that I'm working for a salary today because I hadn't any better judgment than to go into the army and then spend all the money I had taking post-graduate work and learning something, while you salted down your war-time collections.

"But all this is not important. What is important is this: you've got a patient who has developed a uniformly fatal disease right under your nose and you wouldn't know it yet if I hadn't put a note on his chart yesterday. It hurts your pride and makes you sore to have a laboratory man tell you things like that.

"Whenever DiPallo has been in the hospital, I've put reports of his blood counts on his chart. Any time you took the trouble to look for them you could have seen them. I didn't discuss the case with anyone—not even with Miss Compton or Farquhar here—until ten minutes before you came in this afternoon. I haven't criticized you to Joe. I did advise him not to have his teeth taken out but I did it in such a way that he thinks the extraction was the dentist's idea and not yours. I've leaned over backwards trying to be ethical, and you've got no kick coming."

The fat man still stood motionless, in the middle of the floor, his porcine face blank with astonishment.

"I know what I'm trying to do," continued Richard. "I'm trying to find out something. Nobody can cure primary anemia today; in spite of everything we do, every patient who has it dies. I've got a hunch—never mind how I got it; that's none of your business—that Joe DiPallo has developed typical pernicious anemia right under our eyes. I'd be a fool not to learn all I can from him."

Now that Cameron paused for a moment, Steinberg pulled out a handkerchief and mopped his face and began to sputter.

"How do I know he's got pernicious anemia? You ought to 've asked me before you started bothering Joe. He's my patient and naturally I didn't want a big lab bill run up on him. What else was I to think you were up to?"

"That's exactly what I'd expect you to think," replied Richard drily. Then, seeing a look of suspicion creeping over Steinberg's fat features, he went on, "Come over here a minute and let me show you what we've got on Joe. I've got all the counts and stomach examinations tabulated in the order in which they were done. Look at them."

Steinberg bent down and peered at the paper on the work bench.

"Don't you see what's been happening to Joe? Four million reds in August, three and a half million in October, less than three by Thanksgiving, and now less than two million. And the color index crawling up, and the red cells getting every size and shape you can imagine. There's never been any free hydrochloric acid in his stomach all the while I've been following him. He's been getting weaker month after month; now he can't eat and his tongue is sore and his hands and feet are tingling. It's the classic textbook picture, right out of Osler's 'Practice.' Even a laboratory man couldn't miss it."

Although he could say nothing against Cameron's argument, Steinberg was too stubborn to admit he had made a mistake. The most he would do was to say that he would have someone in consultation and talk the laboratory findings over with Ascot when he got home. Then, grumbling and muttering to himself, he finally went away, much to Farquhar's relief.

The small Scotsman looked at Richard with profound respect; he admired people who could face physical danger with such boldness, it seemed so much finer than his own passive resistance. Suddenly Cameron straightened up and, seizing Farquhar by the shoulder, began to shake him gently back and forth.

"Sandy, I see how I can manage it. If I can't get dogs at the University, I can try it out on Joe. It can't do him any harm. I'll start in now, before Steinberg gets around to do a transfusion. If I can only get a week's start of him, I believe it'll be enough. I'm going to do it, Sandy."

Farquhar stared at the excited freckled face so near his own with brown eyes in which admiration still persisted.

"What are you driving at now?" he demanded nervously.

"I'm going to begin treating Joe Pallo this afternoon. I'll stuff him full of meat on the quiet, without Steinberg knowing anything about it. The head dietitian is a friend of mine; she'll help me work it. And I'll bet you anything you like that Joe will be on his feet before old Blowhard finds out what's going on."

Panic-stricken, Farquhar shook his head. He became eloquent: he pointed out how foolhardy such an undertaking would be, how it could not possibly be concealed from Ascot and Steinberg, what would become of Richard's job when those two found out what he was doing.

But Cameron was adamant.

III

At the March meeting of the Safe Harbor Hospital staff, the principal paper was by Oscar Steinberg. This in itself was enough to insure small attendance. As one of the doctors said, it was not that he objected to going to medical meetings but that he did not care to be bullied after he got there.

"We're over-organized anyhow. Good Lord, if I went to all the meetings I'm supposed to, I'd be sewed up five evenings out of seven. What with the County Society meeting twice a month and the special sections getting together at odd times and most of us on two or three hospital staffs, a man hasn't a minute to himself. And then they put that loud-voiced, pin-headed leather-neck on the program!"

But in spite of all the unreasonable demands on their time, forty-five loyal staff members listened perfunctorily to Steinberg's discussion of "Blood Transfusion in Pernicious Anemia." If several of them talked to one another in low voices and a few fell asleep and one or two snored audibly, it was not surprising, for the opening section of Steinberg's paper was an uninteresting history of transfusion and after that he rambled on through a long, confusing account of the technique used in various methods. More than once he lost his place and had to repeat himself, but he labored on with grim determination to read all he had written. Like many other doctors he thought this sort of public appearance was necessary now and then to maintain his professional standing.

Not until he began to describe his own illustrative case did the listeners stir slightly in the hope that he would soon finish. From his seat in the rear of the room Richard Cameron watched

Steinberg with an enigmatic light in his eyes and an otherwise expressionless face. From time to time he looked about to see how the audience endured boredom. Far over in one corner he could see Sandy Farquhar, also alone; once or twice he caught Sandy's eye and winked at him, but the Scotsman was too disturbed to wink back.

Samuel Ascot, scowling darkly, also sat by himself. Not only did he find Steinberg's paper dull but he was harassed by a familiar problem: his new assistant was proving almost as unsatisfactory as his predecessors had been. He was cocky and self-confident; furthermore, he knew too much. As the months passed, Ascot disliked him more and more. But it was going to be very nearly necessary to keep the fellow through the summer because Ascot had planned a four weeks' trip to Alaska and he dared not leave his laboratories in charge of a stranger during his absence. Nevertheless he could not endure seeing how the doctors were beginning to listen to Cameron. That was the intolerable thing about assistants—they always wanted to be in the limelight, when what they were paid for was to work and not talk.

Ascot heard only snatches of what Steinberg was reading.

". . . Italian, male, aged thirty-nine . . . got tired before noon . . . not much good with the women anymore." There was a solitary guffaw, and several of the doctors turned to glare at the man who found that statement amusing. ". . . physical examination negative . . ."

But then there came a few sentences that registered on Ascot's touchy self-esteem.

"I got a lot of long-winded laboratory reports that told me nothing except that he had only four million red blood cells and no free acid in his stomach. That's the trouble with bringing people into the hospital for observation. These lab men like Ascot and Cameron and the Xray men like Farquhar write you a book full of rot about the shape of the blood cells and the hydrogen ion concentration of the urine and the rate at which the patient's stomach empties, but they never tell you what's wrong with your man. Myself, I don't think they know half the time what the stuff they say means, any more than I do."

Steinberg paused as though he thought this might get a laugh, but when he caught a glimpse of Ascot's angry red face he hurried on again.

"Anyhow, the point I'm getting at is that it was almost a year after I first saw this man before I was sure he had pernicious anemia."

"Why didn't you call a doctor?" inquired a disrespectful voice.

Steinberg stopped, his face more bewildered than indignant. The chairman rapped with his gavel.

"Let us have no interruptions during the paper, please."

"Well, last month his red count was down to 1,855,000, his skin was lemon-yellow, he developed a sore tongue, and the diagnosis of pernicious anemia was made. So I had his blood typed and gave him a transfusion of 600 cc of citrated blood."

Here Steinberg walked over to the door and, putting his head out into the hall, whispered loudly, "Bring him in now, nurse."

"The remarkable thing," he went on, "is the rapid and uninterrupted improvement the man has made since the transfusion. Usually blood must be given several times at intervals, but one transfusion was all we needed in this case. Judge for yourselves, gentlemen."

Steinberg waved a fat hand toward the door in what he meant to be an impressive gesture and the eyes of all the doctors in the room turned upon the broad, swarthy man who was coming in.

"Sit down, Joe. That's it, nurse. Get him a chair. . . . Now, I doubt whether any of you would think Joe was sick if I hadn't told you." There was an expression of intense self-satisfaction on Steinberg's round face. "You feel good, don't you, Joe? . . . And you can walk around without getting short of breath like you used to? . . . And eat anything you like? . . . Feel like the old Joe, eh?"

To each query the smiling, dark-eyed Italian said "Yes," and Steinberg looked at his audience in triumph; it was not often that he could show off so satisfactorily.

"Any questions any of you want to ask?" he boomed. "Come on up here if you want to, and look Joe over. He won't mind, will you?"

The Italian shook his head and grinned goodnaturedly. A few of the doctors came to look at him more closely. Steinberg had not exaggerated. Joe DiPallo did look perfectly well. He was not pale, his skin was not yellow, he was not thin, his eyes were bright, he gave the impression of vigor. Cheerfully he submitted to minute inspections of the color of his skin and the whites of his eyes, and answered all questions politely.

Among the men who came up to examine him was Richard Cameron. Farquhar, who was at his heels, nervous and jumpy, saw him lean over DiPallo and heard him ask in an undertone, "How are you coming, Joe? You haven't been to see me for a couple of days."

"I been away, doc, on a little trip. But I'm O.K."

"Following orders?"

"Sure." DiPallo made a grimace with the side of his mouth away from Steinberg. "Raw in the morning and cooked at night. It ain't bad. I don't mind it."

Richard put a hand on the Italian's arm and squeezed it a little.

"Good work, Joe. Come out and see me tomorrow night. I've got a proposition to make you."

DiPallo winked at Cameron as he turned away with Farquhar following him.

When the two men had settled themselves together in the back row of seats, Farquhar whispered nervously to Richard.

"Gosh, but you've got a nerve—talking like that right under Steinberg's nose. You're going to get into an awful jam if you go on with this thing."

"I don't see how, Sandy. I've got Joe back on his feet and Blowhard hasn't the least idea I did it." Cameron laughed aloud and one or two men nearby glanced around at him curiously; then he looked at the apprehensive little man beside him with kindly eyes. "Cheer up, fellow. I'm doing fine."

"I don't think so," objected Farquhar. "I think that insane

sense of humor of yours will drive you to do all sorts of other crazy things too. If only some other man than Steinberg had this case or you were working for anyone but Ascot!"

Richard slid down on the small of his back and crossed his long legs.

"I can't help having a sense of humor, Sandy. Surely you don't think it's my fault that some of my good Scottish Covenanter ancestors got shipwrecked on the Irish coast and stayed there long enough to acquire a sprinkling of Irish blood before they came on to America."

But Farquhar shook his head and withdrew into melancholy brooding.

Richard glanced at him affectionately. In this thin, nervous, worried little man he saw something that no one else seemed to see—a sort of desperate stamina under his surface timidity that, in a crisis, cast out fear and held Sandy Farquhar loyal to self-imposed standards of a type rare in the modern world.

By this time all the other doctors had resumed their seats and Joe DiPallo and his nurse had left the room. The chairman called for discussion of Dr. Steinberg's paper. One or two men asked rather inane questions about the typing of blood for transfusion and another made a little speech calling attention to the unusual rapidity of improvement after only one transfusion.

"If the diagnosis had not been so definitely confirmed by typical blood findings, I should be tempted to question whether the doctor was dealing with a true pernicious anemia. Certainly this patient should be followed up with the greatest care. I hope Dr. Steinberg will do this and report to us again, a year from now, what his condition is."

Finally Richard Cameron got to his feet.

"If I may, I should like to ask a question or two. In the first place, I should like to hear Dr. Steinberg describe the stomach findings more fully. I'm sure we all realize that achylia is almost invariably associated with pernicious anemia. That was demonstrated as long ago as 1870 by Fenwick, or perhaps even earlier. Many patients, we are told, go for years with no free acid in their stomach contents and then develop typical pernicious anemia. Will the doctor tell us whether he had a gastric analysis done when he first saw the patient, and if so, what were the figures?"

There was something in the quiet assurance with which Richard spoke that caught the attention of the more alert physicians in the group, and some of them looked around toward him with apparent interest. At this, Samuel Ascot frowned more morosely than ever. Cameron was getting more arrogant every day, it seemed to him. What business was it of his to be discussing Steinberg's paper? What did he know about pernicious anemia? He was almost as bad as that runt, Farquhar, who was always insisting that he was first of all a doctor and after that an Xray specialist. Before long Cameron would be as intolerable as Featherstone had been. Ascot drew himself up in his chair and stared straight before him: he would not give that upstart assistant of his the satisfaction of turning around to look at him.

"Another thing," Cameron went on. "Has the doctor ever considered dietary treatment in this case? There has been some very interesting work in California recently on experimental anemia in dogs, and there are several men both in this country and abroad who have reported good results in the primary anemia of human beings with a high protein diet—lots of milk, eggs, and meat. The California experiments suggest that there are certain meats, especially liver, which induce a remarkably rapid regeneration of the blood, similar to that described in Dr. Steinberg's patient."

In closing the discussion Steinberg spoke rather petulantly of Cameron's questions. He said he had been at the annual convention of the American Medical Association two years before when the digestive symptoms in pernicious anemia had been discussed thoroughly; it had been the consensus of opinion among the biggest men there—and he mentioned several of them by name—that the low gastric acidity in these cases was a secondary condition of no great moment. Personally, he was content to take these men's word for it: they certainly knew more about it than anyone at this meeting.

As for the diet of meat and eggs or liver, he called the attention of his listeners to the fact that the experiments Cameron spoke of had been done on dogs and that Joe was not a dog. A lot of this experimental stuff was the bunk anyhow: some fellow got a bunch of rabbits or a cat or two and fed them something or cut something out of them and then wrote it all up and published it in a medical journal and expected doctors to believe it. For his part, rumbled Steinberg, he had no notion of trying any new-fangled dog diet on his patients. If Cameron was so anxious to see it tried, perhaps the veterinarians could help him. Or, it would be still better if the doctor would confine his attention to his laboratory work and let clinical medicine alone.

Steinberg considered this a clever rebuttal of Cameron's suggestion and he could not understand why the best doctors in the room went up to the fellow after the meeting adjourned and talked with him. Of all the men who had come to Seaforth since the War, Cameron was in Steinberg's opinion the most pestilent. He wondered why Sam Ascot kept him on.

CHAPTER IV

I

Early one sunny Thursday afternoon the following June Cameron stepped into the elevator on the top floor of Safe Harbor Hospital, cheerfully intent on getting outdoors as soon as possible. That morning he had found himself in one of the irrationally jubilant moods that always set him hunting adventure. Breakfast had tasted better than usual, his work in the laboratory had gone with more than ordinary speed, and now he was bound for a half-day in the open.

At first it had been a problem to find a free afternoon. Ascot took Saturday afternoon and Sunday off because he liked to spend a night away from Seaforth when he chose; by long habit Mary Compton took Wednesday afternoon, and by almost equally long precedent the technician in the downtown laboratory had Friday. There was left for Richard only Thursday or a half-day early in the week. For a time he had disliked this arrangement but now he had begun to appreciate the breathing spell out of Ascot's sight midway between Monday and Saturday.

Glancing at himself in the narrow mirror on the side of the elevator cage, he adjusted his tie, buttoned up his new gray tweed jacket, fished from a pocket a pair of brown cape gloves, and slapped a rakish gray tweed cap against his trouser leg. Outside the hospital entrance he paused to sniff the air and look about him. Below, on the driveway, stood the blue roadster with red wheels that he had bought the previous autumn. He would put the top down, he decided, before he went to lunch; the sunshine was too good to miss.

At the bottom of the steps he very nearly collided with a young woman who had come out of the building a minute or two before. A pettier man might have thought she turned deliberately into his path but Richard saw in the greenish-blue eyes raised to his a surprise as complete as his own.

"Why, Dr. Cameron! Imagine meeting you in Seaforth!" Snatching off his cap, Cameron recalled the wariness that had prompted him last August to conceal his destination from this girl, but the smile with which he regarded Miriam Brooks was—in spite of this—gay and untroubled.

"Miss Brooks! This is certainly an unexpected pleasure. You gave me the impression last summer that you were wedded to Spokane."

The girl looked approvingly at the man who stood before her with the sun shining on his copper-colored hair. He had given her an excellent dinner on the train and had kissed her disturbingly the same night.

"You must be a very busy man—to judge from the pace at which you came down those steps just now."

"I am," agreed Richard. "Very busy. But not this afternoon. I'm just going to lunch now. Won't you come with me? I'm fed up eating with men. Please do."

Although he did not touch her, Miriam could feel him guiding her toward the blue roadster. Not unwillingly she went with him. She felt it would be hard to escape this red-haired man with the gay voice and she did not want to try. He had attracted her when they first met and now, after an autumn and winter during which she had been respectfully adored by a young man too diffident to do more than hold her hands, she was ripe for masculine domination.

"Aren't you high-handed, doctor—abducting a lady in broad daylight? Or is this the way they do things in Seaforth?"

It was on the tip of Cameron's tongue to answer that he was not sure whether she was a lady, but he only laughed and said, "Oh, I always act like this and women always like it." Then he began loosening the side-bars of the top. "It's too gorgeous a day not to ride out in the sunshine. And, besides, blondes like you and me need our ultraviolet."

Miriam sank down in the deep leather seat and smiled at him. Her memory of this man had been right: he was not in the least like any of the boys she went around with in Spokane. He was older, there was something bold about his nose and chin, his red hair seemed to crinkle with energy. The movements of his lean body and freckled hands were quick and deft and casual.

They lunched together in a restaurant where Richard found a booth that sheltered them from too direct observation. Miriam could not help noticing how smartly he was dressed, and she was pleased with herself for having on her new cape whose flowing lines were suited to her slender height and whose soft green color brought out the yellow lights in her hair. No man so well-groomed himself could be indifferent to a woman's clothes.

She was quite right: Richard was not indifferent to her. Indeed he found himself pleasantly excited by her presence. There was something softly sensual about her that stirred his senses and he made opportunity to touch her hand; she did not withdraw it at once and neither did she move her foot when he put his ankle against hers. He smiled and asked what she was doing in Seaforth.

"Oh, an aunt of mine is ill. Mother couldn't leave home just now so she sent me over instead. Auntie is in Safe Harbor. That's how I came to be at the hospital this morning."

Cameron was annoyed: if the girl had to sit with a sick relative, she would have little time for him. But it soon appeared that Miriam had no intention of returning to the hospital that afternoon.

"Auntie has to be very, very quiet. And I know I'm in the way even though the nurse was too polite to tell me so, in so many words."

Richard's annoyance ebbed away. The last few poverty ridden years he had seen comparatively little of women and now his eyes rested lingeringly on the curve of Miriam's red mouth. Suppose the color was lipstick, he still wanted to kiss her. He could imagine bending her head far back on his arm and putting his mouth on her pale throat, not gently but roughly so that she would cry out and push her hands against him. While they were dawdling over coffee and dessert, this picture hovered in his mind. He could feel tenseness growing up between them, and suddenly he realized that he was going to do something that afternoon far different than he had expected. He grinned to himself as he thought of it.

Early in February, shortly after his talk with Professor Carey at the University, he had seen an advertisement in the Sunday paper of a place for rent just outside the city limits on the north. Going to see it, he found a fairly well-built, four-room cottage painted brown with a green roof, a shed for an automobile and fuel, and two acres of tillable land. Inside there were built-in shelves, and a work table and a kitchen stove, a bed, a cot, and a chest of drawers had been left by some previous tenant. On impulse he leased the place.

His next free afternoon he bought a chair or two and a library table at a second-hand store and moved into his new home. Then he went to the city pound and brought away two healthy young mongrel terriers to whom he took a fancy. These animals he installed in the back room of the cottage. On Sundays he took them walking or drove with them in the back of his car, and three nights a week he cooked their basic ration of rice and potatoes. Since it seemed to be necessary to research single-handed he meant to waste no more time, but the care of the animals made a heavy drain on his limited leisure.

After the hospital staff meeting at which Dr. Steinberg had

so proudly displayed Joe DiPallo as a case of anemia cured by one blood transfusion, Cameron suggested to the Italian that he come out to live with him and help with the dogs. This plan not only rescued Joe from the drudgery of the shoe-shining parlor where he had been employed but also lightened Richard's work and made it possible for him to keep DiPallo under constant observation. Joe slept in the fourth room of the cottage on the cot and cooked the dogs' food and cleaned their quarters and took them out for exercise every day. He also consumed twelve ounces of liver or kidney himself every day. On this régime he had continued entirely free of symptoms since March and now looked as sleek and healthy as the dogs he cared for. Sometimes Cameron laughed to himself as he watched the man, for he knew that Joe did not realize that he, and not the dogs, was the prime experiment.

Today Richard had planned to go home directly after lunch and load DiPallo and the dogs into the car and drive off into the country for the afternoon. But instead he bought a packet of the cigarettes Miriam confessed she liked best and drove away with her around the north end of Lake Donovan toward the hills.

Since it was the middle of the week there was little motor traffic. The blue roadster sped smoothly through the little town of Springville, swept past small farms and modest country homes, and began to climb into the wooded uplands east of Seaforth. There was just enough wind to blow the dust away, the sun shone brilliantly as though to make up for the dreary winter.

Cameron thrust aside the rational part of his mind that persisted in saying that he was on the verge of making a fool of himself. As the girl beside him burrowed down in the seat so that her arm and thigh touched his, he put his foot down hard on the gas and the speedometer shot up to fifty. His tautened senses urged him to make love to the girl. He knew that she would not repulse him, that she half expected him to do this very thing, half wanted it. But all the while some thing seemed to whisper in his brain, "Then you haven't learned anything since 1912, after all."

It seemed impossible that it was eleven years since he had

seen Evelyn Darnley. She was a tall, slender woman with thick ropes of ash-blonde hair wound about her head, whom he had met at the home of a mutual friend. A sort of seductive helplessness and the plaintiveness of her soft blue eyes drew all men to her. It soon developed that she was unhappily married and on the verge of beginning divorce proceedings against a complaisant husband who made no effort to conceal his own affairs of the heart.

Richard Cameron, twenty-three and infatuated, laid siege to Mrs. Darnley, who was a year older and had the advantage of not being in love with him. He neglected his studies, dropped dangerously near the foot of his class in medical school, spent the money that should have gone for room and board on candy and flowers and perfume and auto rides.

Flattered by his devotion, Mrs. Darnley gave him much of her free time for several months but, for fear of arousing gossip before her divorce was granted, she used discretion. It was not until summer that, out of sheer boredom, she consented to follow Richard to the resort where he was working in northern Michigan. Here for two months Evelyn had been his mistress and he had lived in paradise. Once it was stirred to life Mrs. Darnley had her share of physical passion, but before the summer was over her lover's adoration had begun to pall on her. The following autumn her divorce was granted and the next December she married a man twice her own age who possessed what Richard lacked—an income.

This experience had throttled something that had been very winning in the boy Richard Cameron. It also put an end to his idealization of women. In the concessions he made his body there was no longer any sentiment: he considered certain indulgences preferable to constant preoccupation with sexual desire. But when he encountered married women or divorcees he went the other way.

Something in Miriam Brooks brought Mrs. Darnley vividly back into his mind but that annoying whisper persisted, "Just as big a fool as you were twelve years ago."

On a Sunday trip in May with Joe and the dogs, Richard

had driven this road and stumbled on an isolated spot toward which, half-consciously, he was now veering. At four o'clock he came into the side-lane which led down to the little stream he had found before. He turned in off the highway and stopped the roadster under two huge firs. With the engine shut off, he could hear the creek—not more than a hundred feet away, but invisible from the machine—splashing over rocks and boulders. Just beyond the car the lane stopped and a winding trail began only to disappear after a few yards into a wall of green undergrowth. There was a deep stillness in the place; only now and then a bird chirped or a squirrel squeaked cheerfully.

Cameron turned toward Miriam. Something in the curve of her neck, the droop of her shoulders as she sat there whiplashed his senses into a fury. She was Evelyn over again—a little more sensuous than Evelyn had ever dared to be, or perhaps only a bit more honest.

"Well," he said in a voice so hoarse that it surprised the girl.

She looked up into his dark gray eyes, now all black, blazing pupils, half afraid and half pleased with what she saw there. She put a warm hand on his arm and moved the fraction of an inch nearer him.

"I didn't bring you all the way out here," he went on with an effort, "just to sit and admire the scenery and listen to the birds."

Miriam did not move, did not speak.

Richard reached out suddenly and pulled her toward him and held her tight against his body, but his savagery held a curious suggestion that it was actually directed less toward the girl than toward himself. He pressed his mouth down hard against the white skin of her neck until he felt her draw a deep gasping breath and go limp against him. She reached up blindly to pull his head down and turned her red lips toward his. But, as she did so, the image of Evelyn Darnley once more thrust itself into Richard's mind.

She too had been tall and fair and slender; she too had groped for physical intimacy once he had broken down her half-hearted defense; she too had surrendered her body to him in the interval between the surrender to her first husband and that to the second. The parallel was too much. Suddenly the woods of northern Michigan blotted out the firs and cedars of the Far West, and the past plaintiveness of blue eyes obscured the present longing in the oval greenish ones so close to him now. The remembered touch of Mrs. Darnley's body destroyed his desire for Miriam's.

Empty of passion as a deflated balloon, Cameron dropped his arms and pushed the girl back to her side of the car. All he could think of for the moment was how near he had come to making an utter fool of himself again.

"Well, well, my dear girl! That was once your virginity had a close call. If it hadn't been for the dear old Westminster Shorter Catechism which I remembered just in time . . ."

The girl flushed scarlet, then grew pale again. She sat staring straight in front of her without speaking. Presently a faint sense of shame invaded Richard's consciousness.

"I do beg your pardon, Miriam," he said less flippantly. "I suppose you won't mind my calling you Miriam? I believe it's customary under these circumstances. . . . I see you don't understand. Well, neither do I. Why didn't I go through with what I started? I can only tell you that I didn't feel like it when I got right up to the edge. However . . . Well, suppose we have a smoke. Maybe that will calm our razzled nerves."

He held a match for her cigarette before lighting his pipe and was a little surprised to see that his fingers did not shake. Then he leaned back and watched her—his hair shining in a patch of sunlight, his freckled hands loosely clasped about one knee, his dark gray eyes curious, his teeth set firmly on the stem of his briar pipe. The girl smoked silently, as though she scarcely knew what she was doing. Now that Richard was no longer obsessed by physical passion, he saw that she seemed younger than he had thought her, not over twenty-two or -three at most. Not only that, but she had been pretending a sophistication greater than she really had.

When at last she turned and looked at him, the dark pupils of her green-blue eyes seemed to him to be wide with dismay and regret. "She's predatory by instinct—and curious. But that's about all there is to it." He reached over and patted her hand with deliberate carelessness.

"Tell me something, Miriam. Are you the brazen hussy the modern girl is supposed to be or the sweet old-fashioned thing our mothers would like us all to believe they were? The method of science appeals to me, naturally: try it and see. But I didn't find out much this afternoon—except that a man, once scorched, dreads fire.... And now suppose you tell me what I can do to entertain you during the shank of the day that remains and the evening that lies before us?"

Try as she would, Miriam Brooks could get no other serious word out of Cameron during the remainder of the fortnight she spent in Seaforth. He was an assiduous attendant, buying good dinners and theater seats, and taking her for long drives in the moonlight; the most ardent Seaforth booster could not have found fault with the way he showed the girl the lakes and boulevards and hills and harbor. But not until he came to tell her goodbye did he kiss her again.

"For old time's sake, Miriam. You know, last summer at Butte." He grinned. "Don't trust the men, my dear girl, and don't trust yourself. We're, all of us, slaves to biology. And we can't help it."

If he had ever half-expected to be dogged by recollections of this interlude with Miriam Brooks, he was pleased to find that she receded rapidly into the background of his mind and that the invitation to her wedding which he received early in September did not disturb his cheerfulness. Indeed, by that time, he was so engrossed in the results of his diet experiments with the dogs and in Joe's continued good health that even the memory of his fleeting June madness had become vague. Furthermore, he was exchanging very interesting letters about his anemia experiments with Dr. Thornton in Northdevon and was laying new plans for the future.

II

A week before Dr. Ascot was due to return from his Alaskan

trip, Richard met Steinberg in the doctors' room in Safe Harbor Hospital. At sight of the fat man Cameron grinned: he knew that Steinberg disliked him, had for him the distrust of the stupid for the intelligent, and it amused him to watch the big man endeavor to conceal the animosity for which there was no generally known reason.

"Good morning, doctor," said Richard. "Have a good vacation?"

A slow smile spread over the fat red face above him. It seemed even more unpleasant than Steinberg's usual smile.

"Yes, sure. I had a fine trip, all right. Ask your friend, Farquhar, if I didn't. He'll tell you. He knows." The little bloodshot eyes narrowed. "He thought he was so damned smart, jumping on me like he did. I never forget a guy like him."

Something in the way Steinberg rolled his words in his mouth was so coldly malignant that Cameron rose hotly to his friend's defense.

"I suppose you mean the time last year when you hit Farquhar because he wouldn't change a report on a fracture case to suit you. You didn't know I heard that row, did you? Well, I did. And I remember that right afterward you had a consultant and put the patient's leg in a weight-suspension apparatus and got an excellent result. If you're asking me, I'd say that Sandy did you a good turn that day. He probably saved you from a malpractice suit."

"Yeah, Cameron. I guess that's what you would think. You've got to be kinda thick with that fellow. But you won't be asked for your opinion, so you can keep it to yourself. Only I'll just give you a tip: you'd better keep away from Farquhar a little more. He won't be around here much longer, and you might lose your job too, all of a sudden, if you're mixed up with him too much." Steinberg drew down one side of his face into a leering grimace and opened the door into the corridor. "Well, so long, Cameron. Hope you enjoy the news I just gave you."

Until now Richard had always been too eager to find out what lay beyond the next corner of the road to worry about the future or to take vicissitudes, his own or those of his friends, too seriously. But he was startled to find how much Steinberg's clumsy hints upset him; this threat to Farquhar's security disturbed him more than he liked to admit.

Sitting at his little desk in the hospital laboratory during the noon hour, he pondered the situation. The shy little Scotsman had made a corner for himself in Cameron's life that would be appallingly empty without him. Sandy knew his specialty and his professional opinions were always worth listening to; his reports were marvellously complete and still compact to the point of curtness. He never lost his temper with the most unreasonable of patients, he never complained about emergency work at night or on Sunday. He had a caustic, witty tongue which he exercised in private at the expense of the University, the rotting Shipping Board vessels tied up in Lake Donovan, the stupidity of medical men and of life in general. But, beyond and above all this, he was honest. Timid as he was, he clung to his own standards of conduct through thick and thin.

Bit by bit Richard had come to know a good deal of the man's history. Part of it Sandy had told him, and considerably more Cameron had put together for himself. Far from being the spineless creature Ascot thought him, Farquhar had had to develop an inordinate courage in order to live at all. Small and frail from infancy, fear early took possession of him. He worried lest he fall ill and lest he fail in his studies, and each time he finished another lap of his education at the head of his class he was astonished. He was forever haunted by the fear of being without a job.

He was dogged by other phobias as well. Loud noises had always terrified him, thunderstorms threw him into a panic. He dreaded swimming and mountain climbing. But with an obstinacy equal to his fears, he stuffed his ears with cotton and practiced revolver shooting at a mark, and forced himself to open the closet in his department at the hospital every day or two in order to listen to the terrifying roar of the electric transformer housed therein. Perspiring with terror he drove himself up the shale slopes of the Olympic Mountains and flogged himself into the icy waters of Puget Sound.

Nor was that all. He was afraid of himself, of certain quirks in his own personality. He dreaded the suggestive hints people dropped about his failure to marry after his mother's death; he fled from women and lived quite without intimates of either sex. There seemed to be a sort of barrier between him and other people: it was as though there were a "No Admittance" sign over his private life. Most of the time he was unapproachable; he had none of the free-and-easy, give-and-take manner that distinguished Richard. If he tried to tell a smutty story, he was so ill at ease himself that he made his listeners uncomfortable too.

Thus Farquhar's whole existence had been a mosaic of fear and inner conflicts and outer bravado. Ascot did not know this and, if it had been explained to him, he could not have understood any more than Steinberg did. Cameron did not understand all of it either, but he had liked Sandy from the moment he saw the little man at bay but still defying the blustering Steinberg. Characteristically, Richard never stopped to analyze his friendship for Farquhar; he liked and disliked people by instinct. "My friends," he sometimes said, "can do no wrong, my enemies can do no right."

Cameron remembered how Sandy had implored him to avoid an open clash with Steinberg, to be tactful with Ascot, to be cautious about his experiments, and to talk less freely at staff meetings. And yet Farquhar constantly compelled himself to do things he dreaded and on occasion he even turned on those men whose good will he advised Richard to cultivate. Sandy was no coward—so much was certain—and yet Cameron knew he was afraid of something.

Some weeks before Sandy had hinted that he might be leaving Seaforth soon. "I've been here at Safe Harbor for five years. That's a record for me. I never stayed anywhere else more than two years. I loathe the idea of settling down; it's staying put in one place that ossifies a fellow's brain." But Richard recalled now that, when he said those words, Farquhar's muddy brown eyes were full of fear.

Thinking of the menace to Sandy's security made Cameron

restless and resentful. Impulsively he ran across the hall into the Xray department to talk to the little man and, finding him out, left a note on his desk asking him to share a bachelor dinner the next evening. Even though Farquhar might have nothing to say about his own predicament, he had something to tell the little Scotsman that would make him open his eyes.

III

Since Seaforth was in the midst of one of those periods of overcast skies and cool, cloudy weather that frequently occur in the Pacific Northwest in summer, Richard and Farquhar settled themselves in front of Cameron's small open-front coal stove after they had finished a supper of steak, fried potatoes, and peas. Before lighting his pipe, Richard brought from a shelf in his closet a bottle of liquor and put it down within his friend's reach.

"Have a drink, Sandy? It's bootleg, but the fellow I get it from supplies a lot of men around town who are perfectly well and healthy. Better take a chance on it. It'll do you good."

Before Cameron's banter Farquhar's hesitation faded and soon he was visibly thawing under the influence of the mixture of gin and vermouth.

Sitting there before the fire in a chair too large for him, Sandy seemed to shrink still more in contrast with Richard's long arms and legs. Farquhar's hair, nondescript light brown, was already thinning over the crown, and it straggled in a pale fuzz down the back of his neck. His brown eyes, lusterless during the meal, were just beginning to brighten a bit. His thin shoulders were hidden under the padded outlines of his coat, which rode up after he sat down until the collar approached his ears, and his thin fingers twitched as he raised his glass to his lips. "He's no beauty," thought Cameron. "Father would have called him a motheaten sorrel." But Sandy's appearance had nothing to do with Richard's liking for him.

After a silence during which both men finished a glass of contraband liquor, Cameron threw a chunk or two of coal on the fire and then inquired in an offhand fashion whether Farquhar had decided to leave Seaforth as he had hinted he might. At this, the small man started and looked sharply at his host, but Richard's eyes were on the match with which he was carefully lighting the tobacco in his pipe-bowl, and after a moment Farquhar relaxed again and managed to smile.

"Why, I wouldn't be surprised if I pulled out of here anytime after this month. What makes you ask?"

There was, it struck Richard, an excessive nonchalance about this answer. Probably things were bad then, just as Steinberg had hinted.

"Oh, you said last summer that you might be moving on later in the year. Don't you remember? I think you're right, too. You've outgrown Safe Harbor and Seaforth, too, for that matter. You belong in a bigger place—some medical center or a big clinic where they know an Xray man is something more than a glorified photographer."

Farquhar was astonished.

"That's the first time anyone ever encouraged me to move on," he exclaimed. "Usually people say what a bad reputation a man gets who doesn't stay put." Then he grinned thinly. "Maybe I do belong at the Mayo Clinic, but I haven't heard of Will or Charlie falling over themselves to offer me a job there."

"Well, you don't give yourself a chance," retorted Cameron. "You know as well as I do that a doctor is known these days by what he publishes and reads at medical meetings. Now, you've shown me some swell case reports and Xray films you've worked up, but you don't even try to get them into journals for other people to see. How do you expect anyone to know you exist? Hell, Sandy, it's all right to be modest, but you not only put your light under a bushel but—for fear the bushel might have a hole in it—you put a blanket over the whole works. I almost think you're hiding out from somebody."

Once more Farquhar looked sharply at Cameron but Richard's profile was motionless under this scrutiny.

"What I want to know, Sandy, is why you don't try promoting yourself? Get on programs, write papers, publish stuff. That sort of thing has put over many a false alarm. Why not use it for a man with brains, for a change?"

But Cameron could see that this talk made Farquhar more nervous and jumpy than ever. And presently he fell into a stubborn silence that defied all Richard's efforts.

After a pause Cameron said in quite a different tone, "I'm fixing up a swell surprise for our friend, Ascot, when he gets home."

Farquhar jumped. "Now, Rich," he cried, "for the Lord's sake don't go stirring that man up as soon as he gets back from his trip. I've known him to be almost human for three or four weeks after his vacation. You just made a new contract with him this summer. Why can't you play safe until the new agreement expires? In 1924 you'll be just that much more ahead of the game."

"I wonder." Cameron laughed a little. "I've had a hunch about this new contract all along. Ascot was in such a devil of a hurry and my first year wasn't up yet when he started to talk about it. What if he were just trying to make sure things would be O.K. this summer while he went to Alaska and figuring that he could fire me whenever he felt like it after he got home?"

Farquhar was startled.

"Well, if you've thought this all summer, I must say you're a cool customer. Losing your job mustn't mean very much to you."

"I don't take this job very seriously, if that's what you mean, Sandy. How could I? That fat, pompous, bad-tempered, conceited ass I've been working for isn't worth it. When I was a kid my father used to call the weasels and gophers and other pests around the farm 'varmints.' Well, that would be a good word for Sam—a 'varmint,' touchy and full of his own importance."

"That's all true enough, but you're working for him and your job depends on him. He can fire you on a month's notice any time he wants to. I know." Into Sandy's voice there had crept an edge of bitterness.

Cameron stole a look at him: the little man had pulled himself up erect in his chair and was staring straight ahead into the coal fire.

"I know—from experience. You work like hell, with all the skill you've got, at night, on Sundays, on holidays, after hours. You watch the corners and cut expenses to the bone: you use small films and economize on the number of them, you screen patients instead of making films, you watch your solutions and keep the tanks covered and put off making fresh developer as long as you can. You wear your brains out trying to word reports so that stupid fellows like Steinberg can understand what you mean. And then he says your reports are incomprehensible, that you don't know yourself what you mean. And knocks you down because you won't change them to suit him."

The insignificance of Farquhar's face was gone; his eyes were blazing with the bitterness of the superior man who knows that, in spite of his superiority, he will always be a failure.

"These doctors here expect me to take patients, without any history, and within twenty-four hours tell them exactly what's wrong and what ought to be done about it and when. That's what they expect of an Xray man at the same time they're complaining that Xray examinations are a useless expense.

"They bleat about keeping the fees down, and then when I do as they suggest and screen a chest and miss a beginning TB by doing it they damn me. They monkey around in their offices with those little, one-horse Xray outfits salesmen high pressure them into buying and—because they're too ignorant to know what they're looking at—they tell people they're well when they're sick and sick when they're well. Then, afterwards, when I go over the same patients and find old lesions, the doctors demand that I put on the soft pedal and save their faces."

Farquhar had forgotten Richard was there; his eyes were far away.

"And I know all about hospitals and hospital superintendents too. I ought to. I've been working for them for more than eleven years, and even I can learn something in that length of time. How often have I listened to a superintendent assuring some family that it was the Xray man—or the laboratory man—who made the unfortunate mistake? And even when they admit that I work hard and know my stuff and do better work than any other man they've ever had or ever will have, they still come around one day and tell me that it is their painful duty to suggest that I hand in my resignation.

"If I have nerve enough to ask why, they say something vague about my personality, and how I don't get on well with some of the surgeons, or bring up some inane complaint by some old fossil who graduated in medicine in 1880 and hasn't learned anything since then. They've nothing personally against me. Oh, no! They hate to see me go, and they'll be happy to give me references. I mustn't feel down-hearted because I just didn't happen to fit into their particular institution; that is no reflection on me, in any sense of the word. Of course not."

Farquhar pushed back his chair roughly and sprang up. From the glitter in his usually opaque brown eyes Cameron knew the man was beside himself. His quiet voice was slowly rising to a shout.

"Oh, man, don't I know about these things? Don't I? I've been through it often enough—being fired by mealy-mouthed superintendents who did the dirty work for their trustees. I know my stuff and they know that I do. But what good is that for me? They've got the whiphand because they control the money while I haven't got any. They want to get rid of me, and what's it to them whether I get another job or starve?

"If a man wants to be sure he'll get his head knocked off, the way to do is to stick it up above the rank-and-file. Then everybody will be after you, hot-foot. People won't leave anybody alone who isn't just like them and just as stupid. They think—God help them!—that they're normal. They measure everybody else by themselves. If you want to read different books or live differently than they do, then you're dangerous or abnormal. You're a Bolshevik, a degenerate, and you must be suppressed—by all the good 110% Americans! Normal, average, wholesome! I'm sick of the words. Who knows what is normal?

You think you're normal, and I think I am, and they think they are. My God, what a mess! It makes me want to vomit!"

Cameron did not speak or look up; he smoked silently with his eyes on the bowl of his pipe. But his mind was busy with Steinberg's innuendoes of the previous day. What had this man discovered to use against Farquhar?

For a minute longer Sandy stood transfigured, glaring into space at the people he hated; then slowly the glow began to fade from his face to be replaced first by apprehension and then by a scared retreat within himself. He sat down and looked about as though to see whether Richard had taken his outburst seriously.

Cameron's instinct told him to continue being casual, so he got up and fixed the fire, knocked out his pipe, found his tobacco pouch, and offered Farquhar another drink.

Then he said, "Let me tell you you're some speaker, Sandy. You ought to be on a soap box down on the skidroad. You'd convince people you meant what you said. You almost made me think that you belong to the downtrodden proletariat of laboratory men."

But no chaffing could lighten the gloom that had settled on Farquhar's face.

"Who's been talking to you about me?" he demanded.

"Nobody," lied Richard cheerfully. "But I heard you might be leaving the hospital soon."

"Well, that's right. I am going—in October, I guess. I've been here five years, it's time for me to move on. I guess I'd got to feel too settled here. I might have known better." Again the bitterness came into his voice. "I ought to have known better—from experience."

There were questions Cameron wanted to ask, but the recollection of certain words Sandy had used kept him from it. He made his queries along other lines.

"Well, all this doesn't disturb me a particle. Something good is going to turn up for you, and it won't be in Seaforth. What had you thought of doing when you left the hospital, Sandy?"

"I'm not making plans. I can't, Rich. Not this time. Somehow the starch has gone out of me. I haven't the foggiest idea where I'll go or what I'll do." The man's voice was heavy, flat with despondency.

"But I have, you see. That's why I'm not upset." Cameron leaned forward with his elbows on his knees and his head in his hands. His red hair shone like bright copper in the firelight. "I'm not gassing, Sandy. I mean it. You may think I never look ahead or plan anything, but sometimes I do. And this is one of the times."

He grinned at Farquhar.

"From the first day I walked into Ascot's lab I knew we'd never get along, and I began right then to figure how I could get out of here none the worse for him. My methods may be queer but they're working. And Ascot is due for a jolt: for the first time in his life, an assistant is going to get the best of him. And the beauty of it is that I'm going to step into something big, really big."

"That's fine," said Farquhar with genuine pleasure. But in a moment dejection engulfed him again. "I wish you luck but I'm going to miss you like hell!"

"Oh, no, you're not. That's just the point. I've got it all doped out. Long before October you'll be telling the fat superintendent your own plans and jolting him a little, for a change. Now, listen, and I'll tell you all about it."

At first Sandy paid little attention but gradually as Cameron talked on animation began to creep back into his brown eyes and pale face. Then for a time he seemed to be swept into the current of his friend's enthusiasm, but before long doubt reasserted itself.

"You can make anything sound good, Rich, but it won't work out. I don't take any stock in the dreams of an optimist like you."

"An optimist! Like me!" Cameron threw back his head and laughed until he shook the chair in which he sat. "Optimists like me! Oh, that's the best one I ever heard you pull, Sandy. The very best. Why, bless you, it's you that's the optimist, not me.

"Yes, you are," he insisted, seeing denial shaping itself on

Sandy's lips. "You're an idealist, a reformer, at heart. You see the world and the people in it—how silly and stupid it all is. And you're outraged. Why?

"Think a minute, man. You're outraged because, in spite of your thirty-nine years and all your experience, you still think maybe something might be done about it and you ought to try to do it. In other words, you don't think humanity is hopeless. You still believe that people might be bribed or persuaded or bullied into using their brains and living decently. Then, when every attempt to get them to do any of these things fails, you get angry and rail at them for their stupidity. You're a defeated uplifter, Sandy, berating the heathen because they won't be uplifted. And you call yourself a pessimist because you're always disappointed.

"Now that's where I'm different. I know most people are stupid, and I know they can't help it: they just haven't got any brains. And I know the few that have brains seldom use them. They don't dare. If they did they'd be thrown into jail or an asylum or a concentration camp. I know that every baby when it's born has certain characteristics that it will never be able to get rid of, and I know that every child is pitched into a family and an environment that are almost always bad. I know these poor creatures will be from infancy in the grip of emotions that dominate their actions and I know that at puberty—if they live that long—they will be thrown headlong into a maelstrom of sexual passion and desire that will whirl them helplessly round and round until old age brings them at last into the safe harbor of senility.

"I know that every man on earth tries to grab what he can for himself as he is swept along by this current of emotions—pleasure, success, sexual satisfaction, money, power, what not. All human beings are trying blindly to satisfy an urge that was born within them. And so the world men have built up around them is a wild jungle with everything growing pell-mell, trying to crowd out all its competitors for space.

"There's no use lecturing people, Sandy. They're what they are, and they can't help it any more than you can help being what you are. All of us are born 'as is.' I'm afraid the man was right who said that this probably is the best of all possible worlds.

"But the whole thing is entertaining in a way, providing you can maintain some degree of detachment. And you can do that by not taking things too hard, by not trying too hard to make money or be a success, by taking life as an adventure and not expecting it to bring you much happiness. Then you can laugh, Sandy, laugh at the world and the people in it and the jungle they've made out of life. That's why I laugh, instead of railing at the fat-heads as you do. By the same token, you are a disappointed optimist and I am a pessimist because I'm never disappointed. I never expect anything more than a kick in the seat of the pants. But sometimes the fellow who thinks he's kicking me finds out that he's really kicking himself."

An hour later, the alliance of Cameron and Farquhar for purposes of offense and defense was christened in another serving of bootleg gin and vermouth.

CHAPTER V

I

On the next afternoon after Sandy's visit, three women members of the local Society for the Prevention of Cruelty to Animals met Joe DiPallo as he was coming back from his daily walk with the dogs. Word had come to their organization, so they informed the Italian, that Dr. Cameron kept animals for purposes of vivisection and they had been appointed to investigate. Joe possessed an alert mind and, when he wished, could assume a monumental stupidity. He did not know what the letters S.P.C.A. which these three women used stood for but he was sure they meant Cameron no good, so he instantly became an ignorant Italian who neither understood English well nor spoke it intelligibly. He flatly refused the committee entrance to the house and after a quarter-hour of futile argument the three women got into their car and drove away.

DiPallo was convinced that they would come back and this prospect worried him, but when he told Cameron about it Richard only laughed at him and said, "All right, Joe. Let them come."

The following evening the committee did return. Their appearance as they stalked across the lawn toward his cottage entertained Cameron vastly. Number One, evidently the leader, was stern-visaged and officious in manner; Number Two was lean and sour-faced; Number Three was fat and vacuous-looking. Some years later when he first saw Grant Wood's picture, "Daughters of Revolution," Richard decided that some such group as this must have posed for the painter. There was about the faces the same middle-aged sagging of the jowls, the same smug obstinacy, the same dunder-headed assurance.

Without apology the committee brushed past Cameron into his combination kitchen and living room, which they surveyed haughtily. The room was long, since it formed the entire front of the house, and it was scantily furnished, but except for a big, heaped-up library table at one end it was clean and orderly. Besides the straight chairs at the small dining table there were but three others. With sardonic civility Cameron offered these to the women and sat down himself on one corner of the library table, cleared for this purpose by a sweeping gesture of one arm. The committee continued to scrutinize the room with eyes that seemed to expect cowering famished animals and implements of torture.

"May I ask the occasion of this call?" inquired Richard in a voice that did not conceal his amusement. "Have I met any of you before?"

These questions went unanswered. Confronted in the flesh by this long-legged, composed man whose dark gray eyes were full of humor, the committee could not immediately put their errand into words. The spokesman temporized with the first query that came into her head.

"Do you live alone here, young man?"

"No," answered Cameron politely. "There are four in the family."

"Indeed!" said the spokeswoman, raising her eyebrows and looking at the other members of the committee as though this answer suggested further and hitherto unsuspected immorality. Then she braced herself for the attack but, seeing the direction which Richard's mocking gray eyes had taken, she hesitated once more.

Having looked the three up and down, Cameron had transferred his gaze to their ankles. He had once read somewhere that this maneuver made women nervous and it occurred to him that this was a good time to try it out. Almost immediately he saw that the information was correct. Although skirts in 1923 had not attained the levels of 1929, they did uncover most of the lower leg when their wearers sat down, particularly if the hemline was irregular. Each of his callers Richard saw at once was disturbed by his steady contemplation of her ankles.

"Perhaps, ladies, I ought to introduce myself," he said softly. "Give you my dossier, as it were. Name: Richard Boniface Cameron. Only I never use the Boniface: it sounds like a complexion lotion. Age: thirty-five. M.D. in 1912. Two years in Cook County Hospital. Three years in Montana. Two years in the service abroad. Three years' post-graduate work in Northdevon. One year in Seaforth. Prison record: none. Unmarried, childless, and at present free from entangling alliances."

He saw that these women were not dull enough to miss the bantering quality of this speech and waited for the stern-faced leader, goaded by indignation, to go into action.

"This, young man, is neither the time nor the place for levity."

But Cameron interrupted her. "The name is Cameron or Richard, if you like. And would it be too much to ask you to use the title, 'Doctor?' I worked for it too long to dispense with it now."

Number Two, the lean, sour-faced woman, frowned angrily and cleared her throat.

"Let us get to business," she said sharply. "We are not interested in this nonsense. It has been reported to the Society for Prevention of Cruelty to Animals by . . . uh . . . uh . . . interested parties that you keep a number of dogs about your cottage, Doctor . . . uh . . . Cameron."

"Yes, that is quite true," admitted Richard cheerfully. "I like dogs, you see. At present I own two nondescript terriers that I got from the city pound where they were to be killed because they were unclaimed. It's very kind of your society to take such an interest in my pets."

The committee looked at each other and then at the mocking, freckled face of the man who perched on the corner of the library table, swinging one leg carelessly. They seemed to find their errand thicker going than they had anticipated. But Number Two was not to be intimidated. Sourer than ever, she glared at Cameron through narrow, dark, slit-like eyes.

"Enough of this, young man. We did not come here to . . . uh . . . to . . . uh . . . make foolish jokes. Let me point out to you that it is a serious matter to be reported to our society as you have been. We shall insist on a thorough investigation."

"And of what, madam, may I ask? My sanitary arrangements, my morals, my health?"

The chairman, wrath shining in her small pale eyes, seized the leadership again.

"The S.P.C.A. has been reliably informed that you keep these dogs ostensibly as pets but in reality in order to mistreat, abuse, and torture them. There are, let me remind you, many humane persons in this city who feel it their duty to come to the defense of helpless animals tortured in the name of so-called science."

"Ah, I see. Another evidence of the kindly interest of my neighbors," murmured Cameron. Then his voice sharpened, lost its undertone of raillery. "And I wish to remind you, ladies, that the world is full of people who go about putting their noses into things that are none of their business. If you were men I'd throw you out of my house on your necks. You are presuming on your sex to do something I would thrash a man for trying."

Paying no heed to the startled indignation on the faces of the committee he went on, "But now that you are here and have forced your way into my home, I too shall insist on a thorough investigation. Before you leave, you shall look under every bed and into every cupboard and closet." He crossed the room with a long, quick stride and flung open the door into the animal quarters.

Slowly the committee followed him and peered past him into the kennel. Joe Di Pallo stood at a table cutting slices of cooked meat and putting them on two clean enamel-ware plates. He looked up in apparent confusion.

"Go on, Joe," said Cameron. "Don't mind us. These ladies are . . . dog-lovers. They're interested in what we're doing here."

Richard pointed to two large wire cages in one end of the room. In them stood two alert terriers, their ears stiffly erect, their eyes glued to DiPallo, their tails vibrating with eagerness. Joe wiped his hands on the denim apron he wore and went to unlatch the cage doors. Both dogs dashed out and began to jump against his legs and whine. He put down the plates of meat on the floor and the animals fell upon their food lustily.

"You will notice how afraid they are of us," said Cameron to the women, pointing to the sleek, well-nourished dogs. "Also how emaciated they are and what poor appetites they have. They are really almost on the verge of collapse from weakness."

The committee could not help seeing that the kennel was clean and well-kept; it was lighted and ventilated by windows on three sides and the cages were spotless. While the dogs, having gulped their meal, frisked about the room barking and chasing each other, Cameron displayed the drinking water supply and the arrangements for the disposal of wastes.

Then he led the women back into the living room where he insisted that they look into all the corners and shelves and into the kitchen fixtures as well. He took them into Joe's bedroom and his own, and made them examine the bathroom and his clothes closet. He opened boxes and bureau drawers and tumbled out their contents for scrutiny. From a window he pointed out his roadster standing in the small garage; he even went out and brought in the two black cases he kept in the car.

"My drugs and instruments," he explained. "You'd better look them over too while you're here."

By this time the fat vacuous member of the committee, who

had not spoken a word since she entered the house, was visibly nervous and anxious to get away; the sharp faces of the other two wore an expression of exasperation. Cameron saw that they knew he had been poking fun at them; their eyes told him how greatly they resented his lack of that deference which American women demand from their men. (Later the sour-faced woman, describing the evening rather inaccurately to the society she represented, said that Dr. Cameron had been very impolite, and that he had the "typical Continental manner." She even went so far as to hint that he might be a dangerous alien who had changed his name and acquired an American accent. Of this she felt she was eminently fitted to judge, because she had spent a fortnight soon after the World War on the continent of Europe and ten days in Great Britain.)

Even the stern-faced chairman of the committee seemed to feel that it was useless to look longer for covert evidence of torture and vivisection. The thing was to find a way of retreat that would save their faces. She suddenly recollected something Richard had said earlier in their call.

"You said there were four in the family, doctor, but I've seen only yourself and this man." She nodded toward the kennel where Joe could be heard talking to the dogs. Her pale eyes suggested that she still suspected skillfully-concealed iniquities.

"Oh, yes. I believe I did forget to tell you about Rebecca and Ivanhoe."

The women exchanged glances of bewilderment with an air that indicated a certain nebulous familiarity with these names.

"You see, ladies, I am fond of history. If I had children I'm sure I should call them for historical characters. But I have no children, so the best I could do was to name the dogs for Scott's heroine and her lover."

At this the committee stiffened. All differences between the sour face, the fat face, and the stern face disappeared. It was plain from their reaction to the word "lover" that they suspected this was either a foul joke or a proof of Cameron's depravity. But neither individually nor collectively could they deal further with the situation. Nervously they retrieved handkerchiefs and gloves from their handbags and turned their eyes anxiously toward the door.

But Richard had no intention of letting them off so easily.

"Before you go, ladies, you must allow me a few words. You have not found what you came looking for because it isn't here. I am not a sadist and I don't torture dogs any more than I torture patients. If you had come out here because you honestly believe that experiment and research are wrong and unnecessary because human life is neither worth living nor worth saving, I might have granted you the honors in the argument. There's a good deal to be said for that point of view.

"But you came because you imagine that other people are like you, because you think I must enjoy tormenting animals as much as you enjoy pestering your fellow citizens.

"If it were possible to reason with you, I'd tell you a little of what animal experimentation has taught us about tuberculosis and diphtheria and syphilis and cancer and diabetes and other diseases. But I couldn't convince you; the facts about these things have nothing to do with your opinions or your actions. But I, for one, would find your overdone sympathy for laboratory animals more impressive if you had some human kindness about you.

"Why do you cry over guinea pigs and white rats when you don't care that there are kids in this town that haven't enough to eat or decent clothes on their backs or homes fit to live in and are going to die of preventable diseases before they grow up? Why don't you try to make Seaforth a place fit for youngsters to live in, instead of sticking your fingers into things like research that are beyond your comprehension?"

Although these words stirred them to deep resentment, the women of the committee made no retort, no attempt to refute Cameron's implications. With such dignity as they could muster they fled the house. Watching as they hurried toward their car, Richard thought he saw in their still backs a sort of ludicrous resemblance to the foolish virgins of the New Testament fable.

But he knew that their departure was not an admission of defeat, but only a temporary tactical retreat. They would be back again one day, better armed.

Laughing to himself, he went back into the cottage to find DiPallo waiting anxiously for him. Unable to conceal his worry, Joe asked the question that had been agitating his loyal soul all evening.

"What the dames goin' to do to you?"

Cameron looked reassuringly at DiPallo and flung himself into his armchair.

"Oh, hell, Joe. They won't do anything. They'll sputter a lot, but they won't have a chance to do anything else. Go to bed and forget about them."

Richard lighted his pipe and blew out a great cloud of fragrant smoke which drifted in white wreaths above his head. The look on his face was the one with which he confronted new problems or old difficulties that sprang up to harass him anew.

"You know, Joe," he said to the man who was still waiting in the doorway, "this business of fixing liver so it tastes good is a sticker. People are going to be a lot more finicky than Rebecca and Ivanhoe about eating it every day. I notice you don't think it's so hot anymore yourself. But how a fellow that doesn't know any more about cooking than I do is going to invent some new way of dressing it up to taste nice is beyond me."

II

When Dr. Ascot returned from his Alaskan cruise the first of September, he found a huge pile of letters waiting for him. Before leaving for the North he had inserted in the Journal of the American Medical Association an advertisement for an assistant physician and had asked for the answers to be sent to his residence rather than to the office. It seemed better to him for Cameron to know nothing of his intentions.

Now he sat down and spent his first evening at home going over the letters of application. Many of them were clearly impossible—illegibly written on cheap paper or poorly typed or lacking important details of training and experience—but there were a half dozen that Ascot thought worthy of further investigation. These he put aside to take with him next morning, resolving to keep his project a secret for the present.

This resolution he might have kept had not Mrs. Ascot at breakfast next morning passed on to him a bit of gossip told her by the cook. This woman, it appeared, was an intimate of a maid whose mistress was a member of the Society for the Prevention of Cruelty to Animals; the maid, it also appeared, had overheard the ladies of the committee that called on Richard discussing their experience. In the cook's recital of this second-hand information there was little resemblance to the facts: Cameron was made out to be not only a torturer of animals but a most ill-mannered person who swore and used obscene language in the presence of ladies.

"I suppose you'll have to look into this, Sam. Of course what the cook told me is probably nothing like what actually happened. You know Mrs. Sampson loves to make up stories out of whole cloth. But it would be bad for her to go around spreading things of this sort about Dr. Cameron."

Ascot immediately lost his temper.

"Damn the fellow!" he shouted. "I won't have him around another day. He's worse than Featherstone. No telling how much business this tale will lose me if it once gets around. I'll throw him out on his neck, that's what I'll do. There are plenty of men who'll be glad of his job."

Mrs. Ascot, appalled at this threat, tried to quiet her husband.

"But, Sam," she expostulated, "there probably isn't more than a shred of truth in the whole story. It would be too bad to let Dr. Cameron go when he handles the work so well. With a new man you might not be able to get out of town so often."

She would have liked to add that she liked Richard and had come to hope that he might stay on permanently and perhaps become a junior partner one day, but she did not dare. She knew too well what an explosion that would provoke. But her efforts to placate her husband were futile; Ascot went downtown bent on getting rid of his assistant at once.

His immediate task was a double one: to write to the most promising applicants and the persons they had given as references, and to consult his attorney about the new contract he had made earlier in the summer with Cameron. To dictate the letters was easy but the interview with the lawyer was difficult.

"If all you wanted was to tie the man up for a few weeks while you went off to Alaska on this trip and still be able to fire him whenever you wanted to as soon as you got home, why didn't you say so when you had me draw up the contract? Good Lord, Ascot, you said to make it tight, and I did. Unless Cameron has fallen down in his work or done something grossly unprofessional, he can make you trouble if you try to throw him out now."

Ascot flushed brick red and began to sputter. What was the use of having a lawyer draw up papers, he demanded hotly, if he didn't put in a way to evade them? This was all nonsense. He could hire and fire whom he liked and as he pleased. He didn't like Cameron and he was going to get rid of the fellow, contract or no contract.

"What's wrong with him?" asked the lawyer curiously. "He seems to me like an upstanding sort of chap. And my brother Henry thinks he's unusually competent; he tells me the staff at the hospital like him very much."

This remark vexed Ascot afresh. He had at times felt that it was a mistake for him to have an attorney whose brother was on the Safe Harbor staff, and now he was sure of it. Just like Tom Stone's brother Henry to fall for a smart guy like Cameron!

"I don't give a damn what Henry thinks!" he cried. "I've always run my business as I liked and I don't need any advice from him—or from you either. All I want of you is to tell me how I can discharge Richard Cameron."

The lawyer shrugged his shoulders.

"Well, Ascot, I guess you'll just have to fire him and trust to luck that he won't make trouble. You said to make that agreement hog-tight, and I don't intend to figure out ways for you to break it. Unless Cameron has failed to do his work properly or committed some gross breach of professional ethics, you have no grounds on which to discharge him. If you do it anyhow, he'll have grounds for action against you. That's all." Stone rang for his secretary. "Let me know what you want to do when he starts suit."

Fuming, Dr. Ascot rushed back to the downtown laboratory where he spent the next two hours quizzing the harassed technician about Cameron's work during July and August. By noon he had worked himself up to the pitch of discharging Richard that afternoon in spite of the good record of the last eight weeks. It was while he was eating lunch that self-regard began to assert itself and counsel caution. Autumn was coming on, the golf course would be in prime condition for several weeks still, Saturday afternoon football games would soon begin, and a little later there would be the sporting events in Rainier National Park and the other mountain resorts. If he had no competent assistant to take charge of the laboratories, he could not get away from the office as often as he liked and he would be obliged to work part of every Saturday afternoon and stay in town on Sundays.

On second thought it might be better to keep Cameron on for another month or two; by that time he would have heard from the applicants he had written to and perhaps have completed arrangements with one of them. Then he could throw Cameron out and take his own time about breaking the new man in. Half-wistfully Ascot looked about the restaurant but he saw only a few men to nod to and none he knew well enough to confide in. A wave of self-pity engulfed him. Here he was eating his first luncheon after his vacation alone. There was no such thing anymore as friendship, it seemed to him.

Drearily he plodded back to the office, feeling that everything conspired to spoil his happiness. It did not improve his mood to learn from the girl in the reception room that Cameron had been detained at the hospital to make a frozen section report on a surgical emergency. By the time Richard came in at a quarter past two, Ascot's resentment had risen very nearly to its post-breakfast level. He called the younger man into his private room and complained that the volume of work had not increased materially while he had been away and that Richard had allowed the stenographer to use a rubber stamp of his signature on the reports instead of signing them each with pen and ink in his own hand.

With some difficulty Cameron controlled both his temper and his sense of humor.

"During July and August when so many of the doctors are out of town it is almost impossible for business to pick up much. So far as the reports are concerned, I had both laboratories to take care of and I didn't have time to read all the reports and sign them too. So I left off the signature. That seemed to me less important than checking them to make sure they were correct."

In spite of himself Ascot recognized a certain fairness in this and was slightly mollified. After all, Cameron was reliable and his work was good. If only he hadn't started trying to make a reputation for himself, if he could only have been content to work and keep his mouth shut, the fellow might have stayed on indefinitely and perhaps stepped into his shoes when he was ready to retire. This half-melancholy thought softened Ascot's petulant expression a little and Richard smiled to himself.

"Did you notice, doctor," he asked quietly, "that Browning came over to us in July?" He threw this inquiry out casually as though he did not know that Ascot had angled for Browning's work for years.

"No!" exclaimed Samuel Ascot. "Did he? The girl didn't tell me." There was genuine approbation in his words. "Well, well! How much did he send us in August?"

"A little over two hundred. If you'll wait a minute, I'll bring the ledger in and you can see the total for yourself."

Ascot looked eagerly at the entries in the account book. Yes, there it was under Browning's name—$215.50. That account would average nearly three hundred a month the year round, between three thousand and thirty-six hundred more coming in next year. Ascot suddenly realized that this would pay an assistant's salary—a new assistant, of course, not Cameron. He had foolishly raised Richard from three hundred a month to three hundred and thirty in that new contract last June. But a new man he could start off at two hundred and seventy-five, and then Browning's work would cover it.

Ascot had a moment of rosy dreams. Perhaps next spring he could afford a bigger car and in another year or two he might be able to build a more pretentious house. These reflections mellowed his mood and his pale blue eyes became almost friendly. On the spur of the moment he resolved to give Cameron a good reference; after all, he was smart, no question of that.

But this fit of good temper did not last out the afternoon. At half-past four Dr. Ascot went into the main workroom with a test tube of blood for a Wassermann and experienced an impulse to boast a little to the technician about Browning's accession. That young woman, who was busy with a nitrogen determination, was annoyed at the interruption and, without realizing the seriousness of what she was doing, she said that Dr. Browning had decided to send his work to the laboratory because of a clever diagnosis Cameron had made for him at the hospital early in the summer.

In a rage Ascot rushed back into his office. So that was it! More of this supplanting, the instant he was out of sight! Perhaps the two had an understanding that Browning would take his work away again if Cameron were to leave the laboratory. That was what you had to expect from assistants. They were alike, all of them: not one could be trusted. It was enough to make a man insane.

In his anger Ascot quite forgot the extra income Browning's work would mean, his pleasure at having Browning weaned away from his competitors at last. He shook his fist toward the small room where Cameron usually worked in the afternoons, he cursed and swore in a shrill voice that penetrated both the workroom and the reception room and caused the technician to frown over her calculations and the secretary to hasten back over the letters and reports she had finished typing for possible errors. Finally, Ascot called his attorney on the phone and told him what had happened. To his disgust Tom Stone began to laugh.

"Man, you're crazy! Most fellows would be glad if a man who was working for them could pull in business, not trying to figure out a way to fire him for it. If you're wise, you'll cool down and forget it. That's my advice."

But Ascot could not cool down. On the contrary, he boiled up into a fury that drove him out in search of Cameron.

"Why, I supposed you knew Dr. Cameron had been called back to the hospital," said the secretary. "Some emergency, I don't know just what."

"Emergency !" snorted Ascot. "Emergency! And not a word to me! He rushes off just as though it was his laboratory, not mine. Who do they think they are at that hospital, calling him all the time? Dr. Cameron, Dr. Cameron! A . . . a . . . ah!" Purple in the face, Ascot rushed back into his private office, leaving a handful of patients in the reception room staring after him in an astonished silence.

"I'm sick of that fellow, of his name, of everything about him!" he growled, throwing himself into his desk chair. "Sick of his grinning around here all the time, with his damned freckles and his persnickety clothes. He can't get away with this."

He seized the telephone and called the hospital number. But before the call was completed, his eye fell upon an envelope addressed to him and marked "Personal," which was tucked into one corner of his desk blotter. He could not remember having seen it there when he came in from lunch. He turned it over and found Cameron's name and address on the back flap, then tore it open with trembling, angry fingers. The date at the top of the typewritten sheet was that of the previous day.

"My dear Dr. Ascot:
   "I wish to tender my resignation as of the above date, to take effect on October first of this year."

The next lines ran together and blurred in Ascot's vision. He did not hear the switchboard operator at the hospital calling "Safe Harbor Hospital, Safe Harbor Hospital" over and over. Mechanically he replaced the receiver on its holder.

"For some months I have felt that I was not a suitable person to continue here indefinitely as your assistant. However, after our agreement of last June, I thought it might be well for me to finish out a second year before leaving. Longer than that it would have been out of the question for me to stay in any event because any real increase in the volume of work done in these laboratories is impossible for reasons connected with your personality.

"But my decision to leave Seaforth this fall was precipitated by an opportunity to go into the Fifer Research Institute in Northdevon to work in the Department of Physiology with Dr. Thornton on a problem I have been interested in for some time.

"Should it be convenient for you to permit me to go before October first, I shall be glad to do so.

"It may be of some interest to you to know that Dr. Farquhar plans to go east with me to do graduate work in radiology.

"Very truly yours,
"Richard Cameron."

The blood vessels in Samuel Ascot's brain during the next thirty minutes were called upon to undergo a terrific strain. Usually he shouted and waved his arms and stamped up and down the floor until he worked off a rage, but today he sat glowering and brooding, hunched over his desk, incapable of speech. The emotions that surged back and forth in his mind were too conflicting and too vehement to be expressed in words, but now and then he emitted a sound like the growl of a beast.

This, it seemed to him, was the last blow of fate—that an assistant of his should resign before he could be discharged. Nothing more insulting or more humiliating could Ascot imagine except the possibility that the fellow might tell some of the other doctors what he had done. The secretary and the technician slipped stealthily out of the suite at five-fifteen but Ascot simmered and stewed in his own sour juices until six o'clock when he finally made shift to go home. At nine that evening he called Richard on the phone and told him not to report at either laboratory again.

Ascot never understood how Cameron had managed this thing. Not for an instant did he admit that the man had been clever enough to foresee what was coming and act accordingly. At times he was inclined to suspect that Tom Stone had tipped Richard off. He quickly forgot all the work Cameron had done, all his accuracy and speed in the laboratory, all his overtime and night work, and all the Sunday calls he had taken without complaint. In Ascot's mind the younger man changed swiftly into a crook, a schemer, a swindler. He did not notice that many of the hospital staff shied away from him when he vented his wrath at Cameron in their hearing.

He did not observe that Mary Compton was pale and absent-minded, and if anyone had told him that her engagement to one of the younger doctors in Seaforth, which was announced just before Hallowe'en, had any connection with Richard's departure, he would have said the notion was insane. He fumed and sputtered for days that there "was something funny" about Cameron's liking for Sandy Farquhar, concerning whom Oscar Steinberg was busily gossiping.

III

All this was a matter of indifference to Richard. He was very busy exchanging telegrams with Dr. Thornton about Sandy's matriculation in the Graduate School of Medicine, arranging to surrender the lease on his cottage, and superintending the construction of a trailer in which he could haul his belongings.

The cool sunny morning on which the Cameron-Farquhar expedition started for the Atlantic coast found a week left of September. The cavalcade was an unusual one: in the blue roadster were Cameron and Farquhar, in a seat built into the space in the rear of the car originally intended for luggage sat Joe DiPallo, bright-eyed and vigorous, and in the closed trailer, bringing up the rear, were Rebecca and Ivanhoe, unaware that they were leaving forever the city of their nativity.

From the foothills beyond Lake Donovan, before beginning the climb toward the summit of the Cascade Mountains, Richard stopped the car and looked back at the city sprawling over its steep hillsides. He had always liked Seaforth's way of overrunning bluffs and leaping across ravines. "I wonder what it'll be like a hundred years from now," he thought. Then he laughed and jabbed Farquhar in the ribs.

"Better say goodbye to Seaforth, Sandy. You won't be there anymore. You too, Joe," he added as he glanced back at DiPallo.

On his own side Cameron leaned far out of the machine and put one hand against his nose in a gesture of contempt.

"That's for you, Sam Ascot. And may you choke on a fishbone!"

Then he let in the clutch and started up the long grade, headed east.

BOOK II
NORTHDEVON

CHAPTER I

I

Although Northdevon was one of the oldest and largest cities in the United States it was not built up into the air and down into the ground like its neighbor, New York. Instead it sprawled over a great deal of flat land near the Atlantic seaboard and depended for transportation on clanking surface street cars and a handful of double-decked buses. Its inhabitants proudly called it a city of homes and regarded the lack of subways as due to the stability of their characters rather than the slowness of their wits. In the newer suburbs the streets were broad and even in the old residential sections they were often lined with trees, but the Damon Fifer Research Institute was not located in any of these quarters. It reared its seven stories of dark red brick in the southwest corner of the city, among the slums.

Early one morning in late October Richard Cameron, just descended from a Poplar Avenue car, stood on the curbing across the street, looking at the Institute. There was something aloof about it. With its austere façade and the flight of broad white steps that led up to the entrance, it stood out among the old, two- and three-story tenements of the neighborhood as though it were the twentieth century's conscious substitute for a cathedral. Soft autumnal sunlight shone on rows of white-trimmed windows and the whole building seemed to exude an atmosphere of cleanliness appropriate to a temple of research.

Once more Cameron was embarking on adventure. Behind that dignified façade worked men who had ideas, and he was to be one of them. Fifer stood high in the scientific world and was reputed to have almost unlimited financial resources; it meant much to be appointed an associate there. Richard was sure he would find endless opportunity: when the anemia problem was solved there would be others waiting for him. He could think of many things he would like to study: typhus, cancer, the common cold, tuberculosis. At the prospect his inveterate curiosity made him smile.

For a fleeting instant as he walked up the white steps of the Institute it occurred to him that it might have been better to wear a plain blue suit this morning than the rough brown tweed he had on; the dignified atmosphere of the place seemed a reproof of the angle at which his soft brown hat clung to the side of his head. Perhaps his addiction to bright colors and loose-woven tweeds and homespuns was inappropriate in a man about to make his official début at Fifer. But this feeling was suddenly swept away again by a rush of justifiable pride. Three months ago he had been trying to do two men's work well enough to escape verbal excoriation by Samuel Ascot, and today he was walking into the Damon Fifer Institute to be formally installed as associate in physiology.

Besides his pride in this achievement, he was almost equally pleased about Sandy Farquhar. On the way across the continent Farquhar had been despondent about his own future, but three days after their arrival in Northdevon, with the help and advice of Dr. Thornton, Cameron had pushed him into matriculating in the Graduate School of Medicine. Now, within three weeks, Sandy was a different man; he was engrossed in his work, he was less nervous about meeting people, and the fear that had lurked in the back of his muddy brown eyes when he was in Seaforth had died down. He had found a two-room apartment near the medical school where he did his own cooking and lived in solitary independence, and he told Cameron that he would like to spend two or three years in Northdevon. "There are no better teachers anywhere in the country than Penfield and Draper," he said. "If I put in three years with them I'll have as good training in radiology as anyone could ask, and I might not always have to take filthy little jobs in two-by-four hospitals."

As Cameron stepped into the entry, a blonde girl glanced out of a window marked "Information" and said "Good morning, doctor." That in itself was evidence that he was known as a man who had a right to be there, he reflected, as he went on into the main lobby.

This was a large square room from which two long corridors and several small waiting rooms opened. One of the corridors ran toward the rear of the building where the outpatients' clinic was held, the other ran off at a right angle into the wing that housed the executive offices. The waiting rooms, of which there were several, were cut off from the lobby and separated from each other by a white wainscoting three feet tall, surmounted by glass partitions that went up to the ceiling. Sitting in them Richard could see a motley throng of men and women, most of whom seemed to exhale an atmosphere of hopelessness. Now and then a brisk, white-clad nurse would lead one of them away down the corridor toward the clinic, but Cameron saw none come back. It struck him that it was as though they had been sucked into the maw of a huge machine from which there was no escape, but before he had time to ponder this impression Dr. Thornton came in and joined him.

James Alexander Thornton, more often known as Jim, was a thick-set man of forty-odd with a round genial face, keen blue eyes, and a deeply cleft chin. About his large bald spot grew a fringe of sandy hair and he had the air of being vastly entertained by almost everything he saw. When he found that Richard had been waiting for him, he grimaced.

"You're too confounded punctual, Cameron. Remember I

have to drive in twelve miles every morning. That's the price I pay for living in a snooty suburb like Cornwallis. And if you keep this up, your punctuality will get under my skin.... Well, suppose we go along and see if we can see Dr. Hastings now."

As he followed Thornton, Richard suddenly realized that he was nervous. His buttocks and the backs of his thighs tingled and seemed to shake inside. It was not an ordinary matter for an obscure fellow like him to meet a person as famous as Thomas Allen Hastings, Director of Fifer Institute.

Hastings' anteroom proved to be a small square cell lined with filing cabinets and bookcases full of bound scientific journals. From a handsome walnut desk where she was going through a card index, a middle-aged woman with carefully waved, bobbed gray hair looked up and nodded impersonally.

"Good morning, Dr. Thornton. Will you be seated, please? Dr. Hastings will be free in a moment."

She did not speak to Richard or take any apparent notice of him, but went back to her work. Cameron was annoyed. Twice in the last three weeks he had been introduced to this woman and still she ignored him. He wondered whether she simply did not recognize him or whether she regarded mere research associates as beneath her notice, and told himself that this would probably be another of the things he would never learn. He sat down, crossed his long legs with an elaborate display of indifference to all secretaries, and ran a hand exploringly over the short wiry red hair that covered his head like a close-fitting cap. Then he discovered some dust on one brown oxford and was just rubbing it off on the back of a trouser leg when the door of the private office opened and two men came out.

The one who was taking his leave Richard knew by sight to be Ralph Lanister, who had charge of the General Clinic. He was a dark, saturnine man of middle height, dressed in a double-breasted blue suit that bespoke an expensive tailor. He was speaking in a low voice to Dr. Hastings, a much older man.

"I think, then, that I'd better go on with the original plan."

The elder man smiled nervously through his spectacles.

"Yes, yes. I think that will be best."

"Montagu will object—violently." Lanister gave a short laugh in which, it seemed to Richard, there was a good deal of compressed cynicism.

The gray-haired secretary, who had leaped up the instant the door opened and begun to flutter about the two men, now interrupted them.

"Pardon me, please, Dr. Lanister," she said in a tone in which Cameron liked to think he could detect a note of fear. "But Dr. Hastings has an appointment."

Lanister looked at her as though she were a bothersome insect and said to Hastings, "Very well, then. That's understood." Then he looked around and nodded to Thornton. "Hello, Jim. How's everything?"

"Fine, thanks. I've brought down my new associate, Dr. Cameron, to meet Dr. Hastings and you. He's going to work on anemia. I discussed the problem with you, Dr. Hastings, before you went abroad last spring, you remember."

"Oh, yes," assented Hastings vaguely. "Now that you mention it, I do recall the occasion, although I had forgotten it.... Well, well, Dr. Cameron, I'm glad to meet you. Do you know Dr. Lanister of the General Clinic?"

Richard could feel Lanister looking him up and down. There was a vast difference between his sophisticated brown eyes and Hastings' mild blue ones.

"So you're going to be Jim's 'Man Friday,' are you?" Cameron thought there was a flicker of amusement on Lanister's dark, lined face. "Well, I wish you luck. I hope your job will be more cheerful than mine: I'm the fellow who tells people they're going to die and we can't do anything more for them."

Lanister's voice was smooth and slightly flippant but the long-fingered hand he held out gripped Richard's firmly. Cameron felt an instant liking for this worldly-looking individual. If he ever said anything complimentary, it would mean something. But no less than he admired Lanister's sophisticated appearance, Richard was struck by the weariness that seemed to hover over him.

"You'd better bring Dr. Cameron to the staff meeting, Jim.

He might as well see all the animals at once. I think they'll be in good form this morning."

"I believe he's to be introduced today, Ralph."

Lanister nodded at Thornton and Richard, bowed slightly to Dr. Hastings, and walked quickly out of the room.

"Mrs. Harlow, will you see that I am not disturbed for a few minutes?" said Hastings. "Thank you. And now, gentlemen, if you will come in."

Hastings was a short, slight man of fifty-nine with a pleasant pink-cheeked face and small hands and feet. He was obviously a gentleman, and the books that lined his private office suggested to Cameron that he was a scholar as well. His white hair was brushed neatly across a wide forehead above two mild blue eyes and his small white mustache was closely trimmed. Leaning back in his desk chair, he smiled genially at Richard.

"I'm sure that you will find your work here profitable, and I hope you'll enjoy your associations in the Institute. There are some fine men here. Of course you're familiar with Dr. Montagu's studies in tuberculosis. He and Fergusson have done some brilliant work in heredity recently. And Lanister whom you met outside just now is an authority on diseases of the lungs."

Richard found himself wondering whether this pleasant elderly gentleman was trying to play the salesman.

"You'll find an open door in every department, doctor.... Let me see. Didn't Dr. Thornton tell me you'd been in general practice?"

"Yes, sir. I practiced in the country, out in Montana, for three years."

"Oh, yes, that was it. Montana. Well, well! I recall crossing Montana some years ago when I was on my way to Yellowstone Park. It seemed an extraordinarily large state."

Cameron felt an impulse to laugh: he was sure that this mild little man would find more extraordinary things about Montana than its size if he were to live there.

"And you were in the service too?"

"Twenty-three months in France, sir."

"I see. And you were fortunate enough to come out with no injury?"

"I was not wounded but I did pick up an osteomyelitis in one leg."

"But you have recovered?"

"I think so, sir."

When Dr. Hastings turned to Thornton with some questions about the Department of Physiology, Richard glanced about the room. It was quite large and one side was covered from floor to ceiling with open book shelves. On the wall above Hastings' desk hung a number of signed photographs, some of which Cameron recognized as those of famous European scientists whom he had seen at medical conferences in Paris during the War. On the other two sides of the office there were windows and one of them, surprisingly enough, looked out on a tiny plot of grass with a tree or two. Richard found something cheering about this unexpected little island of green tucked away among Northdevon's old, red-brick slums.

Presently Thornton brought the interview to an end.

"If you'll excuse us, Dr. Hastings, I think Cameron and I had better be getting back upstairs. I have some work to finish before staff meeting."

"I'm glad you came down, both of you," said Hastings cordially. "I enjoy contact with men who are active in research more than any of you realize, I believe."

Outside, in the waiting room, held at bay by the efficient gray-haired secretary, were four men with briefcases or catalogues. A less astute observer than Cameron would have seen as he watched them spring up and surround Hastings that the man dreaded them. Richard found himself half pitying the white-mustached director confronted with these high-pressure salesmen.

On their way up to the Department of Physiology on the third floor, Thornton looked with fresh interest at his new associate.

"You never told me you'd had anything the matter with you while you were in the service."

"Well, I saw no reason for you to be interested in my tibia. It's in my leg, not yours. Besides, I never think about it myself anymore unless someone asks me a direct question."

"Haven't you tried to get compensation?"

"No. This wasn't the result of a wound, and I might have had a bone infection just like it if I'd stayed in Montana and never gone near the War. The government took care of me while I was sick and that's enough. I don't want any more help from them.""

"Don't you belong to the Legion?" asked Thornton, pulling back the door of the automatic elevator.

"No. I'm not a joiner. The fewer things I belong to, the fewer strings there are on me for people to pull."

At this remark, Jim Thornton laughed aloud.

"You're a queer veteran.... But you may be right, at that.... Come on into my room, Cameron. I want to have a talk with you."

Richard hesitated.

"I was just going to take a look at Rebecca and Ivanhoe and see whether Joe had showed up yet this morning."

"You don't need to do either now. Johnson told me last night that he'd never had as good a helper in the animal rooms as your Italian. That means a steady job for him from now on. And the morning report from the kennel shows both your dogs in good shape."

Cameron was openly pleased with the new arrangement for DiPallo.

"I've been afraid he might get away from me here in Northdevon. And I'm depending on him to convince you that I'm on the right track about pernicious anemia."

"That's just what I want to talk to you about, Cameron. Come on back to my office."

Fifer Institute was a conservative place not given to many changes in personnel or physical arrangement. Thornton's predecessor had cut up the greater part of the Physiology Department into small rooms which looked more like cells than offices, each of them devoted to the housing of some one division of the work under progress. One cubby-hole was full of records of rachitic rats and another of hundreds of Xray plates and films of growing bones. In the three years Thornton had been in charge, he had made a good many changes in the way work was carried on, but, as yet, only a few in the actual arrangement of floor space. He had, however, knocked out a partition between two adjacent cubicles to make a room of reasonable size for himself and was about to do the same for Richard.

Another evidence of the innate conservatism of the Institute was that only in the executive wing downstairs were the offices furnished with modern desks and chairs. On the upper floors the desks were home-made ones secured years before from the manual training department of one of the Northdevon high schools. They had once been painted black but now they were scarred and battered from long use. The chairs were the sort of light armchairs with perpendicular rungs at the backs and sides that were popular at one time in rural hotel lobbies. They, too, were worn and shabby.

But, although the desk was ancient, Thornton's office was a trim, tidy place with windows on two sides and filing cabinets and bookshelves of green metal. A typewriter table stood against one wall and there was a stereoscope for the examination of Xray films. Thornton motioned Richard into a chair.

"I'm hard to convince, Cameron. I never believe anything until I can't help it. One swallow doesn't make a summer and your Italian doesn't prove your case. How do you know he isn't in one of the spontaneous remissions that characterize pernicious anemia? The answer is that you don't know. You hope, you believe, you think—but you don't know."

Richard nodded soberly. "You're right, Dr. Thornton."

"Well, then, admitting that, suppose we find out exactly what we do know. You've been trying to confirm the findings of those men who experimented with artificial anemia in dogs, and I've been working along the same line recently. Between us we've got six dogs we've made observations on. Now, just what are you sure of? What have you proved to be true?"

"Four things, Dr. Thornton. First, a meat diet increases the flow of bile and cuts down the output of bile pigments; starches and sugars do the opposite. Second, dogs made anemic by bleeding regenerate blood after the first bleeding quickly no matter what they eat, which means that they must have saved up somewhere in their bodies blood-making material for a day of need. Third, anemic dogs regenerate blood better while fasting than when they're on a diet of sugar. Fourth, dogs made artificially anemic will stay that way for a long time on a diet of bread and milk or of rice, potatoes, and milk that is ample to maintain them in good flesh and good general condition."

"You've left out something, haven't you?" Thornton smiled quizzically.

"You said only the things I'd proved," retorted Richard, laughing, "And it may be a coincidence that these dogs re-build their blood with such startling rapidity when they eat meat."

"Don't take my criticisms too literally," advised Thornton.

"Well, Rebecca and Ivanhoe have done this sort of thing three times in succession. Fed meat, especially beef hearts or liver, after bleeding, they've regenerated their blood much faster than they ever did on enormous doses of iron added to the diet of bread and milk, or rice, potatoes, and milk."

"And you reason therefore that you're dealing with cause and effect. I admit the logic of the argument. But there are many things that aren't logical. And there are many things you don't know yet about this blood-making. How much liver does it take in proportion to the animal's weight to produce a given increase in red blood cells? How soon does improvement begin and what are the first signs of it? What sort of meat is best? Ought it to be cooked or is it better raw?

"When you've learned by experiment the answers to those questions—and that might take a long time—you still won't know whether the same thing that cures experimental anemia in dogs will cure pernicious anemia in a man. The two are far from being the same thing, you know."

"All you've said is true, Dr. Thornton. But didn't you ever know something was true before you could prove it? If you'd been watching Joe DiPallo since last February as sharply as I have, you wouldn't think he was in a spontaneous remission any more than I do.".

Thornton laughed softly. "Perhaps not," he admitted.

"From the start I've had a hunch that this is going to be something big." Richard leaned forward across the desk and looked straight at the keen blue eyes of his chief. "Don't ask me why I think this, for I can't tell you. But deep down inside of me I know it."

Jim Thornton looked intently into Cameron's face; there were animation and eagerness there, and there was also stubbornness. This man with his red hair and wide cheekbones and long firm chin had the air of one who would never turn back once he had started to prove a point or do a certain thing.

"I think you're on the track of something important, too, Cameron. It might turn out to be almost as big as insulin. But that's all the more reason we must be careful. We mustn't let anything leak out until we're sure of our ground. We mustn't publish anything beyond the plain objective record of our animal experiments.

"You see, my father was a doctor too and he happened to be in Europe studying when Koch announced that he considered tuberculin a cure for tuberculosis. Father told me how frantic patients rushed the sanatoria demanding to be treated with tuberculin, and how hospitals had to lock their supplies of it up in their safes. Then it turned out to be a false alarm. It was the same sort of thing with the Friedmann turtle serum: that was a pure fake but it raised many people's hopes and set them on the wrong track and so helped, in the end, to kill them. We mustn't do that sort of thing, Cameron. We mustn't talk until we know. I've taken no one into my confidence except Lanister. In a general way I told Hastings something of our plans but he didn't seem to be especially interested.

"There's something else, too, that you've got to take into consideration, Cameron. The Institute has no hospital of its own; it has to depend on other institutions for beds for patients. But Ralph Lanister knows the ropes in Northdevon; he's lived here all his life and he has a lot of influence. If the experimental work looks promising he'll help us get hospital connections. Otherwise, we'd never have a patient except those well enough to come in to our clinics downstairs.

"One thing more. This is your job—not mine. I've got a lot of other things to look after, and I want you to go ahead with this anemia work on your own. You thought of it before I did, and it's yours so far as I'm concerned. . . . No, don't argue with me about it. I mean what I say. I'll help you whenever I can, but that's all. Now, get out and get busy. . . . and don't talk."

For five minutes after Richard left the room, Thornton sat drawing little triangles thoughtfully on his desk blotter.

"I like that fellow. He's sure he's right. But he doesn't get sore when you ask him to prove it."

II

After he left Thornton's office Richard went to see Rebecca and Ivanhoe. In the animal rooms he found the dogs curled up in their cages fast asleep and Joe DiPallo clad in one of the long green-gray denim coats that were the uniform of the working personnel of the Institute. Joe seemed happy: he told Cameron that he had found in the Italian quarter nearby some old friends of his father who had lived in the same village in the old country. Besides, he was glad to have a regular job again, and something coming in every Saturday.

"It's fine, Joe. The best thing that ever happened to you. You'll have more money than I could afford to pay you and still be right here where we can keep an eye on you."

So far as Richard could find, there was but one drawback for DiPallo. Eric Johnson, who had charge of all the animals in the Institute, was not an Italian, and Joe had cherished a blanket animosity for Scandinavians in general and Johnsons in particular since a Swede of that name who had had more to drink than was good for him had beaten Joe up for charging him twenty cents for a shine on the ground that number fourteen shoes rated an overcharge.

"This Johnson, he's a Swede. I don't know if I like him. But ..." Joe shrugged his shoulders expressively and promised to try. "Maybe I learn more than him and get his job someday."

Perhaps Cameron was not so disturbed as he should have been at this evidence that DiPallo was being Americanized. He had come down to impress on Joe the necessity for not talking about his own health or the work at the Institute. The voluble Italian might say things to his friends that would eventually filter into current gossip or even get into the papers. So Richard talked earnestly to him of these dangers and DiPallo gave his word to keep watch on his tongue.

From the animal rooms Cameron went to the library which was on the top floor of the building. Hearing the peculiar rumble which attested that the elevator was in use, he ran up the stairs that wound about the elevator shaft and arrived at the seventh floor considerably out of breath. As he paused at the half-open door of the library, he heard a high-pitched male voice in loud talk.

"Now, Miss Emerson, this is important. Dr. Montagu is anxious for me to get this paper written at once and I have those others promised for December, as you know. You'll have to see what you can get for me at the Academy of Medicine and the University library, and then let me have the abstracts in the morning. I certainly hope you won't be going away again, Miss Emerson. The substitute was hopeless. She couldn't read French and she couldn't make abstracts and they wouldn't let her have anything at the Academy because she lost a book we'd borrowed there just before you left."

All this seemed to have been said without stopping for air and Richard peered in curiously at the person who had such excellent control of his breath. Leaning over the counter that formed the front of the librarian's alcove, he saw a large man in a ragged, green-gray laboratory coat. The man had a big head and a round, flabby, over-sized face with small gray eyes that darted from the librarian to Cameron and back again. His voice was ill-tempered and sharp, and Richard was annoyed by it no less than by the untidiness of his hair and the raggedness of his coat.

"Now, Miss Emerson," repeated the man fussily, "be sure you don't forget. I must have these references this afternoon."

The young woman who stood behind the librarian's counter did not betray the slightest vexation; she smiled politely at the agitated man and reassured him that she would not fail to do as he wished. The low voice in which she spoke struck Cameron as being unusually melodious and pleasing.

"All right, then, we'll leave it that way for the present." The flabby-faced man seemed to begrudge this civility, he hesitated a moment longer and cast a suspicious glance at Richard, who had gone on about his own business and was busy at the card catalogue.

"Is there anything else you wanted me to do for you, doctor?"

Again Cameron found himself listening involuntarily to the young woman's musical voice.

"No. I guess that's all." The big man managed to inject into these five short words an astonishing amount of displeasure. He glared for an instant at the librarian, glowered once more in Richard's direction, then rushed out of the room with coat tails flying. "Flounced" was the word that flashed into Cameron's mind as he watched the exit.

He stole another look at the girl. She was standing as she had been throughout her interview with the unpleasant man in the ragged laboratory coat; her hands and forearms were extended on the counter before her and her face was half turned toward the door. It was a pleasant, attractive face with a wide forehead and a small but firmly set chin, but at the moment its expression reminded Richard of the faces of young mothers who are trying to quiet obstreperous offspring in public while promising themselves a more satisfactory seance as soon as they got home.

In spite of his sympathy for her, Cameron grinned to himself. This girl was evidently the regular librarian. He put her down as a great improvement upon the elderly spinster who had been in charge during the few weeks he had spent in the Institute before going west.

Judith Emerson had dark brown hair that lay in soft, waving lines along her cheeks. Her skin, usually pale olive, was now touched with a bright flush that seemed to round out her cheeks. Her eyes, set wide apart, were large and warmly golden brown. She did not so much as flicker an eyelash but, from the cover of the card catalogue, Richard saw the fingers of one hand close on the pencil she held until the knuckles seemed to whiten. With an effort he turned back to his search in the card index.

When he looked up the next time, Miss Emerson had sat down in her alcove and only her head and shoulders were to be seen above the counter. Observed thus in profile, her head was beautifully shaped. She wore a blue frock with a round white collar and a windsor scarf tied in a loose bow under her chin, and now that she was sitting down so that he could see only the upper part of her body, she seemed absurdly young.

"May I ask you something, Miss Emerson?" said Cameron, approaching the alcove with several slips of paper in his hand.

The girl looked up, obviously surprised to hear herself addressed by name by a person she had never seen until ten minutes before, but she smiled courteously and came forward at once.

"Perhaps I should introduce myself. My name is Cameron. I'm working with Dr. Thornton but I only came this month so I don't know much about the Institute yet. Can you tell me what this cabalistic sign on the book cards means? I've found it on several of the references I've been looking up."

At this question Judith Emerson's face flushed and she seemed to hesitate before answering. When she did speak there was a definite acidity in her tone.

"I put that mark on the cards of the books Dr. Fergusson or Dr. Montagu have taken out and never returned—or lost. I don't know which."

"Oh!" said Cameron somewhat embarrassed. "I see. . . . Well, pardon me. I didn't know."

"No, of course not. How could you?" Judith paused an instant and then went on in the low, musical voice that had attracted

Richard's notice in the first place. "I'm sorry, Dr. Cameron. I didn't mean to be rude. Won't you let me see your list of references? Perhaps I can find the missing volumes at the Academy or the University when I go there to look up Dr. Fergusson's material this afternoon." Swiftly she checked over the slips. "If you'll let me keep these, I'll be glad to see what I can do for you."

Richard folded his arms on the counter and smiled at the girl as beguilingly as he knew how.

"That would be very kind of you, Miss Emerson. I'm afraid I'm being a nuisance very early in my career in the Institute." Then he added curiously, "Was that Dr. Fergusson who just went out a moment ago? You see, I don't know many of the men on the staff yet."

Judith nodded.

"Well, I'll be damned!" exclaimed Cameron softly.

The young woman had no answer to this ejaculation, she merely stood as though waiting for him to ask further help or advice about using the library.

Richard was astonished. He had not heard Judith address the ragged man by name and it had never occurred to him, until she spoke of going to the Academy of Medicine for him, that this objectionable person might be Fergusson. He had heard much of Fergusson's work on heredity and had read several of his papers on the effect of Xrays on fruit flies; it seemed incredible that a man capable of such brilliant research should also be capable of such childish behavior. "Spoiled kid," he thought. "Not enough hair brush for him."

Then he looked at Judith and laughed.

"I might have known that any man who signs himself M. Carr Fergusson would have a screw loose somewhere."

The girl kept her lips firmly closed and, realizing that she had no intention of being drawn on the subject of Dr. Fergusson, Cameron returned to the matter of his references.

"I'm working on anemia, Miss Emerson, and I've been handicapped by being on the west coast, out of reach of the large medical libraries. I want to lay my hands on everything of any importance that's ever been written about the blood in anemia. Will you help me find the stuff?"

For the next half hour they were both deeply engrossed in going over his bibliography and the Cumulative Index since 1917.

"I'll go through the Index Medicus year by year as I get time," promised Judith. "It's an awful mess, but I've gotten so used to it now that I can almost always dig out what I want, eventually. You're not in a hurry, are you?"

"Oh, no. I'm starting on a problem that's likely to take years to work out. A few weeks or months mean nothing to me."

He smiled at the girl. The longer he looked at her the more attractive she seemed. She was tall and she had wide shoulders and long hands and feet. She wore a long-waisted frock of dark blue; the skirt fell in fine pleats and there was a round white collar above the cross-tucked yoke. It was clear from her talk that she knew her business thoroughly, but she seemed ridiculously young to be concerned with such subjects. Cameron presently ventured a little talk unconnected with pernicious anemia, and by the time a doctor came up from the General Clinic downstairs to inquire about the latest diet in epilepsy, Judith and he were on friendly terms and he had offered to drive her to the Academy of Medicine after lunch.

"Good heavens, Miss Emerson, if you did find that stuff Fergusson wants, you couldn't drag it all the way over here in your arms on a street car."

To her protestations that she had often done so, he remained deaf.

"I'll pick you up at one-thirty on the corner above Timball's and take you first to the Academy and then to the University library. It won't take half the time it would for you to go by street car."

For her part Judith suggested that he fill out the proper blank of which she had a supply—requesting permission to use the library of the Academy of Medicine—and get Dr. Hastings to countersign it at staff meeting.

"It will take several weeks to get your reader's card anyhow.

They look up everything about you back to the Mayflower. So the sooner you start, the better."

III

Forty-five minutes later, when Thornton and Richard went into the staff room which divided with the library the top floor of the Institute, most of the staff were already scattered among the lecture chairs which faced a low platform with a desk and a blackboard. The stratification of this gathering was easily seen. Next to Lanister in the front row of chairs sat a man whom Cameron recognized from published photographs as B. C. Montagu. He was a slight, angular man with a pale, narrow face, and he was dressed in a shabby dark suit and an old-fashioned standing collar with a black bow tie. Richard was surprised at the insignificant appearance of the man whose textbooks were studied in scores of medical schools and whom Geoffrey Kendall had always regarded as his only real rival in pathology. It seemed incongruous that he should be the great Montagu.

Beyond him was Fergusson. Now that he was in the presence of his superiors in rank, his back gave the impression of subservience rather than truculence. Occasionally he leaned across Montagu to speak to Dr. Lanister in the shrill penetrating voice Cameron recognized at once, but Lanister seemed to pay little attention to him.

Four other men in white coats sat beyond Fergusson; they were chiefs of the sections of the General Clinic downstairs, Thornton whispered to Richard. Behind them were the associates and assistants who had been able to get through their work in time to attend the staff meeting. In this group conversation seemed to lag. One or two of them had the detachment and wore the well-cut clothes of well-to-do men but most of them were clad in the long gray-green coats Cameron already knew as a sort of Fifer uniform.

Further back was a cluster of nervous men in white smocks, doctors, as Richard soon learned, who worked half-time in the clinics. Some were young and some were middle-aged, but all had small incomes and spent their afternoons in hospitals or other clinics in the city. In the extreme rear of the room sat two much younger men, Fellows, Thornton explained, in the pathological and Xray laboratories. They were recent graduates in medicine who were now working for advanced degrees under the tutelage of Montagu and Fergusson. Fellows were not usually admitted to staff meetings but these two had some special "drag" and were permitted all sorts of liberties in the Institute. In the same row as the Fellows but nearer the door sat the head nurse and her first assistant.

At the stroke of eleven Dr. Hastings came in, followed by a girl with a stenographer's notebook, and the assemblage fell silent except for Fergusson's querulous voice. Hastings tapped gently with the gavel that lay on the presiding officer's table. Fergusson glanced up as though surprised to see the Director and subsided into silence.

When roll-call and minutes had been dealt with, Dr. Hastings made a little speech. He told the staff how glad he was to be home again after nearly seven months abroad, how he had seen some remarkable things in Europe but had yet to find an institution where finer work was done than at Fifer. Since his arrival in Northdevon he had had but four days in his office; this was not long enough for him to clear up his accumulated correspondence, to say nothing of visiting the staff and talking over their problems, but he wanted to assure them once more that he was personally interested in each of them and that his office was always open to any man who cared to come to him for advice.

Having finished with these formalities, Hastings introduced first the new associate in physiology and then the two Fellows in pathology and roentgenology. Amid perfunctory handclapping Cameron stood up in his place and bowed and said "Thank you." There was a sting of disappointment in the realization that this introduction which meant so much to him seemed to mean so little to the other men that he might as well have worn a sheet and safety pin as his new brown suit. The applause for the two young Fellows in the back seat, however, was even more desultory.

With these matters out of the way, Dr. Hastings said there was something to be brought before the staff which he would ask Dr. Lanister to present. The slender chief of the General Clinic rose to his feet and stepping up to the platform began to talk in a surprisingly casual fashion, thrusting his hands into his trousers pockets and perching part of the time on one corner of Hastings' table, swinging a trim black-shod foot. About him Richard sensed again a curious mixture of energy and fatigue.

Lanister said that he had been watching the outpatient clinics for months. They were attracting more and more patients and the work of the examining physicians was growing heavier. The clinic doctors were overloaded; they had too many people to see every morning, they had no secretarial assistance, they were obliged to carry their records home and copy their entries at night in order to keep up their paperwork. Furthermore, their salaries were small.

"There are two alternatives before the trustees, gentlemen. Either to put these men on full time at double their half-time pay, with offices on one of the less crowded floors and individual stenographers. Or to continue them on part-time with a twenty-five per cent increase in pay and secretarial service during the hours they are in the clinic. The first of these alternatives would make it possible for them to give their whole energy to the Institute and would raise the standard of work in the clinic very definitely. I bring this matter before you at the request of the trustees because, as you all know, it is their policy to get the reaction of the staff on all professional changes."

Richard glanced at the little group of white-coated men in the back of the room: these clinic physicians, he saw, were pleased with Lanister's statement of their case.

"I suggest that we have an expression of opinion by the various men," concluded Lanister, with a meaning look at Hastings.

Almost before Lanister could reach his seat, Dr. Montagu sprang up. This was Richard's first full-face look at him. His features had not changed, his cheeks were still flat and pale and his lips were still thin and straight, but no one could have thought him insignificant once he began to speak. His deep set gray eyes shone from their sockets with a strange glassy brilliance that illuminated his whole narrow face, and his spare, angular body seemed to vibrate with passionate protest.

"Gentlemen, I for one cannot approve of either proposal Dr. Lanister has put before us," he said in a low, hoarse voice that barely carried to the back of the room. "This is not a hospital, it is a research institute. There are many clinics and many hospitals in Northdevon, but there is only one research institute. The examination of the public is not our business and their treatment is not our responsibility. We are here to study the causes and characteristics of disease. The only reason for having the clinics is to filter out patients who offer an opportunity for fruitful study. It is illogical to put more money into the clinics when we are always short of funds for the laboratories."

"Will you suggest what we should do with the other patients who come in, then, Dr. Montagu?" asked Lanister quietly from his chair. "I mean the ones who are ill but have no interesting or extraordinary disease."

"Do with them?" exclaimed Montagu in that low strangled voice that barely reached the rear of the room. "I don't care what you do with them. I'm not interested in them. It's sentimentality to grieve over them. Send them to some hospital or some other clinic in town. Our duty here is not to individual patients but to the world. If we were to discover the cause of one disease this year, we would do more good than if we were to spend all our time on these unfortunates in the clinics. It would be indefensible to take money from the laboratories and use it in the clinics, Dr. Lanister."

Montagu's eyes blazed as he looked at his listeners. Suddenly it came to Richard that this man was a crusader born out of his time, a crusader with a fanatical devotion to the task he set himself. And yet he was an incongruous mixture—that pale, narrow, flat-cheeked face, the hoarse, barely audible voice, the angular body, the eyes burning with fanaticism.

Slowly, almost indolently, Lanister rose to his feet again.

"There is no intention on the part of the trustees to interfere with your work, Dr. Montagu. There is no real conflict, as they see it, between clinical medicine and research. But if the examinations downstairs are inadequate for lack of time, some of the very cases you might be able to use to the best advantage in your study may be missed. Slipshod work in the clinics may easily mean less material for research."

Montagu stood where he was, thinking. Cameron could feel the man struggling to be fair, unbiased.

"Yes, I see what you mean.... There may be a good deal of truth in it, too.... It would be unwise, extremely unwise, to lose good cases for the laboratories.... Well, then, why not give them the twenty-five per cent raise and a stenographer every other forenoon?"

"Would you like to have your secretary give her time every other morning to the clinic work, then?" queried Lanister smoothly.

"That is ridiculous!" retorted Montagu sharply. "As I have pointed out this Institute has research for its purpose—not the care of the sick poor. They are not our responsibility. We want only those patients who can give us material for investigation. It is a waste to pour money into the clinics downstairs when we need all our resources for the work in the laboratories. All of us—the doctors in the clinics as well as those of us in active research—should be willing to sacrifice something for the sake of science."

Lanister glanced drily at Hastings who stirred nervously in his chair and asked if there was any more discussion. Montagu, who seemed to have forgotten to sit down, still stood on the low platform staring at the men before him. Some uncanny influence flowed from him; everyone watched him and no one said anything.

"Then," said Dr. Hastings uneasily, "perhaps it would be well to consider this matter again next week at the regular meeting. Before that time all of you will have time to think the question over more carefully. Meanwhile, Dr. Lanister will report today's discussion to the trustees.... Now, if there is nothing more to come before the group this morning, a motion to adjourn will be in order."

The half-time doctors scurried out of the room talking excitedly to one another, hurrying off to get their lunch before rushing away to their afternoon's work in other institutions. Montagu buttonholed Hastings; Fergusson approached Lanister and pulled out a sheaf of papers from his pocket. He managed to convey the impression that he was brandishing these papers defiantly in the face of his superior. Cameron heard snatches of the talk between them.

"... only one company represented here ... prices seem high, Fergusson..."

"Oh, of course ... if you must go into every detail ... this machine will last for years and ..."

"Now, Fergusson, you know it won't be three months until you're wanting another one ... this will be out-of-date before spring...."

As Lanister took the papers and turned away, Cameron saw Fergusson scowl peevishly at his back.

Then Thornton brought up two or three other men and introduced Richard to them. Most of them were in their thirties but one or two were older and had an air of discouragement and fatigue. They were all polite to the newcomer but Cameron suspected that they were not particularly pleased to see Thornton getting another addition to his staff, and he was glad when his chief suggested leaving.

"There is a dining room in the cellar where they serve lunch to the nurses and any of the doctors who care to stay. But I see enough of these fellows without eating with them every noon. So I usually walk over to Oak Street unless the weather is too sloppy. There isn't a decent restaurant in the neighborhood of the Institute and the walk makes a nice break in the middle of the day, besides helping me keep my waist line under control."

When they came down the broad white steps at the entrance to the building, they saw Lanister driving away in a taxicab.

"There's one of the finest men on earth," said Jim Thornton. "Don't let his hard-boiled surface fool you. He's grown that shell standing off Montagu. Otherwise B. C. would go through him like a hot knife through butter."

"I liked what I saw of Dr. Lanister this morning. When I was here before I guess I got the wrong impression of him."

"You probably did," assented Thornton drily. "Most people do. But I know too much about him to be fooled by that sardonic face of his. He shells out money right and left to help the poor devils that get turned away from the clinic here, but if anyone mentions it he gets sore. . . . Sometimes I think it might be a good thing if B. C. got a chronic disease too."

"I don't see what you mean."

"Why, don't you know about Lanister?" exclaimed Thornton in surprise. "I took for granted you knew. It's just fourteen years ago now that he came back from his European training considered to be the most promising young diagnostician in Northdevon. But before long he broke down with diabetes. For several years he was in such bad shape that he had to get out of practice altogether. Then when he thought he could go to work again, old man Fifer—who was a distant relative of his—put him in the Institute as chief of the General Clinic and made the stipulation that the job was to be his for life if he wanted it.

"The man was really never well until insulin came out, but he's got one of the keenest minds I've ever seen in action. He's independently wealthy, he's a bachelor, he lives alone in the old family home—an eighteenth-century house on Delaney Street. He's sorry for Hastings and keeps the wolves off him as much as possible, he respects Montagu although he never agrees with him, he dislikes Fergusson but never interferes with his work. There's the situation 'interpreted,' as the social workers say."

"I see," said Cameron thoughtfully. "I admire Dr. Lanister . . . but there's something about Montagu . . ."

"Yes, damn it, I know there is," agreed Thornton. "Whenever he gets up and begins to talk in that cracked-pot voice of his with his eyes shining like headlights, I can feel myself slipping. He should have been an early Christian: he'd have hypnotized the lions and walked out on the Romans."

"But what the man says is right," insisted Richard. "Finding the cause of disease is the first step toward prevention and effective treatment, and in the long run it saves more lives than curative medicine ever can."

"I know that as well as you do, my dear Cameron, and as well as Montagu does too. Lanister's point and mine is, why not do both things? By all means give Montagu a free hand to pound away on his TB research and Fergusson on fruit flies and heredity and you and me on anemia. That's fine. But let's have a decent clinic downstairs too, where we can do what there is to be done for poor devils who have ordinary uninteresting things wrong with them."

By this time they had come to the corner above the Institute and Richard paused to look back. Autumnal sunlight, filtered through the pall of smoke that hovers over all great cities, fell gently on the dark red walls and shining, white-trimmed windows. Even at this distance he thought he could feel the dynamic zeal that drove Montagu to hold to the path of pure research. This burning-eyed zealot had made a deep impression on Cameron; he felt that here was a man dedicated to the pursuit of facts and ready to make any sacrifice of himself or anyone else, without compunction. It was this fanaticism that made him, physically insignificant as he was, stand out in comparison with the men about him. Of them all only Thornton and Lanister, it seemed to Richard, could endure that comparison without losing caste.

"Come along, Cameron, or we won't have time for a decent lunch," urged Thornton. "You can moon over Fifer any time you like during the next ten years or so. And go on admiring B. C. Montagu. I do . . . in spite of being under the same roof with him for four years. . . . But, if you get into a tight place and want help, go to Ralph Lanister."

CHAPTER II

I

For the next few months Cameron turned every ounce of energy he had toward the things Thornton had told him must be done to clear the way for the closer study of blood regeneration. First of all, he worked out a standardized diet which would maintain dogs month after month in good general health although constantly anemic. As soon as this basic, compound food had been satisfactorily tested, Thornton turned over to the anemia work several animal rooms and thirty-six vigorous young dogs of a bulldog cross, born and bred in the Institute kennels. Each animal had its own cage and each was fed every afternoon by Richard or DiPallo. The quarters where they lived were large and airy and were kept at a temperature constantly between sixty-five and seventy degrees Fahrenheit. Every day that was not too stormy Joe exercised the dogs on the roof. They were all likeable animals but Cameron never felt the same affection for them that he did for the mongrel terriers he had brought from Seaforth. Because he knew so well how they would react to changes of diet and loss of blood he kept Rebecca and Ivanhoe for specially important investigations.

Richard had already found that fasting animals manufactured red blood cells and blood pigment out of materials they had saved from the ordinary processes of bodily chemistry and that, on favorable diets, they stored up reserves of these ingredients against future necessity. This bank balance, the nature of which was still obscure, appeared to be held in the liver, the kidneys, the spleen, bone marrow, and muscles. There was, therefore, as Cameron pointed out to his chief, a logical basis for feeding these tissues to animals suffering from anemia.

When some months' work established the rate of blood formation both during periods of fasting and periods of standardized subsistence diet, one of the assistants in Thornton's department used these figures in testing a new drug, germanium dioxide, which had recently been reported to be of spectacular benefit in anemia. Examined in this way it proved to have no consistent effect whatever on blood manufacture in experimental animals and was eliminated as a possible treatment for pernicious anemia.

By this time there had been discovered in the clinics down stairs twelve patients with pernicious anemia whom Richard had put on diets containing several hundred grams of liver or kidney a day besides ordinary meats such as beef or mutton. All of them were chronic cases who had been ill for months or years, and all of them had had many sorts of treatment and more than one blood transfusion. Without exception they began to improve within a fortnight after beginning this diet and maintained a state of comparatively good health so long as they stayed on the meat diet. But some of them did not like liver or kidney and a few did not care for meat of any kind and so persisted in trying to go back to vegetable foods. Whenever they did this, they promptly relapsed.

Cameron sat up nights reading cookbooks and cudgelling his brain for new ways to cook liver and kidney or make them palatable while raw. But Thornton took this difficulty less seriously. "Ye Gods," he exclaimed one day when Richard was talking of these culinary difficulties, "if these people don't care enough about being alive to eat a little liver or kidney, let them curl up and die. You've got something more important to do now than humor their finicky appetites."

The great problem that confronted Cameron was to find out what it was in liver and kidney that stimulated blood formation and whether this substance existed in other foods as well. Once that had been discovered, it might be possible to make an extract of the tissues that would contain the active principle in a form that could be swallowed in a capsule or made into a pill or injected hypodermically; it might even be possible to manufacture it outside the animal body altogether.

One of the first possibilities that came to Richard's mind was that meat might contain a mineral that influenced blood formation, but laborious experiment showed that the only minerals that could be proved to promote blood making were iron and copper salts. The other minerals studied—calcium, magnesium, sodium, potassium, aluminum, antimony, zinc, and silica—were all found to be nearly inert. Even copper, when added to the basic, inert ration, had but slight power to stimulate blood production. Iron salts, however, proved much more potent when given in large amounts. When he realized that the old-fashioned doctors who gave their anemic patients big doses of Blaud's pills were more scientific than those more modern physicians who gave smaller amounts of iron by hypodermic injection, the iconoclast in Richard was amused.

He next investigated the green vegetables. He had always hated lettuce and spinach, and it was a great pleasure to find that these vegetables as well as greens and cabbage and asparagus had little power to build new blood. These discoveries having stimulated his iconoclastic proclivities, he proceeded to study milk and dairy products and learned that neither milk, cream, nor cheese compared in potency with liver and kidney.

After that Cameron embarked on an orgy of experimentation

on meats of many kinds. In this way he found that steaks and roast meats were much less powerful stimulants to blood building than heart muscle, and that heart in turn was less potent than beef stomach or chicken gizzard. Bone marrow, spleen, brains, and sweetbreads all caused some blood formation, but liver and kidney were superior to all other meats.

It was just at this point that another of Thornton's assistants turned up with two facts that startled Richard. The first was that fish liver seemed to be almost inert and the second was that apricots were more effective in stimulating blood manufacture than any of the meats examined except liver, kidney, and chicken gizzard. The potency of apricots could not be explained by their iron content for they contained less iron than useless fruits such as raspberries. When apricots were burned, the active principle remained in the ash, which, as Cameron complained to his chief, "didn't make sense either." But the clinic patients, who showed a profound lack of interest in the why of their treatment, were pleased when he reduced somewhat their daily ration of liver and kidney and added instead a certain quantity of apricots.

It occurred to Thornton that it might be possible to reduce the amount of liver and kidney these people had to consume every day still further by adding to their diet a large amount of iron. Eventually this proved to be the case, but it took many months to work out the exact dosage required for the best results.

Through all these busy days of experimentation and speculation, Richard was nagged by the persistent question "Why?" Curiosity consumed him. The things he had found seemed so bizarre. What was it in liver and apricot ash that stimulated the body to build new blood? What had liver and kidney to do with ordinary blood making in health? What about that old finding that people who had pernicious anemia also had digestive symptoms and little or no acid in their stomachs? Where did the stomach come into the picture anyhow? Could it be that something that ought to be absorbed from one's food was not so absorbed when gastric acid was below normal, or did the lack of acid allow something poisonous to go through the stomach wall and intestine to destroy the blood cells? To himself he seemed to be groping in a maze of half-knowledge. Of only one thing did he feel sure—the blood-building power of liver and kidney and chicken gizzard and, to a less extent, apricots—and to this fantastic but well-established fact he held fast.

The year after he joined the Institute staff, Cameron refused a vacation. A Northdevon summer, hot and muggy as it was, was to be preferred to the risk of leaving someone else in charge of his experiments. During the long, hot days he watched his dogs, all of whom were still fat and happy, weighed their food, counted their red cells and measured their hemoglobin, and perfected the methods by which he would be able to detect the very beginning of improvement in anemic blood. In the library he pored over articles on anemia and other diseases of the blood in the current medical literature.

As the weeks passed Judith Emerson began to worry over him. Hot weather, loss of sleep, and nervous strain took a good many pounds off him by midsummer; he grinned less often and frequently sat staring into space with his lips moving slightly. From the gossip of laboratory assistants she heard that he was working seven days a week and eating for lunch only a sandwich brought from his boarding house in a paper sack. His suits, always loose fitting, began to dangle about him and his skin turned pasty, so that his freckles stood out more distinctly than ever.

One day as she watched him with troubled brown eyes, it suddenly came to her that perhaps he had the disease he was studying so hard.

"If you would only tell me more about your work," she said to him, "perhaps I could help you more than I do. At least I could go over the journals for you. I know the library staff at the Academy of Medicine so well that I'm sure they would help me find the important articles as they come out. That would give you more time and perhaps you wouldn't need to work so hard."

Richard grinned at her in his old impish way.

"But you're always so loaded up with Montagu's stuff and Fergusson's."

Judith flushed.

"They've both gone away for the rest of the summer, so you see I'm not 'loaded up' just now. And it would really be a pleasure to do it . . . if I knew just what it was all about."

So it was that at five o'clock that afternoon she went down to Richard's office to learn more of what he was trying to do. She found the room stuffy with the warm, humid air of a Northdevon August. Cameron's battered old desk stood facing a windowless wall, half of which was lined with shelves stacked with books, and the other half covered from the ceiling down with charts and graphs.

Jim Thornton and Richard were standing near one of the two windows talking when she came in and she drew back, but Cameron saw her and called out, "Come on in, Miss Emerson. You're not afraid of Dr. Thornton, I hope. He's not as bad as he looks. I've been working for him almost a year now and he hasn't bitten me once."

Thornton smiled at Judith; he had never forgotten the welcome change she had made in the Institute library.

"I'm glad you're coming in on this, too, Miss Emerson," he said. "Cameron has been working all day and reading all night, and the combination is beginning to leave its mark on his disposition."

Richard laughed. "That's no exaggeration," he admitted. "Yesterday Rebecca growled at me."

Judith looked at him with surprised brown eyes.

"Rebecca is Cameron's number one dog," explained Thornton jovially. "The one he started out with, on his career of bloodletting." He looked from the girl to Richard and back. "Well, I must be getting out of here. My wife has some people coming in for dinner tonight and she warned me this morning I'd have to dress. Think of me in a boiled shirt about seven o'clock and pity me. . . . And don't forget to eat sometime tonight yourselves."

When he had gone, Richard drew up another chair to his desk.

"This exact spot is the coolest in the room. I spent a good deal of valuable time figuring out just where what little air comes in those two windows is most likely to strike. Sit down, Miss Emerson, and let's see what we can dope out together."

Judith Emerson had more than the average woman's intelligence and tact and, besides that, she was genuinely interested in Cameron. There was something attractive about the man himself and now there was an undercurrent of excitement in his manner. It had seemed to her when she entered the room that there were things of importance brewing there, and when she sat down beside Richard she thought she could feel a sort of excitement flowing into her, too.

Richard leaned back and stared up at the ceiling above his chart-covered wall.

"There are just one or two basic things for you to keep in mind, Miss Emerson, so that what I say as I go along will be clear to you. Pernicious anemia," he said slowly, "is a disease of the blood-making tissues, especially the bone marrow. Not enough red cells are manufactured and those that are turned out are not normal. When the red count keeps going down, each red cell that's left has to carry more than its usual load of hemoglobin—the coloring matter of the blood—because that is the only way the blood can absorb oxygen from the air in the lungs and carry it out into the body. Without oxygen a man dies, no difference whether there's no oxygen in the air or whether he hasn't enough red blood cells to transport it into his body tissues.

"Everyone who gets pernicious anemia dies of it, unless an automobile runs over him first. Drugs do almost no good. We can keep the patient alive for a while with transfusions of blood from healthy people, but always in a few months or years he peters out and dies. That's why I'm so interested in this disease: it's always fatal in the end.

"Now, let me show you what we've found out so far." He

sprang up and seized a long pointer from the corner. "Just look up here, to start with. This first chart . . ."

Cameron was soon in full swing on the things that just then interested him more than anything else in the world; he talked well, his language, unconventional and often slangy, was vivid and expressive. His dark gray eyes shone with suppressed excitement and his voice suddenly seemed boyish. As she watched and listened, a conviction came to Judith: this man was like Montagu, with the fanaticism left out. In spite of his unreasonable demands upon her time and his carelessness about borrowed books and journals, she had always thought Dr. Montagu a great scholar and respected him for his scientific achievements. The way he drove everyone about him to superhuman exertion was inhuman, that was true—more than one man in his department had broken down under the incessant strain—but he had no more mercy on himself than on others. He was as thin and haggard and worn as his assistants, but he never stopped, never rested, never thought of saving either himself or them.

Cameron was like that—and yet unlike. Judith fumbled for the word that would differentiate the two men. Montagu was a fanatic, a scientific fanatic, consumed by the fire of his own zeal for research and blind to everything else. She had heard him say more than once what he thought of people who wasted their evenings at theaters or dances or concerts. A fanatic. Like Paul—that was it! Bent on saving people in spite of themselves, whether they wanted to be saved or not.

This man too was a searcher after truth, he was excited about the thing he and Thornton were trying to do, he was working too hard and getting the same sort of glitter in his eyes that blazed so fiercely in Montagu's. The same? No, not quite the same. That was the point. Like Montagu, yes, but not the same. Judith pondered the subtle distinction she felt between the men but could not find words to express.

Richard was talking rapidly, pointing to graphs and charts to support the assertions he made. As the light in the room became softer his red hair seemed to shine more brightly. When he went from one chart to another, his long, lean body moved jerkily as though it were mounted on springs, and always there was that undertone of excitement in his manner. But he did not raise his voice. It went on and on, mellow and soft.

Judith found herself thinking that he ought to sing, that he would have a baritone suited to songs of adventure. Adventure—that was it. She sat up straighter in her chair. Why hadn't she thought of it before? This man was an adventurer—not a crusader, not a fanatic, not an inhuman driver of lesser men, but a man who might better have lived in the sixteenth century and been a buccaneer in his Queen's service. She smiled to herself, pleased with her discovery and with Richard because she liked adventurers more than crusaders.

"And so, you see, Miss Emerson, where we are now. There were a lot of difficulties we didn't foresee; I guess there always are. Thornton is going to drop his other research for the present anyhow and concentrate on the basic physiology of blood formation, and I'm going to start applying what we've learned to people who have pernicious anemia. That's the set-up as it stands today. What do you think of it?"

Judith started guiltily. She had meant to listen carefully to all he said and ask questions until she was sure she understood it all, but instead she had forgotten the words in the man himself. She saw at once, however, that he did not suspect this and set her quick wits to prevent his finding out.

"It's all most interesting, Dr. Cameron—fascinating, really, when you tell it. But it's rather complicated. I wonder if you won't ask your stenographer to abstract the most important points so I can have them to refer to? That would help me a great deal in going over the literature for you."

Richard thought this an excellent idea: this girl, he told himself, really grasped what he was driving at, what he was trying to do. Talking to her was stimulating, it was even better than talking with Thornton. They must have more of these evenings together. He could feel new ideas bubbling up in his mind. It did a man good to put into words for an intelligent, interested listener the facts he knew and the theories that grew out of the facts.

It was nearly eight o'clock when Judith and he drove away from the Institute together.

II

After Cameron took over the clinical testing of the liver diet and gave into Thornton's hands the animal experimentation on which it was based, he found his human subjects much harder to control than the dogs had been. He was constantly confronted with people who, having improved, forgot how desperately ill they had been and vowed that they would rather die than eat a pound of liver, raw or cooked, every day. At first he could scarcely believe that people so soon forgot the menace of impending death, but before long he came to the conclusion that the average clinic patient had a memory lasting six to eight weeks and no longer.

These refractory individuals he dealt with as best he could, coaxing, imploring, bribing, and bullying them into eating the life-saving meat. One woman who insisted that she was made desperately ill by swallowing liver—although she never proved this by demonstration—said she would eat an equivalent amount of chicken gizzards if she could get them. For weeks thereafter Joe DiPallo patrolled the poultry stores of southwest Northdevon, collecting these tidbits for her. When, despite these efforts, she relapsed, a social worker sent out from the Institute brought back word that she had been selling the gizzards among her neighbors for a good price.

Nor was the difficulty of getting people to eat the necessary amount of meat the chief one. An even greater was the rising price of liver. The majority of the patients who came to the clinics at Fifer Institute were poor, many of them were immigrants or second-generation Americans of Central or South European stocks. Among the families of these people rumors spread rapidly: hearing that liver had been good for Jan Sienkowski they concluded that it would be good for them, too. Thus there arose an unprecedented local demand for liver and, to a lesser degree, for kidney, and on the heels of increased demand came higher prices.

Before long Cameron found that he was buying out of his own pocket nearly twenty dollars' worth of meat a week. He did not begrudge the money, but his salary at Fifer was no larger than it had been in Seaforth and so much out of three hundred and twenty-five a month left less than he wanted for scientific journals and books in addition to clothes and rent and gasoline. Consultation with Thornton and later with Lanister led to an arrangement for a daily delivery from a packing company of sufficient fresh liver and kidney to supply all patients financially unable to meet the rapidly mounting prices of these foodstuffs.

During the autumn Rebecca turned temperamental and refused to eat either liver or kidney. Twice Richard coaxed her back to normal by enticing her to live on chicken gizzards for two or three weeks, but this proved so nerve-racking for both of them that he decided to give the dog a long vacation. In boarding kennels some miles outside the city he found a foster home for her.

Finally, just before Thanksgiving, these petty annoyances were climaxed by the appearance of a patient who was a vegetarian by conviction and professed himself determined to die rather than to eat animal flesh of any sort. This man resisted all arguments and all forms of moral suasion; he also resisted his own increasing weakness and was taken to a hospital in a very serious relapse from which he was temporarily rescued only by repeated blood transfusions which bled both his family's veins and pocketbooks thoroughly.

"Roberts is the biggest fool alive," said Cameron to Jim Thornton early in December. "He can't hold enough apricots to get his blood up to normal, and yet he won't eat a hunk of liver to save himself from dying. Still I've got to admit that he's got guts—whether he has brains or not."

After Roberts was taken home from the hospital Richard went now and then to call on him in the hope that he might one day relent, but weeks passed without relapse, physical or moral.

All these experiences made Cameron more and more anxious to develop a liver extract that could be swallowed in a pill or injected hypodermically like insulin: the cost would probably be less than that of a pound of liver a day, it would be less repugnant to fastidious persons, and it might make it possible to evade vegetarian protests. But to see the advantages of an extract and to make one were two different things. Pacing back and forth in his room at night or talking the problem over with Sandy, Richard puzzled over this dilemma—how was one to make a liver extract when one had no idea what the active substance in liver was.

Months before, Thornton had pointed out the handicap of having no hospital beds in the Institute; as time went on, this disadvantage became more and more apparent. Only people who were able to be out of bed and on their feet could come to the clinics; this, in turn, meant that only the milder cases of pernicious anemia came under Cameron's observation. A year after he began to use liver diet in treatment, although he had twenty patients all of whom were in good health, he had never yet had the opportunity to test liver in an acutely ill patient and saw but little prospect of doing so.

It was at this juncture that Lanister sent for him one late winter afternoon. Richard straightened up slowly and pushed away the microscope over which he had been hunched all day, studying blood smears.

"Lord, but it makes a fellow's back ache, sitting screwed up like this," he muttered to himself as he pulled off the long gray-green denim laboratory coat which he too now wore in the Institute. "Some day I bet I'll go crazy, hunting for reticulocytes and nucleated reds. And to think I was once an innocent young medical student who thought a red blood cell was just a red blood cell and had never heard of megaloblasts and erythroblasts and normoblasts and reticulocytes."

Cameron found Dr. Lanister alone. He had just finished signing a batch of letters and he pushed the last of them aside and motioned Richard to a chair. Insulin had put Lanister on his feet again: he looked much better than when Cameron had first returned to the Institute fifteen months before, much less sallow and not so thin. But his dark eyes were no less sardonic than they had always been.

"How many cases of pernicious anemia have you treated to date, Dr. Cameron?"

"There are twenty under treatment now. Five who dropped the diet after beginning it and improving to some extent, I have traced and know to be dead. Four others have been transfused in various hospitals and have not returned to the clinic. A few others who dropped out I have lost track of, I'm sorry to say."

"Um." Lanister seemed to ponder this quick definite answer. "Keep pretty good tab on your human 'guinea pigs,' don't you? I suppose that's the only way you can ever learn anything from them." He paused an instant and laughed shortly. "Good word for them—'guinea pigs.' It's the only use most of them will ever be to the world. . . . Well, I've got another 'guinea pig' for you—if you want him."

Something in Lanister's lined dark face sent Richard to his feet.

"You mean . . ."

"I mean a man nobody cares enough about to object to anything you may do to him. You haven't had a case like that, have you?"

"No. All the patients we get here in the clinic are able to be up walking around, and none of the hospitals wants to risk doing without transfusions in people that have relapses. That's been our biggest drawback."

Lanister's eyes did not flicker.

"This man is in the state prison at Oldcastle, under death sentence. I understand the powers that be are anxious to keep him alive long enough to execute him with due ceremony. Do you want to go up and see what you can do?"

"What about the papers? Won't they get hold of it and raise a stink about it?"

"No. I've already talked to the authorities and the prison doctor. It's safe. Don't worry about that. Do you want to go?"

For a long time after Cameron had gone, Ralph Lanister sat staring at the blank wall before him. He knew what it was to live with death just around the corner, and something pricked him for having sent Richard to Oldcastle to bring back to life a man who must be executed in three weeks' time. It seemed like taking a rotten advantage of him. But... Lanister laughed shortly to himself. This was another of the occasions on which he envied Montagu his conviction that a scientific purpose justified all means.

III

It was a week before Cameron got back to Northdevon. Sandy Farquhar had just gone to bed one night when he was roused by the impatient ringing of his doorbell, and when he stumbled out in slippers and bathrobe to open the door he found Richard in the hall. Over a bottle of alleged Canadian whiskey in Sandy's dinette fifteen minutes later Cameron told him the story.

When he arrived at Oldcastle the prison doctor met him and told him about the prisoner who was ill. Charley Morrison's last blood count, done three hours before, had showed less than a million reds; the smear was typical of perniciousanemia. When Richard said that what he needed was a meat grinder, raw liver, and a stomach tube the prison doctor looked at him strangely but went at once to get them.

While he was gone, Cameron read over the summary of the prisoner's history. Morrison, it seemed, had been a rather mediocre mechanic and three years before he had quit his job and started west. With him he took a woman—apparently a common whore he'd picked up on the street—and the two of them drove across the country, staying nights at auto camps along the way. They drank a good deal and quarrelled incessantly so that one night the manager of the camp where they were stopping went to their cabin and ordered them to shut up or get out. That was the last he heard of them.

The next day about noon someone found the woman alone in the shack with her head hammered in and a tire wrench on the floor beside her body. Charley and the car were gone. But he was not a clever fugitive and within forty-eight hours the state police had arrested him. He was convicted on circumstantial evidence for he could not be induced to confess even with the liberal use of the third degree—but his family had the case appealed, and one way and another it dragged on through one court after another until finally Charley fell ill. For a time no diagnosis was made, but at last a bright young doctor with a jail contract made a blood count and recognized pernicious anemia.

After that Morrison was kept alive with blood transfusions until his last appeal was heard. But he had severe reactions and after the last two transfusions he had very nearly died. When the appeal was denied and the governor had refused clemency, on the ground that enough of the taxpayers' money had already been wasted on a criminal, Charley was sent to Oldcastle to await electrocution. In the death house he had developed an acute relapse and the prison physician had conceived the idea of trying out on him the new treatment of which Dr. Lanister had told him a little when he visited Oldcastle at Christmas. Furthermore, if justice was to be served, Morrison must be kept alive for seventeen days longer.

The prison doctor came back with the meat grinder and the liver, and stood watching Cameron chill and mince the red brown meat and make it into a thin porridge.

"Looking at it one way," he said slowly, "it seems funny to go to all this trouble to keep that fellow alive just to execute him in less than three weeks. I never thought of it before, not till this afternoon when I saw him the last time."

But Richard did not falter in his preparations.

The prison doctor presently led him into a little room where Morrison lay on a narrow infirmary bed. Charley had never been much to look at, and now his skin had turned the ghastly lemon-yellow color of pernicious anemia and had become pasty and greasy as well. He lay curled up on one side in a semi-stupor, drawing shallow rapid breaths that scarcely lifted his chest wall. Now that his shifty eyes were closed, his face lost its hard lines and his mouth curled up a little at the corners. Against the pillow lay a disorderly mass of long straight blonde hair. When the doctor shook him and roused him from his coma, Charley started up panting for breath and his hair fell down on either side of his face in a great tumbled mass of yellow. Then, seeing the things in Cameron's hands, he cowered back on the cot.

Richard had asked the prison physician to help him, but when they laid their hands on the convict he threw himself about with the last of his strength and cried, "Go away! Leave me be! God damn it, leave me be!"

Something in the shrill, hoarse voice made Cameron think of the screams of horses burning in a stable fire he had watched years ago; there was the same hopeless agony, the same protoplasmic horror. He looked down at the terrified creature on the cot, doomed by nature and condemned to death. If Morrison were brought back to life now, he would go to the chair in seventeen days.

Perhaps Charley saw the hesitation in Richard's face, perhaps some instinct told him that here was a man who was essentially kind, perhaps he was too sick and too stupid to know what he did. But he stared up with wild eyes and shrieked, "Go away! I died too many times already! Leave me be!"

"Sandy, I tell you I couldn't do it after that. The fellow was right; it wasn't fair. It was right enough, so far as I was concerned, that he should forfeit his life for killing that woman. But Charley Morrison had gone through all the conscious part of dying every time he'd had one of those awful reactions to a transfusion and every time he'd gone into coma. And over and over he'd been revived and brought back alive to go through the whole thing again, to go back to jail and into court. To kill him once would have been all right, but to make him die a dozen times was too much.

"I stayed on and pretended I was trying the new treatment because the prison doctor is a decent sort of chap and he didn't want to risk losing his job. But he felt the same way I did about things. Charley died yesterday—in coma. He never knew when he went out."

After Cameron finished, Farquhar sat pale and shaken. Suddenly he shivered as though he saw Charley Morrison before him in the flesh.

"There's nothing people won't do to other people, Rich—people that they hate. Men are cruel to . . . other men."

CHAPTER III

I

The next morning when Cameron reached the Institute he found on his desk a note asking him to see Thornton at once. The physiologist was in an expansive mood; his round face and bright blue eyes shone with satisfaction. Even when Richard told him what had happened at the state prison, he was no less cheerful.

"Forget it. The fellow's dead, and that's that, Cameron. I've got real news for you." He took from a desk drawer a long, important-looking envelope and extracted a document from it. "Item number one. Take a look at that."

Cameron unfolded the sheets of heavy paper and found clipped to the upper left-hand corner of the inner one an oblong slip of yellow paper. It was a check for five thousand dollars made out to James A. Thornton. Richard looked over at his chief with unbelieving eyes.

"I never saw that much money all at once before," he said,

turning the check over with skeptical fingers. "Five thousand dollars. Five thousand, not five hundred."

"From the Livestock Council of America," explained Thornton. "For our anemia research and particularly for the development of a liver extract. Lanister and I have been after these people for six months. I wish you could have heard us selling the idea to them. Remember when we went to New York together last fall? Well, that was when we met the president of the outfit. Ralph, I believe, could sell anything if he wanted to. He had the old man almost weeping over the duty of industrial leaders to foster research and the prestige it would give the Livestock Council to back this project and the advantages of finding a use for extra liver—at a good price. But the check was so long coming that both of us began to get nervous for fear our industrial 'maggot' had changed his mind."

Richard looked up sharply.

"Any strings tied to it?"

"Not a string. They tried one or two but we wouldn't have it. No, it's on the level. Five thousand smackers for you and me, and not a cent of it earmarked for B. C. or Fergusson."

Cameron handed back the check as though he feared it might evaporate.

"Then we can talk to Waldheim, can't we?"

"Yes. In fact I called him up two or three days ago while you were away. He's ready to start tearing liver to pieces for us. He's a damn good organic chemist and he'll furnish us with chemical fractions of liver galore. You can test them out on patients and I'll go on hammering away at the basic physiology of blood making."

Thornton leaned back and gazed at Richard with the air of a man who has boundless faith in the future, but Cameron sat with his eyes on the floor, blindly fumbling with a key ring.

"If I only had somebody except these clinic patients to work with," he began.

"You don't listen very well, do you?" interrupted Thornton. "Didn't you hear me mention 'item number one' when I flashed that check on you? Haven't you any curiosity about 'item number two'? Better come out of your trance, Cameron, and listen to me. Ralph has wangled you a ward at the University Hospital."

"What?"

"A ward at the University Hospital and an appointment as assistant physician in charge of it. Didn't I tell you that when you needed help he was the man to go to?"

Richard could not speak, there was a queer tightness in his throat and in his eyes a stinging strangely like that of tears. Watching him, Jim Thornton's face became exultant.

"You've earned it, Cameron. For fifteen months you've worked like a nailer, not to prove your point, but to find out the truth about the relation of diet to blood making. So far as I'm concerned I want you to know that I'm convinced of part of your theory. There's something in liver and kidney and chicken gizzards that stimulates the building of new, healthy blood. I don't know what it is and neither do you—yet. But you'll find out, with Waldheim's help."

The fervor with which these words came from his lips surprised Thornton himself; he felt a desire for Richard to realize how much both of them owed Ralph Lanister.

"You see, this anemia project interested Lanister from the start because of his own experience with diabetes. After he broke down in the first place he never knew what a well day was for thirteen years. Then he heard about insulin—medical gossip first, and then a meeting where Banting made some sort of preliminary report. I remember that Ralph seemed different when he came home. I know now that he must have felt like a prisoner whose death sentence has been set aside.

"As soon as insulin was available, he began to try it on himself. I can imagine the fear and suspense when he first began to use it, the relief that must have crept over him gradually as he realized that he was no longer in daily danger of going into coma and dying. Think of the load of dread he carried all those years, Cameron, think of it!

"Then you came along with the prospect of beating another chronic incurable disease, and he was interested right away.

After he'd watched you a little while and made up his mind that you were all right, he told me he meant to see that you got your chance. And what Ralph Lanister says he'll do, he does."

"I see he does," said Richard soberly, thinking of his old misunderstanding of Lanister's apparent indifference and cynicism. "I'm afraid I haven't appreciated him before."

"Nobody does," cried Thornton. "And it makes me sore."

Then he went on to discuss their plans for the immediate future.

"Waldheim had an idea of how to start. He calls it 'chemical dissection.' He'll begin with raw minced liver at pH 9 and extract all the water-soluble elements. If they prove to be inactive in blood forming, he thinks we should try next the proteins precipitated from his liver pulp by acids. After that, he'll make extracts from raw liver that's been treated with acid. But, before he starts, he wants to be sure you've got a way to tell quickly whether these chemical fractions are any good or not. I wasn't quite sure about that."

"I worked on that point all last summer, Dr. Thornton. Don't you remember how I was groaning around about reticulocytes? Well, they are the cells that are the forerunners of healthy red corpuscles. When those little fellows with their bright blue chromatin network begin to increase in the blood smear, the bone marrow is getting ready to turn loose normal red cells by the hundred thousand."

"And how long does it take to tell ?"

"Three or four days, or a week. Liver works fast."

Thornton settled back in his chair with an expression of satisfaction and enthusiasm.

"We're on our way, Cameron, at last."

A little later when he heard Richard go down the hall, open the elevator door and close it again, and listened to the whine of the slowly ascending lift, Jim Thornton's wide mouth broke into a broad smile; he knew that his assistant was on his way to the library and he thought he knew why.

II

The ward at the University Hospital proved to be a small one in the old building which had recently been partially evacuated for the new modern skyscraper across the street. By comparison the old building with its stained gray stone walls looked very small and unimportant, but Richard knew that not a little of the fame of Northdevon's medical school stemmed from it. He had seen alumni—gray-haired men—come back to stand and stare with nostalgic eyes at the place where they had served their apprenticeship.

Had he been less the adventurer than he was, Cameron might have been disappointed with Ward B. But instead, he stood on its threshold the first morning with dark gray eyes sparkling in excitement as they surveyed the domain that was to be his.

The ward was deserted. Its ten beds stood empty, their heads against the wall and the bedside tables between them naturally clean and tidy. At one end an old-fashioned bay window jutted out over the scrap of lawn beside the entrance four stories below. The ceiling was high, the floor was covered with dull green linoleum, the lower half of the wall was painted a harmonizing shade. Near Richard was the nurses' desk with its rows of empty chart holders. Off the corridor to his right was a smaller room with four beds in separate cubicles and at his left a still smaller room for blood counts and other simple laboratory work.

It was all very plain but to Cameron it was the place of dreams. Already in his imagination he had filled every bed. There were twice ten patients who belonged here. Some who were slipping downgrade because they didn't eat liver enough or didn't take it regularly or fried it to a hard chip before they ate it. Some who were improving but not so rapidly as they ought; if he had them here under daily observation perhaps he could find out why. Then there were one or two who were in acute relapse and had been sent to other hospitals or were at home under the care of doctors who had never heard of liver diet. There were still others—middle-aged people mostly—who had come to the clinic at the Institute for various reasons and had been found to have little or no free acid in their gastric juice; they ought to be watched to see whether they would develop pernicious anemia as Joe DiPallo had done.

Suddenly the ten beds in the ward and the four in the smaller room seemed absurdly few. There were so many people who had this disease and there were so many things to learn about it. He stood running over in his mind a list of his patients, trying to decide which ones to bring in first. More men than women had pernicious anemia, the men therefore should go into the ward beds. But that left only the four beds in the small room for women. Too bad. He frowned regretfully.

He could see them, lying there in the white beds, comparing symptoms. Each would be eager to explain the course of his illness to nine others, all intent on doing the same thing. He could imagine them unifying their complaints into a vociferous protest at having cream and sugar and butter cut down and being forced to eat liver and kidney every day. They might all of them join in a revolt, the women from their quarters inciting the men and the men bragging about what they would say to the doctor when he came in on rounds. Rebellion would gather ground until one day a rebel would lapse into coma and be wheeled out of the ward into the private room reserved for the critically ill. Thereafter, until the passage of time dulled this memory, everyone else would gulp down his allotment of liver in a panic.

The swiftness with which people forgot the imminence of death never failed to astonish Richard. Only let a man whose tongue had been so sore he could barely swallow, whom the least exertion rendered breathless, who was on the verge of coma, improve until he could walk about comfortably and, in a few weeks, he would be calling God and man to witness that he would rather die than eat another pound of liver or kidney. It was all nonsense, he had decided, to think that rare juicy steaks were not good blood makers. Why, anyone could see the blood fairly oozing out of the meat! Then this stuff about liver and kidney being the only things that would make blood cells was nothing but a notion of the doctor's; he didn't know half as much about it as he thought he did. Probably the butchers paid him a commission on the liver and kidney they ate in the ward every day. Didn't doctors always keep their patients ill as long as possible—if not make them sick in the first place—in order to batten on their necessities?

Richard had often wondered why the human being, sick or well, found it so hard to have faith in anyone. Why so many of his own patients did not see that it was an incurable itch to understand that drove men like him into laboratories and hospital wards. But his sense of humor always rescued him from this fruitless speculation. Had he not wondered ten years ago, when he was driving the hot dusty roads of Montana, why people had such an aversion to paying a doctor for his work? If he was ever to learn anything about anemia he would not have time to answer either of these questions.

Full of pride he looked at Ward B. It was not large but it was his. Only fifteen months ago he had come from the west coast, an obscure man with an *idée fixe* about pernicious anemia, and now he had a ward in the University Hospital. Then pride softened into something more generous. If it had not been for Jim Thornton he would never have had his first opportunity, and if Ralph Lanister had not owed his life to insulin he would never have had a chance to try liver feeding on hospital patients. Failure now would mean letting down not only those patients but these men as well: Thornton—cheerful, keen, friendly; Lanister—dark, worn, sardonic. Very different they were, and yet very much alike.

The world had need of men like them, of clear brains unmuddied by wishfulness, of undismayed realism, of cool heads hard to convince of anything. The days of the old frontier were over, the last wilderness had been conquered or discarded. One needed no longer to be an axeman, a quick shot with the rifle, an adept at rough-and-ready living. War had turned into a problem of ballistics and an exercise in trigonometry, and death in battle had become a wallowing in mud and one's own bodily filth. There was adventure left for only the men who were not content to punch a cash register and add up figures in a checkbook. The crusade against disease still led through unknown country toward an unknown goal, it was still beset with invisible and unknown perils.

But many had travelled that way before, to fight pestilence and death. Jenner, Laennec, Koch, Pasteur, Semmelweis, Schaudinn, Rollier, Finsen, Ehrlich, Walter Reed, Carroll, Lazear, Biggs, Gorgas, Wright, Paul Lewis, Noguchi, Banting, Roentgen, the Curies, Opie, Trudeau, Welch, Baetjer—a line that stretched unbroken from the forbidding past through the unlovely present into the unseen future. A line of various men of all races and creeds and colors—some admirable, some vicious, some kind, some cruel, some generous, some envious, some sweet of heart, some bitter and disappointed, some lovable, some hateful, some forthright, some wily, some brave, some craven-hearted, some famous, and some forever wretched and obscure. But all of them adventurers!

And he, Richard Cameron, had chosen to join that band in search of knowledge, knowing that there would be no discharge from its ranks except by death, without dishonor. That morning in the bare little ward in the old hospital, emotions and hopes that had been smouldering within him broke into open flame. In that hour he knew that he had chosen well. The modern world offered nothing else that could compare with the quests of science. He was not alone; about him in the empty ward were all the men who had cleared the trail ahead. It seemed to him a holy place.

III

Dr. Cameron stared down into the stubborn, slate-colored eyes of his patient, John Roberts, retired grocer, fifty-seven years old. It was now three years since Roberts had broken down and ten months since he had first come to the clinic at the Institute because of vague rumors of a new treatment for pernicious anemia, but he had not yet swallowed a mouthful of liver. He looked up with loathing at the yellowish-brown material in the glass Richard held.

"I prefer to die," said he in a weak voice, "rather than eat animal tissue of any sort. I am not afraid to die. Leave me alone. I will not take that stuff!"

Roberts' dull gray eyes met Cameron's without flinching. He meant exactly what he said, there was no doubt of it. And he had been face to face with death many times in the last three years.

So gradually had disease crept upon him that it was long before he realized how weak he had grown or how short of breath it made him to walk up the stairs at home. Then, one day, he noticed the strange yellow color his skin had turned. This he took to be jaundice and so he swallowed box after box of "liver pills" from the corner drug store, but he steadily grew worse. Finally, when he could scarcely eat for distaste of food and his hands and feet had begun to tingle and feel numb, he went to a doctor who told him he had pernicious anemia and advised blood transfusion.

From then on his existence became a series of oscillations between periods of severe illness and periods of improvement after transfusions. Fortunately one son and one daughter belonged to compatible blood groups so that it was unnecessary to pay a professional donor each time Roberts was transfused, but nevertheless the financial strain on his family was severe and the emotional strain on his wife very heavy. Recently it had become essential to put him in the hospital at each relapse and inject healthy blood into his veins on several days in close succession. But in spite of this treatment he was slipping steadily downhill.

Now he lay in bed, too weak to think connectedly, but roused to protest by Cameron's appearance with a glassful of raw liver pulp in orange juice. His flabby yellow face drew into obstinate vertical lines along his nose and the outer corners of his mouth.

"Doctor," he said feebly, "you are a stubborn man."

Cameron laughed. "The same to you, Mr. Roberts. If I've

been trying to get liver down you for ten months, you've been equally dogged about not taking it. The honors, it seems to me, are even."

"I can't understand why animal flesh should be forced on me when I'm sick," retorted the patient in a fretful voice. "I've lived on vegetables all my life and always been perfectly well before."

Richard shrugged his shoulders and set down the glass of liver pulp on the bedside table.

"You could understand if you wanted to, Mr. Roberts. I've explained to you over and over that the proteins in meat are better adapted to use in the human body than those in vegetables. It isn't a matter of justice or right, it's just a fact. Why can't you recognize it as one? The human being wasn't made to live on grass and plants: he hasn't the dental equipment or the proper length of intestine or even the ferments to digest the cellulose fibers of plants. And none of that has anything to do with duty or conscience."

Roberts shook his head.

"We have no right to kill and eat sentient things," he whispered. "It is not fitting that man should kill in order to eat."

"When you cook plants and vegetables you kill living tissue. And, for all you know, they may have as many emotions about being cooked and eaten as animals."

But this semi-facetious comment made no impression on Mr. Roberts.

"It is not proteins I need, Dr. Cameron. I've eaten beans every day for months and they contain proteins."

"Yes, Mr. Roberts, but not the right proteins. All proteins are not alike, any more than all people. You are a human being and so is Miss Worrall." Richard glanced up, smiling at the nurse who stood at the foot of the bed. "But you don't look in the least alike or act alike or even think alike. No more are all proteins like all other ones."

"I don't believe you," asserted the sick man. "Why should some proteins be no use to man when God made the whole earth to be our footstool? There is no reason why one protein should be better than another. Why don't you go away and let me rest?"

"I will, gladly," said Cameron, "the instant you swallow this liver pulp. It's iced and mixed with orange juice, it isn't hard to take. Come on, just this once, anyhow."

"If I did, you'd be back tomorrow with more. I know you, young man. You are stubborn and persistent. I dare never yield unless I mean to go on doing as you order. I won't take the stuff. Put it down."

"But, Mr. Roberts, it wouldn't be three days before you'd feel better. You know how fast the patients in the ward improve. Not one of them has gone bad on me for weeks."

The sick man turned slowly on his side and doubled the pillow under his head. His implacable little slate-colored eyes hardened.

"All my life I've lived as I should and eaten properly. I've been just to man and beast. If I am sick now it is God's will, and for some purpose of His. And you shan't interfere. Go away and leave me alone." He glared up at Richard with all the stubbornness of a small soul. "Go away!" he repeated. The fact that he spoke in a barely audible voice made his determination none the less evident.

Cameron and Miss Worrall walked out together and into the small laboratory at the left of the ward entrance.

"Come in and tell me what I shall do with this man," said Richard, grinning down at the nurse.

"If you're asking me, I'd say drown him," she answered. "For sixteen years I've been taking care of sick people and I've seen some queer customers, but never one like Roberts."

"It seems a bit late to drown a man nearly sixty years old," objected Cameron. "For the sake of argument I'd be willing to admit that a little judicious drowning at birth might do a lot of good, but . . ."

The nurse looked curiously at Richard's smiling freckled face and dark gray eyes. "Why do you bother so much with Roberts? Why do you care whether he gets well or not?"

There was a long pause before Cameron answered.

"Women," he said at last, "have a way of asking questions no man can answer. I think you enjoy putting us on the spot. How the devil do I know why I want to get Roberts on his feet? And if I did know, why the devil should I tell you?"

But almost before he finished the words, the laughter in his dark gray eyes died out and his face sobered.

"Roberts might be the means to an important end, if he wasn't so pig-headed. He could tell me something I need to know. If we could only get that liver pulp down his throat, we could soon prove that this treatment will bring back patients who are at death's door, Miss Worrall. That's why I want to jam liver into him when he doesn't want his life saved and I suspect that it isn't worth saving. Why, he's down to less than a million reds and if I could pull him out of this slump it would show that no case is ever too desperate for the meat diet."

Richard stood with his lanky body leaning against the end of the shelves above his work bench and his long legs crossed. In their deep sockets his dark gray eyes smouldered. As she watched him the nurse's face was overspread with a mixture of amused surprise and pride.

"You take a lot of abuse from Roberts," she said, "and you never seem to resent it. But I've been so angry at him when he went off on one of his rampages that I could hardly hold my temper."

"Well, there's no use getting sore at the man, Miss Worrall. It isn't his fault he hasn't got any sense. He was born with a vacuum between his ears, and he's been stuffed with half-baked religious notions. He can't control his cockeyed feelings. You can't really get angry at a man who hasn't any brains."

The nurse nodded.

"I won't argue with you about it, Dr. Cameron. But it's a relief not to have you tell me all the usual hooey about any life being precious and worth saving, and how noble the nurse's calling is. I'm sick of all the gush that's peddled about the way we find our greatest reward in simply doing good. It's an insult to any intelligence we're supposed to have."

"I know," said Richard. "People fall for awful stuff. There's one sort—like a committee from the S.P.C.A.—that once waited on me that imagines we torture animals and patients behind closed doors for the fun of it. And another gang that thinks we are consecrated to the pursuit of truth and as pure as the antivivisectionists' helpless animals. There's no use trying to tell them they've got us wrong. It's beyond them to understand that we are just human beings who want to find out things instead of making money. They must give us a motive much higher or much lower than curiosity, you see; they have to turn us into saints or ogres, whichever appeals more to them."

"And what am I to do with Roberts? Get a special now or wait until he's unconscious? I hope you remember how he acted the last time we put a special on and he came to and saw her in the room."

"I remember, Miss Worrall." Cameron's voice was grim. "I'm not likely to forget that set-to with our friend. . . . Oh, I guess there's nothing for it but to transfuse him again. Call his family this afternoon and see if any of them want to be stuck for blood. If they don't, get the office to arrange for a professional donor at nine o'clock in the morning. You see, I can't let the man pass out now. There's an idea floating around in my head and one of these days I'm going to want Roberts alive so I can try it on him. That's the only way he'll ever pay for the trouble he's been to the world in general."

CHAPTER IV

I

Richard Cameron was in a glow of approval of his companion and himself and his own good judgment. Judith Emerson of Fifer Institute and Judith Emerson on Sunday afternoon were two different women. Trim as were her working frocks of dark blue with white collars and cuffs, they could not set off the slender straightness of her figure as did this suit of dark gray with its high collar of squirrel fur. Cameron particularly liked the splash of crimson on her black tricorne hat and the diagonal slashes in her coat through which he could see narrow strips of flaming red. Bright colors, he knew, were one of his weaknesses, and it pleased him to find that Judith shared at least that failing.

Northdevon still had its blue laws: theaters and movies did not open on Sunday and concerts to which admission was charged were also forbidden. On winter Sabbaths there was little to do except go to church, drive in one's car, go to the Zoo, or window-shop. On this brisk, chilly Sunday afternoon in January Judith and Richard had elected the third of these alternatives, and later they had walked down Poplar Avenue and up Oak window-shopping and finally come to rest in Rindbooker's restaurant, famous for good food and unpretentiousness.

Richard had thoroughly enjoyed the afternoon. They had walked to the Zoo over sidewalks crusted with snow and had entered through a little-frequented gate at the far end where the deer and elk were kept. These animals, browsing at their piles of hay, glanced up with quick brown eyes and then went on eating, as though they knew there was no danger from these two red-cheeked human creatures.

"I suppose you've hunted deer, out west," said Judith.

"Why, yes. A little." Richard looked sideways at the girl's soft cheek buffetted to scarlet by the wind. Something in her way of speaking made him vaguely uncomfortable. "But I'm not enough of a shot to be any menace."

Judith's lips, he saw, curved into a smile.

"I've known doctors who were great hunters—or tried to make me think they were—and it always seemed so incongruous for a man who tried to save lives when he was at work to go out and shoot animals for fun on his vacation."

Richard was about to inquire whether she approved of fishing, which he liked more than hunting, but thought better of it.

"I suppose women expect men to be incongruous—or least contradictory."

Judith looked up quickly into his smiling freckled face.

"I never expected to find a man who knew that, Dr. Cameron, or would admit it if he did."

"But I am an unusual man. I've been waiting patiently for months for you to discover this, Miss Emerson. I'm so unusual that I don't believe there's anything a human being could do foolish or silly enough to surprise me."

Under the raillery Judith caught sight of a more serious meaning.

"Then you don't think we human beings are rational."

"Oh, once in a while an individual uses his reason, such as it is, in purely personal affairs like picking out a suit or deciding where to live. But most of the time he does things because he wants to or because he dislikes the idea of doing the opposite." Richard paused to look speculatively at the elk munching their hay. "That being the case, he can't help being contradictory. Because now and then he does something reasonable—usually by accident—most of the time he is zig-zagging back and forth between what he likes and what he dislikes. If a man was to try to live by reason, he'd start by suppressing his desires, and then when the reaction came along he'd fly off to the other extreme in an orgy of emotion."

Judith's golden-brown eyes turned thoughtfully toward Richard's face.

"You don't seem to admire the human being or the society he has built up around him, Dr. Cameron."

"I don't. Can you tell me any good reason why I should? This homo sapiens, as the intelligentsia call him, wallows in halfbaked ideas, suppressed emotions, and uncivilized impulses. He wants to be thought reasonable and moral and respectable—above all, respectable. But I'd think more of him—I'd think more of myself—if I was as frank and open as those animals in there." He pointed with his pipe at a large elk who was pushing a small one away from the hay rick. "That fellow isn't trying to disguise anything. He wants that hay himself and he isn't evoking any law or any court to get it for him; he's simply going to keep that other chap away from it. If they get angry enough—or hungry enough—they'll fight it out, and they won't call it a war to make the world safe for small elk either. Animals, you see, live by instinct and so their lives are unified and they don't get neurasthenia from conflicting emotions tearing them apart."

"Then you don't believe in progress, do you?"

"I can't. I've seen civilization peel off too many people in a crisis. A doctor meets human beings in the raw, Miss Emerson—in the 'forked radish' state, you might say. I believe in change, if that's what you mean by progress. But I doubt whether there's any constant direction in the change. Have you ever read Veblen? . . . You ought to, every American ought to. He has no reverence for anything and that makes him good for us. What I started to say was that Veblen never uses the word 'progress'; he always says 'cumulative change.' You have to make up your own mind whether we've been going up or down. My hunch is that, on the whole, it's been down. I think the ordinary man or woman today in the United States is apt to have a less satisfying life than he would a hundred or two hundred years ago. Not less comfortable, but—by and large—less satisfying."

"Living together in masses is hard on people, I know that," admitted Judith. "But I think I'm glad there are some restraints on impulse. I don't believe it would do any good for me to follow my instincts when Dr. Fergusson loses a valuable book I've talked the Academy into loaning us. I'm afraid I wouldn't be enthusiastic about a life of untrammelled impulse, Dr. Cameron."

It was not until they stopped at the pond where the seals were fed every afternoon at three o'clock that Richard returned to this point.

"Did you mean to imply that women are less creatures of impulse than men are? I was always told that women knew things and understood what to do by instinct. Isn't that what one means by 'feminine intuition'?"

Judith smiled broadly. Her mouth was wide and sensitive and her lips were very red; they gave the oval of her face a sort of piquant strength.

"Certainly women are creatures of impulse, just as men are. But they don't go to pieces under the strain of civilization as often as men do because they don't try so hard to subdue their instincts. They don't even very often try to sublimate them, as high-minded males are likely to do. Instead, women camouflage their impulses and desires so that they look respectable and can go on operating without arousing suspicion."

Richard looked very puzzled. "I don't see at all what you mean."

"Well, suppose I illustrate. They used to tell us in school that women reason by analogy rather than logic.... Possessiveness in men results in the visible accumulation of property and display of wealth, either of which often arouses envy and dislike in others. But in women possessiveness frequently masquerades as mother love, and men write poems and shed tears over it."

Cameron laughed at this until his face and the muscles of his scalp began to ache.

"After that, I shan't argue with you, young woman. My only refuge lies in foolishness. So I'll buy peanuts for the monkeys and apples for the bears, and we'll go to see the lions and the tigers and the elephants and into the snake house. Anything is justified that will get your mind off mother love and make you talk in a way appropriate for a male listener."

When they came out of the Zoo at five o'clock the brief winter afternoon had drawn into dusk and the chill of the sunless air was sharp. Richard suggested dinner at Rindbooker's and tentatively mentioned a taxi, but Judith was not pleased with this proposal.

"I like to walk and I love the smell of cold air at night. All week I live in the stuffy library at the Institute where the only possible change of odors is a whiff from the animal rooms."

So they walked from the Zoo all the way down Poplar Avenue through the shopping district and then back up Oak to the restaurant. The street lights came on, the darkness deepened between the pools of radiance about the lamps. Busses with lighted windows and street cars rattled past them, and automobiles swooping around corners flung their headlights into the dusk. Only here and there walked a couple or a little group. Richard felt a comfortable solitude, as though Judith and he were isolated, a moving island of privacy in the stream of motor traffic.

There was something primitive about walking that appealed to him: he enjoyed feeling his legs swinging rhythmically back and forth, like pistons, under him. There was a little fire in his veins that kept him warm in the face of the chilly wind that swept up the Wardell River from the sea. Into his mind there flashed a familiar picture—young work horses unharnessed on Saturday afternoon on the farm and turned loose to thunder off down the lane toward the pasture at a headlong gallop. He wondered if they might not be driven by the same sort of energy, the same fire of life in their limbs. Perhaps it was that which made all emotions possible—happiness and grief, passion and despair. Perhaps it was when the fire of physical vigor died down that nothing mattered. Perhaps that was the greatest of all personal tragedies—that one grew old so that nothing any longer could matter very much.

They crossed a bridge high above the river that divided the city into halves. In the dim reflected light of the street lamps the water seemed cold and dark and greasy. How hideous people contrived to make streams that ran through cities! This water below them, now full of sewage and factory wastes, had once been beautiful—a clear limpid creek with wooded banks. But that was before white men came. Perhaps the white men would have done better to stay at home, in Europe, where they belonged.

At the thought Richard laughed to himself. Those white men who had come to America had been full of curiosity, they had been tormented by a desire to know what lay beyond the curve of the sky upon the sea, they had been adventurers. And if he had lived then, he would have been like them, he would have gone with them in search of the new world. It was not becoming in him to be critical.

"What're you laughing at?" asked Judith. "It isn't fair to hold back jokes."

"This isn't a joke. At least I don't think so. I was just wondering whether it wasn't the same sort of thing to hunt a cure for pernicious anemia as it was to discover America."

On Poplar Avenue there were many shops distinguished by the restrained elegance of the two or three objects displayed in their windows, jewelry stores with century-old names in small letters on their doors, shops with women's gowns and lingerie seductively arranged. Rare china, old silver, pewter ware glistened in soft, cunningly directed lights. Water colors and etchings and books enticed the passerby. Judith paused to look at a photograph of the original Alice for whom Lewis Carroll wrote *Alice in Wonderland*. On the opposite side of this shop was a window filled with travel books. Cameron was staring at them hungrily.

"When I was a kid I wanted to be an explorer. I wanted especially to go to Antarctica. I'd have given anything to be with Scott or Amundsen at the Pole." His voice was far away, his eyes dreamy, when the girl stole a glance at him.

"Isn't that why you like research? Because it's a sort of expedition into the unknown?"

"Yes. Curiosity drives one man to Antarctica and another into the laboratory or the hospital. You never know what will happen, what you'll stumble over in either place. And yet it's more than ordinary curiosity." Richard seemed to be fumbling for a word. "I had a chief once who called it 'the itch to know.' I guess that's probably as good a definition as there is."

When at last they came to Rindbooker's the warm air inside the restaurant was soft on their cold cheeks. The room was not crowded; a sort of brooding quiet hovered over the white tables and the silverware.

"This isn't a fancy place," said Cameron. "But how they can cook meat! I had some mutton chops here last fall that I'll never forget—an inch thick, with their tails curled around them, and broiled over a hardwood fire!"

Judith laughed at what she called his "lyrical outburst in praise of mutton chops."

"I enjoy eating so much," resumed Richard when he had satisfied his first hunger, "that sometimes I'm afraid I live to eat. That's why it cheers me up to look at you, for then I know that something besides food still appeals to me."

"I feel sure I ought to blush at such plain speaking," replied Judith, "but I'm not going to. I like my new clothes myself so much that I sank a month's salary in them."

"It wasn't the clothes I meant," retorted Cameron. "I've seen a good many women who'd look like scarecrows even in that get-up. But I'm pleased with myself for having sense enough to know that you are good to look at, Miss Emerson."

Cameron grinned at the flood of color that spread over the girl's clear, olive skin. There was something very satisfying in her face, in her warm, golden-brown eyes, in her firm oval chin. Her skin was pale but her lips were full and wide and very red. Richard remembered that she had suggested walking across town, that she had kept pace with him all the way. He could see her tall, straight, flat-backed, and he suddenly thought that here was a woman he would enjoy taking west to tramp with on mountain trails. She could hold up her own end of the stick.

He held out a cigarette case.

"I'm sure it's quite safe here. I don't believe the trustees lurk about, spying to see if the women on the Institute staff smoke in public, do you?" He struck a match for her. "That old stuff about women pretending they didn't smoke and then going home and puffing up the air wells and in the bathrooms was the bunk! There can't be anything so awful about a little fire on one end of a paper full of tobacco." Cameron looked up at the smoke ring he had blown from his own cigarette. "Of course, I prefer a pipe myself. I get more kick out of it."

"I believe I would like to smoke a pipe," said Judith, her golden-brown eyes twinkling. "But you wouldn't like that, would you?"

Richard paused an instant, then looked at her with a grin.

"Well . . . no. I don't think I would. Which is only one more proof of what we were saying this afternoon about reason and impulse. My reason tells me it's quite all right for you to smoke a pipe if you want to, but I know I'd hate seeing you do it. So here I am—inconsistent, contradictory, unreasonable, and all the rest of it."

"You see, Dr. Cameron, that I was right when I said it was much better to do as women do—keep their instincts in one compartment and their reason in another, so that they won't intereferе with each other."

"I believe you are right. I keep trying to reason with people about their likes and dislikes when these things have nothing to do with reason. For instance, folks who don't like liver and don't want to eat it even when it's the price of life for them. I don't get anywhere arguing with them, and I expect I never will."

Judith nodded agreement. She was not the sort who considered it essential to chatter every minute she was in a man's company, and now she watched the changes that came over Cameron's face. He had turned half away from her and was staring toward the front of the restaurant where people were coming through the revolving entrance doors. She wondered what it was about his profile that stirred her. His nose jutting out so boldly that, although it was perfectly straight, it gave the impression of being turned up a little at the end? The crispness of the wiry red hair that was so nearly curly? The perpendicular creases back of his lips that promised a certain sternness in his forties? Or was it the air of zest for life the man exhaled that made him more attractive than most men?

"Dr. Cameron," she said, obeying a sudden impulse, "do you feel any sort of responsibility for the things you may discover, the uses they may be put to?"

Richard turned slowly back toward her as though he had been recalled from a far country.

"No, I don't think I do. Why should I? Is it any of my concern what the people I may cure of pernicious anemia do with the years I give them? Some of them might be better off dead, but that is a thing I can't decide. And if they make fools of themselves, should I consider it my fault because I saved their lives? I suppose you're thinking of what some people call the responsibility of science, the irony of things being turned to horrible uses the inventor never dreamed of. Well, that's the world's fault. Nobel isn't to blame for high explosives. If people haven't got sense enough to use scientific discoveries decently, that isn't the fault of the scientist."

The man's gray eyes were shining; something in their expression gave Judith a physical thrill swiftly succeeded by an expectant tenseness that pervaded her from head to foot. Cameron was looking at her queerly, he was unconventional, he did not care for security, he was drawn to the unknown, the unexplored. She could feel part of herself rushing out to meet the explorer in him.

"I am seven kinds of a damned fool!" he burst out in a voice that stifled all these speculations of hers in an instant. "And the whole thing is as simple as A, B, C. You see, Miss Emerson, Roberts is a vegetarian and he won't eat liver . . ."

Slowly, as he went on talking headlong, the glow died out of the girl's olive face and golden-brown eyes. She had a sudden impulse to break out laughing. All the while she had been watching him, so thrilled and expectant, Cameron had actually been thinking of a male patient fifty-seven years old who had pernicious anemia.

II

Most of that night Richard spent in the library at Fifer Institute. This was the first time he had roused the watchman to let him into the building at midnight but so intent was he on finding corroboration of his new idea if possible that he brushed past that surprised functionary with brief apology. Throwing off his hat and overcoat, he pulled from the library shelves volume after volume of the Cumulative Index. His blunt, freckled fingers flicked over the pages and traced down the columns of fine print. "Stomach, digestion in; stomach, ferments of; stomach, function of; stomach, mucosa of; stomach, secretion in." There were a devil of a lot of men writing about the stomach, and probably there wasn't a thing in all these articles, he thought, that he didn't already know. But no matter. He must make sure no one else had thought of this before.

The chill of the fireless building finally penetrated his consciousness sufficiently to make him put on his overcoat again, but he plowed doggedly through his list of references. Slowly his thin face grew gray and tired but when he finished his fruitless search of the scientific journals at six-thirty his eyes were alive with increasing excitement, for it began to seem that no one had ever thought of the thing that was in his mind. Certainly there was nothing of it in recent medical literature and no reported precedent in laboratory experiment.

Before he left the library he wrote a note and left it on the counter in front of the librarian's alcove.

"My dear Miss Emerson:

"Would you mind looking up the digestion of meat in the human stomach for me? Here is the list of the articles I've already read, so you won't duplicate them. Thanks.

"Cameron."

Judith's desk, he noticed half-consciously, was neat and orderly: against the wall stood a row of books primly ranged from large to small and the calendar was already torn off at Monday's date. Just beyond the counter hung a shabby smock she wore when she had to rummage through old, dusty files.

Deep inside him there welled up a strange warm glow at sight of these things she handled every day, and he put out one hand and touched the yellow smock gently.

In front of the Institute his blue roadster stood at the curb of an almost deserted street. The air was raw, the sky was dull gray with the promise of snow, and there was a cutting wind whistling up from the river, but Cameron forgot to button his overcoat and put on his gloves. There was something more he must make sure of as soon as possible. Only ten minutes after Miss Worrall came on duty in Ward B he reached the hospital.

"Good morning," he said brusquely to her as he paused at the door of his little laboratory. "Can you bring me some arrowroot cookies right away?'"

Miss Worrall had long since ceased to question any order of his and so she went without comment to do as he asked. When she returned with the wafers she found Richard setting up the burettes and reagents for examining stomach contents and for a moment she wondered vaguely what he was about, but idle speculation gave place to surprise when he said abruptly, "Would you mind passing this stomach tube on me before you go?"

No sooner had she done this and fastened the end of the little tube to his cheek with a bit of adhesive than Cameron spring up from his stool.

"Thanks, Miss Worrall. That's all just now. But when you get time I wish you'd stick Roberts again for a red count and hemoglobin."

Closing the laboratory door behind her, the nurse looked thoughtfully down the corridor. Something was brewing, she was sure. There always was when Richard came in with that air of suppressed excitement and talked in short, clipped syllables.

As soon as she could leave the ward, Miss Worrall went to Roberts' room and peeped inside. Yes, the old devil was awake at last. Yellow as a lemon again and his blood count very low. Transfusions didn't seem to do him much good any more, he didn't react to them and his relapses were coming closer and closer together. But then the man was a fool not to take liver as the other patients did; what happened to him was his own fault. Though, of course, if he wanted to die that was none of her concern.

"Good morning, Mr. Roberts," she said with professional cheerfulness. "I'm glad you're awake, for I want to take a blood count. Will you turn your head so I can get at your ear, please?"

The sick man directed a baleful, jaundiced stare at her.

"Dr. Cameron took blood from me only Friday. Why do you bother me again today? I think you're experimenting on me. I know doctors do experiment on their patients. I don't believe any of you know what you're about."

Taking the lobe of the man's ear between strong fingers, the nurse felt she would be justified in pinching it. There was nothing Roberts didn't complain of: when they made a blood count every day he felt abused, and when they did not he felt neglected. She found something repulsive in the bit of flabby yellow flesh but she pricked it as swiftly and carefully as though she loved it. If Dr. Cameron, she told herself, could hold his tongue and his temper with this old fool, so could she.

When she took the little pipettes of blood into the laboratory, she found Richard drawing gastric juice out of the tube in his mouth. He explained that he was taking a sample every ten minutes, measuring the amount of acid in each, and making a graph to show the acidity level and its fluctuations during an hour or so.

"Good stomachs run in my family," he said as he made a dot on his chart and connected it with the rest of the curve. "This is perfectly normal—at least, this far. But I'll be glad to get rid of this thing." He tapped the end of the thin rubber tube that dangled from the corner of his mouth.

"I thought you took it unusually well. Most men—even doctors—fight it."

"And why shouldn't a doctor gag when a stomach tube is pushed down his esophagus? We have the same reflexes other people do." Cameron grinned but with the tube protruding from his lips the effect was not as engaging as usual. "I've seen women—and nurses, at that—who didn't swallow the things like little woolly lambs. . . . How's Roberts this morning?"

"He doesn't look well, doctor. That last transfusion didn't do him much good. Do you suppose his bone marrow is past being stimulated?"

"Probably it is. That is, by transfusions. The question is, will anything else stir it up? The old chap is sliding downhill pretty fast the last few days." Before he had finished the words a gleam of excitement flickered up again in his dark eyes.

It was nearly five o'clock that afternoon when Cameron was notified that two doctors from out of town were in the Institute lobby asking for him. Although their names meant nothing to him, he hurried down and found waiting for him two plump, well-dressed, middle-aged men, one of whom was almost entirely bald while the other wore a reddish-brown toupée.

"You are Dr. Richard Cameron?" inquired the bald one. "My name is Worden, Oliver Worden, and this is my brother Thomas."

Richard held out his hand while his quick eyes made note of the sallow tinge of the speaker's face.

"We are both physicians," went on the bald brother. "And

we both have had pernicious anemia for some time. Out our way, in Nebraska, we've been hearing rumors lately about a new treatment for this disease. Medical gossip, you know. It travels almost as fast as the other kind. But, to be quite frank with you, doctor, we came to see you because we know we'll die if something isn't done for us and we thought we might be of some use to you. Anything would be better than puling around in bed like a pair of ailing tomcats. Couldn't you use a couple of co-operative guinea pigs who speak English?"

In spite of the gloomy future Oliver Worden pictured for himself, his bright blue eyes twinkled at Richard.

"We're serious about it," said Thomas Worden. "Ollie always sounds like he's joking, but he isn't this time. Can you use us?"

"Can I use you?" cried Cameron. "Can I use you? You don't know how much you look to me like angels in disguise. All day I've been trying to make up my mind to try something, and now you come walking in." He looked from one brother to the other, "You mean you wouldn't mind if I . . ."

"Tried things out on us?" finished Oliver. "My dear Dr. Cameron, that's exactly what we came here for."

After evening rounds at the hospital that night, Richard told Miss Worrall about his good fortune.

"Can you imagine such luck? Just like an answer to a maiden's prayer, the two of them appear at the Institute. 'A couple of co-operative guinea pigs who speak English.' They're coming into the house tomorrow. They'll have that two-bed room on this floor and they're going to keep their own records and help with the laboratory work. One of them will start liver right away, and the other one . . . Well, I've got an idea about Thomas. It may not work but it's worth trying."

III

With a sigh of relief Miss Worrall sat down and smiled broadly at the young woman in lounging pajamas who lay on a couch before a grate fire in a suite in the Nurses' Home.

"I certainly am glad to see you out of bed, Connie, and I'll be gladder yet when you get back on the ward. Ever since you've been sick I've had a succession of dumbbells on night duty. I've lost so much sleep the last three weeks, trying to look after everything, that I'm walking around in a daze. I wouldn't know a compound cathartic pill from an aspirin tablet. There's just one thing I'm absolutely sure of when I see it. Liver!"

From the pillows behind her oval face, Constance Manning smiled at the other nurse.

"You sound awfully upset, my dear. What's the matter? Don't tell me you've fallen for Dr. Cameron at last or that the patients have all gone on strike against liver and kidney." Then a sudden thought seemed to come to the girl and her hazel eyes filled with curiosity. "Has old man Roberts passed on?"

Miss Worrall shook her head and bent over to untie her white oxfords.

"My feet are simply killing me, Connie. This is the first minute I've been off them since six o'clock this morning. I guess I'll have to reduce. Arches that were meant to carry a hundred and twenty-five pounds don't do well under a hundred and fifty." She burrowed deeper into the club chair in which she sat, stretched out her feet, slipped off her shoes, and wriggled her toes in evident pleasure. Then she looked over at the curious young face against the pillows on the couch. "No, Roberts didn't die. But if anybody was ever any closer to the angels' choir, I never saw it."

"Now, you are just trying to get me excited. It isn't fair to hold out news of the ward. What happened? What about Roberts? What went wrong with him?"

"Plenty," said Miss Worrall emphatically. "You don't happen to have any cigarettes, do you?"

The younger woman stared. "You asking for cigarettes!" she cried.

"Yes," answered Miss Worrall half-ashamed. "Oh, I know I always said I'd never smoke and scolded you girls who did. But I've found out that when you have to wait and watch and wait again, smoking helps you hang on to yourself." She reached for Miss Manning's case and took out a cigarette which she lighted with a trace of awkwardness. "Then you don't know what happened in the ward since you've been away?"

"No. Really, I don't. The first week I was too sick to care about anything except the way I felt. And the girls over in the surgery don't know anything about the rest of the hospital anyhow except what they hear in the nurses' dining room. You know what sort of tripe that is."

Miss Worrall nodded. "It was just as well, Connie. A person your size with a ruptured appendix and a tummy full of drains shouldn't be listening to gossip. . . . Had the Worden brothers come in before you collapsed that night?"

"Oh, yes. They went into that two-bed room on our floor. Don't you remember I went in and found one of them with his hair off, brushing it?"

"Of course, I'd forgotten that was you." Miss Worrall laughed softly. "It's Thomas who takes his hair off. The other one, who hasn't any hair of any kind, is Oliver. They're not much to look at but the probationers all think they're 'swell guys,' I understand. Well, the same day you went to surgery Oliver began the liver diet but Dr. Cameron put Thomas on something new he fixed in the laboratory. The Wordens did their own blood counts and it was only about four days before they began to feel better and then their red counts began to rise and they developed perfectly ravenous appetites, both of them.

"I never saw Dr. Cameron so pleased about anything before. In the evenings he'd come in to check over the Wordens' counts and hemoglobin, and I'd see him hanging over the microscope and then suddenly jumping up to pace back and forth, talking to himself under his breath. Then he began bringing Dr. Farquhar in with him—you remember that little sandy-haired fellow who's been in the Xray department—and the two of them would go into the laboratory and lock the door after them. And three times a day Oliver Worden ate liver and his brother took the thin, reddish stuff Dr. Cameron left for him in a flask in the incubator."

"But what was it?" interrupted Constance Manning.

"Don't try to hurry me," reproved Miss Worrall. "You've got to get this straight as you go so you can appreciate the way it worked out.... Well, everything went on like this for a week. And then that poor creature who took your place on night duty called me up one morning at four o'clock to say that Roberts had gone into a stupor. I went right over and sure enough the old man was unconscious. He had less than a million reds and he looked like the wrath of God, so I rang up Dr. Cameron. He came and took one long look at Roberts and then went into the lab without giving any orders at all. You can imagine how that made us feel. I didn't know what to make of it, but I waited a while and then decided I'd knock at the door and ask what he wanted me to do. But just then he came running out with a flask of the same stuff he'd been giving Dr. Thomas and a big Luer syringe and a long nasal catheter. I helped him pass the tube and fastened it to Roberts' cheek so it would stay put, and then Dr. Cameron began putting his new preparation into the man, a syringeful at a time.

"When I went down to breakfast, I asked them to send up a tray for the doctor, but when it came and I carried it into the lab I found him there with Farquhar, and both of them had stomach tubes in their mouths. I suppose I must have looked startled, for Dr. Cameron stammered out a very lame explanation. That was the first time I'd ever seen him at a loss for words. But I knew he didn't want me around so I put down the tray and got out. But after that nothing could have got me away from the ward until I found out what was going on."

Miss Worrall glanced at the interested face of the girl on the couch and went on with obvious enjoyment.

"All that day Dr. Farquhar was running in and out of the ward and Dr. Cameron sat hunched up in the lab studying blood smears whenever he wasn't talking to Farquhar or the Wordens or hanging over Roberts. He kept on putting the reddish liquid down the tube into Roberts' stomach until he used up all he had fixed for Dr. Thomas, but still the old man didn't come out of his coma.

"That night I went back to the ward after supper. You know

how you have a feeling when something's going to happen. They sent up a good supper for Cameron and he ate it like a starving Armenian. Roberts' family came in during the evening but they left about ten o'clock. I didn't blame them for not staying; they've done a lot for that old devil. After that Dr. Cameron sent Farquhar and the Wordens off and told me I'd better go to bed too, but I didn't do it. I stayed in the night nurse's cubby-hole and every half hour or so I'd go and look into Roberts' room.

"Dr. Cameron had brought in a chair and he sat there beside the bed, watching. Roberts was alive but still unconscious. Midnight came and one o'clock and two, and still no change. The doctor padded out to the laboratory. He hadn't been home all day, his clothes were wrinkled and mussed up, he hadn't shaved, and his face was tired and so pale that his freckles stood out like searchlights. But all of a sudden as I watched him coming along the hall, I thought how solid he was and how I'd like somebody like him around if I was sick and ready to give up. It seemed to me that nothing but his determination was pulling Roberts back and keeping him alive.

"You've seen that picture, haven't you—the Country Doctor, I think it's called—where there's an old doctor in whiskers and a frock coat sitting beside a sick child, and a scared father hovering in the background? I always disliked that picture, I was sure the doctor didn't know what to do; that he was just sitting there being sympathetic and good for nothing. Well, it came to me that night how different Dr. Cameron was. He didn't look sad or sentimental; he was all the time thinking and planning what to do next, and there was an undercurrent of excitement about him, mixed with a sort of grimness.

"You've been around these patients enough to see how soft and flabby they get to look. It seemed to me that Roberts hadn't a bone left in him. He sort of ran down together into the middle of the bed, a heap of flesh that breathed but didn't move. He looked so repulsive, so sort of—obscene, somehow, that I couldn't make myself care whether he died or not except for Cameron.

"It got awfully nerve-racking sitting there, watching and waiting for something to happen. About three o'clock I think it was the doctor nodded to me to come with him into the laboratory. He sat down on a stool and tucked up his feet on a rung and got out his pipe, and then he jerked open a drawer and took out a package of cigarettes. 'If you won't go to bed like a sensible woman, for heaven's sake smoke,' he said. 'It'll help—take my word for it.' So I had my first cigarette and, believe it or not, it did seem to quiet me down a little.

"In spite of his determination I could see that Dr. Cameron was worried and finally I asked if he thought Roberts would ever come out of this coma. He frowned and said in a queer, smothered way, 'I don't like the way he looks, but I'm not giving up.' Then he got up and went back to the old man.

"I stayed in the ward until six o'clock and then came over here to my room and took a shower and put on a fresh uniform before breakfast. When I got back upstairs everything was just as it had been all night. I'd ordered a tray for the doctor, of course, and he gulped down everything on it and asked for more. 'I can go without sleep,' he said, 'if only I can have plenty to eat.' Then Farquhar came and they went into the laboratory together and locked the door."

Miss Worrall tossed the stub of her cigarette into the grate and reached, unconsciously, for another. Her voice had been dropping in pitch and was now vibrant with feeling.

"An hour later Dr. Cameron called me. Roberts had his eyes open and was saying feebly that he was hungry. It wasn't ten minutes until he was grumbling because we couldn't produce exactly what he wanted at a moment's notice. I knew from that that he wouldn't die then. . . . You may think I'm crazy when I tell you the rest, Connie, but I'll never forget Cameron's face as he stood beside that bed. I once saw a man who'd given blood to save his son's life; he was marching up and down, his face white with exhilaration, saying over and over, 'I did it, I did it.' Only the doctor said, 'It works! By God, it works!'"

She leaned down and began to tighten her shoe laces. When, a minute or two later, she looked up at Constance Manning, her face was once more composed and matter-of-fact.

"I shall get up and burst my incision wide open," cried the girl on the couch, "if you don't tell me what it was that brought Roberts back."

"Oh," exclaimed Miss Worrall, flushing a little. "I forgot about that. Why, it was hamburger."

The younger woman stared up at her in blank amazement.

"Honestly, I'm not kidding you. Truly, I'm not, Connie. It was hamburger mixed with gastric juice pumped out of Dr. Cameron's own stomach and Dr. Farquhar's. They put the two together and add some hydrochloric acid and keep the mixture in the incubator for two hours and then neutralize it and filter it before giving it to the patient. It works as well as liver, perhaps better. Both Dr. Thomas and Roberts have done remarkably well on it and now we're trying it on several other cases."

"But where . . . who . . . ?"

Miss Worrall chuckled. "Well, for a little while Dr. Cameron and Dr. Farquhar and I managed to furnish the gastric juice, but the best we could do wasn't enough. So last week some of the senior medical students volunteered to help. They come into the lab in the morning and take histamine to stimulate the secretion of their stomachs, and then we pump up all the gastric juice there is. The boys are developing quite a rivalry to see who can give the most."

By this time Constance Manning had found her tongue again. "But Roberts won't eat hamburger, will he, any more than liver?"

"He wouldn't if he knew it was hamburger," admitted Miss Worrall. "But he doesn't know that. He thinks it's a vegetable purée. You see, we color it green with the sort of stuff they use to color cakes and sweeten it with saccharin to disguise the flavor of meat. The Wordens are sworn to secrecy and no one else besides Dr. Cameron and Farquhar and I know what the new treatment is. I have to laugh when I hear Roberts crowing over us because he's getting well without liver."

"You don't mean to tell me that he's getting well!" The girl's face was as incredulous as her voice.

"He went home today with his red count almost up to four

million," answered Miss Worrall proudly. "I don't know when I've enjoyed anything more than I have putting this thing over on him in spite of himself." She glanced at her watch, then stood up and smoothed down her uniform. "I've got to run, Connie. I'm late now. Please don't tell on me—about the cigarettes. And go on home and have a good rest so you can get back on the job before I lose my mind entirely struggling with these substitute night nurses. You've got more sense than all of them put together, even if you do look like a débutante, and you ought to be glad you're on Ward B. No monotony there, always something new. Why, there's no way of knowing what may happen before you get back!"

CHAPTER V

I

Early in Cameron's second summer at Fifer, Sandy Farquhar came to the Xray department of the Institute. Dr. Fergusson was abroad on a four months' leave of absence when his assistant, Peter Wesley, broke down and Ralph Lanister appealed to the Graduate School for a roentgenologist to fill in the emergency.

"I'm almost sure Sandy will be recommended," said Richard to Jim Thornton. "He had eleven years' experience in Xrays before he came back here to study two years ago, and I know Draper and Penfield consider him the best student they've had for a long while."

Cameron's prophecy came true and Farquhar was asked to carry the Xray work until Fergusson returned from Europe in the autumn, and was promised a research Fellowship after that as part of his work for a doctorate in radiology. On the last Monday in May, therefore, Sandy descended from a Poplar Avenue car across the street from Fifer at ten minutes past eight. Although work in the laboratories did not start until eight-thirty, Farquhar was, as usual, making a point of being beforehand.

The little Scotsman was almost cheerful; there were times those days when he felt that his luck had changed and that life would be different in the future. This post at Fifer and the Fellowship to follow had almost banished his habitual gloom. That morning while he was dressing and getting breakfast he had whistled "The Campbells Are Coming"—a performance that marked the top level of optimism for Farquhar. Now he said a cheerful "Good morning" to the colored woman who was scrubbing the white steps of the Institute. Astonished, she sat back on her haunches and stared after him; that must be a new gentleman, she thought; no one else would have been there so early or spoken so politely.

In the lobby Sandy found other negro women busy cleaning. The waiting rooms, empty as they were, seemed still to retain like a sponge some of the despair and hopelessness of the countless patients who sat in them from year's end to year's end. Farquhar could feel depression creeping from them as he hurried down the corridor toward the rear of the building.

At the fourth floor he let himself out of the elevator cage and walked briskly to a door labelled "Xray Dep't., Entrance," but as his hand fell upon the door knob a presentiment of disaster swept over him so strongly that he paused, reluctant to enter. Disgusted with himself, Sandy straightened his slight shoulders and put resolute fingers on the latch. But the door did not open. He applied more force but still it did not yield, only rattled on its hinges. He had started to turn away when he heard steps inside the laboratory; in another instant the door swung open a few inches to disclose a small weazened dark face under a crop of kinky gray hair.

"I must have come too early. I'm the new man in the Xray department and I was to begin work today."

The colored woman, dust mop in one hand, looked sharply at Sandy.

"You suhtainly come early, all right. You the new doctah, you say? Ain't nobody heah yet except me."

"I'm sorry," said Farquhar. "But perhaps you could show me my office or desk or . . ."

The negress smiled at him; people were not often so polite to her.

"Oh, suah. Just you come along with me, doctah, and I'll show you where you's been put. I was gettin' it ready for you yesterday." She spoke in the soft slurring voice which, after many years in Northdevon, still retained the musical accent of her youth. "Youah Doctah Farquhar, ain't you?"

She scuttled off ahead of him through a room full of filing cabinets and viewing boxes for Xray films and darted down a narrow passageway lined with doors on either side. This hall, after some thirty feet, unexpectedly expanded into a small rectangular cul-de-sac which was surrounded on three sides by little, built-in booths. There was no window in the cul-de-sac itself and at first Farquhar could see nothing distinctly but, as his eyes accommodated themselves to the dim light, he made out a battered desk to which there clung fragments of black paint, a rickety chair, and a series of built-in drawers behind the chair and between two of the booths. The furniture he recognized as the counterpart of that in Cameron's office on the third floor, but the smallness of the cubby-hole surprised him. There was, indeed, barely room to squeeze between the desk and the stack of drawers.

"This is youah place, doctah. Leastways that's what they told me to clean it out for. Doctah Cohen used to sit in heah befoah Doctah Wesley come." Then, perhaps disquieted by the surprise on Sandy's face, she hastened to add, "I's done the best I could to clean it up for you, doctah. And I fixed a place for you to hang youah things in." She pushed open the narrow swinging door of the first booth at her right and disclosed a sort of closet with built-in drawers across one end and a few hooks on the wall. Above the drawers Farquhar noticed a small window of frosted glass; evidently this and similar windows in the other booths were the source of the dim light that pervaded the cul-de-sac.

"Thank you," he said to the negress. "Thanks very much. I'm sure you did the best you could. This is fine. I'll be all right here."

The cleaning woman turned slowly to leave, looked searchingly at this courteous little man with the friendly brown eyes, then shuffled off down the hall and out of sight.

Left alone, Sandy threw his gray felt hat on the battered old desk and sat down in the chair. He could see that the place really had been cleaned up for him: the stack of drawers was spotless and when he pulled one of them open he saw it was lined with freshly folded newspapers. The desk had been thoroughly dusted and the concrete floor was still damp from scrubbing.

Farquhar had changed since the day he set out from Seaforth with Richard Cameron. He had gained a little weight and his neck was not quite so scrawny or his shoulders quite so thin; he was more neatly dressed and his thin, light brown hair was more closely trimmed. But there was a greater change in him than these. Sanderson Farquhar would never be attractive, he would never possess assurance, but he had lost much of his old diffidence and part of the fear that had hidden for so many years in his muddy brown eyes. There was now in his voice and manner a bare hint of the confidence born of recognized skill.

Leaning back in his chair, he noticed a number of framed photographs hanging above the desk: Osler, Aschoff, Virchow, Roentgen, Mme. Curie, Baetjer, Pancoast, Pfahler. They had been left there by Peter Wesley, no doubt. Sandy looked steadily up into the faces of these great doctors, and as he did so his own face changed. The small nose, the insufficient chin, the pale skin, the opaque brown eyes seemed to alter; they became hopeful.

"This is the chance I've waited for, half my life," he whispered to himself. There was an intensity of longing, an agony of hope in the small man's expression and in the small, thin hands that mechanically twisted and untwisted about each other. "Oh, Christ—if there is a Christ—don't let me muff this, too. Keep the hounds off me—until I can dig myself in! That's all I want, all I ever wanted!"

At that moment Farquhar had left about him not a vestige of insignificance—only the passionate longing for life of a handicapped animal in a world of foes.

He was still sitting there when a tall, thin man walked down the corridor and stopped in the neck of the cul-de-sac.

"You're Dr. Farquhar, I suppose." The thin man held out a hand which in Sandy's grasp felt feverish. "I'm Wesley. Julia said she'd brought you back here. I'm sorry I didn't get those pictures out before you got here, but I couldn't manage all the things I should have done."

Sandy could see that Wesley had been hurrying; his pale checks were flushed in the center, he breathed rapidly and at intervals gave a hacking cough.

"It isn't much of a place. I can imagine how it strikes a fellow coming in." Wesley glanced down at Farquhar's wistful face. "But the whole floor is awfully crowded. You see, it was intended for a clinic and these closets were to be dressing rooms. And then they turned it into a laboratory. But the Institute can't afford to remodel the place just now."

"No, I suppose not." Sandy felt that this was not a brilliant reply but he could think of nothing better at the moment.

"Wouldn't you like me to show you around the department? That's really what I came into town for this morning."

Farquhar felt that he ought to expostulate with Wesley: Richard had said he had a cavity in one lung and might have a second hemorrhage as bad as the one that had heralded his breakdown if he was not careful. But before Sandy could remonstrate, Wesley turned back into the hallway.

"Dr. Fergusson's office," he said, pointing to a closed door on the right. "The fluoroscopic room here." He opened a door and disclosed a dusty, windowless room with black walls and an upright fluoroscope with a screen dangling in front of a wooden panel and an enclosed Xray tube behind it. "The place is dirty as hell, but Julia is terrified of the Xray apparatus and absolutely refuses to dust it. I'm supposed to police this room but lately I've felt too rotten either to clean it or use it. The outfit works better than you'd think from the looks of it.... That room over there is the one where Montagu and Fergusson have their conferences on the heredity research." Wesley muffled a series of spasmodic coughs in his handkerchief.

Farquhar regarded the closed door with awe. Montagu was a name to conjure with; his work on tuberculosis and its spread had established his reputation, and now the study of heredity he was making in collaboration with Fergusson attracted the attention of the whole scientific world. Sandy felt a thrill at the thought that he might listen to the great Montagu talking over plans and methods of research and conclusions.

"When are the conferences held?" he asked eagerly.

"Oh, you won't get in on them." Wesley smiled bitterly. "I have never been asked to sit in on a conference in the five years I've been here, and you're coming in to take my place. Dr. Fergusson doesn't want his assistant to know too much of what's going on."

Before Farquhar could answer, Wesley hurried on. "Here's the main radiographic room, doctor."

He led Sandy into a huge, high-ceilinged, oblong room, cluttered with chairs and tables and drying racks for films and viewing boxes with ground-glass fronts and electrical machinery. It reminded Farquhar of a careless farmer's machine shed in winter. Later he was to find some order in this apparent chaos but that morning it seemed an insane jumble of Xray apparatus, old furniture, electric batteries, and switchboards.

"This is Fergusson's idea of an Xray laboratory," explained Wesley. "That thing in the corner that resembles a coffin is an exposure switch that operates with the impulses of the alternating current. On the ordinary sixty-cycle set-up you can make an exposure as short as one one-hundred-and-twentieth of a second. If you've got two or three people to help you and nothing goes wrong and the patient isn't too scared to do what you tell him and no one starts the elevator and God is with you, you can make chest films with it that would knock your eye out. I'll show you some I'm particularly proud of. You see, the shortness of the exposure overcomes the movement due to breathing and heart movement." Wesley's voice was full of an enthusiasm that veiled its slight huskiness. "You couldn't get better lung detail if the patients were dead."

By this time the technicians had arrived and Fergusson's secretary, and Wesley introduced them to Sandy. Two of the technicians made the exposures, the third did the dark-room work. The secretary wrote letters, typed the reports on Xray examinations for the clinic downstairs, answered the telephone, and put the films into the viewing boxes to be studied.

"You're expected to do all your fluoroscopy in the forenoon," explained Peter Wesley. "And as much as possible of the radiographic work too. Then in the afternoon you sit in here and examine films and dictate reports on them, while Fergusson has his conferences with Dr. Montagu."

"Doesn't Dr. Fergusson go over the films with you and at least tell you what he thinks of your interpretation?"

Wesley smiled acidly. "He hasn't any of the time I've been here. I write my own reports on the films, then Fergusson reads what I've said and scratches the reports up and changes them to suit him before they go down to be put on the patients' charts. But in five years he's talked over just one case with me and told me why he changed what I'd written."

"Then a man isn't taught anything down here," said Farquhar slowly. "He just has to learn what he can for himself."

"That's it," agreed Peter Wesley. He gave a short, sharp laugh that brought on a fit of coughing and forced him to sit down and rest.

Shortly after nine o'clock a thin stream of patients began to trickle into the department from the clinics; with a word or two of advice from Dr. Wesley the technicians went ahead with the examinations requested.

"These films will be sorted out and ready for you to look at tomorrow afternoon," explained Peter. "Yesterday's crop will be waiting for you when you get back from lunch today. Don't try to get out reports the same day the films are made—unless it's that rare thing, a real emergency. If you once start doing that, they'll run you ragged, sending people up from the clinic at 10:10 and expecting a diagnosis ready at 10:20."

Going back through the main radiographic room, they paused to watch the two technicians make a chest film of a squalling negro baby. Expertly these women focussed the Xray tube, adjusted the factors of distance, voltage, and amperage, held the squirming infant face down on the cassette, watched its breathing, and flashed the exposure at the end of inspiration.

"That was a fortieth of a second," observed Peter. "And it will be a good film, too."

As he followed Wesley, Sandy heard one technician say to the other, "Isn't it quiet and peaceful around here when Fergusson's away?"

II

Occasionally that summer Farquhar went out to the suburban town where Peter Wesley lived. In spite of his physician's advice, Peter refused to go at once to a sanatorium; since his first profuse hemorrhage he had raised blood only three or four times in small amounts and he was coughing very little. The fact that Xray films of his chest showed a cavity in one lung he chose to disregard, for the time being.

"If I get worse I'll go up to Saranac in the fall and have that lung compressed," he said. "But this summer I'm just going to lie around and loaf. This is the first chance I've had to be lazy since I was a kid." Then, seeing Sandy's disapproving eyes upon him, he went on, "And don't worry about my wife. I know how to keep from handing my TB on to her."

Farquhar enjoyed talking with Peter Wesley. His five years in Fifer Institute had given him a certain cynical wisdom but, underneath that shell, Peter was deeply interested in his work. He was particularly concerned over a large number of Xray films of lungs removed at autopsy which he had accumulated without Fergusson's knowledge. With each film, he told Sandy, there was a typed copy of the post-mortem findings. There were nearly a thousand of them and Wesley was distressed lest they should not be used, and, at the same time, determined not to turn them over to Fergusson.

"He hogs everything that's done in the department and always has. Publishes it under his own name. So I got fellows I knew in two or three of the big hospitals around town to save lungs for me, and I used to go around late in the afternoons in my car and gather them up and Xray them on the quiet. I got away with it because Fergusson isn't very sharp at catching on to things like that."

"But where are all these films stored?"

"Down on your floor," answered Wesley, grinning. "Thornton is a good pal in time of trouble."

"And you're sure Fergusson would be sore if he knew about it?"

"If I'd ever published an article about anything I learned from those films, M. Carr would have thrown me out on my neck. I know that."

When, a little later, Peter turned over these roentgenograms to Sandy, Farquhar found on them something that piqued his curiosity. In many of the films he noticed small round white spots which he had been taught to interpret as calcium deposits in the lungs or the lymph nodes of the chest, but when he read the autopsy reports he often found no mention of any such calcified areas. This discrepancy, occurring over and over, set him thinking. What could these tiny densities be if they were not calcium deposits?

After pondering this point for some days, Sandy went to one of Wesley's obliging friends at the Wardell Hospital and asked him to save more lungs from cadavers, tying off the blood vessels in one lung before removing it from the body and leaving the vessels in the other lung untied. Then, during the hot summer nights, Farquhar worked with the Xray films of these excised lungs in a viewing box before him, patiently sectioning the air-filled tissues in search of the things that cast round, dense shadows on the films.

Presently he bought a water-bath and a quantity of paraffin. The paraffin he melted and moulded into rolls the size of a small slate pencil. These tiny rolls he mounted on a sheet of cardboard, some standing on end, some lying on their sides, others twisted into figure eights and semi-circles. Then, with nervous fingers, he made an Xray exposure of the cardboard. In the dark room while he stood waiting for the film to come out of the developer, his heart pounded in excitement and when finally he saw on the cleared roentgenogram the sharply outlined densities that corresponded to his rolls of paraffin his knees went weak under him.

"God!" he whispered to himself. "I was right after all."

From that night on, Farquhar became almost ghoulish in his desire to Xray and then dissect the lungs of dead people. Between times he experimented with his little rolls of paraffin and pawed over the files of chest films in the department. Week by week, the conviction grew within him that most of the round white spots he had been taught to regard as deposits of calcium in the lungs and evidence of old tuberculosis were really nothing but blood vessels lying in such a plane as to be seen in cross-section on the films. Bent on confirming or disprov ing this theory, he worked feverishly during July and August. At last he felt so sure of himself that he told first Peter Wesley and then Richard what he was doing, and asked Wesley's help.

"We must publish this before someone else beats us to it. I'll speak to Dr. Penfield in the fall and ask him if he can't arrange for us to read a paper before the Northdevon Roentgenological Society this winter. But we must get an article in one of the Xray journals too. I haven't time to do any writing now but you could work up a couple of papers—one short, for the local society, and one longer, for publication. I'll furnish all the dope and you can do them right here in bed."

By this time Farquhar was so sure he was right that he spent every moment he could spare from his routine work in the laboratory making films of his paraffin rolls to be used as illustrations for the article. He buried these rolls in chunks of meat, he laid them beside specimens of calcium borrowed from the Chemistry Department at the University, he compared the shadows they cast on Xray films with those made by arteries full of clotted blood and found them to be almost identical. Slowly he accumulated more and more evidence of the correctness of his interpretation. The Xray films he carried out to Peter's house overflowed the bookcases and piano top and library table, and the shapes into which he twisted paraffin cylinders in order to Xray them were legion.

Early in September he showed some of these films to Dr. Penfield. The older man was impressed by Farquhar's thoroughness and he announced himself more than willing to arrange for a preliminary report of the work to the Northdevon Roentgenological Society. For seventeen days thereafter Farquhar trod on air, and then Fergusson came back.

Between the two, instantaneous dislike flamed up. In Fergusson's flabby face and pale eyes Sandy thought he saw a soul as small as Samuel Ascot's and a temper as malignant as Oscar Steinberg's. He wondered whether Fergusson had had a haircut while he was abroad. More vexatious than his untidiness was Fergusson's habit of closing his office door ostentatiously whenever Farquhar came down the hall; Sandy told himself over and over that it was not his fault that he had to use the bulbous end of a corridor for an office and that Fergusson had no reason for suspecting him of eavesdropping outside his door. Finally, one day, when he found on the clinic patients' charts the terse reports with which he had taken such pains scrawled over with comments and corrections in Fergusson's handwriting, his anger rose to new heights.

From the first Dr. Fergusson had an antipathy for his new assistant. It had been annoying to receive word the first week he was in France that Wesley had had a pulmonary hemorrhage and must resign. If Montagu had been in Northdevon he might have arranged for a successor to Peter Wesley, but the great man was in the West Indies on a cancer survey, and so—reluctantly—Fergusson had been obliged to leave matters in Ralph Lanister's hands. When he learned that the man who was taking over the department for the summer had just finished two years' study in the Graduate School of Medicine under Draper and Penfield he was more vexed than ever, and when he learned that Farquhar was a friend of "that upstart, Cameron" in Thornton's laboratory he was infuriated. If he had not had four months' leave on full pay Fergusson would have come back to Northdevon at once, but since he did not want to do that he maintained complete silence about Sandy's appointment and the research Fellowship that was to follow it.

But, once back in the Institute, Fergusson felt the situation in his department would soon become intolerable and went downstairs to tell Lanister what he thought of the emergency Xray appointment. To his intense annoyance Ralph Lanister brushed him aside and promised active opposition to any move on his part to discharge Farquhar.

The same day Dr. Montagu said something that appalled him. "Surely, Dr. Fergusson, you wouldn't allow personal likes and dislikes to shape your opinions. You don't know enough about this man's work yet to form any judgment of his ability. Personalities must be subordinated to performance in research. The chances are that he's pretty capable or Penfield and Draper wouldn't both have recommended him to Dr. Lanister."

This pronouncement Fergusson dared not defy: he owed his reputation as well as his job to Montagu. But he grew increasingly nervous and irritable. He criticized the technicians for trifling errors in technique, he shouted at his secretary when he gave her dictation. When he heard Farquhar moving about in his little cul-de-sac at the end of the hall, he drummed the desk with his thick fingers and twisted the buttons on his vest.

But there were other sources than depravity for these reactions. All his life Fergusson had been poor, and above all things he dreaded a return to economic insecurity. He had a wife and two children and he knew it would be almost impossible to find another position with the prestige and the income which Montagu's protectorate assured him at Fifer. He had established his professional reputation with his work on heredity in association with Dr. Montagu's study of tuberculosis, and he wanted to spend the remainder of his working life in the Institute. It was not only that the combination of security and professional recognition tempted him but that research itself attracted him with such compelling force that it drove him to disregard everything except his own advancement and the security of his family. Mentally gifted but torn by suspicion and jealousy and fear, Fergusson soon realized that it would be more politic to obstruct Farquhar's attempts to go beyond routine than to discharge him outright.

He protested that the pressure of the clinic work in his department made it necessary to retain Sandy as assistant rather than make him a research Fellow. He concentrated on keeping Farquhar busy with the monotonous routine of the laboratory. Finally he bobbed up at the November staff meeting with a proposal to Xray the chests of all high school students and medical school students in Northdevon for evidences of childhood infection with tuberculosis. This project, thoroughly meritorious in itself and supported by Montagu, was approved by staff and trustees, and the first of the next year Sandy found himself going around the city with a portable Xray machine and two public health nurses making chest films of thirty or forty school children a day. This project, Fergusson felt sure, would keep Farquhar out of mischief, and slowly his shrewd eyes refilled with assurance.

Now and then he even took the trouble to stop in the viewing room when Sandy was working there and comment not too caustically on the quality of the films made with the small, portable machine. Strangely insensitive to the emotional undercurrents among his subordinates, he never recognized the covert hostility in the eyes of his secretary and the technicians. Sometimes he fancied there was smouldering resentment in Farquhar's face, but he was so sure he had the man safely pocketed for two or three years at least in this tuberculosis survey that he contemplated his own clever stratagem with pride.

III

Bitterly disappointed as he was, Sanderson Farquhar kept his chagrin to himself. Richard was engrossed in the anemia research, his struggle to keep down the retail price of liver, and the failure thus far to discover among the liver extracts made by Waldheim a usable one. Coming upon him once or twice in the library with Judith, Sandy felt a dull suspicion that his friend was in love with this young woman. These things kept Farquhar from asking advice or help of Cameron and there was no one else in the Institute whom he could bring himself to approach.

Lanister's sardonic dark face did not invite confidences, Hastings he knew only by sight, with Thornton he had but a speaking acquaintance, Peter Wesley had gone to Saranac Lake to a sanatorium, and Montagu was Fergusson's sponsor. As for confiding in the assistants in the other departments, that never occurred to him. Grimly he set himself to work with his school children, carrying home at night armfuls of chest films to study and writing page after page of notes as material for the thesis he must prepare if he was ever to secure his doctorate in radiology. On those week-ends when he knew Fergusson was out of town he spent his time at the Institute, plugging doggedly at his calcium deposit-paraffin roll research.

In February Penfield asked him to give his paper on calcium deposits in the lungs at the next meeting of the Northdevon Roentgenological Society. The hesitation with which Sandy consented soon changed into unshakeable decision. Between them he and Peter Wesley had done this work; he would read the paper in both their names and later publish it the same way. Then, no matter what happened afterward, their names would be linked with the subject and their priority established. He wrote Peter what he meant to do; this news ran Wesley's pulse up and put him back at bed-rest for a fortnight but he sent word to Farquhar of his gratitude.

Farquhar told Richard about the meeting and Cameron broke a date with Judith to be there. She didn't expect a man to give up professional things for social engagements; that, Richard told himself, was one of the things that made her different from any of the women he had ever fallen in love with. It was, he felt, much more satisfactory to have a woman friend than a sweetheart; he determined to steer clear of love the rest of his life. And when he shook hands that evening with Sandy and found how damp with sweat the little Scotsman's palm was, he was glad he had come.

Farquhar had on a new double-breasted blue suit, neatly polished black shoes, and a fashionable red-and-blue striped tie. He had also had a hair-cut recently. Richard grinned as he took notice of these efforts to minimize the shortcomings of a defective physique. But by the time Farquhar was fairly launched on his paper Cameron became conscious of a feeling of pride that was stealing over him. Sandy had proceeded steadily from accidentally observed facts to a theory that would account for those facts and, finally, to the proof of that theory. The audience gave him close attention. Mounted in illuminated viewing boxes on the platform, Sandy had his illustrative Xray films and, as he warmed up to his subject, he seemed to forget himself and to change before Richard's eyes into a cool, collected scientist who had something to demonstrate to his colleagues. His words came easily, he was calm and at the same time convincing, he forgot his diffidence. When he concluded his paper exactly thirty seconds before his allotted twenty minutes was up there came a round of sincere applause.

Joining in the hand clapping, Cameron chided himself: he had always shown Farquhar a tinge of patronage, he suddenly realized. He had drifted into an attitude of half-conscious superiority because Sandy had always seemed so definitely an under-dog. And now the man had come out with a piece of work that these experts in Xray interpretation evidently regarded as important. Richard remembered how little he had seen of Farquhar since he came to the Institute, how little he knew these days of what was happening to him or what he was doing; he resolved to wait for Sandy and drive him home and invite him to dinner one night next week to meet Judith.

But when the meeting broke up, Sandy was surrounded by men who wanted to discuss his paper and ask him questions and look at his films, and later when the crowd had melted away Cameron found to his chagrin that the little Scotsman had slipped out unnoticed. The impulse to drive out to Farquhar's apartment and wait there for him he discarded in favor of going past the University Hospital for a last look at the anemia ward.

"No telling how long it would be before Sandy got home," he told himself. "But I've got to get hold of the fellow soon and have a talk with him and find out how things are going."

IV

While Cameron was drifting off to sleep, Farquhar was standing on Poplar Avenue in the shadow of a three story brick house, looking up at the dark bulk of Fifer Institute. He remembered the first morning he had come there to work. Although things had seemed promising that day, he had even then recoiled in apprehension from the locked door of the Xray department. He recalled his introduction to the cul-de-sac in which his desk still stood, the words he had said while he stared at the photographs Wesley had left on the wall. "Oh, Christ—if there is a Christ—don't let me muff this too. Keep the hounds off me till I can dig myself in!"

Christ hadn't done it, of course. He had been a fool to think it possible. Those three summer months and the first weeks of September when he had worked alone on his dead lungs and his paraffin rolls would always be the high point of his happiness. Whatever happened now, he had at least done that piece of work and it would be published under his name and Peter Wesley's. For that he had Dr. Penfield's word given not two hours ago. And to that knowledge he clung like a tired swimmer to a floating timber. This no man and no combination of circumstances could take away from him.

But the fact remained that he had flung down a challenge tonight which Fergusson would not ignore. Sandy's paper before the Roentgenological Society and the forthcoming article in the Journal of Radiology would seem to the man deliberate insubordination and disloyalty. There was no blinking that. But the thing was over and done; even if he wished, Farquhar could not recall the evening just past. He drew up his thin shoulders under the new blue coat with a trace of pride, then looked about as though to make sure he was unobserved.

Before him in the dark he could see Fergusson's face when he saw that article of his and Peter's. "The Identification on Roentgenograms of Calcium Deposits in the Thoracic Viscera." That was a good title, but Fergusson wouldn't think so. He would be furious, he would bawl at his secretary and yell at the technicians and storm out to see Montagu. Thievery, he would call it, thievery and arrogance. How dare Farquhar come out with such an article without the sanction of his chief? It was unheard-of effrontery.

Sandy knew he would sooner or later be discharged. Montagu's cold fairness which made for impartial discussions in staff meetings would never supply motive power for the defense of an underling. Richard was in no position to save him, he was only an associate himself. Thornton had plenty of personnel problems in his own department, Lanister hardly knew him, and Hastings was putty in the hands of Montagu and Fergusson. Farquhar drew a long breath. It had been a good bout while it lasted; he had given Fate a run for the money this time. But he knew the fight had gone against him.

In Seaforth Cameron had seized command, told him what to do and furnished the energy to do it. But now ... Sandy shook his head slightly. He had the conviction that it was no use, that it never had been any use. He had done all he could, taken every turning that presented itself and every chance that came to him; he had studied hard, worked hard. Penfield considered him worth putting on the program tonight and he and Draper had recommended him to Lanister; they would see to it that his paper was published and that he had credit for this thing he had discovered. But they couldn't change the future because they couldn't change the past or make him a different man. Neither could he. He had tried. Yes, damn it, he had always tried. But the thing had been impossible from the first. Why not admit that, once and for all?

In his pocket Farquhar could feel the little notebook he had carried for years. In it he set down now and then ideas that came to him. He remembered the first entry in the little book, made when he was twenty. "My body is an incubus and my fears are born of it. But it is possible for the possessor of a defective body to remain unbroken by the disasters that overcome it because he has it always in his power to escape his servitude, his subjection, to his body. And I think it is his right. What a horror life would be—all life!—if there was no end to it!"

Sandy rubbed one thin hand across his eyes and stared up at the dark building across the street. Here and there, in hallways and corridors, a dim night-light shone. The polished brass plates at the entrance reflected the feeble rays of the street lamps. It seemed to him that he could see through the walls of the Institute and through the men who worked there. In that institution dedicated to the study of disease and the discovery of truth, the inevitable had occurred. People—all people—were short-sighted and selfish and greedy; scientists were no exception. Fifer Institute was a web of entangling alliances, interwoven prejudices, conflicting motives, and clashing purposes. It was honeycombed with jealousy and bickering. The achievements that stood to its credit—and there were a goodly number of them—had been accomplished in spite of these things, and more would be attained in the future. But how pitifully insignificant they were, compared with what might have been done! If men could only learn not to knife each other, not to hate each other, not to trip each other up! If they could only work together, face things squarely as they were, set reason a guard over their conduct!

But they had not learned to do these things and it seemed to Farquhar that they never would learn. Poor foolish humanity, wasting time and energy fighting one another, while all around them rolled a magnificently implacable universe bent on destroying them! Turning the little span between birth and death into a torture chamber! What a sublimely ridiculous spectacle man was—this infinitesimal midge on an insignificant planet in one corner of the universe! Sandy's lip curled in a grim smile.

But there were men who were not midges, though they did live on an insignificant planet. There was Richard. And Jim Thornton whom Richard admired. And, queerly enough, there was Ralph Lanister—dark, sardonic face, cynical eyes, and all—and beside them B. C. Montagu. Four men out of the twenty and more who worked in the Institute were real. They had learned things, they were learning now, they would go on as long as they lived. And they passed their knowledge on to others. They did not work for money. They were adventurers, crusaders, men nagged by an insatiable desire to know and to understand what they knew. They were not intolerant of other men in search of truth.

It was possible then for men like that to maintain an existence in the hostile modern world—precarious and impecunious, but still an existence. So much was sheer gain, to be set down to the credit of man. Not much, it was true, but something. And all the other men who reported at the Institute for work were sycophants, parasites.

Sandy Farquhar laughed silently and turned his overcoat collar up about his neck before he walked slowly away down Poplar Avenue alone. He did not belong among the parasites, but he was there—with Fergusson. But for a different reason.

CHAPTER VI

I

The next months were full of misgivings for Cameron. He had begun to distrust his dietary treatment of pernicious anemia: such a simple, elementary thing as feeding these sick people liver and kidney and predigested raw beef must surely have been tried by someone else long ago. He was sure that some Italian scientist must have followed up the work of Pirera and Castellino and he clamored for blood studies from Italy until Judith Emerson came to wish that country had never survived the Middle Ages. Richard was invited to give a paper on the treatment of pernicious anemia with diet at the next annual meeting of the American Medical Association and after that he developed an obsession that someone would rise on the floor of the meeting and publicly demolish his whole theory. The fact that he had now almost fifty patients—among them Joe DiPallo—who had been alive and well on the liver treatment for periods of months or years did not dispel his anxiety, nor did the growing security of his position and an increase in salary to four hundred dollars a month give him composure. Slowly he grew less cheerful and came to be ironical and sharp-tongued.

One factor in the tartness of his mood was the constantly rising price of liver. "Damn the butchers!" he would cry to Dr. Thornton. "Damn the packers! How do they think clinic patients can pay a dollar a pound for liver?" He urged people to eat more kidney and Miss Worrall sometimes suspected he resented the fact that chickens have but one gizzard apiece.

Then he had begun to fear that a practicable liver extract could never be made. Patiently Waldheim, the chemist, split liver into this chemical fraction and that, and patiently Richard tried them all out in turn. But one after another proved worthless. Not until Waldheim combined an extract of acidified minced liver with exactly the proper quantity of absolute alcohol did he get a precipitate that contained the active principle he needed. Successive dilutions and precipitations and washings eventually gave him a material he called "Fraction M," which was extremely potent but which, as he pointed out to Cameron, undoubtedly consisted of as many distinct chemical substances as Northdevon had inhabitants.

Injections of this liver fraction promptly caused a rise in the number of red blood cells, but unfortunately it also produced pain and tenderness and sometimes abscesses at the site of the injection, while if the extract was introduced directly into the patient's blood stream he was likely to have nausea and chills and fever. Although they were dissatisfied with rigid daily rations of liver and kidney, many of the men and women in the ward resented Richard's attempts to use "Fraction M" hypodermically. They insisted that they were "being experimented on" and complained bitterly of the soreness following the injections. When, now and then, in spite of Cameron's carefulness, abscesses formed, they threatened legal action against him. They were apparently incapable of understanding that, since laboratory animals are not subject to pernicious anemia, all treatment of this disease must be finally evaluated by its effect on human patients. But when, in desperation, Richard put them all back on liver and kidney feeding, they did not cease complaining.

Three alternatives presented themselves at this time: the use of a permanent liver and kidney diet in these cases, the development of the use of a mixture of raw beef and normal gastric juice such as Cameron had used so successfully with Roberts and Thomas Worden, or the improvement of Waldheim's liver extract. Upon the second and third of these possibilities the chemist and he bent all their energies but, as winter dragged on, it seemed to Richard that, for all their efforts, they were gaining little ground.

Roberts and Thomas Worden had, to be sure, made spectacular recoveries. The Worden brothers had long since returned to Nebraska in good health and Roberts still came to the hospital six days of the week to take his incubated mixture of raw beef and gastric juice through a stomach tube. More than once Miss Worrall suggested to him that he might take the preparation by mouth like any ordinary medicine "I'm sure he'd never realize there was meat in it, Dr. Cameron; it tastes so strange"—but the vegetarian, always negativistic, refused to do this. He enjoyed coming to the ward and talking with those patients the nurse would allow him to see, furthermore he suspected that she disliked passing the tube on him so often; consequently he insisted that the treatment be carried on precisely as Cameron had started it.

Now and then the nurse thought Richard limped as he walked and once or twice she felt sure that he was really ill. One day in midwinter she ventured an inquiry but was answered so savagely that she forbore any further questions about his health. Nevertheless, as winter wore into spring, she became convinced that Cameron, whether he knew it or not, was physically unfit. Over and over he would begin his day's work with all his old gaiety only to have his good humor turn into cynicism before he had finished filtering the gastric juice given each morning by the volunteer medical students.

"All this 'bigger and better' stuff makes me wild, Miss

Worrall," he said one forenoon. "How can you be sure anything is better than something else? There's no progress—nothing but change. A fellow might think this anemia treatment represented progress but I doubt whether it does. How are people to get money for liver or extract? And how are we going to find anybody to give us gastric juice after the novelty wears off? The boys are getting fed up on it already. I'm in a blue funk, I suppose, but sometimes I wonder whether there's any use going on here this way."

Moodily he jerked off his laboratory coat and took his hat and hurried out of the laboratory. Miss Worrall looked after him anxiously. He certainly was not himself these days and for the last week or two his limp had seemed definitely worse.

II

But the next morning when he rushed into Ward B with his face flushed from running upstairs instead of waiting like a sensible man for the elevator, she decided she must have been mistaken about the limp. And when he told her in a torrent of words what he had thought of during the night, she too was caught up in the flood of his enthusiasm.

"I don't see why I didn't think of it before. It's so simple. But I expect that's just the reason. I don't see the simple things because I'm looking for complicated, outlandish things. I've always known it was absurd to expect healthy people to volunteer their stomach contents for anemic patients perpetually. Now, while it's still experimental, we can get the medical students to do it, but they'd be bored stiff with the whole thing as soon as it got to be established technique."

"Anybody would," said the nurse pertly.

"That's just where I've been bone-headed not to think of this before. I ask you, Miss Worrall, where does the stuff we've been pumping out of our stomachs come from if not the mucous membrane that lines our stomachs? Isn't that where all gastric juice is manufactured? Where else could it come from? All right, then. The next question: won't there be gastric juice in the lining of animals' stomachs when they're fresh killed? Answer: there certainly should be. Finally, question number three: how can we find out about this? Answer: I am now on my way to the slaughter houses of the mercenary packers to get a bucketful of pigs' stomachs. Can you take care of the boys this morning without me?"

"Of course," exclaimed Miss Worrall. "Do you know, Dr. Cameron, I have a feeling that this is the real answer to your problem. I believe you can grind up pigs' stomachs and make a powder people could take in a capsule." She made an expressive gesture with her hands. "What a relief to be rid of liver! Do you know I've got so I almost turn sick at the sight of it myself?"

"Now, now, Miss Worrall, don't you turn nutty on me! You're the balance wheel of this ward, you know. I'll be on my way then. Don't say anything about this to the students. The whole thing may be a false alarm."

But neither of them believed that. In Cameron's mind, as he drove to the packing house district, a warm comfortable sureness sprang into being and on Miss Worrall's usually collected face there shone all morning as she moved about among the gastric juice contributors a superiority born of the knowledge that she knew something important which they did not even dream of.

Within the month Richard's idea had proved correct even to the minor detail of the closer resemblance between hog stomach and human stomach than between the stomachs of cattle and men. The organs, quickly removed from freshly killed pigs, were washed before Cameron brought them to the laboratory; there they were washed again and dipped for a moment into boiling water. After that they were ground up and mixed with fruit juice or tomato juice, and this mixture after being chilled was ready to give to patients.

Two new patients were treated first of all and both responded rapidly. When Cameron suggested to Joe DiPallo that he might try the new treatment, he was interested but not enthusiastic.

"I got so I like liver," he said. "It saves the trouble of decidin' what kind of meat to eat, when you always take liver the way

I been doin'. But if you want me to, I'll try out the new dope and let you know what I think of it."

With Mr. Roberts Miss Worrall had better luck. Tomatoes were one of his pet foods; to them he attributed all sorts of uncanny values. When the nurse showed him the tomato juice mixture and told him it combined all the virtues of the purée he had been taking for so long, his habitual reluctance to follow suggestions weakened.

"I guess this will about end the liver business," he said gloatingly. "It sure makes me laugh when I think of Dr. Cameron lecturing me about eating that stuff, trying to make me think I'd die if I didn't. And here I am, perfectly well, and no animal tissue has ever passed my lips." He drank the glass of tomato juice and looked calculatingly at the nurse. "These are not local tomatoes, Miss Worrall. They have a flavor that tomatoes grown in this part of the country never develop. I am a connoisseur of tomatoes. I can always tell the two kinds apart; one taste is enough." Then his small slate-colored eyes glittered with sly curiosity. "What did you put in with the juice?" he demanded.

But Miss Worrall was not to be caught by his cunning. "It is treated with hydrochloric acid and certain enzymes."

"What are enzymes?" Roberts was instantly suspicious.

"Ferments. They digest food and produce chemical changes. They're a good deal like yeast."

"Oh, yeast. Yeast cakes like you buy in the stores? . . . Well, I always knew this meat eating was just a notion. If God had intended us to live on animal tissues . . ."

But the nurse knew better than to let him start on one of his interminable tirades about the sin of eating flesh and blood; she hastily invented an errand to the diet kitchen and maneuvered Roberts out of the laboratory. Later, over a friendly cigarette, she laughed with Richard over the outcome of Roberts' obstinacy.

"The old devil has been a God-send," said Cameron. "If it hadn't been for his pig-headedness I probably would never have found out about raw beef plus gastric juice, or pigs' stomach either. And now we can have our choice of treatments: give the patients liver and kidney to eat, or fruit cocktail or tomato juice with pigs' stomach ground up in it to drink, and get equally good results whichever we do. And one of these days Waldheim will have a liver extract that we can give in a hypodermic injection two or three times a month. It's coming, Miss Worrall. I know it." And so it was, but something else which Richard did not foresee came first.

III

The next day Lanister sent for him. Richard found the chief of the General Clinic alone in his office. Lean, dark, sardonic as ever, the man's face was far more alive than it had been when Cameron first saw him. Then he had still been in the shadow of chronic invalidism while now his energy had risen to a new level.

"Well, Cameron, sit down," he said, turning smouldering, quizzical brown eyes toward Richard. "Sit down and prepare for a shock."

The younger man slid into an armchair facing Lanister. "I'm ready," he said. "Shoot the works!"

"Day before yesterday a man I've known slightly for years sent his mother-in-law to me. She's been sick for twenty-five years. She's got pernicious anemia, Cameron, she's never had any specific treatment for it, and yet she is alive at sixty-five."

"Impossible!" Richard sat up with a jerk. "She must have had transfusions or something. Maybe she eats a lot of meat or is fond of liver or kidney or sweetbreads or gizzards."

"She flatly denies all these allegations, Cameron, and so do her daughter and son-in-law. They assure me that she hates all 'insides' and that she has never eaten much meat. They also told me that of recent years, since her weight has shown a tendency to increase, the old lady has lived chiefly on salads, brown bread, and vegetables. So what?"

Richard sprang up and began to pace up and down, dragging one foot a little and running his hands through his hair.

"I don't believe it. It can't be so. Vegetables and fruit—except apricots—can't do that. There must be something phoney about the woman, Dr. Lanister. She must have something else wrong with her, some sort of secondary anemia."

Lanister shook his head and smiled.

"Here's the blood count, Cameron. Done forty-eight hours ago, right here in the Institute, 2,700,000 red cells. And look at the hemoglobin. No such figure as that goes with any kind of secondary anemia I ever heard of. And I brought you some smears to study for yourself." Lanister took three glass slides carefully wrapped in thin paper from his pocket. "If this isn't the blood of pernicious anemia, I'll stop taking insulin and agree that I had the pip all these years instead of diabetes. Besides, the woman has no free acid in her stomach."

Slowly Richard took the slides; his mind was a welter of conflicting thoughts and emotions. If this were true, he had been going the wrong way all these years. If this woman had a way to control pernicious anemia without eating liver or kidney or any kind of meat, all his plans and castles in Spain would tumble. He wouldn't dare present a paper to the A.M.A. or go on with his feeding ward at the hospital or urge Waldheim to make simpler, purer liver extracts. He would be back again where he was when he resigned his job with Sam Ascot and left Seaforth.

But how could that be? There was Joe, well for over three years on liver and still well on swine stomach. There was Roberts, well on hamburger and normal gastric juice and now on ground pigs' stomach and tomato juice. There were the Worden brothers and others—nearly fifty of them—who had been snatched from imminent death and kept not only alive but free of symptoms on liver diet or one of these other newer methods. There was something Lanister hadn't found out about this old woman, something she hadn't told, something nobody knew. Nothing else was possible.

Richard stopped in front of Lanister's desk and looked down into that dark, agnostic face. "Either your old lady hasn't got pernicious anemia or else she's holding out on you."

Lanister smiled slowly. "You may be right about that, Cameron. But go over the slides anyhow and tell me what you think of them. Then, if you like, I'll try to get her into the University Hospital where you can get at her yourself."

Richard took the slides and started for the door. "I'll run over them right away."

Lanister, looking after him, noticed his halting gait. "What's the matter, Cameron? You've got a game foot today."

Richard glanced down at his leg and grimaced wryly.

"It's that bone infection I got during the War flaring again. Damned nuisance right now, too, when I've got so many irons in the fire. But it'll probably quiet down again in a few days . . . I'll let you know about these smears right away, Dr. Lanister. Then we can make some plans about your old lady."

The footsteps that took him away down the corridor were uneven and lagging.

CHAPTER VII

I

A few days after Lanister told Richard about the puzzling old lady with pernicious anemia, Judith gave him four or five clippings from small-town newspapers.

"I've got so used to looking for the word 'anemia,'" she explained, "that when I saw it in an advertisement in the personal column of a paper my cousins send me occasionally from up-state New York, it struck me as worth looking into. I put a clipping bureau on the job and they've turned up these from New York and the Middle West. I think you'll be interested."

"Let's see," said Cameron quickly. He ran through the eight lines of small print in the first clipping.

> Pernicious Anemia need no longer be a Fatal disease. After eight months' Research I found its Cause and Cure. I can remove the cause in ten (10) days. If cause is removed they recover. If not removed, Never. A. W. Newton, Appelford, So. Dakota.

"Maybe Dr. Lanister's old woman uses something like this. She must take something, I know."

"Knowing a thing and proving it are not the same, Dr. Cameron."

"Don't I know it?"

Judith smiled at the tone of Richard's voice. "Mr. Newton has been doing research too. Eight months of it. Just think!"

"Let's see what else he has to say." Cameron read the next clipping.

> Pernicious anemia is caused by intestinal worms called "anemias." It is no more a disease than "cooties." I studied for eight months before finding the cure, and cured myself and two friends before I put my treatment on the market. When I took it I found 450 "anemias" in 6 days, several hundred of them fully destroyed. After that I got better. In 6 weeks I gained 15 pounds and could carry 2 buckets of water. I am 60 years old and in better health than for 20 years past. "Anemias" can not remain in your body if you take my remedy. It is harmless to everything but the "anemias." Sample sent upon request. A. W. Newton, Appelford, So. Dakota.

Amusement and indignation struggled in Richard's face.

"Barnum is still right, Miss Emerson. Only there are two born every minute."

> When food is ground up in the stomach, the liquid extract of it passes on into the small intestine where there are tiny tubes to take it up and distribute it through the system to make flesh and strength and blood. But there, lying in wait in the intestine, are from 300 to 700 "anemias," many as large as the end of your finger, and they absorb the extract of the food. They Get Theirs First! The system gets what they leave. This makes what the doctors call malnutrition. And for once they are right. The system has no show whatever with a herd of "anemias" getting all the nourishment. My treatment positively guaranteed to remove the cause of Pernicious Anemia in 25 days. Satisfaction or your money back. A. W. Newton, Appelford, So. Dakota.

"Mr. Newton has you beaten," observed Judith with smiling eyes. "He can see the 'anemias,' some of them as 'large as the end of your finger.' Isn't that wonderful?"

"Do you know what he charges for killing a 'herd of anemias'?"

Judith ran hastily through the remainder of the clippings.

"Here it is. Thirty dollars for a course of treatment 'positively guaranteed to remove the cause of your disease in 25 days.' Have you collected that much from your anemia patients yet?"

"Ye Gods, woman, I'd've been dead of starvation if I had to depend on income from patients. Thirty dollars, my word! I wonder what he'd send a fellow for thirty dollars cash. Probably Epsom salts scented up to smell like …"

"Dr. Cameron," interrupted Judith suddenly. "Why not write to this man and ask for a sample? Then we could have it analyzed and find out what's in it."

Richard nodded slowly.

"Suppose you do that. It might give us a clue to the latest development with Mr. Roberts. He called Miss Worrall a few days ago to tell her that he had found a man who knew what caused pernicious anemia and cured it by removing the cause instead of stuffing liver and yeast down people's throats. I took for granted he'd fallen for one of the local quacks, but it might be this Newton." Cameron pulled out his billfold. "Write to him and send ten dollars and beg him for a sample at once because you are desperately ill and nearly penniless. Promise to send the other twenty as soon as you can raise it. I'll give you a list of symptoms and a blood count to give him. Can you get the letter off today?"

"Certainly I can," laughed Judith. "How I'd love to see his face when he finds there's only ten dollars instead of thirty. Shall I send it air mail?"

Richard shook his head. "If you do, it will reach Newton later than the regular mail. Whatever time they save flying is lost before they get around to delivery in these small places. Besides, ten dollars and two cents is enough to waste on the stuff."

Six days afterward the answer to the decoy letter arrived. It consisted of a long, poorly-spelled, badly-typed dissertation by

Mr. Newton in which he called her attention to the fact that he did not make a practice of extending credit but would make an exception in her case, that the "sample treatment" was not enough to produce noticeable improvement, and that before he could send her the remainder of the course she must remit the balance of twenty dollars in cash. The "sample" proved to be a small pasteboard box full of something that looked like coarse sharp sand and a three ounce bottle of green liquid.

At sight of this bottle, Cameron began to laugh.

"I'll bet Roberts fell for this green stuff. We used to dye his raw beef-gastric juice mixture green, you know, so he'd think it was a vegetable concoction. He thinks he's getting the same thing we gave him—or something better."

"And I," exclaimed Judith, "am perfectly sure that he feels the 'anemias' being slain in his duodenum."

"Oh, undoubtedly. By this time he has probably counted their dead bodies by the hundreds."

"But what can you do about it, Dr. Cameron?"

"Well, there are several spokes I might put in Mr. Newton's wheel. First, I'll have Waldheim examine this stuff and tell us what it is. Then I'll turn the report over to the Journal of the American Medical Association; there's a department whose business it is to investigate patent medicines. And if Newton does business by mail, as he probably does, the Pure Food and Drug administration might be interested in him."

A week later Waldheim reported that Newton's "sample treatment" was worth perhaps three cents. The powder was feldspar, a common constituent of most crystalline rocks such as granite and basalt, and the green liquid was a watery solution of vegetable matter containing chlorophyll. Armed with this analysis Cameron went to call on Mr. Roberts.

He found his former patient in a small neat apartment on the west side of the city. The sick man looked pale and his skin had already become pasty and yellow although it was only fifteen days since he had discontinued treatment, but he was as stubborn as ever. When Richard showed him the chemist's report, Roberts merely sneered.

"I recollect that when you began giving me that vegetable purée that first put me on my feet, you said it contained chlorophyll. And you told me that chlorophyll was a coloring matter very much like the hemoglobin of human blood and might be useful in making new hemoglobin in a person with anemia. For once you were right. What of it, if this medicine is watery and green? So was yours."

Cameron saw that Roberts meant to turn against him the false arguments he had used to induce him to take the mixture of ground beef and gastric juice. Valiantly he urged that the value of his treatment had been proved by Roberts' improvement, that it cost very little now that hospitalization was not necessary.

But the sick man had his answer ready. The mere fact that he had improved meant nothing: he had had periods of feeling better before he ever saw Cameron—temporary, it was true, but definite nevertheless. The fact that a doctor helped you didn't prove that he was the only one who knew anything about your condition. As for the cost of the treatment, it was well known that one got precisely what he paid for; nothing cheap was ever much good.

Roberts, indeed, seemed to enjoy the situation thoroughly. It was a pleasure to unburden himself of distrust and suspicion and ill humor. In his previous encounters with Cameron he had always been at a disadvantage, and it was intoxicating to hold the whiphand for once. He outdid himself in pure invective. He pointed out that Richard had never told him the cause of pernicious anemia or offered to remove that cause whereas his new doctor could do both, that he had never known exactly what was in the vegetable purée or the tomato juice cocktail of which he had consumed such quantities and that Cameron had no right to criticize the new medicine because its composition was a secret, that he had been experimented on and used as a test animal, kept in the hospital when there was no necessity to do so, and that other anemia patients also had been similarly experimented on and kept in the ward. He hinted that Richard was probably being subsidized by the packers who wanted to boost the sales of unpopular meats and that proof of this bribery would be produced when needed. All the while his slate-colored eyes gleamed with approval of his own cleverness.

As Cameron told Judith afterward, he had never quite realized the utter stupidity of which the human being was capable or the utter futility of trying to reason with such a person until he spent that afternoon with John Roberts.

II

Having sent to the American Medical Association headquarters his information concerning Newton's "cure" for pernicious anemia, Richard turned his attention to Mrs. Standish, Dr. Lanister's mysterious patient, who was now quartered in the University Hospital for investigation.

"I wish you luck," said Lanister. "The old lady is a descendant of the Puritans and if there's anyone harder to handle than a Puritan reincarnated I've never met one."

Within the week Richard heartily agreed with him. Charity Standish had always been hard working, thrifty, and independent; at sixty-five she was as stubborn as John Roberts although not so devoid of civility. When, her lips bent into a half smile, she sat up in bed to talk with Cameron, she answered every question he asked and told him nothing he wanted to know.

"When you were first taken ill, Mrs. Standish, what symptoms did you complain of?"

"I didn't complain. That was never my way. It might have been better for me if I had. But women of my generation could stand more than these modern flibbergibbits."

"Yes, yes, Mrs. Standish, I understand. But can't you recall how you felt when you were first ill? Did your ordinary routine work tire you more than usual?"

"Well, I was tired all right. But I guess that wasn't strange, with a husband and six children to look after. I don't think I knew whether I was just worn out or sick."

"Perhaps you can remember whether you got out of breath or had a feeling of weakness when you hurried or walked up stairs."

"Young man, I used to work from six in the morning until midnight. I made all my own clothes and the three girls', and shirts for my husband and the boys, and did all my housework besides. At night, after the rest had gone to bed, I sat up and sewed. Seems to me it wouldn't have been much wonder if I felt weak."

"Did your hands and feet ever tingle or feel numb?"

Old Mrs. Standish laughed a little. "I guess you don't know our part of the country, Dr. Cameron. Anybody's hands and feet would 've been numb in the winter. We didn't ride around in automobiles with heaters in them while I was raisin' my family."

With an effort Richard forbore mentioning his own fifty mile drives in Montana when the thermometer stood at forty or forty-five degrees below zero. But he shifted the angle of his questioning.

"Tell me something about your diet, Mrs. Standish. What did you eat?"

"I ate what my husband could afford to buy and what was left when the children got through." The sick woman peered sharply up into Cameron's thin, freckled face, tapering down from its wide cheek bones. "Of course we didn't have fresh things in winter then like people do now."

"Did you eat meat or did you live chiefly on vegetables and starches?"

"Well, now, young man, whenever we had any meat I guess I got my share."

"Then you didn't eat starchy foods to excess?"

"Well, I can't say I know just what you mean. I always ate bread and potatoes when there was any, but I don't reckon it was to excess."

"Were you fond of fats—butter and cream and things like that?"

Charity Standish cackled in derision.

"I can tell you never tried keeping butter enough in the house with six children around! And we never had candy either, except at Christmas when we got some for the young ones.

"Biscuits, cake, doughnuts, macaroni, foods like that . . ."

"My land, cake and doughnuts didn't last overnight around our boys. And I never held with macaroni, a foreign dish if there ever was one."

"What sort of meat did you usually buy?" persisted Cameron.

"Well, not porterhouse steaks and prime ribs, I can tell you that."

"No liver or blood sausage or brains or sweetbreads or chicken gizzards?"

"No, none of them things. I never liked 'insides' and neither did my husband." Mrs. Standish shook her head positively. "Of course, if we had a chicken, there was a liver and a gizzard, but that wasn't much for a big family like ours."

"Were you in the habit of piecing between meals or eating at night before you went to bed?"

Richard was sure he detected a flicker of hesitation in his patient's answer.

"Piecing . . . between meals? No, I never believed in that. We used to eat apples in the evenings but I never was one for piecing."

"What about apricots?"

"I never liked them much. Always tasted to me like little, dried-up peaches."

Cameron could have sworn that there was relief in Mrs. Standish's face. He had an uneasy feeling that he had missed a clue somewhere in matter of diet and he went back again and again to that point in the succeeding days. But his questioning was fruitless.

Almost equally unsatisfactory was the patient's account of her illness and its treatment. From her daughter—the only child remaining on the east coast—Dr. Lanister had learned that Mrs. Standish had from time to time taken liquid medicine that stained her teeth if she did not drink it through a tube and another drug which she measured in drops. These, Richard knew, were iron and arsenic preparations time-honored in blood diseases but quite incapable of keeping pernicious anemia under control. The statements Mrs. Standish made concerning the various physicians she had consulted were also vague.

"He said my blood was thin" or "He told me I had a tendency to be anemic and gave me some more of the drops." According to her story, no one had ever done a blood count on her; this Cameron found hard to believe.

Questioned about her complexion, Mrs. Standish denied ever having been jaundiced. "All my people are kinda sallow," she asserted over and over.

When a week had gone by in this unsatisfactory fashion and Richard had convinced himself by repeated examination of her blood that the woman had true pernicious anemia, his suspicion that he had not dug out an accurate history of the case was confirmed by Miss Worrall's observation that Mrs. Standish was not as well as when she entered the hospital.

"I can't put my finger on what it is that makes me think so, doctor, but I'm sure she isn't quite as strong."

Cameron looked up with quick interest from his microscope.

"And her blood count has gone down a little. It all fits in together. She does something at home that she can't do here, and I've got to find out what. Here's a woman with pernicious anemia for twenty-five years, and not only is she not dead but most of that time she's been in fairly good health. Unless I can find out how she's done it, I can't go to the American Medical Association and read that paper of mine on liver diet."

"Why, Dr. Cameron," cried the nurse in genuine distress, "you've got fifty cases all worked out and every one symptom-free on meat feeding."

"But one patient alive for twenty-five years without liver or kidney or pigs' stomach or chicken gizzards or blood transfusions—nothing but iron and arsenic now and then—ruins my whole theory. Mrs. Standish ought to have died long ago, but she didn't. On the contrary she's been fairly well most of the time. Her case blows up the whole paper and all the work we've done the last three years here and at the Institute. Thornton's work and mine, too."

Miss Worrall saw that the man's shoulders drooped in discouragement and she heard in his voice the sharpness of bewilderment.

"I can't understand it," he continued slowly as though he were talking to himself. "There must be something I haven't found, something she won't tell anyone. If I can't get it out of her, it's going to be just too bad." With an effort he rose from his stool and buttoned up his white laboratory jacket. "I'll have to give her the third degree, I guess, Miss Worrall," he said, and walked out with the dragging little limp that was becoming habitual.

But, despite Cameron's efforts, it was the nurse who unearthed the first important clue to the Standish mystery. A woman less alert might have dismissed as unimportant the information that two years before a niece from Iowa had lived with Mrs. Standish for several months, but Miss Worrall carefully allowed three or four days to pass and then casually referred to the niece again. Then she relayed to Richard the news that this young woman had now returned to Iowa where she was teaching English in a country-town high school.

That evening Cameron left Northdevon for Chicago and on the next afternoon but one reached Belleplain, Iowa. As soon as school was dismissed for the day he went to the high school building and inquired for Miss Nora Standish. The girl, naturally enough, was astonished to find confronting her a man of whom she had never heard, who demanded intimate details of her aunt's life, but she had a sense of humor and when Richard had explained his errand she was amused and interested. Something made her want to help this tall, red haired, thin-faced man who walked so rapidly that his limp seemed only to catch up with him occasionally.

"Let me think, Dr. Cameron. I'll try to reconstruct Aunt Charity's typical day. She's very methodical, you know, and whatever she does one day she is likely to do every day. She always got up early and when I was living with her she had breakfast ready by the time I had bathed and dressed. Then she had a regular schedule of cleaning and marketing. Of course, I was away from a little after nine until four-thirty or five in the afternoon except on Saturday and Sunday, but . . ."

But with Nora's best memory of her aunt's daily life there seemed to be no item upon which Richard could seize as pertinent.

"There's just one other thing, Dr. Cameron. It seems almost too silly to mention, but whenever I was awake after Aunt Charity went to bed I used to hear her get up and go out into the kitchen and open the refrigerator. You see, her apartment had the guest room next to the kitchen, and so I could hear her cross the floor and open the door of the refrigerator softly and close it again. I never thought anything of it because she always kept a pitcher of water in the ice box to cool; she never drank water straight from the tap if she could help it. Now that I've talked with you, this seems a little queer but at the time I thought nothing of it."

In Richard's brain ideas clicked together into a pattern: ice box, the unlikely pitcher of water cooling there the year round, the secret raids upon the refrigerator each night. Here was the solution of the puzzle, not in detail but certainly in outline.

Two days later he once more marched into the cubicle where Mrs. Standish lay, with Miss Worrall at his heels. He bent down and looked into the sick woman's eyes.

"Mrs. Standish," he said sternly. "I want you to tell me something. What was it you used to eat every night at bedtime? I know there was something. You might as well tell me about it now and save time and trouble for both of us."

To the nurse's surprise the old woman's stubborn defense dissolved in the twinkling of an eye and she poured out a stream of disconnected phrases.

". . . sure it wasn't good for me . . . such rich food . . . not fit for an invalid . . . so expensive . . . I couldn't afford it . . . I didn't want anyone to know, doctor . . ."

Miss Worrall watched Richard standing beside the bed, looking down at the sallow face on the pillow, at the humiliation written there. She saw the man's own face suddenly soften, saw him put a thin, long-fingered hand on Mrs. Standish's frail blue-veined wrist, heard him speak in a voice that had lost the cutting edge the last few weeks had given it.

"You've done nothing to be ashamed of, Mrs. Standish. Nothing wrong. Only, why didn't you tell me before? This is what I've been trying to find out ever since you came into the hospital. Just what was it you ate every night before you went to bed?"

"A sandwich," whispered the woman. "A sandwich . . . with *pâté de foie gras*. You see"—her words grew so faint that Miss Worrall had to strain to hear them—"I had some at a party once, just about the time I was taken sick. And I liked it so much, I just seemed to crave it after that. I simply had to have it. But it is disgraceful to want anything that way just as bad as a drunkard with his whiskey. I was ashamed of myself. I couldn't . . . bear anybody to know."

The nurse saw Richard's freckled fingers close gently on the old lady's thin hand; she was sure there was in his throat the same tightness that had suddenly seized hers.

"Listen, Mrs. Standish," said Cameron softly. "Your *pâté de foie gras* has saved your life. Yes, I know exactly what I'm saying, and I mean it," he went on as a look of disbelief began to spread over the sallow face of his patient. "There's goose liver in it. You didn't know it, but you were giving yourself the only treatment that's worth a tinker's damn in pernicious anemia."

In the little laboratory, five minutes later, Richard looked at Miss Worrall, ruffled his hair into a hundred copper colored tufts, and then threw back his head and laughed in his old, light-hearted way. An instant later the nurse joined in and they both laughed until their faces ached.

"A secret passion for goose liver which she conceals as disgraceful saved her life! This makes my case foolproof. I'm all set for the American Medical Association and all its wiseacres who know everything about pernicious anemia. And I ask you, lady, mightn't the whole thing have come straight out of 'Alice in Wonderland'?"

III

As long as he lived the next day was in Cameron's mind a series of disconnected tableaus. The chilly weather he had encountered on his trip to Iowa had given him a cold; his eyes were sandpaperish, his nose stuffy, his throat sore. Besides this, the dull ache he had had for weeks in his ankle turned into waves of hot sickening pain that rolled up toward his knee whenever he put his foot to the floor. Feeling illogically that to refuse acknowledgment of illness might somehow stave off collapse, he did not take his temperature but dragged himself to the Institute.

He always remembered how Lanister and Thornton laughed when he told them the unexpected dénouement of the Standish-*pâté de foie gras* mystery, and how Thornton looked sharply at him and advised him to go home to bed. But Richard protested crossly that he had work to do, letters to answer, memoranda to write, charts to read, consultations to hold with the clinic doctors over new cases of anemia.

"You look to me as if you ought to be in bed, nevertheless," insisted his chief. "You'll be passing your infection on to your patients, very likely, and you know what acute infections do to these anemic people."

This sensible advice vexed Cameron.

"I'm not going out to the hospital, if that's what you're driving at. I've got to go to Overholt . . . to see Rebecca. She's sick."

Early that morning DiPallo had told him the dog was ill. Richard remembered being surprised that an animal of Rebecca's age had distemper.

"It seems like some pup come in," Joe tried to explain. "And they didn't know it had distemper. I guess from what they told me it must take quite a while to be sure. Anyhow this pup give it to some of the other dogs they got there boardin' besides Rebecca. And I thought you'd oughta know about it, because I don't think she's goin' to get well."

But Richard refused Thornton's offer to drive him to the Overholt kennels.

"Joe's going with me. And besides, Jim, I feel better than I did. I always get sick all of a sudden and then I get well again the same way."

"Well, for God's sake, don't come down here again until you're all right, Cameron. You should have gone to the hospital before this and had that leg Xrayed and found out what's wrong with it. The first thing you know you'll be hobbling around here minus a foot."

"What if I am?" cried Richard feverishly. "It's nothing to you, is it?"

He heard Thornton mutter something about the obstinacy of the Scotch-Irish who inherit stubbornness from both strains in their make-up, and then he found himself going up to the library. But Judith was not there.

"Miss Emerson left for Boston day before yesterday," explained the serious-faced substitute. "The national association of librarians meets there this week, you know."

This made Cameron more than ever aggrieved. He had gone to the library expressly to tell Judith about Mrs. Standish and Rebecca, and she was not there. Why had she gone away like this, and left no word for him? She might have known he'd be back from the Middle West by this time, even though he hadn't written her while he was gone. He couldn't write letters, rushing about as he had been. And now she had gone to Boston, of all places, to a convention of librarians! Damn the librarians! He wanted to talk to Judith and she wasn't here. He felt lonely and abused. His head ached and his back hurt and hot pains shot up his right leg and his chest felt tight and queer.

With little chills rippling up and down his spine, he stumped stubbornly down to his office on the third floor and attacked the heap of charts on his desk. The rest of the day was a gray plain of pain with here and there a sharply outlined scene, like a bright patch of sunlit hillside seen through fog.

Rebecca was a pitiful sight. Her dry eyes peered out between crusted lids, on her thighs pea-sized pustules gave off an offensive sweetish odor, she coughed and struggled for breath. When she heard Richard's voice and DiPallo's, she stopped trying to drink and sprang toward them, but her paralyzed rear quarters and dragging legs would not hold her up and she toppled over and lay, panting, on the floor. Her tail vibrated feebly and her brown eyes, dotted over with tiny ulcers, looked up at the two men standing over her.

Cameron felt tears in his eyes. Angered by this lack of self control, he knelt down and put one hand on the dog's dry, rough coat. Over her thin body passed a little quiver of delight. Then he saw that Joe had knelt down too, on the other side, and that his dark eyes were wet.

"Damn it all," said Cameron, "Rebecca deserves something more than this. She's saved fifty lives already and we're hardly started."

His feverish hand met DiPallo's short, thick one on the dog's shoulder. There was something damp on both of them.

Rebecca jerked spasmodically when she coughed, her eyelids were thick and festered. The veterinarian explained that he had done all he could but that she had not responded to any form of treatment. "I'm sorry, Dr. Cameron," he added. "We all like the dog out here."

Joe thought they ought to go. "You oughtn't to stay here, doc. You're sick, and we can't do nothin', anyhow."

But as he watched the dog's thin body twitching in convulsions, Richard knew that she deserved at least this much of him, that he should stand by until she passed the way of all flesh, and he would not leave the kennels until she had died.

Then, suddenly and unaccountably, he was in his own apartment, sitting on the side of the tub in his bathroom, with his hat and overcoat still on, singing "Hey, diddle, diddle, the cat and the fiddle" and shouting for DiPallo to bring him a drink.

"Give me a drink, can't you, when I ask you? Damn it all, I tell you I want a drink! . . . No, I'm not going to bed now. I've got to write a letter yet tonight. D' you hear me, Joe? A letter. . . . To Boston. She's gone to Boston. Now why the hell d' you suppose she wanted to go there?"

A hand that did not belong to him poured stinging liquor into his mouth and he looked up into Sandy Farquhar's pale face.

"Have a drink, Sandy? ... Oh, that's all right. Help your self. I got plenty. Another quart, anyhow.... Quart? Quart? ... 'The quart's in the middle of the cat and the fiddle and the cow.' ... That's funny!"

Farquhar's face grew huge and hazy and grotesque, and behind him fantastic little beings began to skip over the walls and dance in the corners of the room. A gleam of reason flickered into Richard's brain again.

"I'll go to bed if you want me to, Sandy. It's time to check out, I guess. I'm seeing things."

CHAPTER VIII

I

Five days afterward Cameron drifted slowly back out of chaos. It was night but about him there was a dim radiance from street lamps outside his window. Aimlessly he moved his hands over the contour of his body and presently found the edges of the narrow bed on which he lay. With difficulty he turned on his right side. Opposite him was a door half-open and through it he saw an oblong strip of pale light. Tired from the exertion of moving, he rested, breathing quickly.

He heard muffled sounds, rubber soles on linoleum, the soft hissing of rubber tires. A white figure pushed a cart across his line of vision, the faint footfalls died away.

He felt weak and tired, and he seemed to recall that he had been ill. Then he became aware that there was something queer about his right ankle and put out the other foot exploringly. It encountered a bulky, damp dressing. Presently he moved the right leg a little and thrust it out into the cool air.

He tried to recall what had happened after Rebecca's death

but everything blurred together so that he had no idea how much time had passed. Now that his eyes were accommodated to the dim light he saw a tumbler of water and a drinking tube on the bedside table and realized that he was thirsty. But when he put out his arm he could not reach the glass. As his hand fell back on the coverlet he frowned. A moment later he reached out again. This time he curled his finger tips under the edge of the table and pulled. The stand slid toward him and he closed a hand around the tumbler, but to his disgust he found that he could not lift it.

He grunted in vexation. Too weak to lift a glass of water! Absurd! How could he have grown so feeble in what must have been only a short illness? He would have to ring for a nurse to get him a drink. It was hard to admit that he was reduced to such dependence. He put his head down on the pillows to think.

Suddenly he noticed that a towel covered the table top and a little grin twitched at the corners of his mouth. There was always more than one way to kill a cat. Taking the edge of the towel between a thumb and finger he tugged at it carefully. Together towel and glass moved toward him, and a minute or two later, when his nurse came into the room, he was propped up on one elbow with the drinking tube in his mouth.

"Dr. Cameron," cried the woman hurrying toward the bed, "you mustn't do that. Let me help you."

"I'm all right. I'd rather do it myself."

Richard grinned up at her and took another swallow.

The nurse was distressed. "I left the room for only five minutes, doctor. You'd been so quiet all night that I never dreamed you'd wake up before I got back."

Cameron took the tube out of his mouth and drew a long breath.

"You don't need to apologize to me. I'm all right, I told you. And the water tasted fine. Now I think I'll go back to sleep."

Next morning Sandy Farquhar told Richard that he had been in the hospital for nearly a week.

"You've had the 'flu'—the good old 'flu,' like we saw in 1918.

You've been toxic as the devil and crazy as a coot, Rich. You kept singing that fool song about the cat and the fiddle and the cow. We all expected you to develop pneumonia but you didn't do it."

"I seldom do what I'm expected to, Sandy. Don't you know that yet? But what about this ankle that's all done up in dressings?"

Farquhar looked sternly at the man in the bed.

"A sinus opened up in that ankle the day we brought you into the hospital. And it isn't the first one. There are scars all over that foot. And here I thought you hadn't had any trouble with your ankle for years."

Cameron smiled sheepishly into the accusing brown eyes.

"Now, don't get sore about it, Sandy. I've had sinuses open up and discharge a little now and then but they never made me sick. And I got an ultraviolet lamp and treated myself at night and kept the infection pretty well quieted down that way. But the last few weeks I've known I was in for trouble with it again."

This good-humored acceptance of misfortune did not mislead Farquhar.

"I should think you would know it! When it comes to your own health you haven't got any more sense than a bum on the streets. I'm ashamed of you, Rich."

Within the next twenty-four hours Ralph Lanister and Dr. Penfield called in a bone surgeon and sent to Baltimore for a man who had developed a way to treat bone infections with maggots, and the four of them went to Cameron's room to discuss his treatment. They found their patient sitting up in bed, studying the Xray films of his leg made the previous afternoon.

Richard listened attentively to all Penfield and the two surgeons had to tell him. In his thin, freckled face, the hollow cheeks threw his long chin into prominence and his dark gray eyes looked steadily from one specialist to another. It was as though he gave courteous, impersonal consideration to some technical problem which had no connection with himself.

"How long will it take the maggots to clear up this infection?" he asked the surgeon from Baltimore.

The great man cleared his throat uneasily. "That's hardly a fair question, Dr. Cameron," he protested. "Every case is a law unto itself. It all depends on your resistance and general health."

But Richard insisted on an approximation. "I don't mean to be unreasonable," he said, "but you can tell me whether it's likely to be weeks or months. And then"—he looked at the other surgeon—"I must have some idea of the length of time your work will take. I know you'll have to do a lot of reconstruction to make a usable ankle, and it just happens in this case that 'time is of the essence of the contract,' as the lawyers say."

That night, having sent his nurse away—telling her that he could sleep more soundly alone in the room—Cameron sat up in bed to face the problem set for him by the answers he had wrung out of the consultants that afternoon. All about him was the hushed busy life of a huge modern hospital. Suddenly he felt himself at the very heart of it. But whereas he usually found the subdued bustle a stimulus and enjoyed in a disembodied fashion the professional matter-of-factness, tonight he had a prickly horror of the place.

Although his door was closed, he could hear soft-footed nurses hurrying up and down the corridor, picture friends and relatives torn by fear tiptoeing through the halls. He knew that orderlies were rushing about on lowly errands, that internes wearing a pose of indifference were striding past on rubber-soled shoes with stethoscopes sticking out of their pockets. Through these passages life and death stalked each other, and on another floor of the building birth held the balance of power between them. Curious place, a hospital.

Long bare corridors, wide wooden doors at mathematical intervals, small bare-walled rooms with metal furniture, crisp white uniforms, the artificial cheerfulness of floor supervisors, the white-clad residents concealing under a mask of assurance their conscious ignorance. Richard felt himself revolting. This hospital was like a factory: it too was dedicated to mass production so many abdominal operations, so many deliveries, so many autopsies, so many Wassermanns and blood counts and Xray examinations a month. It was too business-like, too impersonal, too efficient. The human being was naturally neither efficient nor impersonal, especially when he was ill.

Those specialists this afternoon—the surgeon and the man with the maggots—had not been interested in him as a person; they were concerned, one with reconstructing damaged bones and joints, the other with worms. They did not consider him as an individual but as a body containing a chronic infection, one more case in a series that might establish a new thesis on bone diseases and their treatment. It was not that he objected to being an experiment in osteomyelitis. Not at all. But he had something else he must consider.

A sort of crepuscular light filtered in from the street through the open window. He could hear the street cars and automobiles passing the hospital, and he braced himself to think collectedly. He must make his own decision, he reminded himself, and he must not be influenced by hopes or wishes or emotions; the mere fact that it was his leg and not some other man's must not sway him. What the specialists advised would, by their own admission, consume weeks, perhaps months. But the nub of the matter was this: when they had finished with him, would he be well or would he be prone to recurrent attacks of infection that would make him a chronic intermittent invalid?

His mind seething in conflict, he lay back against his pillows. It was true that he had been unwise to neglect himself, and it was also clear that it would be a major undertaking to reconstruct a useful ankle. In the end the question boiled down to this: should he follow the advice of the surgeons or do the thing that haunted the background of his consciousness?

It was at the very moment he was thankful he had no family to consider in making his decision, that Judith Emerson entered his thoughts. For the three years he had been at Fifer Institute he had been too busy, too engrossed in his research to think about himself and his emotions, but now he realized that he loved this girl. He imagined her near him, in the room, dressed in one of her working frocks of blue with white collar and cuffs, her brown eyes thoughtful, her dark brows drawn in concentration. The sudden violence with which he desired to see her and hear her voice surprised him no less than the eagerness of his hope that she would approve his decision.

At nine-thirty the next morning Lanister and Sandy Farquhar came into his room together.

"Dr. Baird had to go back to Baltimore last night," explained Lanister. "But he'll come up and set his maggots to work whenever you say the word, Cameron. I think he and Nason will do as good a job for you as anyone in the country."

Looking at Richard, Sandy saw in his gray eyes and long, firm jaw the dogged determination with which he faced difficult situations. From far down in his toes Farquhar felt a tingling thrill start upward.

"Oh, Baird and Nason know their stuff," he heard Cameron say. "If I were going to be conservative, there's no one I'd rather have. But I can't lie here for weeks or months while Baird's maggots and Nason's surgery make me a leg I can walk on. Besides, where would I be when they finished?"

"Well," asked Lanister, "what do you think?"

"I think I'd be an invalid about half the time. And you think so too, both of you." Richard's gray eyes sharpened as he looked from Lanister's dark ironic face to Sandy's pale one. "This damned infection has been hanging around now since 1919. In that time I've seen a good many other people with osteomyelitis. They have an operation and the infection quiets down, then it flares up again and back they go to the hospital for more surgery. Year in, year out, it's like that."

In Lanister's dark eyes there was a strange brilliancy and on his mouth a twisted half-smile.

"Well, I can't live like that, these next few years. There's all this stuff about powdered pigs' stomachs to be worked out. There's Waldheim's liver extract nearly ready to go into production. There's the whole treatment of pernicious anemia to be standardized. I can't be an invalid with all these things going on. Besides, chronic infections raise the devil with your kidneys and liver; amyloid changes, they used to call it, when I was in school. I don't want to run the risk of going to pot with a chronic bone infection I can't get rid of."

"Yes, Cameron. So what?" Sandy felt his heart quicken at the expectancy in Lanister's voice.

"So this," answered Richard. "I'm going to have this foot whacked off. I'd rather be minus a foot and be well than have two legs and this cursed infection in one of them."

There was a trace of defiance in Richard's manner but Farquhar saw that Lanister's eyes were dark with irony.

"I suppose by all the rules of the game I ought to appeal to you to change your mind, to think this over more carefully. But I'm not going to, Cameron." Lanister paused and laughed a little. "You see, you're doing exactly what I'd do if I were in your place."

As they left the room Sandy looked back. Richard was holding the Xray films of his leg up to the light from the window. It struck Farquhar that he was very likely trying to decide at just what level the amputation had better be done, and in the same instant Sandy saw that it was impossible to be sorry for a man who took life in his stride and turned what would be catastrophe for someone else into a mere inconvenience to be overcome and then forgotten. Richard Cameron with a foot gone would still be unbeaten and undismayed.

II

That summer Richard made his first appearance on the program of the annual meeting of the American Medical Association. The title of his paper—"The Treatment of Pernicious Anemia by Diet"—was unassuming and his name meant nothing to the great majority of the 6,273 physicians in attendance, but there had been enough underground gossip in medical circles for a year or two about the experiments with meat feeding at Fifer Institute to insure a good audience in the section on "Practice of Medicine" that particular morning.

During the presentation of the two papers that preceded his, Cameron sat in the wings on one side of the platform. He was still awkward in the use of his artificial foot and had to help himself along with a cane; as a consequence he avoided crowds and the necessity for hurrying. From the chair provided for him offstage he peered curiously at the segment of the auditorium within his field of vision.

There was quite a crowd but he thought most of them had probably come to hear the first two papers and would leave before his turn came. He found his mind full of questions as he watched the audience. Why did they scatter out so? Why didn't they bunch together up front where it was easy to hear? Why did so many of them get up and go out during the reading of papers, and why did others come in when a man had half finished? Doctors, Richard reflected, were strange creatures. He ought to know; he had been one for over twelve years now. By all odds, they seemed to him the most nonconformist group he knew. Stubbornly individualistic, they could hardly be organized into professional associations, and it was almost impossible to get them to agree on anything. And, in spite of that, they were the world's prize respecters of authority. Trained to accept this man's pronouncements on skin and another's on heart disease and another's on tuberculosis, they became followers who waited for a master's voice and then obeyed it. Only now and then did one among them think for himself, work out an original theory or devise an original method of treatment. For the most part they did so-and-so's operation for this and another's for that, followed Mackenzie or Lewis in the interpretation of cardiac irregularities, and went on doing the classical repair of inguinal hernia.

And yet Cameron could not see that they could be blamed for this or that it could be helped. The average patient was not dangerously ill and what he needed was quick relief—not profound scientific acumen. If a doctor were to succeed in practice, he must know certain routine things he could do with the skill of long experience which he could depend on to relieve most cases he was called to treat. New things, difficult diagnoses, obscure conditions formed an insignificant fraction of the average doctor's practice and the patients who had them did not stay with their family physician anyhow. They rushed off to the Mayo Clinic or to Chicago or Boston or Philadelphia or Northdevon or Baltimore.

Richard almost wished he had not come to this meeting. Could he prove that it was liver and not some other unrecognized substance in the diet that caused the spectacular improvement in his patients? Was it wise to broadcast the liver and kidney diet at this time? Would these doctors take it seriously? Could they bully their cases into eating a pound or half pound of liver every day? It was still too soon to say anything about the powdered swine stomach to be swallowed in capsules or the liver extract to be given hypodermically; these refinements had yet to be proved uniformly dependable. Briefly he felt his old dread: feeding liver and kidney to these desperately ill people seemed such a silly thing that he always expected to find that it had been tried and rejected long ago by some obscure scientist. But the recollection of his fifty cases followed for periods ranging from three months to over four years banished that fear again: all these patients could not be well unless the treatment they had received was specific for their disease.

The paper immediately before his was on secondary anemia and Jim Thornton was scheduled to discuss it and to break ground for Richard's presentation of liver diet in pernicious anemia. Fifer Institute was well represented on this year's program: Lanister had spoken on diabetes, Thornton was discussing anemia, Montagu and Fergusson were to speak on tuberculosis and heredity. Conscious of a little glow of loyalty to the Institute, Cameron smiled.

But far back in his mind flickered a tiny flame of apprehension: things were not right with Sandy. Instinct warned Richard that Fergusson was holding something over Farquhar. The article on calcium deposits in the chest had come out in the Journal of Radiology a month ago, there were haggard lines about Farquhar's mouth again and the old devil-ridden look was back in his brown eyes. Yet when Richard had suggested a long vacation together during the coming summer, Sandy said it was impossible.

"I can't go, Rich. You see, while Fergusson is away from the Institute this summer, I want to finish some work I started last winter. I'll have three months alone in the department and I must get this thing done then or never."

Something in the Scotsman's reedy voice made Cameron recall the day he had seen him defy Oscar Steinberg.

"Then promise me you'll take a month off after Fergusson gets back. You'll have your degree by that time and you must get away for a while. You slaved all last summer in that damned Xray laboratory and you've no business doing it again. You're getting too much radiation."

Sandy laughed a little.

"Oh, I'm sure I can get a vacation in the fall, Rich. By that time Fergusson will be glad to give me a permanent leave of absence."

Cameron remembered the edge of bitterness with which Farquhar had said this.

"Now, see here, Sandy, you're not going to be thrown out of the Institute just because Fergusson doesn't want his assistant to publish anything without his O.K. on it. I'll see Thornton about it and he'll talk to Lanister. We'll put a spoke in Fergy's wheel for once. He's an ass, anyhow. I never have liked him."

But Farquhar protested.

"Please don't stir up anything, Rich. It'll be worse if you do—worse for me, I mean. Honestly, it will. This may blow over without a fight. Besides, things are different with me than they were in Seaforth that time. I've got Penfield and Draper behind me now and there are lots of openings for good Xray men these days. I'd rather leave Fifer Institute than have a row. For that would make it harder to find the sort of position I want."

But, despite Sandy's plausible arguments, Cameron had worried over the little man, and one day during the convalescence from his amputation he had talked to Jim Thornton about Farquhar's situation. Thornton's promise to go to Lanister in case of need had quieted Richard's fear at the time, but now, for no reason he could have specified, Cameron felt a wave of misgiving pass over him. He had not seen enough of Sandy since they came to Northdevon, he had been so engrossed in his own work that he had neglected his friend. But if Farquhar's security was to be threatened once more, he meant to intervene and see that justice was done. This determination occupied Richard's mind to such a degree that he did not hear the chairman call on Thornton; it was only when Jim's round cheerful face came into his line of vision that Cameron realized his own time was near.

When he crossed the platform from his chair in the wings to the speaker's stand, Richard was surprised to see that many men were hurrying into the room and but few going out. The chairman came up to him and whispered that it would be well to wait until everyone was seated before beginning. Obediently Cameron stood looking over his audience and wondering how much the time keeper would take off his allotted twenty minutes for this delay. Standing thus, he chanced to see a familiar red face under a thatch of tumbled gray hair in the front row of seats. Startled, he looked again more closely, then ducked his head lest anyone see his expression. For, only a few feet away, waiting to hear what he had to say about pernicious anemia, was Samuel Ascot.

The rows of faces turned up toward him were curious. Evidently rumor had been busy spreading word of something new to be divulged. Instantly all doubts were swept from Cameron's mind. This was just the county medical society multiplied. He knew his stuff, he had his facts in order, there was nothing to worry about. Calmly he began to talk to the men before him just as he had often talked at hospital staff meetings.

Swiftly, with no fumbling for words, he told them how, basing his theory on animal experiments partly done elsewhere, he had begun to feed liver and kidney to patients with pernicious anemia, and how in the fifty cases he was reporting today symptoms had promptly vanished and health returned. Only when they neglected to eat the requisite amount of meat had any of these patients relapsed. He exhibited lantern slides to show the spectacular increase of red blood cells and hemoglobin on liver diet and their no less spectacular maintenance at or near normal levels. He asked his listeners to try the treatment for themselves and report their results, favorable or unfavorable, directly to him at Fifer Institute.

Full of the pleasure of speaking to a responsive audience, he stuffed the manuscript he had not found it necessary to use into his coat pocket and reached for the cane that hung on the side of the speaker's stand. A burst of applause rolled up to the platform. The presiding officer hesitated a moment, then rose and beckoned Richard to wait. On the floor a man had risen and was trying to attract the chairman's attention. When the hand clapping died down, he shouted, "Will Dr. Cameron answer questions?" The chairman glanced inquiringly at Richard, then rapped with his gavel for order.

"Gentlemen, if it is your pleasure, the next period can be turned over to a discussion of this paper. The essayist who was to have presented a paper on methods of transfusion has been called away and has cancelled his space on the program."

It was well after twelve o'clock before Richard could escape from the last group of doctors who waylaid him to ask questions.

III

Cameron's paper formed the topic of much discussion during the remainder of the meeting. Little knots of men gathered in the dining rooms of hotels, in restaurants, in the corridors of hospitals and auditoriums, on the streets, to argue, to criticize, to disagree. Those of small repute waited to see what famous doctors thought of liver and kidney diet in pernicious anemia and then talked these opinions over among themselves. One man who had once held a Fellowship at Fifer stopped B. C. Montagu to get his reaction to the new treatment.

Austere and angular, Montagu looked coldly at his questioner. His pale, flat-cheeked face and thin-lipped mouth seemed more withdrawn than ever; only his deep-set, smouldering eyes betrayed any interest in the subject. Pausing to reach the considered answer that was his habit, he at once became the magnet about which a cluster of doctors quickly formed.

"As a matter of fact," he said slowly in his strange, hoarse voice, "I know almost nothing about the work and almost nothing about Dr. Cameron. He is connected with a different department at the Institute and I have had no contact with this research."

There was a murmur of surprise in the group about him and one or two men started to turn away.

"But I know Dr. Thornton well and he is the head of Cameron's department. Furthermore, I know Dr. Lanister, head of the General Clinic at the Institute, where the treatment was first tried. If both these men back a thing, it is safe to assume that it is sound. My judgment is that you should accept this work with an open mind. Further investigations will soon either confirm or disprove it."

With that statement, Montagu turned his back and walked away, apparently buried in thought. No one else approached him although now and then some man whom he passed would mutter to a friend, "There goes Montagu. You know, the pathologist." Unaware of the stares of these onlookers, the scientist walked on until, turning a corner, he came upon another group of men and had to swerve to avoid them. Arrested by the sound of a shrill, high-pitched voice that came from the center of this cluster, he stopped in his tracks and listened.

"The evidence is not sufficient to support the conclusions or at least, if it is, it was not presented. The investigation should not have been turned over in the first place to an unknown, poorly trained man of this caliber. He has not even considered the bearing of heredity on this disease. Pernicious anemia runs in families, there is a distinct constitutional predisposition toward these blood dyscrasias. I have been studying heredity for years but Cameron has never once asked me for advice. He comes out with this absurd treatment based on his own preconceived ideas. It is ridiculous!"

Dr. Fergusson, it was plain, felt himself outraged. His round, flabby face was flushed and his pale angry eyes darted back and forth over the puzzled men around him; his big hands fumbled nervously with the buttons of his wrinkled vest.

"Fifer Institute is not to be held responsible," he cried. "It is not our policy to put out unconfirmed theories. Cameron's work will immediately be reviewed and a corrected statement of it will be published as soon as possible."

No one had noticed Montagu standing at the edge of the group, but now his hoarse voice interrupted this tirade.

"Dr. Fergusson, have you forgotten yourself?"

Startled by his stern words, his pale face and blazing eyes, the men nearest him drew back and, through the gap thus made, he walked straight toward Fergusson. The big man seemed to shrink and run together inside his clothes; his face turned white. Montagu looked up at him scornfully.

The cluster of doctors did not wait for anything more to be said; as rapidly as they could without giving the impression of flight they melted away, leaving Montagu alone with Fergusson.

"Whatever your private opinion of Cameron's work may be," said Montagu severely, "you have no right to air it without observations or experiments of your own to confirm your criticisms. You have allowed jealousy to drive you into conduct unbecoming a scientist, Fergusson. You must retract your attack on Cameron's paper at once. At once! Do you hear?"

Montagu swung on his heel and walked away without a backward glance at the baffled, resentful face of his subordinate.

It was a few minutes later that Dr. Hastings encountered Samuel Ascot in the lobby of the auditorium. Hastings had been much pleased at Cameron's excellent presentation of the anemia research; by instinct a scholar, trained in Germany during the great days of the 80's and then associated with Welch and Osler at Johns Hopkins, he had always during his years as executive director of Fifer Institute looked back wistfully at his own attempts to do original investigation and regarded the men actively engaged in research with peculiar respect. When he met Ascot wandering disconsolately about, he was struck by the man's unhappy face and had an impulse to help him.

"Is there anything I can do for you?" he asked genially. Then, taken aback by the scowl with which Ascot looked at him, he went on, "Pardon me for accosting you so informally, sir, but I thought perhaps you were a stranger and had lost your way."

Ascot snorted. This pink-cheeked elderly man with his well-brushed gray hair and well-cut blue suit he instantly assessed as a fumbling nobody. But even a nobody could serve as a safety valve.

"I'm a stranger here all right," he roared. "And I'm glad of it. But I'm not lost. I'm just disgusted. Here I've come all the way across the continent to listen to a whippersnapper I fired out of my own office."

The bewilderment in Hastings' friendly blue eyes wiped out all other expression.

"You mean . . ."

"I mean that man Cameron. Didn't I fire him out in Seaforth three years ago? He's absolutely worthless and as conceited and cocky as if he knew something. Funny that a fellow I had to fire can come back here and put it over on all of you like that."

Dr. Hastings' kindly face hardened a little.

"We feel at Fifer Institute that we are fortunate to have a young man of Cameron's caliber," he began. "But perhaps you don't know who I am."

"No, I don't. And what's more I don't care. But I can tell you one thing—if the A.M.A. can't get up better programs than this, it had better meet on the west coast. Why, right in Seaforth, we've got a man who punctured this fool liver diet of Cameron's over three years ago. Oscar Steinberg, his name is. It's time you easterners woke up and took some notice of what we do out home."

"Very likely, that is true," said Hastings as coldly as he could.

"Oh, you just say that to be polite. I bet you don't know

anything about the West. I bet you don't even know whether Seaforth is in Oregon or Washington."

"Why, I . . ." Hastings hesitated.

"What did I tell you?" crowed Ascot, torn between pride in his own astuteness and anger over Cameron's triumph.

Watching him bustle pugnaciously through the crowd between him and the exit, Dr. Hastings shook his head in commiseration. "That's the unhappiest man I've seen in a long time," he thought. "Poor fellow! . . . I'm afraid Fergusson is a good deal like him."

IV

Being devoid of pretended modesty, Richard found the attention his paper had aroused very pleasant. Wherever he went men pointed him out to each other, spoke to him and asked questions. He suddenly found himself instead of an obscure research associate the acclaimed discoverer of a cure for a hitherto uniformly fatal disease. This unexpected fame might have gone to the heads of some people but Cameron knew that these other doctors were interested not in him but in the work he had done, and that many other men had been very close to the dietary discovery which he had finally made. So he went about quietly and cheerfully, answering the innumerable and often repetitious queries of the men who constantly waylaid him.

Some of the younger doctors found out the story of his recent illness and looked at him with a touch of hero-worship in their eyes, but a few of the older physicians shrugged their shoulders and suggested that the whole thing might have been a grandstand play. But the rather inaccurate accounts of his misfortune did not impair his newly won prestige, and at the few social functions he attended during the convention he found the ladies present eying him with distinct interest.

It was at the dance following the annual banquet that he caught sight of Judith Emerson. Before his operation she had sent him a book by Stephen Leacock with a note saying that she hoped it would make him laugh, and during his convalescence she had come to see him twice and had brought him each time some abstracts from foreign journals on anemia. But he had been embarrassed in her presence. Only sheer stupidity, he told himself, had kept him from recognizing long ago that he was in love with her and now it would be unsportsmanlike to speak to her when he had just lost a foot. Technically he fell into the category of cripples and for all he knew she might have an aversion to cripples.

Besides, a hospital room was a poor place to talk confidentially to a young woman: the nurses were always popping in, there was a litter of papers and bottles on the bedside table, and it was always possible that some probationer had left a bedpan in a conspicuous spot. Furthermore he never seemed to be able to get the barber when he needed him.

Richard told himself that there was something "phoney" about this thing of men falling in love with their nurses: no man in his right mind would fall in love with a woman who had seen him half-naked and stripped of all masculine independence. He found that he did not enjoy entertaining feminine visitors in a short hospital nightshirt even though blankets did swathe the lower half of his body. "A fellow feels so damned helpless without his pants," he said to Farquhar one day.

But now that he was back in normal life and had given his paper and become a marked man in research circles, he meant to do something about Judith, and when he saw her the evening of the banquet he was glad he had worn a tail coat. Thornton had warned him to have a new dress suit made to replace the one he had worn since he got out of the army, and he looked down proudly at his white waistcoat and shrugged up the collar of his swallowtail coat. Not that he was comfortable—for the June night was sweltering hot—but that he stood out among the other men, most of whom were in dinner coats and black ties.

During the banquet he had not seen Judith. He sat at a table with Jim Thornton and Mrs. Thornton and two doctors from

New York, one of whom had his wife with him. Neither of the women appealed to him: they both tried to look slimmer than they were and they both wore unbecoming shingle bobs. The conversation bored him, although he should have learned many things from it. He was told that the Philadelphia Sesqui-Centennial was going deeper into the red every day, that there was a rumor that Dempsey would fight Tunney in the autumn in an effort to stem the tide, that the Hall-Mills murder trial was to be reopened, that Aimee Semple McPherson had been kidnapped, that Queen Marie was going to tour the United States, that the "Private Life of Helen of Troy" was simply a scream. And the one or two attempts he made to mention anemia were promptly blocked.

When the tables had been cleared and the tiresome speeches all made and the more tiresome responses listened to, and it was at last possible to get up off the spindle-legged chairs on which a thousand people had been crowded together in stifling proximity for three hours, Richard made his escape from the banquet hall as rapidly as he could, intent on getting outdoors. But in the hall ahead of him he suddenly saw Judith and another young woman. Judith was standing with her profile toward him and he was conscious at once of his pleasure in her slender figure. She did not bulge and neither did she wear her hair plastered down to her scalp. She was dressed in a long-waisted, yellow gown and at her back there was a huge bow of black that made Richard think of the obis worn by Japanese girls in the chorus of "Madame Butterfly."

Judith was laughing and talking with the girl beside her and instinctively Cameron started toward them. But before he reached them, two young men appeared with glasses of punch in their hands. Not wishing to intrude, Richard waited, pretending to study the murals that adorned the walls of the corridor. But when the punch was finished, the young men stacked the cups on a convenient window ledge and led the girls away into the ballroom.

Following them slowly, Cameron went and stood in the

doorway to watch the dancing. After a few minutes, he shrugged his shoulders, pulled down his white waistcoat, and turned away smiling ironically. "Strike one against a wooden leg," he said to himself.

CHAPTER IX

I

The months that followed Richard's appearance before the American Medical Association saw the beginning of a wide use of liver diet in anemia. Almost at once Cameron began to get mail from doctors throughout the United States and Canada and very shortly reports started coming in from Europe as well. Everywhere men wrote of patients who had been saved from lingering death and restored to normal activity. Occasionally a caustic letter told of failure with the meat diet, and now and then a critical article appeared in some medical journal, but in most of these cases Richard was able to trace the difficulty to faulty technique or inadequate amounts of liver and kidney. From many journals came requests for articles and there were numerous inquiries from Scandinavian and Finnish doctors who see much pernicious anemia in their homelands.

Level-headed Dr. Thornton, observing all this, gave Cameron sound advice.

"Take every opportunity to publish that comes your way and

answer every letter you get. When your reputation gets big enough the trustees of the Institute will do something because they'll be afraid some other outfit will get you away from Fifer. You don't belong in my department, you're not a physiologist. You ought to have a lab of your own."

Lanister proposed Richard for membership in the National Association of Physicians, a sort of honor society for doctors who refrain from doing surgery. His election to this group pleased Cameron more than any other recognition he had yet received.

"I never expected to get into a highbrow outfit like this," he said to Jim Thornton.

At this remark his chief roared with laughter.

"Good Lord, man, sometimes you seem more like a child than any of my kids. You can't be as naïve as you sound or you'd have to have a guardian."

But although Cameron was seldom as disingenuous as he seemed on this occasion, he was constantly surprised at the acclaim he received for the liver feeding. It seemed incredible that the medical world should take this simple régime so seriously, but not only did he get ample confirmation of his claims for this diet but he saw liver extract go into commercial production within three months after he read his paper to the medical convention.

Elihu Cloverley, president of Cloverley & Co., a small manufacturing pharmaceutical house in Northdevon, was a man in his middle sixties. The son of an English chemist from whom he inherited the conception of pharmacy as a profession, he migrated to the United States as a very young man and located in a suburb of Northdevon. Gradually his business grew and presently he abandoned the retail drug trade and began to manufacture in a small way. When the World War cut off the supply of the products needed in the treatment of syphilis, he co-operated with the chemists at the University to develop new methods of producing organic arsenicals, and after the War was over became the leading American manufacturer of these drugs. But in spite of the volume and variety of the business, Cloverley

& Co. was still under the active direction of its founder when Waldheim and Cameron deposited their liver extract formula, like a foundling, on its doorstep.

At that first interview Richard conceived a liking for Elihu Cloverley which never changed. Cloverley was a short stout man with a round red face and shrewd blue eyes, who bore a close physical resemblance to the John Bull of cartoonists, but his transparent honesty and good will robbed his shrewdness of sinister implications. Silently he listened to Waldheim's description of the extract, studied the chemical formulæ, and gave close attention to Cameron's tables and graphs showing the results of his treatment in pernicious anemia.

By this time Richard had divided his patients, who now numbered over one hundred, into three groups. The first of these comprised those patient individuals who ate liver or kidney every day without complaint; the second consisted of people who found these meats unpalatable and substituted for them powdered pigs' stomachs in tomato juice; the third included the persons who were taking Waldheim's extract. All three groups, he pointed out to Mr. Cloverley, maintained equally good health so long as they continued their treatment systematically.

"Don't ask us why any of this works, Mr. Cloverley," said Waldheim. "I don't know. Perhaps no one ever will know. The extract I'm making now in the laboratory for Dr. Cameron—#279—is a yellow powder which dissolves readily in water, and the active principle in it I believe to be a polypeptide or a nitrogenous base. But what does that tell us? Nothing, precisely nothing." The chemist shrugged expressive shoulders.

"Another difficulty, Mr. Cloverley," added Richard, "is that so far we have no way to test the extract except to try it on patients. We need an extract we can be sure is potent, concentrated so the dose will be small, and pure enough that reactions will not occur when we give it hypodermically. And cheap enough that ordinary people can afford to buy it. That's more than they can do with liver, these days."

Elihu Cloverley smiled. "This is quite an order, gentlemen. I can see that Dr. Waldheim is unable to turn out the amount of extract you are going to need in his small laboratory at the University, but I don't know that we will be able to do all you want, either."

The discussion that followed was terse and to the point. Cloverley saw at once that liver extract was still in the experimental stage and might never be a money maker.

"But I see also that it is necessary to work out a substitute for the liver diet that is so monotonous and repulsive, Dr. Cameron, and I enjoy working out problems. You've brought me one that presents many phases of interest, chemical and commercial. I shall have to tell my sales manager to sell more cough syrup and headache tablets so we can afford to experiment with your liver extract. It will be a pleasure, gentlemen. If we succeed, many people will benefit from it, and if we fail we shall learn something and lose a lot of money in the process."

When they left the Cloverley plant, Waldheim explained still further his choice of this firm as manufacturers of the first liver extract to go out to the medical profession generally.

"Mr. Cloverley is interested in some other things than making money. When he has to, he can drive as close a bargain as anybody, but he really likes research. He thoroughly enjoyed working with us during the War on arsenicals. And whenever he turns out a product it is the best that can be made under the circumstances. His stuff is always a little above standard, rather than a little below. He won't try to make our extract out of horns and hides, and some of these other firms would."

As time went on Richard realized that this was true. Elihu Cloverley himself took an active part in devising ways to refine the extract and increase its potency. The chemists in his plant were a superior group of practical men full of pride in their work. Whenever a batch of extract was found to be defective it was promptly recalled and destroyed and any that was in manufacture according to that process was also discarded, and an entirely fresh supply made. By the second year Liver Extract #279 was in routine use all over the country with excellent results.

II

When Cameron returned to Northdevon in the September following his first appearance at the American Medical Association, after a very satisfactory six weeks in New England and eastern Canada, he had quite recovered his physical equilibrium. Every trace of awkwardness in the use of his artificial foot was gone and he had overcome all tendency to think of himself as a cripple. The only thing that seemed strange was that he could not run upstairs when the elevator was busy.

His first forenoon in town he spent at the University Hospital with Miss Worrall and young Dr. Morgan who had been in charge of Ward B during the summer and was now to stay on permanently as his assistant. Because of the attention attracted by the anemia research another small ward was to be turned over to them for the study of the liver extract soon to be produced by Cloverley & Co.

Well pleased with the season's results, Cameron went immediately after lunch to the Institute. Finding that Judith had not come in yet from her noon hour, he went in search of Farquhar, whom he found alone in his little cubby-hole on the fourth floor. Fergusson, Sandy told him, had not yet returned from his summer's leave.

"And did you finish the work you told me about at the A.M.A. meeting?"

Across Farquhar's pale face flitted the ghost of a smile.

"I did." He opened the drawer of his battered desk and took out a thick, neatly-typed manuscript. "Here it is, ready to go in for publication as soon as I get the prints for the cuts."

Instead of examining the article, Cameron studied Sandy himself. He seemed thinner, paler, frailer looking than Richard could remember ever having seen him. "Been working all day and half the night ever since June," thought Cameron.

"You see, Rich, this is—properly speaking—the logical conclusion of that other paper of Wesley's and mine on calcium deposits in the chest. I've worked out the steps here by which a child gets infected with tuberculosis and shown how we can discover the infection by Xray examination long before the youngster is ill. It's more definite and more accurate than the skin test for sifting out the kids who are likely to break down with TB, and I think it'll be valuable for a long time in public health work. I'm proud of it."

There was a strange mordant enthusiasm in Farquhar's eyes as he told how, for years, he had collected data on childhood tuberculosis without any notion of where it would lead him and how during the past winter and spring he had combined this with all he had learned at Fifer and written it into this thesis. While he talked Cameron found himself listening for something Farquhar was not saying.

Then there came a short awkward pause which Sandy broke with a forced laugh.

"And I've done something else, Rich, something you may not like. I've resigned—like you did at Seaforth before I could be fired."

This, Cameron suddenly realized, was exactly what he had been expecting Sandy to tell him.

"I've had a long talk with Dr. Hastings and fixed everything up to leave the Institute next month. You needn't look so worried, Rich. I've got money enough to tide me over until I can find a job. Things aren't like they were in Seaforth that other time. I've got a degree from the University of Northdevon back of me now, and Dr. Penfield has several possible openings for me in mind. But I'm going to rest for a while, before I go to work again, just as you said I ought to."

Cameron thought of Farquhar in the little cottage in Seaforth, crouching before the fire, crying out, "I'm not planning. I can't! Not this time! The starch has gone out of me." Sandy was not like that today; some perverse sense of humor seemed to have seized him.

"Where do you think you'll go when you leave the Institute?"

"Oh, I'm going to take my time about things. I've worked hard for a long while, Rich, and I feel like being lazy."

The curious smile on Farquhar's face told Richard that advice would not be welcome, and presently Cameron took himself off, uneasily aware that Sandy had not said all that was in his mind.

Later in the afternoon Richard invaded the library again and found Judith working at the card index. He paused in the doorway to watch her. The very sight of her made him happy; it was a pleasure to look at her wavy, soft, dark hair and her warm olive skin and her slender body curved and graceful in the blue frock with its white belt and white guimpe. When she raised her eyes, he walked rapidly toward her, holding out a thin, brown hand.

"Why, Dr. Cameron, how nice to see you again! And how well you look!"

He kept her hand in his, drew her a little closer.

"I've told you before that my name is Richard."

Judith flushed and made an ineffectual attempt to withdraw her hand.

"I've missed you, young woman. Why on earth did you go west this summer of all summers when you knew I was going up to Maine and the White Mountains and points north?"

"Why, Dr. Cameron, I'd planned my trip to Glacier Park and Yellowstone more than a year ago. Surely you wouldn't have had me miss it."

Cameron looked down at his freckled brown hand which still imprisoned hers and smiled.

"My dear, I wouldn't have you miss anything—ever. And you liked it?"

"I loved it! I'd like to go back. It's wonderful country."

"Yes, it is. I loved it too when I lived in Montana, even though I was broke all the time and froze in winter and roasted in summer. It is grand country."

In his voice there was an undercurrent of something warmly personal. Judith felt a surge of blood in her cheeks and made another effort to pull her hand away, but inexplicably found herself closer to Richard than she had been before.

He leaned toward her, his face close to hers, his dark gray eyes questioning. She tried to keep her gaze centered on the soft rough brown fabric of his coat but in spite of all her efforts it crept upward. She turned half away from him and threw out one arm against the filing cabinet behind her, bracing herself to resist the impulse to surrender that suddenly swept over her.

"There..." she began in a low voice. "No, there aren't. I looked to see. There's not another soul here."

Richard gathered her into his arms, up against him. She felt his lean firm body against hers, felt his heart thudding against his chest. Then his mouth came down and found hers.

Judith Emerson had had her share of flirtations and dallying, and she was not a complete stranger to the pursuit vulgarly known as "necking," but the ecstasy into which her whole body flamed at Cameron's touch was new and overwhelming. Her head fell back and her body went limp in his arms. As though from a great distance she heard him saying over and over, "Judith, dear! Judith!" When at last he raised his face from hers, she found herself strangely weak, leaning against his shoulder. But, though a flood of red swept over her cheeks again, she looked into his thin, eager face without faltering.

"I love you, Judith. I've loved you for a long time. Will you marry me ... tonight?"

"Tonight!" Although she prided herself on lack of regard for the conventions, this startled the girl. She pulled herself out of his arms and stood erect. "Tonight! Why, no, of course not! I can't."

"Why can't you? We haven't any time to waste, my dear. I'm thirty-nine years old, and I ought to have found you and married you ten years ago."

By this time Judith had recovered some of her usual composure.

"I was a sophomore in college ten years ago and I'm glad I didn't meet you then and marry you. I'd have hated missing all the things I've done since then."

Despite his earnestness Cameron's eyes began to twinkle at this retort.

"But if we'd been married in 1916 and settled down, we'd have had a home and our family by this time."

"And I suppose you think you'd have turned into a good Republican and a solid citizen," mocked Judith. "Well, I don't believe it. You won't ever settle down. You'll talk about it, but you won't do it. You're too much a buccaneer."

Richard seized her hands and stood looking down at them. They were slender and cool and long of finger. Suddenly he bent over and kissed each palm gently, then folded them shut.

"I love you, Judith. I love you."

His bright hair was close to her face as he bent down, and impulsively she laid her cheek against it; it was rough and stiff and scratchy, but she liked the touch of it.

"Tell me," he said softly. "Do you love me?"

"Yes, dear."

"And you will marry me?"

"Yes."

"When?"

Into Judith's mind flashed the memory of that Sunday afternoon they had gone to the Zoo together and she had fancied he was about to make love to her when he had only been concerned with a refractory vegetarian patient. She laughed a little. "It won't hurt you to wait a few weeks," she answered. "You're like a small boy: you want what you want when you want it."

"One would think I was an ogre and you were afraid of me," grumbled Richard.

Judith put a hand on his arm. "I don't think you're an ogre and I'm not afraid of you. But you won't be easy to live with. You have an aversion to being tied down and you're not interested in making money. I think we'll always be poor and a little disorganized. Do you see what I mean, dear? But I love you as you are and I shan't try to make you over. I'll marry you . . . as soon as I can."

The words were smothered in her throat as he pulled her into his arms again and kissed her with hot, impatient lips. This time she had no desire to resist, she gave herself over blindly to the strange, wild desire that sprang up at the touch of his hands and mouth. But presently he released her.

"Judith, I haven't been any better than I should have been and I've had more to do with women than I like to think of now. I'm not fit to marry you. I know it sounds banal to talk like this. But I am sorry. There's no use lying about it. Only I can't undo what's been done."

"Listen, Richard. I don't want you confessing anything to me, because I don't intend to confess to you. I haven't lived in a convent and I know more about life than you think I do. Neither of us can help what's past. All that concerns us now is the future."

"All I want is for you to love me, Judith. And if—as you say—I am a buccaneer, then I pledge the loyalty of a buccaneer to his queen."

He clicked his heels together and bowed, then he took her hand and kissed it.

III

Two weeks after Farquhar left Northdevon a hoarse voice bawling the Sunday paper on the street below woke Richard from a sound sleep. For a moment he lay stretching his long body and running his fingers through his wiry red hair. He had a date with Judith and he must get up and shave, take a shower and dress and get the car out to go for her. His dark gray eyes wandered first to a colored miniature of the girl on his dresser and then to the new suit that dangled from a hanger on the open door of his closet. It was gray tweed and it was flecked with yellow and green; he yawned and tried to decide whether he should wear a green tie or a red one.

Through the window came again the stentorian bellow of the man on the street, he was coming back around the block. "Extra! Extra! All about the Hot..." Cameron jumped out of bed and banged down the window. Looking out he saw the man riding past on a bicycle with a canvas sack full of papers on his back.

"These 'varmints' ought to be kept off the street on Sunday mornings," he growled to himself. "They raise such a row a fellow can't sleep if he wants to."

But these days nothing could keep Richard Cameron long in a bad humor. Judith was wearing his ring, they were to be married at Christmas. Both research wards at the hospital were showing excellent results. He had three papers coming out in three important journals. A dozen of the best-known clinics in Canada and the United States were trying out Liver Extract #279. Thornton was studying the effects on experimental anemia of various sorts of meat, powdered pigs' stomach, and liver extract. There was but one disagreeable thing in the whole picture: Sandy Farquhar had tried to leave Northdevon without his knowledge.

By chance, one evening early in October, Cameron had run into him just outside the University Hospital, trudging along with a heavy briefcase full of books and papers. Farquhar had been startled and not too pleased, Richard felt, to see him. Quiet as he was with most people, Sandy usually talked freely enough with Cameron, but that evening he was uncommunicative; Richard got the impression that he did not want to divulge his plans. He was equally vague about the date of his departure from Northdevon and that of his return; he did not seem quite sure whether he would come back at all. But Richard did finally extract a promise not to leave without seeing him again.

All the way to his apartment Farquhar spoke only in answer to direct questions and then in a monotone. When Cameron let him out at the apartment house he watched Sandy cross the sidewalk and enter the building with the haunting sense that there was something pathetic in the little man's narrow shoulders and something resembling flight in the way he closed the door after him without looking back. Perplexed and worried, Richard drove away. He must, he decided, take Farquhar in hand again. He was running away from the Institute and from Northdevon, even if he didn't want to admit it. But perhaps it might be just as well to let him go down to Hot Springs in Virginia as he planned: it would do him good. He had always worked like the devil and he had spent too much time with Xrays to do his health any good.

Therefore Richard contented himself for the immediate

present with dropping into Dr. Penfield's office the next day and verifying Sandy's statement that there were in prospect several openings for good roentgenologists.

"I suppose you know Dr. Farquhar well," said Penfield when Cameron rose to go. His tone of voice seemed curious.

"Yes, very well. In fact we came to Northdevon together, from the Pacific coast."

Dr. Penfield hesitated a moment before adding, "His personality is something of a handicap, I'm afraid."

Richard looked at the older man appraisingly: Penfield's face was kind and his blue eyes seemed friendly.

"Yes, doctor, I know it is. But it oughtn't to be; Sandy is square and decent and capable, and that ought to be enough."

Once more Penfield seemed to hesitate before answering.

"It ought to be, Dr. Cameron, I agree with you. But I'm afraid it won't be, even with a man as brilliant as Farquhar. However, I assure you we'll do all we can for your friend. We like him, all of us."

This conversation was still fretting Cameron the following afternoon when Sandy called him on the 'phone to say that he was taking the five o'clock train for Virginia. To Richard's protests he answered sensibly that there was nothing to keep him in Northdevon and no reason why he should not start his deferred vacation at once.

"You're always bossing people, Rich. Telling them what they ought to do." Farquhar laughed softly over the wire. "I feel sorry for that poor girl who's going to marry you. Oh, by the way, will you give her my regards and say goodbye to her for me?"

Finally, under pressure, he promised to write from Hot Springs and to come back to Northdevon without fail some time during November. With this concession Cameron was forced to be content.

This bright Sunday morning while he was dressing, his eyes fell on the three letters with the Hot Springs postmark on them that lay on his library table. They were so sane and cheerful that he felt somewhat reassured about Sandy. Of course he wasn't tramping and riding horseback and swimming and playing golf and tennis as the letters hinted he was, but he did seem to be enjoying himself after his own fashion. It wasn't Richard's idea of a vacation, but if it was what Sandy liked let him have it.

Carefully dressed in his new gray tweed, with shoes freshly shined and a new gray felt hat cocked over one ear, Cameron rang the buzzer at Judith's apartment at ten o'clock. She opened the door at once, dressed for the street in a costume of soft tan woolen with a cape falling from her shoulders and a broad belt of brown suede.

"Judy," cried Richard, "you are beautiful this morning. If I am very careful of the dress, may I kiss you?"

But at the touch of her his resolutions of restraint weakened and in swift succession he kissed her mouth, her eyes, her throat, and the tip of her nose.

"Marry me before Christmas, Judy."

The girl smiled at him but shook her head.

"And Sandy says I boss people and tell them what to do. He doesn't know how completely cowed you have me."

"Richard, you're not fair." There was a hint of tartness in Judith's voice. "You're not cowed and you know it. I've given up all my plans for myself and sunk all my hopes and ideas in you. You know that too." Then, as Cameron began to grin at her, she went on more slowly, "I believe you say things like that deliberately to make me flare up at you. I think you enjoy it."

"I do," admitted Richard. "Is that very bad? I love seeing you 'flare up,' as you call it. Your eyes shine and your voice crackles and you look all bothered and earnest. I think you're the most attractive woman alive when you're like that."

"I'm not," said Judith softly. "But I like hearing you say I am. I hope you'll say nice things to me sometimes after we're married."

When she went back into her bedroom to repair her makeup, Cameron stood waiting for her, whistling softly and practicing teetering back and forth from heels to toes, a maneuver he had found difficult with an artificial foot. Presently his eyes fell upon the Sunday paper on the small wooden stand under the telephone. Black headlines streamed across it as usual. Idly he picked it up to glance at the front page.

At the head of one column was a photograph with a long caption underneath. Cameron stared at the picture for an instant, then shook open the paper and began to read feverishly.

Judith found him there, pale and incredulous, standing as she had left him with the paper clutched in one hand.

"Richard," she cried, "are you ill? What's the matter? What's happened?"

He held the paper toward her.

"It's Sandy. He's dead! Look! Here's his picture."

IV

When Cameron left him Farquhar fled for shelter to his own apartment, but once there found that he was too restless to spend the evening alone. Then the sight of his wall calendar reminded him that this was the night of the first regular weekly concert of the symphony orchestra. One of the few extravagances Sandy allowed himself was a season ticket for the orchestra and now, forgetting that he had had no dinner, he hastily bathed, put on his evening clothes, and went to the music hall. All the way downtown he felt as though he were suspended in a vacuum awaiting catastrophe.

Strangely, the little Scotsman who was usually so conscious of his slight stature and insignificant appearance did not think of them twice that evening. Perhaps it was because the awareness of his seldom worn dinner suit made him feel inconspicuous in the mass of uniformly black-and-white men about him, perhaps it was the nebulous realization that for him appearances were no longer of importance. Sinking into his seat still with that feeling of waiting for something to happen, he glanced idly about and then took up his program.

An instinctive lover of music, Farquhar had tried conscientiously for years to acquire the intellectual basis of the art he appreciated intuitively, and now he gave his attention to the program notes. He saw that the opening number was the Egmont Overture. That was an old friend, or at least an old acquaintance. The comment was that it dealt with Goethe's ironic conception of a martyr who sacrificed himself for others and was hanged for his pains. The second number was to be Saint-Saëns' fourth concerto for piano, and the last before the intermission Gluck's Overture to Iphigenia, neither of which Farquhar knew.

He put down the program to watch the players straggle out on to the platform. He listened to the squealings and tootings and thumpings with which they tested the tuning of their instruments, and something in their frame of mind communicated itself to him. At once he felt uncertain and taut, although he did not know why. There was, indeed, no way he could have known that the orchestra, having been worked to staleness over the *pièce de résistance* of the evening which was to follow the intermission, was now about to perform mechanically the well worn Egmont Overture which all of them had played over and over until it no longer had any emotional content for them. The same perfunctoriness tinged the manner of the conductor when he bowed to his audience and took up his baton, and it persisted throughout the rendition of the entire composition.

Made more restless than ever by this mood which had descended upon him out of the void, Farquhar hoped for relief from the piano number which, according to the program notes, was to mark the American début of Josef Jadowski; but when the pianist made his appearance and sat down with a flourish of black coat tails before the grand piano which had been pushed forward from some mysteriously hidden niche in the wings he felt disappointment engulf him. Jadowski was a tall, cadaverous man who, seen full-face, gave the impression of youthfulness, but when he turned to face his instrument he revealed a poorly camouflaged bald spot that gave his head a curiously frayed appearance.

After two or three false starts he launched into the Saint

Saëns concerto with great vehemence. Sandy sat perfectly still watching the thin black figure bending and swaying as the long black arms stretched over the keyboard. Although Farquhar was an amateur, he knew by instinct that this was a masterly exhibition of technique and nothing more; that behind the impressive façade of performance and virtuosity Jadowski was empty and had nothing to say.

It was a relief when the orchestra reappeared, even though the program notes stated that Gluck's Overture was the quintessence of classicism. Nothing could be worse, Sandy told himself, than that ghastly mannequin at the piano, and at least he could amuse himself by listening for and identifying the instruments he liked to pick out of the ensemble—the bassoon, the oboe, the French horns. They always wailed, laughed, lamented, called to arms; and he always heard them with a quickening heart. But to his distress there was nothing about the Iphigenia Overture that stirred him except certain somber chords in the bass that were repeated over and over until they beat on his raw senses with the battering force of waves on a sea-facing headland. Again and again they came—the wailing of the furies, the outraged dignity of the offended gods.

During the interlude Sandy escaped to the foyer. Here he stood beside a column watching the parade of Northdevon society, but this too soon made him uncomfortable. Laughing and talking, girls and women strolled past and it seemed to Farquhar that when they looked at him they laughed more than ever. Women always alarmed him and tonight they terrified him. He was convinced that to them he seemed not a small, inconspicuous man in a dinner jacket but a clown, an absurd and comical figure forever denied entrance to their world.

He could see himself as he felt he must appear to them—a ridiculous person with the burden of the past upon him. Everyone had a past, of course—a past he carried everywhere, like a pack on his back. But some people had little packs full of pleasant memories and past happiness while others had only horrors in their burdens. He could see them on the men and women who passed him: those who walked lightly with erect shoulders were those whose loads were light and those who hurried along with sad faces and bent backs were those whose yoke was heavy. But everyone had his pack; by looking carefully Sandy could see them just as he could make out on Xray films the vague shadows that spelled disease.

His own burden was large and heavy. It was between him and the wall now. He could feel it there, pressing against him when he leaned against the column. It would get between him and the back of his seat when he returned to the auditorium for the rest of the concert. It was so big that everyone must see it; they were all looking at him strangely now.

In his agitation he fled to the smoking room. On the way he encountered a man who resembled Fergusson so much that Sandy was restrained from flight only by the recollection that no power on earth could drag Fergusson to a concert. In the smoking room he found a little group of young men somewhat under the influence of the liquor they were imbibing from pocket flasks; they were telling one another smutty stories and laughing boisterously. They looked up at Farquhar with what he was sure was contempt and he hurried on into the washroom.

There in the mirror he saw a lined, haggard, white face which he did not at first recognize as his own. While he wiped his hands he realized that he was looking at himself. That hunted, bedraggled creature in the glass was he—Sanderson Farquhar! Hunted—that was the word. He had always been hunted, he always would be. There was no escape with the pack of his past on his back. In a panic he slunk back to his seat in the concert hall.

The only number to follow the intermission was Scriabine's Prometheus, now being performed for the third or fourth time in the United States. On this composition conductor and orchestra had slaved for weeks, and because of it had filled in the first half of the program with familiar selections which required little practice. Keyed to the highest pitch, the musicians approached this tone poem of a spirit striving to reach the unattainable. The grand piano once more appeared and Josef Jadowski with his frowsy, clumsily arranged mane of black hair sat down before it.

At the first chord Farquhar felt something leap up within him in protest and for the entire thirty-five minutes of the performance he was in torment. The composer had used one basic chord through the whole composition and as it recurred and recurred, now for this instrument and then for another, it gave the impression of a futile struggle foredoomed to achieve nothing. All the pianist's brilliant technique, all the conductor's efforts, all the skill of the orchestra could not change or conceal the essential emptiness and futility of the piece, and all the mystic voices calling to Prometheus, reassuring him, could not alter his inevitable doom.

The music rolled over Sandy but he was no longer conscious of it. He felt nothing now but that sense of utter personal defeat. What little faith had survived the years was toppling in ruin tonight. He had been driven from place to place, from job to job, for fifteen years because of something he could not alter any more than he could change the color of his eyes. Gossip, scandal, rumor always drove him on. It did no good to live alone, to make few acquaintances and no intimates; sooner or later someone always turned up to recognize him. And then there was that wretched business of resigning by request to be gone through again, and after that the concoction of a plausible story to account for the resignation and the ordeal of hunting another job without explaining exactly why he had left the old one and, at the same time, without lying about it. Each time he underwent these humiliations his self-respect seemed first to writhe and then to shrink.

After he came to Northdevon with Richard there had been an interval of peace. In the Graduate School no one had seemed curious about him, everyone seemed to accept him as he was, and bit by bit he lost much of his old fear. When he went to Fifer Institute he was untroubled by any anxiety more acute than the chronic one of poverty, and he had actually thought that he might one day attain a niche of modest security. But the first sight of Fergusson told him that this niche would not be at Fifer. It was not only that Fergusson disliked him but that he could not endure an assistant capable of anything beyond the routine of the department.

In spite of his timidity, knowing that it was only a question of time until Fergusson too would find out about him, Sandy refused to cringe before his superior or propitiate him in the hope of keeping his job. From the day Fergusson read the article by Farquhar and Wesley in the Journal of Radiology, Sandy knew that he had made a malignant enemy. Indeed, he had often reflected, he could almost name the hour when Fergusson received the information that delivered his subordinate into his hands.

During the summer's reprieve, in Fergusson's absence, Farquhar had lashed himself to work with a fanatical contempt for human frailty. Some nights he did not go to bed at all, on others he lay in a semi-stupor of exhaustion during the hours of darkness. By September he had finished his long article on childhood tuberculosis and its diagnosis by Xray examination—the fruit of fifteen years' observation and thought. And, going through it with a ruthless critical eye, he knew that it was good.

Then he realized that he could not go through another day of Fergusson's smirking salacious watchfulness. Remembering Richard's tactics with Samuel Ascot, he sent in his resignation a week before Fergusson returned from his summer's vacation.

It seemed to him now that he had lived in a vacuum since spring. His inhuman concentration on his task had numbed him with fatigue and the adroitness required to avert an open clash with Fergusson had occupied all his consciousness. But now this period of marking time was over, something was about to happen. At the certainty of this, he felt his hands tremble and grow wet with sweat.

The music which still surged about him re-enforced the conflict within him. Regret, disappointment, bitterness surged up and overwhelmed him. He was a failure, he had never been anything else. He had been punished and humiliated over and over for something he could not help. He could never achieve his professional ambitions, he was shut out forever from the happy normal life for which he had always longed. He was alone, he would always be alone. He had no friend in all the world but Richard Cameron and he could not bother him asking for help.

A stifling sense of isolation shut down over Farquhar as mist or fog closes down upon a wayfarer. He was an outcast; the pack, red-tongued and savage, was in pursuit. He had no defense against that mob—neither money nor prestige nor influential friends. He had only himself, his own personality such as it was, his love of beauty, and his passion for justice. But over himself he had a power that could defeat the world and deliver him "from the body of this death."

His face flushed, his hands shaking, his heart pounding, he sat motionless, rigidly erect in his seat, drenched with sweat—an inconspicuous mousy little man in a high collar and a black bow tie, whom his neighbors hardly noticed. But from the turmoil within him was born resolution, and this resolution, edged by fear and made cunning by desperation, went with him when he left the music hall.

V

The sound of footsteps at his door made Dr. Thornton raise his eyes from his desk to see Cameron standing on the threshold.

"Oh, hello, Richard," said he, springing up. "Come in. I've been wondering when you'd get back." The last sentence was freighted with embarrassment.

Cameron closed the door behind him and sat down. Thornton stared at him in amazement: he had seen this man gay, he had seen him absorbed and determined and curious and occasionally angry, but he had never before seen him savage. The lean freckled face with its wide cheek bones and tapered, stubborn jaw was grim.

"Jim, do you know whether Fergusson is in the Institute?"

"Why, I suppose he is." Thornton was startled by this demand. "I don't see much of M. Carr, you know. Why?"

But Cameron answered with still another query. "I suppose there's been a lot of stuff in the papers and reporters hanging around?"

Thornton nodded. "But they got precious little out of any of us."

The dark eyes that Cameron turned upon his chief were blazing with pity and anger and self-reproach.

"Sandy went to Virginia to kill himself, Jim. And now he's dead but . . . not a suicide."

Thornton leaned back in his chair and swept the papers he had been working on into a drawer. "Tell me, Richard. I want to know. I always liked Farquhar, what I saw of him."

"I've got to tell somebody, Jim. I can't stand it if I don't. And I trust you."

Cameron flung himself up out of his seat as though he could not bear to sit still and began to pace up and down, dragging his artificial foot a little as he always did when he was tired. "Have you got any tobacco on you?"

Thornton tossed him an oiled silk pouch. "You may fire when ready," said he, and there was no flippancy in this paraphrase.

"I've pieced the story together, Jim, out of what people could tell me and the letters and things Sandy left. I think that when he got down to the Springs and found it was beautiful Indian summer weather he was tempted to live a little longer. But apparently nobody took much notice of him; they never did, you know. The manager of the hotel said he sat around watching people dressed for riding and tennis and golf go in and out, and went tramping by himself in the country. He had registered under an assumed name and address, and for a few days he must have been destroying identifying marks on his baggage and clothing and getting things ready to leave for me.

"He evidently had the date set and everything arranged, and then the sun came up on a magnificent morning and Sandy wanted one more day alive. In his room he left a letter addressed to me and a parcel ready to be mailed to me. The manager told me it was a fine day. You know what fall can be down there, with the hills full of color and the sky sapphire blue and a haze hanging over the distance."

Cameron paused to light his pipe.

"No one will ever know all that happened to Sandy that day, Jim. But up above the hotel a few miles there is an estate that belongs to a man from Pittsburgh. There's a creek along one side of it, quite a stream. Well, this man's son, a boy about ten or twelve, went off that morning for a long hike with his cousin who is two or three years older, and somehow they got lost and separated. The little fellow finally found the creek and followed it down to where he could see his father's estate on the opposite side. He can't swim but he tried to get across on some logs that had fallen into the water, and he says one of them broke or rolled with him. Anyhow he fell in.

"He didn't know there was anyone within miles, he hadn't seen anyone for a couple of hours. But all of a sudden a man showed up beside him and grabbed him and started to tow him ashore. The boy says that when they got to the bank the man pushed him on to it, out of the water, and asked him if he was all right and then said, "Hang on a minute, son. I'll be right with you." Then he cried out in pain and threw up his arms and slipped back into the stream.

"Of course the kid was scared stiff and he was too near all in himself to do anything. He thinks he ran along the bank, looking into the water and yelling, but he must have collapsed before long. I should think it was at least an hour before his cousin found him and raised the alarm.

"They didn't find Sandy until the next day. He was wedged up against some snags a few hundred feet downstream. Then there was trouble identifying him. The chambermaid at the hotel whom he had tipped rather generously had put the letter addressed to me in the mail and there was no label on the parcel and nothing in it to identify him. But he'd overlooked in a dresser drawer, among some shirts, a snapshot of himself and me taken in Seaforth years ago, and that was the picture they put in the papers. The one I saw Sunday morning, before his last letter had been delivered."

There was a long, deep silence in the room.

"Then Farquhar was a hero at the end," said Thornton softly.

"He was always a hero, all his life!" cried Richard hotly. "I don't care how he died because I know how he lived. . . . He was a delicate youngster and the bigger boys bullied him at school and tormented him when he couldn't hold his own with them. That started him being afraid of things. And when he got older, he found out something that put an end to every hope he ever had.

"He'd been an only child, Jim, and his poor health kept him out of athletics and prevented him mixing much with other kids of his own age. I suppose there never was a boy who knew less about the workings of the human body than he did when he went away from home to college. And it was just after that he discovered he was a homosexual."

Cameron ran his hand over his face, through his hair.

"Sandy took it hard. He felt that he must always be an outcast, and he never got a chance to change his mind. He stayed away from men and women both; after that one affair he never had another. He lived alone, made books and music and things like that take the place of people. When he got to medical school he found a fellow there who'd known him in college and spread the word about Sandy.

"Well, he stuck it out and took his degree in spite of everything, but when it came to outrunning gossip he found he couldn't do it. He went into radiology because he thought it wouldn't matter so much in a laboratory what a man's personality was. But wherever he went, scandal followed him sooner or later. If he could have gone in for himself, I think he might have succeeded in the face of all the odds, for he was a grand man with sick people. But he had no capital and so he had to work for other doctors or hospitals all his life. That ruined all his chances because eventually his story would get around and then he'd be forced to leave. 'Resigning by request' was the way he put it."

"Did you know him in school?"

Cameron shook his head. "No, I never saw him until I went to Seaforth. He had the Xray department in the hospital where I worked out there.... He didn't tell me about himself, not in so many words, but I put things together and then I learned a lot, guessed at it, before we came back to Northdevon. And he knew I understood, although we never talked about it."

"Fergusson must have found out somehow and held it over him while he was here and tormented him until it passed endurance." Thornton spoke slowly and thoughtfully.

Scowling at his pipe, Cameron nodded. "Fergusson," went on Thornton, "ought to spell his middle name with a 'u.' M. Curr Fergusson."

"The thing that killed Sandy wasn't Fergusson so much as the thought that, no matter how clean and decent he was, he must always be an outcast. He left some diaries and notebooks and asked me to take what little insurance he had and publish them at my own discretion. He'd always wanted, he said, to do something for people of his sort, something to stop them being hounded and persecuted for things they can't help. What gets me, Jim, is to think that a man like Sandy has to die while all sorts of filthy-minded people who weren't fit to tie his shoestrings go around being respectable. He was kind and honest and brave, he was a good doctor, he loved beautiful things, and, in spite of all that happened to him, he loved people."

Jim Thornton was a tolerant man, slow to wrath, but now his round, genial face had grown hard. His mouth became a grim gash above his deeply cleft chin. Suddenly he struck the desk with his fist and sprang to his feet.

"Come along, Richard," he cried. "I'll go with you to see Fergusson."

VI

No one except the three men who met that afternoon in Fergusson's office ever knew exactly what happened there. But his department was notified next morning that Dr. Fergusson was in bed at home quite incapacitated and that it would probably be some time before he would be able to return to his work at the Institute.

CHAPTER X

I

Late the afternoon before Thanksgiving Judith and Richard were married by an earnest young clergyman in a small chapel noted for its hospitality to unconventional people. They went there alone and came out into the dusk, husband and wife, in time to go to dinner at Rindbooker's a little after six.

Judith watched the man on the other side of the table from her with a feeling that none of the events of the past few weeks could really have happened to her. She had intended to be married at Christmas, but the white, self-reproachful face Cameron wore when he came back from Virginia with Sandy Farquhar's body had weakened her resolution and she had yielded to his entreaties. And now here she was, with a narrow white-gold band on her finger below her engagement ring, and on the opposite side of the alcove was Richard, looking possessively at her. As though this were not fantastic enough, they were to leave in an hour for New York for their honeymoon, which was to last from now until Sunday, and both were to be back at their jobs on Monday.

Judith had rather thought herself unconventional but she had never expected to be married in street clothes before two witnesses whom she had never seen before. She had always taken it for granted that, like other girls of her class, she would have a quiet but orthodox ceremony at the home of an aunt or uncle in up-state New York with the usual preliminaries of invitations and the ordinary aftermath of gifts and a wedding supper and at least a two weeks' trip somewhere.

But she was to have none of these things. Instead, she had run about Northdevon feverishly on two successive Saturdays, accompanied most unconventionally by Richard, buying clothes and shoes and hats, had packed her things early that morning in a fortnighter case, and had rushed home from the Institute at four o'clock to bathe and change before she rode down alone with Cameron in his coupé to the church, to promise that she would love and honor him as long as she lived. Indeed it seemed to her that she had not drawn a quiet breath since the day she had acceded to his pleading that she marry him at Thanksgiving instead of waiting until Christmas; she found herself wondering if tranquillity would ever bless their alliance. But at least it was over and they were married. At the thought, a sudden lassitude enfolded her.

She hardly heard Richard's interchange of words with the waitress. Languor gave place to an impulse to escape. What did she really know about this man across the table? Nothing. He had been born a thousand miles away from her native state, he had been brought up and educated in a different part of the country, he had lived a vivid active life in which she had had no part until three years before. She knew nothing of his family, of his background, of his ideas about women. She admired his gaiety and audacity, his persistence and skill, the way he faced problems and met criticism. But she saw that she did not know the man at all.

Quick panic swept over her. She must invent some excuse

for not going to New York with him tonight. There must be something she could say or do that would give her a loophole of escape.

When the waitress had put down the plates and water glasses and the bread and butter and gone away again with his order, Richard sat back in his chair and smiled at Judith. The strained look that had clung to his face since Sandy's death lifted before the passion shining in his dark gray eyes. He was proud of his wife. She was dressed in dark green with a scarf of rust-colored stuff about her throat and a tall crowned hat cutting at a strangely rakish angle across her forehead. Her soft red lips were slightly parted, her slim narrow hands were folded together on the table before her.

A wave of longing swept over him. His skin tingled and the backs of his thighs twitched. His imagination leaped ahead to the moment when he and Judith would be alone, out of the sight of other people. Since September his passion for her had fed on caresses and restrained physical contact. Now that sort of thing was over, she was his wife. They had no more need to appease Madam Grundy, what they did was no one's business but their own. Breathing hard, he leaned toward her, reaching for her with quick passionate fingers, dreaming how he would take her in his arms, kiss her mouth until it was as soft as water, put his hands on her hair and on the olive skin of her slender body, feel the breasts he could see under her bodice.

Startled by his abrupt movement, Judith raised her eyes and looked into his eager, hungry face. Her gaze did not falter but in it Richard saw uncertainty and a sort of desperate faith. Suddenly it came to him that it was so that Sandy Farquhar had faced the world, with no defense except the other man's decency. But these were the eyes of a woman who had the courage to face whatever life brought her. They did not plead; they looked at him with self-reliant bravery.

Instantly the blaze of physical desire died down. The hand he laid on hers was firm and strong but not hot with passion.

"Judy," he said in a voice so low that it barely reached her ears, "will you always remember that I love all of you? Not just your body, but the woman who lives in it."

She watched him intently—his dark gray eyes, his crinkling copper-colored hair, his freckled face and tapering chin, his wide, eager mouth—and as she looked she recalled the evening he had first told her about his work. She could see him on that muggy summer day in his little office at the Institute, quite unconscious of himself, intent on showing her what he had learned about anemia, talking rapidly, moving swiftly about the room, pouring out words in a voice tinged with excitement. She had seen then that he was an adventurer—not a crusader, and not a fanatic—but an adventurer in quest of truth.

As suddenly as they had risen, her doubts and misgivings ebbed away. They loved each other and they had been married and now they were going away together for four days; after that they would come back and go to work again. But she would not be alone; as long as Richard lived the world could never be bleak and she could never be bereft of companionship. She smiled at her husband. The smile began in the depths of her golden-brown eyes and spread over her olive-tinted skin until her whole face seemed to glow.

Watching her, Richard felt her hands grow limp in his. Again his pulse quickened, and he laughed under his breath. He bent his head and kissed each palm lingeringly; then folded them shut and held them closed.

At the touch of his lips a shiver of expectancy ran through the girl's body. She felt her strength, her self-reliance leaving her. Suddenly she wanted to be alone with him, to feel his arms around her, his lips on her throat, his lean body tense with passion crushing hers into an ecstasy in which pain was sweet.

II

On the next Monday morning many curious eyes observed the arrival of Dr. and Mrs. Richard Cameron at Fifer Institute. It was precisely five minutes of nine when a gray-green coupé stopped before the building and a tall man in a brown topcoat and soft brown hat got out. He ran around the car and opened the door next to the curb, reaching a hand to the young woman inside.

For a moment they stood together talking, then she went up the steps into the Institute while he watched her with his hat in one hand. As soon as the door closed after her, he sprang back into the car and drove away toward the University Hospital. All this was commonplace and if the observers could have heard the conversation that passed they would have thought it also commonplace and altogether unworthy of the newly married.

Said Richard: "I'm sorry, my dear, but I can't get down to take you to lunch I'm sure. Whenever I'm away for a few days, Miss Worrall and Dr. Morgan save up enough things to keep me busy until night instead of the half-day I'm supposed to spend with them. But I'll be here all afternoon and we can go home together this evening."

Said Judith: "I'll be awfully rushed myself, Richard. There are a lot of foreign journals due today. So I won't expect you until about five o'clock. Goodbye, dear."

What the onlookers did not see was the expression of the gray eyes that followed Judith up the steps and of the brown ones that looked into his as they said goodbye. What the onlookers did not guess was the whispered "I love you" that made Judith smile at her husband in a way that caused him to forget that there is such a thing as pernicious anemia. What the onlookers did not know was that deep in her heart Judith knew that this smiling, red-haired man was hers forever. All the onlookers actually observed was that Dr. and Mrs. Cameron were at work as usual.

But one of the stenographers who was romantically inclined told her girl-friend that, just for a moment as he handed his wife out of the coupé, there had been something courtly about Cameron. "Why, say, do you know, he looked just like Rudolph Valentino!"

BOOK III
THE VALE OF ELAH

CHAPTER I

I

Twenty-one months after Cloverley & Co. began to manufacture Liver Extract #279, Elihu Cloverley died suddenly of cerebral hemorrhage, and shortly thereafter his daughters, who now owned a majority of the stock, began negotiations to sell their interest to Pan-American Chemicals, Incorporated. This mammoth corporation, then engaged in absorbing a half-dozen smaller competitors with valuable formulæ, good reputations, or both, found Cloverley & Co. a tempting morsel because of the prestige of its founder and its arsenicals.

The acquisition by Pan-American of a controlling interest changed completely the policies of the Cloverley organization. So long as Elihu Cloverley lived, he ran the business himself, with the aid of capable assistants who owned small blocks of stock paid for out of their salaries or savings and the advice of the most able chemists on his staff. But Pan-American was a vertical trust controlling raw materials and their preparation as well as the sale of a list of products that filled a catalogue three inches thick, and its board of directors comprised not research chemists and benevolent despots like the late Elihu Cloverley, but industrialists and financiers whose sole object was to make as much money as possible. The significance of the change of policy dawned on the scientific personnel of the plant when the executive and sales staff was entirely replaced, and on Richard Cameron when letters began to come in, complaining that Extract #279 was no longer to be depended on. The truth of these protests was soon re-enforced when two successive batches of extract supplied to his research ward at the University Hospital proved to be worthless.

Confident that now, as on previous occasions during Cloverley's lifetime when something had gone wrong with the extract, it would be promptly called in and replaced, Richard called Walsh, the chief chemist at the Cloverley plant, on the telephone, but to his surprise Walsh said he could do nothing since all matters of this sort must be taken up with Mr. Rupert, the new manager. When Cameron tried to get in touch with Rupert he found him a most elusive person, here today and gone tomorrow and never available for consultation. Further attempts to get action through Walsh also proved futile, and at the end of three weeks' jockeying Richard's patience was exhausted.

When he spoke to Thornton about the situation, his chief did not seem surprised at the turn of events.

"The whole idea of these mergers is less expense, cheaper production, higher powered selling, and greater profits. It's easy to see what's happened. The new manager has put the screws on Walsh to turn out cheaper extract, that's all. And Walsh doesn't dare refuse for fear he'll lose his job."

Thornton left off drawing little triangles with his pencil on his desk blotter to watch Richard pacing up and down with his hands dug deep into the pockets of his denim laboratory coat.

"Can't you hold your patients at a normal blood level with swine stomach and liver?"

"Yes, of course. But that is unsatisfactory because you can't control people. If they don't like the taste of the stuff they simply won't take it—or at least they won't take enough. And then there's the devil to pay another way, too, Jim. There still isn't any way to test extract except by giving it to a patient we know has pernicious anemia. That gives the factory a cast-iron alibi, for we can't prove the stuff was no good when it left their hands, you see. But the whole extract treatment will be queered if this goes on much longer."

"Well, Richard, the time has come to get more than one firm making extract and to turn over the supervision of the process to the Medical Association. You can't police the whole thing by yourself. If Elihu Cloverley hadn't died we'd never have gotten into this jackpot. But the world is as it is and there's no use shutting our eyes to it. And neither is there any use getting wrathy about it. The way to handle birds like Rupert is to outsmart them. Why don't you try it? It might be as interesting as chasing reticulocytes or browbeating people into eating liver."

This was why something quite new to him occupied much of Cameron's attention while he was on his way west to speak at the Tri-State Medical Conference in Seaforth. He was familiar with the jealousy and bickering of his own profession but he had only begun to learn about the skullduggery of business and finance. It was true that the Cloverley division of Pan-American Chemicals had capitulated when the supervision of liver extract passed into the strong hands of the American Medical Association, but something told Richard that he was at the beginning of a new phase of conflict with business.

II

Five years had passed since Richard had left Seaforth and he found it hard to believe that he was going back now as the guest of the Tri-State Conference. It was early autumn but the air was soft and warm and the valleys past which the train rushed on its way down the green-clad western slopes of the Cascade Mountains were still brilliantly verdant. With amusement Cameron recalled having said once to Mary Compton that he expected to find himself mildewed almost any day. The memory of this led by association to recollection of his brief episode with Miriam Brooks and, to the astonishment of an observation platform full of tourists, Richard laughed aloud.

"I wonder if she still lives in Spokane," he thought, "and if she still thinks it's the grandest place on earth. It seems to me she got married the same fall I left Seaforth. . . . And I believe Mary Compton married a doctor out there that same year. . . . Well, they've got nothing on me, I'm married too."

Cameron was making the western trip alone because it had seemed sunwise to bring Judith, who was to have a child that autumn. She had worked in the Institute laboratory for a year after her marriage but after that her desire to have a family brought her home. Had her husband been less anxious about her he might have driven west and made a holiday of the trip, but with her in Northdevon he felt he ought get back as quickly as possible. Except that Judith dreaded flying he would have travelled by air, but he could not bring himself to fly against her wishes

Sometimes he wondered whether he would ever again be as carefree as he had been before Judith's pregnancy. Ironically enough, she who had always had excellent health fell ill almost from the moment of conception. First of all, she developed a toxemia and intractable vomiting and no sooner was that under control than she had to be operated for an acute mastoid infection. Her convalescence had been prolonged and stormy, and Richard's resiliency had barely sufficed to bring them through it.

When the invitation came to speak in Seaforth to the Tri-State meeting Cameron had been on the point of refusing when Judith discovered the letter and revived. To her aid came friends with assurances that they would care for her while he was away, but none of this moved him. It was only when Jim Thornton and Judith's own physician urged him to go that he began to consider it.

"Honestly, Richard," said Thornton, "I think Judith will be better off for a little vacation from you. You fuss over her like a hen with one chicken. The girl needs peace, and while you hover around and call her up three times a day to see if she's all right, she can't have it. Turn her over to Powell here for a couple of weeks. He won't let anything happen to her. He's pulled my wife through with three babies.

So at last Richard yielded with the understanding that either Dr. Powell or Thornton was to send him a letter every other day while he was away. His last night at home before starting west he always remembered as a nightmare. He lay in bed thinking that Judith might be taken ill while he was in Seaforth, that she might have a premature delivery, that she might die. For women did die sometimes, even with modern obstetricians.

Driven out of bed by these imaginings, he stole into the hall and crept along it to Judith's door, where he stood straining his ears to hear her breathing. The stillness seemed unbroken. He broke out into a cold sweat. What if she were dead now! Softly he pushed open the door and slipped inside on stealthy feet.

In the shadowy half-light he could see her lying on her side, with one arm flung out across the edge of the pillow. About the pale oval of her face her dark hair made an irregular shadow. He remembered how pallor had crept into her olive skin and blanched her lips; he thought he could see the patch the surgeons had shaved on her head before they operated; he recalled the thinness that had turned the soft curves of her neck and shoulders into faintly angular lines, the swelling that had gradually made her body grotesque in contour.

Trembling, he bent over her. Even now her shallow breathing was barely audible, but it told him she was alive. If at that instant he had not remembered Thornton's dictum that Judith needed a rest from his constant solicitude, he would have fallen on his knees beside her bed, but—remembering—he stood looking down at her with eyes in which compassion had replaced every other feeling.

This was the outcome of the love he had for her, his passion had brought her to this and must yet bring her to more suffering before their child was born. It was terrible, abominable! And yet even now he realized that the pity with which he looked at her was but one step removed from passion. Helplessly he rebelled at that conviction. Must human beings, he asked himself, always be slaves to their emotions, unable to control their lives? Must the hunger of the body always drive men to choose between seeking gratification from women whose persons were for hire and satisfying their desire with the women they loved and whom their love condemned to this? For a passing moment he saw chastity as more splendid than any passion, however great.

Noiselessly he tiptoed out of Judith's room and back to his own, but he was too restless to sleep. He wedged a pile of pillows against the head of his bed and tried to read himself into drowsiness. There were many books about, he turned them over one by one. "The Story of Philosophy," "Island Within," "Death Comes to the Archbishop," "The Bridge of San Luis Rey" were one after another discarded. At first "The Greene Murder Case" seemed more engrossing but it too was soon thrown on the floor beside the others. None of them had any thing to say to a man in a crisis like his; they seemed to him unreal, detached from life.

He switched off the light. Through his restless mind rushed unrelated bits of news, fragments of newspaper stories: Lindbergh's flight to Paris, Chamberlin and Levine's trans-Atlantic flight and Byrd's, the epidemic of marathon dances and flagpole sitting, the "rackets" that were invading the front pages. Somewhere he had heard that Al Capone controlled an annual revenue of sixty million dollars from liquor alone. What would he do with that much money? First of all, he would keep out enough to live on while he tackled the next research problem he had in mind, then he would take Judith to some cool place for the rest of her pregnancy and buy her a Model A Ford—in "Arabian Sand"—and salt down a few thousand for the son about to be born. He would . . . But here his imagination ran down. He had such simple tastes and so little experience with surplus money that he could not even imagine what to do with it.

Then it occurred to him that he might build up an organization for distributing liver extract free to people who could not pay for it. Only when the gray light of early morning began to filter into the room did he comprehend that he had been giving the sort of exhibition he had often ridiculed in young husbands whose wives were going through their first pregnancies. How he had laughed when these conscience-stricken young men vowed there would be no more babies! He could remember telling them sardonically that one baby a year was close enough together.

Something about this flash-back into his country practice aroused the sense of humor that had almost stifled during the night, and Cameron grinned sheepishly to himself as he reached under the bed for his slippers. After all, he reflected, he was no better than other men and Judith herself was not without her share of passion.

III

When Richard was very young he had dreamed of going back in triumph to the small town where he had attended high school and driving through its streets in a large red automobile with the top down, staring arrogantly at the inhabitants who in turn stared admiringly back at the great man who had once lived in their midst. Later he had visions of returning a mighty African explorer, and still later of becoming a public health hero like General Gorgas or Walter Reed.

Now these crude aspirations had taken the subtler form of envisaging the expression on the faces of certain people whom he disliked as they read articles of his or saw his name in the columns of medical journals. But his return to Seaforth as the featured speaker at the Tri-State Medical Conference was like nothing he had ever imagined.

At the station he was met by a committee bent on dividing his entire stay into segments, each of which was to be allotted in advance to some worthy undertaking with complete disregard of such things as sleeping, bathing, thinking, or resting. By the second morning he had resigned himself to living constantly in the presence of spectators. Wherever he went committees and individuals anxious to have a word with him followed.

Whenever he was scheduled to go anywhere, a car, driver, and escort materialized. At all luncheons and banquets he was placed at the speakers' table and whether his name appeared on the program or not he was asked to "say a few words of greeting to old friends and neighbors." He was amazed to see under his picture in the papers a caption describing him as "a prominent former Seaforth doctor who has become world famous."

In anterooms and corridors country doctors and shabby general practitioners loitered to ask the relative merits of liver diet and liver extract, and in the hotel late at night he was waylaid by anxious laymen who inquired into the advisability of bringing their anemic relatives to Northdevon for his personal supervision. He was interviewed by reporters on whom he turned a baleful eye. "You fellows can't get anything straight," he growled to the newspaper men. "If I typed down what I wanted you to print, either you or the city editor or the rewrite man or some other idiot in your office would make hash out of it. Understand I've got nothing against you personally but officially I'll have nothing to say to you."

He attended every clinic in the city, saw every patient in Seaforth who had pernicious anemia, examined innumerable blood smears for individual physicians. He spoke four times for the medical men and once to a mass meeting advertised in the newspapers and by dodgers flung about the streets. To his surprise he found that he liked the public meeting best of all.

Publicity had brought in an audience of three thousand. How much this was due to respect for science and how much to ballyhoo he did not inquire, but he found the crowd responsive. From the start he had their attention. He wore a rough tweed suit and by contrast with the chairman of the evening who was in dress clothes he made a striking figure on the platform.

When he began to talk about research he forgot himself in his subject. The listeners found something stirring in his tall, loose-moving figure, his long arms and legs, the trace of stubbornness in his face. His flaming red hair stood obstinately on end and when he ran his fingers through it in excitement the crowd felt that Richard Cameron was leading them in an onslaught against disease and death.

He told them about the great adventures in medicine, about the discovery of vaccination and the beginning of the measurement of blood pressure, about the discovery of anesthesia and the cause of infectious diseases. He told them about the men who had conquered diphtheria and diabetes and attacked yellow fever and cancer and syphilis, of the men who had made modern surgery possible and turned hospitals from stinking cesspools of infection into havens for the sick. Carried away by his own genuine enthusiasm he swept his audience with him and gave them a different conception than they had ever had before of doctors and the healing art. The applause that interrupted him over and over would have told an experienced theatrical man that Cameron had all the elements of good showmanship. Tired as he was when he finished, Richard felt a strange exhilaration as he followed the chairman from the platform.

That was the high point of his stay. Compared with it, the medical sessions were tame. Before his four days were completed Cameron wanted to get away from these meetings, all of which were as alike as two blackberries growing on the same bush. He would have enjoyed getting together some of the younger men and some of the general practitioners who were interested in diagnosis and talking to them informally in a question-and-answer seminar, but that was impossible.

Amid all the committees and the excessive politeness and incessant speeches, his encounter with Ascot was a positive relief. One afternoon Dr. Ascot was hurrying toward the auditorium, scanning the program which he had in his hand; he did not notice Richard until the younger man put himself directly in his path. Then, scowling irritably at being delayed, he looked up and saw his former assistant.

For an instant Ascot was abashed. For a long time there had been deep in his heart an unavowed conviction that he had been a fool to discharge Cameron five years before, and he had actually come to the point of admitting to himself, though to no one else, that Richard had proved himself a brilliant man. In this moment of abasement Ascot might have held out an olive branch to his old employee had not his eyes taken in the man's clothes.

A thickening body had not decreased Ascot's liking for suits of bold pattern nor his wife's determination that he should not dress himself in so unbecoming a fashion. Therefore he was wearing that afternoon a modest gray suit of conservative single-breasted cut, a blue tie, black shoes, and a panama hat. When he looked at Richard's loose-fitting brown tweed with its dashes of red and bronze and his heavy tan brogues with gay bronze-clocked socks, and saw his tie of Cameron plaid and the smart white tips of the handkerchief in his breast pocket, Ascot was enraged. He did not credit Richard's tall lean figure or fine gray eyes or animated face for any of his attractiveness. He did not stop to think that the man was not to blame for his build or his features or even for his red hair. He simply gave vent to the wrath that was in him.

"You ... you ... tailor's dummy! Get out of my way!"

Then, as Cameron did not jump at command, "What d' you want? Get out of my way, I tell you!"

Richard had intended to speak civilly to Ascot and ask after his wife, but this reception made that impossible. He grinned down at the angry red face so incongruously arched over by smoothly brushed gray hair.

"Well, at least you're plain-spoken and above-board. Damned if it isn't refreshing, Ascot."

Having said this, he strode on out of the building. That was the last he ever saw of Samuel Ascot, or Ascot of him.

IV

One day the next month after his return from Seaforth Richard was called to the telephone by Dr. Powell.

"Your wife sent for me about an hour ago, Cameron, and I thought it best to send her straight into the hospital. If you can drop in there between five and six, I'll meet you. . . . No, no. Everything's all right. Just safety first, you know."

But when Cameron got to the hospital, he knew that everything was not all right. The labor had begun abruptly and bade fair to be prolonged. Judith's pale face distorted with pain made him feel physically ill, but he forced himself to sit beside her bed and talk quietly with her in the intervals between paroxysms.

Dr. Powell came as he had promised, but soon left.

"You'd better come out and have dinner with me," he said to Richard. "Nothing is going to happen here in a hurry. We've got plenty of time."

But Cameron shook his head. "I'm not hungry," he said.

Powell smiled knowingly. "You do the anxious husband so well that I almost forgot you're a doctor yourself."

Richard had no answer; he had forgotten how he had once chaffed men in the same situation. When Powell had gone, he prowled up and down the corridors getting himself in hand to go back to Judith. By this time he was a familiar figure at the University Hospital and one of the floor supervisors who was a vehement feminist, seeing him pacing to and fro dragging his foot a little, made a grimace behind his back.

"The great Dr. Cameron," she observed to another supervisor, "can't endure the sight of his wife in labor! Wishy-washy I call it. He's responsible for her being here."

Later in the evening, after a careful examination, Dr. Powell ordered an opiate for Judith. "No use letting her wear herself out now. She'll need her strength later on. These dry labors are always hard, especially with a first baby."

Judith became quieter under the drug and her husband sat down in the hard rocker in her room and tried to think rationally about her. He had had his share of difficult confinements when he was in general practice, some of them very much like this. He should be able to draft a sensible program but he found his mind wandering from sound medical facts to unreasonable fears. The danger of hemorrhage haunted him. The labor was sure to be long and there was the danger of prolapse and of the child's asphyxiation. He realized that the pit of his stomach was hollow and empty, that the backs of his thighs were tingling, that his body was covered with perspiration.

"Fool!" he called himself. "Powell will bring her through. He has worse cases than this every day or two."

But this imitation of Coué did not bring tranquillity. On the contrary it made him more restless and worried than ever. Every patient was a law unto himself, each was as likely as any other to be an exception to all rules, averages meant nothing in medicine. Had he not said these things over and over in his papers?

Whenever Judith opened her eyes and looked in his direction he managed what he meant to be a smile but was really only a contortion of his mouth. The hours seemed endless but at midnight when the nurses took her away to the delivery room time dragged still more leadenly. Powell had said he would rather Richard did not come with them and, since he could not bear the sight of the empty, freshly-made bed Judith had just left, he descended the stairs that circled the elevator shaft to the floor where his two small wards were, and found his way toward the little laboratory beside the entrance to Ward B.

The nurse on night duty looked up and then sprang to her feet as she saw who it was, but he nodded for her to sit down again.

"Patients all asleep?" he asked.

"Oh, yes, doctor, hours ago. I haven't had a call since ten o'clock."

Softly Richard stole over to the swinging door that closed off the ward and peered through the glass panel. In the dim light the beds stood with their heads against the wall; in them were ten people who had been very ill but were now on their way back to health. Suddenly a sense of mystification came over him. What was it that made men live and why did they die? What was the strange irresistible force that swept into being the instant conception occurred and struggled to persist in the tissues of the body after death had come? Why was Judith straining in the stupor induced by drugs to bring another human being into the world? Where did life come from? Where did it go? What did it mean, this struggling to live, to give birth?

Those patients in the ward, for instance—how did he know that he had any right to interfere with their lives? How did he know that when he cured them of anemia they would not be worse off than before? Might not the things for which he spared them be worse than those from which he saved them? Was not life a drab existence, hardly worth living?

There was Roberts still kept alive by swine stomach in tomato juice since Mr. Newton of Appelford, South Dakota, had given up his cure. When, as eventually he must, he discovered the deception that had labelled pigs' stomach vegetable purée, would he think the price he had paid for life too great? And there was Mrs. Standish. The very secrecy with which for years she had eaten her nightly snack of *pâté de foie gras* had lent interest to existence, and, now that clandestine indulgence had become prosaic treatment by doctors' orders, the old lady had lost her zest for living.

Was he really doing any good at all? Did any doctor accomplish anything beyond prolonging the time in which people might suffer and be unhappy? Save them from diphtheria and tuberculosis and typhoid fever in order that they might die in old age of Bright's disease and high blood pressure and cancer?

Blindly Richard felt his way past the dimly-lighted cubicle in which the night nurse kept her vigil, into the little laboratory where he had done the early blood work after he was given Ward B. He threw up a window, for the air seemed close and stifling. From the internes' quarters across the street he could hear the wailing strains of "Ramona." Didn't those boys ever go to bed and keep quiet?

He sat down on a stool before his work bench. Here he was surrounded by the familiar instruments of his craft—glass syringes and test tubes and lancets and incubators and microscopes and bottles of indicator solutions and retorts and water baths. But tonight they seemed as alien as though he had never used them. They were only the crude weapons with which blundering human beings tried to turn Fate aside.

Mechanically he pulled the microscope toward him but the world of the inconceivably small which that instrument would make it possible to see seemed as unreal and fantastic as life itself. He pushed the 'scope away and sat staring out into the gray dusk of the autumn night, listening to the distant rattle of street cars and the purr of passing motors.

Here at six o'clock they found him and told him that Judith's baby had been born dead but that she was out of danger. That, he told himself, was as it always had been: life gave birth to death.

CHAPTER II

I

Cameron was writing at his desk, his red head on one side, the tip of his tongue between his lips, when there came a sharp knock at his office door. He called out "Come in" and when the newcomer did not at once obey, he glanced up abstractedly. From the doorway a man whose face seemed to have frozen into permanent belligerence was staring at him. Instantly Richard sprang up.

"Mr. Roberts! I didn't know it was you coming up. I thought the girl said 'Rogers.'" He pulled an armchair up beside the desk and said, "Come and sit down. You look tired."

Slowly Roberts shuffled across the room and dropped heavily into the seat, never taking his little slate-colored eyes off Richard's face. In them there was something so malignant and implacable that Cameron felt gooseflesh come out on his back, but simultaneously his professional acumen took note of the man's lemon-yellow skin, his shortness of breath, the erratic movements of his arms and legs as he walked. It was plain that he was in another relapse of pernicious anemia.

His physician's instinct made Richard ask quietly, "What can I do for you, Mr. Roberts?"

The sick man braced himself, planted his feet on the floor as firmly as he could, and seized the arms of his chair in shaking, pasty-yellow hands.

"You can listen to the truth, young man. For nearly three years you have deceived me. I told you over and over I would rather die than live on animal flesh. I should have known better than to take your 'vegetable purées' and 'fruit cocktails.' I always distrusted you and now I know that my suspicions were justified."

Roberts paused for breath. His gasping inspirations drew his flabby yellow cheeks into hollows and pulled taut the muscles of his neck, but although he panted until beads of sweat stood on his face he glared furiously at Richard.

"First you tried to bully me into eating liver. You ground it up in orange juice and tried to force it down me. You told me cock-and-bull stories about animal proteins being superior to vegetable proteins and man being poorly equipped to digest plant tissue. Oh, I remember what you said all right."

There was an overtone of scornful triumph in Roberts' voice as he said these words.

"You had some infernal theory or other you wanted to prove and you meant to use me to do it. You didn't care about me. And when you brought me that sickly sweet, green stuff you said was a purée of vegetables, you finally succeeded in fooling me. I took it."

"And you improved. You hadn't been as well in years as you were when you went home from the hospital that time." There was the barest trace of amusement in Cameron's dark gray eyes.

"That," shouted Roberts as loudly as his weakness would permit, "has nothing to do with it. You lied to me, you deceived me. I believed what you told me and took that stuff every day, thinking it was made of vegetables. Then you sprang that 'tomato juice cocktail' on me. Tomato juice, the nurse said, that 'had been treated with hydrochloric acid and certain enzymes.' Those were her exact words, Dr. Cameron. Don't deny it."

"I won't," said Richard drily. "I see that you have an excellent memory."

At this Roberts scowled so savagely that Cameron resolved to make no more ironical comments. The man was old for his years, he was about to die, and whatever he said must not be held against him. Richard leaned far back in his chair and locked his hands together behind his head, tilting his face up until he could not see the old man. But he could still hear the sharp little hissing sound of his labored breathing.

"I resent your systematic deception, Dr. Cameron. I resent it deeply. There was no excuse for it. There is never any excuse for lying."

"Oh, come now, Mr. Roberts, that's a sweeping statement. There are times when a fellow must lie if he is to be a gentleman, and I believe it is justifiable to deceive a person in order to save his life."

"Yes, your profession teaches that." Roberts conveyed by his intonation what he thought of physicians. "And it may be that you are honest in thinking so." This admission seemed to imply a certain grudging respect for Richard. "But the point is that you haven't saved my life."

"What do you mean?" Cameron started and looked sharply at Robert.

"Three months ago I found out that the 'tomato cocktail' I had been taking since I left off Mr. Newton's remedy consists of swine stomach mixed with the juice. Since then I have taken none of the stuff. I am in a relapse and I shall die very soon. I know that as well as you do. But I prefer it to eating the flesh of animals."

Slowly the man pushed his body upward, bracing his arms on the sides of the chair and steadying himself by clutching at the edge of the desk. Even this exertion fatigued him so that his breath came short and fast.

"I resolved to come and see you, Dr. Cameron, before I am too weak to get about. I wanted to tell you that your deception had come to no good, I wanted you to know that you had not saved my life . . . with your liver and pigs' stomachs."

Roberts seemed to gather all his powers together, he put on his hat, fixed his eyes on the door and staggered toward it. He did not look back, he walked out with his back defiantly erect.

After he had gone Richard found himself in turmoil. He felt he ought to try to get Roberts back into the hospital for a transfusion, he reproached himself for having deceived the man and causing him so much mental suffering; but at the same time his native good sense told him that Roberts would certainly refuse hospitalization, that his response to predigested beef and powdered swine stomach had played an important part in developing the anemia treatment, that he was a misguided fanatic. But, strangely, out of this welter of emotions and convictions, there emerged this fact—he had a profound respect for the intrepidity with which the foolish old man stood by his principles. After all, Roberts—dying for his unalterable beliefs—was no more futile a sacrifice to false gods than the soldier fallen in the delusion of patriotism.

These uncomfortable thoughts drove Richard from his work. Now that Judith was no longer at the Institute he had but two places of refuge there—Jim Thornton's office and the animal rooms. This morning Thornton was busy with his secretary, so Richard invaded the animal rooms in search of DiPallo.

It was now six years since Joe had begun the liver diet and good health seemed to radiate from his flashing brown eyes, his dark face, and white teeth.

"How are things with you this morning?" asked Cameron, putting a warm hand on DiPallo's arm.

"Fine." Joe smiled broadly. "I got a boy last night. Sure enough. I ain't foolin' you." Into his smile crept a tinge of slyness. "That's doin' pretty good, ain't it? I been married just eleven months. I guess old Doc Steinberg'd have a fit if he was to hear about it.".

Richard gave the man a little shake. Stockily built, with wide shoulders, thick chest, and powerful arms, DiPallo did not look his forty-five years.

"Joe, you're my prize patient. Always were, always will be. Are you glad you ran into me out in Seaforth?"

"Am I? Say, I eat everything I want, feel fine all the time. And now I got a kid and maybe more comin' after while. And I'd been dead and buried if it hadn't been for you."

Heartened by the sight of DiPallo as much as by his good news, Cameron went back to his work, balancing Joe's happiness on the opposite side of the scale from Roberts' dour determination to die for his principles. And before night another weight was added to DiPallo's side of the balance.

Richard was just about to leave the Institute when his phone rang and the switchboard girl announced two callers for him.

"They won't give me their names," she said in a puzzled voice. "They say to tell you they are 'a couple of . . . co-operative guinea pigs.'"

Cameron began to laugh. "It's all right. I know them. Send them right up."

The Worden brothers were still plump and middle-aged, Oliver was still bald and Thomas still wore his toupee. But their faces were no longer pasty or yellow and both of them had an air of vigor and well-being. When they saw Richard waiting for them, they smiled broadly.

"Dr. Cameron," said Oliver, the spokesman. "The guinea pigs from Nebraska salute you. We're here to report for inspection and to find out whether we'd better stay with dried pigs' stomach or switch to liver extract."

The infectious good humor in the twinkling blue eyes of the two brothers brought a grin to Richard's face. He drew them into his office, he sent for Thornton to come and see them, he took blood counts, and when the reports came back from the laboratory, he announced with pride that each of them had a normal red count and normal hemoglobin. Then in his turn he was regaled with accounts of practice in Nebraska, how the Worden brothers, by virtue of their personal contact with him, were regarded at home as authorities on pernicious anemia. Finally, he took them to meet DiPallo. All three men took a genuine interest in one another but Joe was so anxious to see his new-born son and his wife that he did not stay long.

"Why not form an alumni association?" asked Thomas suddenly. "There's a hay fever society and all kinds of..."

"The Amalgamated Order of Liver and Swine Stomach Consumers!" cried Oliver. "When you do have an idea, Thomas, it certainly is a unique one."

"Well, here are the charter members—DiPallo and the two of us," rejoined the toupeed brother.

As he listened to their good-natured banter Richard found his thoughts going back to John Roberts with his yellow skin, his implacable eyes, and his scornful, trembling voice. He seemed to hear the man shouting at him over and over, "You lied to me ... deceived me ... I resent it ... I prefer to die!"

II

Cameron was not by nature introspective and he was, ordinarily, but little inclined to think of philosophical abstractions. His mind, as Judith once told Jim Thornton, functioned best when it was attacking concrete, external problems. But after this encounter with Roberts, Richard became increasingly restless.

Although he did not understand the whole cause of his disquietude, the truth was that Roberts had only precipitated a discontent that would eventually have come without him. Cameron was a breaker of new ground and he was suffering from the restlessness that in earlier days attacked the pioneer who found he had neighbors within ten miles. The part of the anemia research that most interested him was completed; the refinements of technique and administration and the theoretical studies that remained did not attract him. For six years he had thought, talked, breathed pernicious anemia and now he was tormented by the emptiness of life without an absorbing central endeavor. Day by day he grew more uneasy and discontented.

Now that he did not have to spend every unoccupied moment studying the literature of anemia, he began taking Judith out nearly every evening. At first they often went to the movies, but Richard disliked the talking films that had invaded the cinema so heartily that they soon deserted the screen for the stage. Northdevon was near enough New York to see many of the current plays either before they reached Broadway or after they left it.

The drama had never meant much to Cameron. He had seen a few Shakespearian productions—usually without enthusiasm—and occasional light operas and musical comedies, but he had had no preparation for the hard-boiled plays of this period. An essentially simple man, he was bewildered by "The Trial of Mary Dugan," "Escape," "Strange Interlude," "Porgy," "Journey's End."

One of the things he perceived was that he was hopelessly out of date in regard to sex—pre-Freudian indeed. He had always thought a moderate amount of sexual indulgence sane and healthful. Having fallen deeply in love with Judith, he had made no attempt to seduce her before marriage and had never regretted his forbearance. Now that he was well-mated he forgot the casual carnal relationships that had followed his early affair with Mrs. Darnley. Accordingly he was not a little startled to find so many modern dramatists and writers belaboring sex as a thing that tortured men and women and twisted life into sinister patterns.

He was glad to see that the new books and plays did not glorify war or see in it the romance and heroism earlier generations professed to have found in organized bloodshed. He felt it was essentially truthful to paint soldiering as filled with evil sights and disgusting smells and, in the end, futile, with a consuming desire for liquor and women its only lighter touch. But he thought it peculiar that so many realistic modernists should regard the United States as the spearhead of progress and consider mass production and installment buying an external evidence of America's superiority.

To be sure, he found books that disagreed violently with these complacent views, but their pessimism was so bleak and bottomless that it repelled him. He could not believe that life was utterly devoid of meaning or that there was always something inherently bestial in the relations between men and women. Certain phrases from these modern pessimists struck him so forcibly that he copied them down in his notebook and pondered over them: ". . . promiscuity or asceticism, two forms of death . . . the fruits of intellectualism—My God!—the morning paper, the radio, the cinema, tanks, trinitrotuluol, Rockefeller . . . befouling the whole world."

All the while he dimly apprehended that his disquiet stemmed from lack of absorbing work. Perhaps too much time to brood and not enough hard brain work was what had made cynics of the current writers. And yet what did most people have to occupy their minds except money-making or golf or ditch-digging? No wonder they were narcotized until they believed the ballyhoo of newspapers and advertising men!

And he was no better than they. All his years in college and medical school, in practice and military service, and in postgraduate study, he had thought of little but narrowly personal and professional matters, and for the last six years he had lived in a world of red blood cells and liver and pigs' stomachs. Now here he was, back to the agonizing question of adolescence: What is it all about? What is life for?

Bewildered, he cast about for an anchor, some point of certainty. But he found none. Science was concerned with *How*, not *Why*. Religion told him nothing of either *How* or *Why* that he could accept. Philosophy repelled him: he was searching for a way to live, not for a theory of relativity. He floundered in the shallows of contemporary thought; however great the depths might be farther out, he could not reach them.

Then one day he remembered an incident in medical school. In his class there had been the usual mixture of ordinary minds and brilliant ones and stupid ones. Exasperated by some display of ignorance by one of the yokels, a faculty member turned savagely upon him and said, "The amount of water you can get out of a well depends not so much on the well as on the size of your cup. . . . And you've got a damned small cup!"

Recalling this, Richard laughed outright and thereby drew upon himself the surprised stares of the people packed about him in the street car.

"That's it," he thought. "The size of a fellow's cup. If it holds only a spoonful, he can't build dams, and if it's as big as a steam shovel he can't dig flower beds. Now, my cup is bigger than some and smaller than a lot of others. I can't expect to empty the ocean with it, and so I'm going to leave the problems of the universe to chaps who enjoy fog and moonshine and have bigger cups. I'll go on doing the sort of thing I can do best—finding out things we need to know, like cures for anemia."

Now one of the rites of the Cameron household was to take exercises every night before retiring. Richard had been addicted to this practice since the age of fifteen and the loss of his foot made him all the more determined not to let himself go into a physical slump. After their marriage he had coaxed and bullied Judith into joining him, and each evening they went through a series of bending, twisting, swinging movements. Gradually it came about that this was a time for mutual confidences as well.

So it was that Richard, lying on his back on the living room floor, glanced sideways at Judith. Her hair lay in a soft dark tumbled mass, her lips were parted, and she was breathing a little more deeply than usual. In the dim light he could see the pale column of her throat and feel his emotions stir.

"Judy, would you like to stay here—in Northdevon, I mean—all our lives?"

"Why do you ask that?" she said after a pause in which she carefully and slowly lowered her body to the floor without letting her heels fly up. "Have you got a chance to go somewhere else?"

Richard laughed. "Not that I know of. But I've got a chance to sew myself up to stay here forever."

"What are you trying to do—be cryptic with me?" demanded his wife.

But he was apparently engrossed in pumping his legs like a bicycle rider and it was some time before he looked over at her and, catching her eye, grinned broadly. Then he hitched over beside her.

"A man with a lot of money—one of the 'Main Line' families—is going to endow a Pernicious Anemia Foundation and he'd like me to be the director of it. He's going to put up a building down near Fifer so the laboratories can work together efficiently."

Judith put a warm hand on his. "Good boy!" she said softly.

"It would fix us for life, Judy—in more ways than one. Six thousand a year to start with, and a gradual increase with length of service up to fifteen thousand, probably."

Judith drew a long breath. "Then—we could have a house and a garden and live outside the city, couldn't we?"

"Of course we could. And you could have a car of your own to go back and forth."

"And you could have a study where you could work at home without always being tormented by telephones and door bells. And there would be money enough to buy the books and subscribe to the foreign journals you want."

"And you could have the right kind of clothes, Judy."

In the little pause that followed, Judith thought, "And maybe I could have another baby—perhaps even more than one." But to Richard she said nothing of this.

III

Only a few days after this Cameron received a note from William Clarence Rupert, manager of the Cloverley division of Pan-American Chemicals, asking him to lunch at the Commonweal Club the following Saturday. This invitation surprised Richard not a little: since the initial difficulty regarding Liver Extract #279 his relations with Rupert had been far from pleasant. Rupert was the sort who effectively boot-licks superiors and bulldozes subordinates while he regales fellow executives with accounts of his prowess with both the other groups. He had consistently denied any attempt to cheapen the extract and he still "pointed with pride" to the historical fact that Cloverley was the pioneer with this product, but he resented any supervision of the extract as it was put on the market, and Cameron's defense of medical control had not sweetened his temper.

"You're honest enough, Rupert, as businessmen go. Now, don't get excited and say I've called you a thief and a liar, for I didn't. But you're in business to make money, not to turn out the best possible liver extract. I know the old rule—'let the buyer beware.' But the buyers of liver extract are not in a position to beware: they're ignorant—most of them—and they're sick. So the doctors have to beware for them."

After a few encounters of this sort, the two men avoided each other, and now Richard wondered what was at the bottom of Rupert's invitation to the haughty Commonweal Club.

"He and I have always been like two strange dogs," he said to Judith as he flung himself into a deep chair in front of the gas-log imitation of an open fire in their flat. "Rupert is an English bull with a thick neck and an undershot jaw, and I'm an untidy Airedale with hair bristling along my backbone. The fellow is up to something, I feel it in my bones."

Judith looked at her husband. His chin was on his chest, his brows were puckered into a frown, and from the crown of his head rose an unruly wisp of red hair. At sight of it, Judith smiled to herself. She had learned many things about this man; she knew he was at once simpler and more subtle than people thought, that he was both young and very old. She felt a sudden desire to protect him from further disillusionment, but she had found that he did not like to be protected, so she contented herself with smiling again at his militant red warlock.

"I wish I knew what Rupert's got up his sleeve," repeated Cameron.

"You won't find it in the gas-log, my dear," said Judith. "I suggest the movies as a more profitable occupation."

But Richard vetoed that proposal. "I don't like Al Jolson and I don't want to hear him croon. The movies used to be dark and quiet and I enjoyed the organ. But now the music is canned and the actors all talk like Northdevon gamins trying to speak Oxford English."

So they played Russian Bank at home and listened to the orthophonic phonograph Richard had inherited from Sandy Farquhar and took their exercises and went to bed at ten o'clock.

Precisely at twelve-thirty on Saturday Cameron walked into the Commonweal Club. Distrustful of his host, he had put on the best suit he owned and worn a tie of his plaid; he told Judith he wanted the moral support of his clan under his chin. He was surprised and not surprised to find that Rupert had a second guest for luncheon—a tall, white-haired man of sixty-odd who proved to be James Wellington Franklin, secretary of Pan-American Chemicals, Inc.

Franklin was everything Rupert was not: slender, elegant, soft of voice, and suave of manner. And his very contrast with the heavy-handed Rupert put Cameron on guard. To his way of thinking there was no legitimate reason why two corporation officials should entertain a research man whose name meant nothing to the general public.

Throughout a leisurely meal in a handsomely furnished private room, Mr. Franklin conducted himself with a nicety matched only by the elegance of his attire. From the breast pocket of his oxford gray jacket there protruded tall, stiff tips of spotless white, in his lapel there was a dark red carnation, his striped trousers hung in faultless creases and broke in precisely the approved British fashion over his pale gray spats. His face was almost benign except when he opened wide a pair of shrewd, pale blue eyes with the hard glint of the bargainer in them.

Franklin appeared to select topics he thought Richard would be interested in. He avowed profound respect for the medical profession and said modestly that he was proud to have a grandson ready to enter medical school. But he felt keenly the passing of the old family doctor such as he had known in childhood.

"There are too few general practitioners today, Dr Cameron. When one goes to a doctor now it is the beginning of a long process. Laboratory work, Xray examinations, diets, tooth-pulling, specialists in this and specialists in that—it goes on and on until the patient is worn out and his pocketbook is empty. Statistics prove that eighty per cent of illnesses can be safely cared for by a general practitioner or left to get well of themselves." He sighed deeply. "Much as I admire the traditions of your craft, Dr. Cameron, I fear that you doctors are yourselves to blame for much of the trouble you find in your practice these days."

Richard smiled at this hoary complaint. Did Mr. Franklin, he wondered, express upon occasion the same profound regret for the passing of hansom cabs and the covered wagon?

"I'm afraid, sir, that being homesick for a simpler world isn't much use. Whether we approve or not, society is being mechanized and the medical profession, being a part of society, must share the process. Mass production is today's gospel. Then why not mass production for the doctors, too?"

Glancing at Franklin's face, Richard saw there a shade of disapproval. "Touched a sore spot," he reflected and turned his attention to the excellent chop on his plate. When he had finished, he said thoughtfully, "I know how medicine ought to be practiced. But for the life of me I can't see how we're to do it that way."

When Franklin politely pressed for particulars, he went further.

"For fifteen thousand dollars or a little less I could equip an office adequately. Then, in order to do my job with an excellence comparable to that of my apparatus, I should see not over four patients a day—or five at most. I don't mean people with a boil or a sore finger, you understand, but those who need diagnosis. That would mean about an hour and a half of my time to each of them. I could take a good history, make a good examination, decide what laboratory work needed to be done, and when I'd finished doing that I would know what was wrong with three out of the four and what, if anything, could probably be done for it. Treatment would follow on other days—sometimes simple, sometimes difficult and time-consuming. But thinking of practicing that way is almost as foolish as dreaming of an honest election in Northdevon."

Richard enjoyed the vexation that had appeared in Rupert's face while he talked and the less overt annoyance in Franklin's. But when the latter deftly changed the subject, he listened politely to the older man's views on modern art and music, both of which Franklin seemed to like even less than modern medicine. Not until the waiter had cleared the table, brought fresh coffee and a box of expensive cigars and closed the door behind him, did Mr. Franklin revert to the earlier topic.

"Physicians make another mistake." he said in his smooth voice, "when they condemn wholesale, proprietary remedies and patent medicines. I don't mean that fraud and misrepresentation should be permitted or that compounds should be allowed on the market that depend on alcohol for their effects. But there are many people who won't go to a doctor until they're half dead."

Richard saw a sort of translucent brightness creeping into Franklin's pale eyes and instantly he was sure that the purpose of this interview was about to be revealed.

"Perhaps, Dr. Cameron, I don't make myself clear. Let me illustrate. I would not countenance the manufacture and sale of a worthless kidney pill, but I would have no scruples about advertising and selling to the general public a pill containing hexamethylenamine. In that way it would reach many people who would never call a doctor."

When Franklin paused, his expression made Richard think of a fisherman who has just put a fresh worm on his hook and sits waiting for a strike. One corner of Cameron's mouth twitched in a fleeting smile but he did not answer.

Rupert broke the silence by clearing his throat loudly. "Mr. Franklin, what you've been saying is intensely interesting to me and I'm sure to Dr. Cameron also." He looked inquiringly at Richard who smiled briefly and nodded. Did this old walrus think he was masquerading successfully as a seeker after truth?

Then the secretary of Pan-American Chemicals launched into an exposition that was first vivid and finally perfervid. There was, he said, a great future for the drug trade in the almost untouched field of popularized medicine. The medical columns in newspapers, for example. Why should not Pan-American research men take them over? They could write the articles and the young women on the office staff could polish them up and edit them for the lay reader. Then there was the matter of mouth washes. The market was flooded with all sorts of fancy-colored nostrums, none of them any good. But a young chemist at the Company's headquarters had just stumbled upon a really remarkable formula. Had Cameron heard of it? ... Well, would he just look over these figures showing how rapidly this antiseptic killed the germs commonly found in the mouth and throat?

Franklin produced from a pocket a mimeographed sheet with long columns of figures and lists of names, among which Richard noticed "Bacillus coli, Staphylococcus aureus, Streptococcus viridans." He lifted grave eyes to the older man's face: there was no use telling Franklin that Staphylococcus aureus did not commonly reside in the mouth and throat. But while the executive had been talking his face had changed: and now the calculating eyes dominated his otherwise benevolent aspect.

There was the radio, he continued, an advertising medium the like of which the world had never seen before, and not yet half exploited. Talks on medical topics—short talks, specially written for the radio audience—could be interspersed with musical numbers—good stuff, not this classical music the public didn't like—and now and then a little discreet publicity for Pan-American as sponsors of the program. If well done, that sort of thing would be irresistible.

Then proprietary remedies to be sold over the drugstore counter to people. Of course it would be better if men and women didn't try to diagnose their own ailments and treat themselves, but they had always done it. Everyone knew that the general public was suspicious of doctors, fearful of that non-existent bogey, the "medical trust." They had always gone to druggists for advice, they always would.

Franklin talked in a persuasive, well-modulated voice and made graceful gestures with his hands to re-enforce his points. The thin column of smoke rising from his cigar seemed an oblation to the god of business, and the uncouth expressions that crept into his speech a part of that god's ritual. Richard found something in the man that fascinated him.

For example, asked Franklin, how many people did

Cameron suppose had gone to doctors and been treated with liver or extract for pernicious anemia? Several thousand, at a conservative estimate. But there were others, perhaps more than that, who had never consulted a physician and never would. Was nothing to be done for them? Were they to be allowed to die, because they were ignorant or prejudiced against the medical profession?

The plight of these unfortunates seemed to touch Mr. Franklin deeply. Something, he insisted, ought to be done for them, something must be done. And presently it appeared what that something was to be. Pan-American was on the eve of putting on the market a liver preparation for direct sale to the public. It would not be precisely the same extract as that sold to doctors, he admitted; it would have to be less expensive in order to return the company a profit and still sell for a price that would ensure a large sale over the counter. But Mr. Franklin was sure it would be made out of liver: as a matter of fact, it would be largely made from the residue left over from the manufacture of Extract #279.

Franklin rose and strolled about the room; as he talked he became more and more expansive. Richard wondered whether this eloquence was due to his powers as a listener.

Bit by bit there grew up in Cameron's mind a picture of Franklin's dream. A huge building, outlined in colored flood lights like a modern Aladdin's castle. Inside it, a broadcasting station handling music and medical tidbits about mouth washes and gargles and liver extracts. Also a medical journalism department, turning out popular, non-technical, medical columns for the newspapers and salting them with discreet references to Pan-American products. A huge, moving sign— "Pan American Chemicals, Inc.—The Greatest Drug Company on Earth!"

And somewhere in this vast hive of business, desk room for Richard Cameron, an obscure doctor who long ago stuffed raw liver down sick people's throats and thereby paved the way for the marvellous preparation to be had today by anyone for an insignificant price. He too would lend his feeble luster to Pan-American's glory. Tucked in among these verbal geysers, he heard something about his formal approval and endorsement of the liver product to be sold direct to the public and his permanent retention as a consultant in the research department.

"You know, Dr. Cameron, slogans are indispensable in merchandising today. Look at 'Uneeda Biscuit.' Now, I've been trying to think of some for us. 'Live with Liver' isn't bad. Or, 'If your bone marrow fails, think of liver.' But that might make people think more of eating the meat than buying the extract. We must have as attractive a trade name as we can. Some of the fellows suggested 'Liverine,' but that seems a little undignified."

Strolling about the room, Franklin came to stand beside Richard.

"Won't you have another cigar, Dr. Cameron? Better take several. I have these specially made for me in Cuba, you know."

Between his fingers Richard felt something that was not foil. He looked down. In his palm lay an oblong piece of paper—a check made out to bearer and signed James Wellington Franklin.

Cameron flushed a brick red, his freckled fingers jerked as though to crumple the check, then suddenly stopped. The other hand which lay on the table turned white over the clenched knuckles.

"Mr. Franklin, it was quite unnecessary to bribe me—and quite useless."

The older man looked up and frowned deprecatingly at the word "bribe." Over Rupert's face flashed a mixture of incredulity and "I told you so."

"You want me to endorse your 'Liverine' or whatever you decide to call it, and you're ready to pay me for that and for other services I can render you. But I'm not for sale and I won't endorse your stuff."

Richard had not raised his voice but it seemed as loud as though he had shouted.

"I may starve, and so may my wife. But I won't do your dirty work for twenty thousand dollars or a hundred thousand. If you think I'd polish the seat of my pants writing advertisements and radio blurbs for you when I might be at work in a laboratory somewhere, you're crazy!"

"But, my dear Dr. Cameron, you misunderstand. Let me explain. I . . ."

Franklin's face was white and distressed, his bargaining eyes were downcast.

"No, I don't misunderstand. I know exactly what you want. And I hope I made my answer equally clear." Then Richard noticed the direction of the other man's oblique glances. "Oh, I see. You want the check back. . . . Well, don't worry about your money, Mr. Franklin. I'll keep the check safe and send it back to you by registered mail on Monday—after I've had a photostatic copy made of it. Just for reference, you understand. It might come in handy sometime. You can't ever tell about things like that."

Rupert stirred himself, his fat face red with indignation.

"What did I tell you, Franklin? This guy is a damned fool. You can't talk business to him about anything."

Slowly, with all the ease and carelessness of movement he could muster, Cameron rose from the table, buttoned his jacket, ran a smoothing hand over his hair. In the softly-lighted room it shone like burnished copper.

"I'm sure I can find my way out alone, gentlemen. Please don't disturb yourselves. . . . And let me thank you not only for the luncheon and the excellent cigars, but also for the glimpse you have given me of modern business methods. The more I see of them, the gladder I am that I'm a doctor."

With one hand on the door latch Richard stopped to look back. Something in the startled faces and slumping shoulders of the two men still at the table made him remember the committee from the Society for the Prevention of Cruelty to Animals in Seaforth. He opened the door gently and went out, laughing softly to himself.

CHAPTER III

I

Little by little Judith came to know that her husband was increasingly unhappy. The discontent that had come upon him did not disappear when the Pernicious Anemia Foundation advanced to the blueprint stage. Instead, it seemed to grow worse. He made innumerable objections to the architect's drawings which, he said, might do very well for a department store but certainly would not fit a research laboratory.

Rumors of the new project having begun to circulate, the mail was filled with letters inquiring about openings with the foundation. "These fellows are pathetic as hell," said Richard to Thornton one day. "Some of them have failed to make a go of private practice and want the shelter of a salaried job, and others have always had a hankering to do research but never managed to get into it. And there are young chaps who haven't any money and can't see how to get into practice for themselves. I'd like to know whose job it will be to turn them down. I hope not mine. But there'll be only three or possibly four men on the staff besides the director and the technicians, and there are over thirty applications in now, before any actual announcement has been made. There'll be a thousand when the news really breaks."

Then the second ward at the University Hospital which he had used in investigating liver extracts was commandeered for a man who was studying the effect of diet on epilepsy, and Cameron was left with only Ward B. The work there was now practically identical with the management of pernicious anemia in the clinics at Fifer Institute: it consisted in bringing the patient up to a normal blood count as rapidly as possible and then working out his maintenance dose of liver extract. Richard's assistant, young Dr. Morgan, and Miss Worrall did this so expertly that Cameron felt at times that he was a sort of fifth wheel at the hospital. He often sat in the little laboratory beside Ward B or in his office at the Institute with the plans and specifications for the new Foundation spread out before him and his eyes fixed blindly on space.

One afternoon in late winter when Judith went to meet him at Fifer and found him already gone, she encountered Thornton on her way out. After they had exchanged greetings he asked her how Richard seemed to her those days.

"He's unhappy," she admitted frankly, "about this Foundation. Of course he won't say so; he always insists that he is enthusiastic over the prospects. But I know him and I know that isn't so."

Dr. Thornton looked with warm approval at Mrs. Cameron. He had always liked her and considered her a most attractive young woman as well as a capable one, and since her marriage it seemed to him she was more admirable than ever. There was about her now a gracious composure which assured him that she would manage to live with dignity in a world she knew was not what it ought to be.

"Richard," she went on quietly, "is an intelligent man, perhaps in many ways a brilliant one. But he is not, properly speaking, an intellectual. He thinks best when he is at work, while intellectuals think better than they work. I suppose he's what is called the 'motor type.' He likes concrete problems and distrusts generalities. He will never turn philosopher or write books about religion and science."

Thornton nodded. "I've been watching him and I'm worried. I think you're right about him, even though I wouldn't have thought of putting it just that way. I'm afraid being a director won't agree with him. I get a kick out of executive work, I really enjoy seeing how much I can get done for a little money, and I enjoy fooling bossy trustees who want to run everything. But Richard won't."

Judith smiled faintly. "No. He feels that his work with pernicious anemia is over. He isn't attracted to the sort of studies you're going on with, you know, and the ward at the hospital runs itself now. So life has lost its savor."

Thornton looked meaningly at her and Judith answered the thing he had not put into words. "No, I can't put meaning into existence for him. No woman could. He must have something to do that seems to him as important as the anemia research did six years ago. He's an adventurer—a decent, lovable one—but still an adventurer. That's why he's stalking around, staring into space and forgetting to meet me here as he promised at half-past four."

After Judith had gone, Thornton sat for a long time thinking of her and Richard. She had looked unusually well that day, tall and amazingly graceful. There was eager anticipation in every line of the animated face that rose from the fur collar of her coat. Into Jim Thornton's honest blue eyes there crept a trace of envy. What must it be like to be married to a woman like her?

But things of that sort do not bear too much thinking about and he plunged into the stack of graphs and charts on his desk. For Thornton was still busy with the basic research into the mechanism by which anemia is produced in an animal's body.

II

Long after Judith had gone to sleep, Richard lay awake in the dark listening to her quiet breathing. Now and then he looked at the luminous face of his wrist watch and cursed the snail's pace at which time crawled past. At last, unable any longer to compel his body to lie motionless, he crept out of bed and stole from the room.

In the living room he knelt on the hearth and stealthily kindled a little fire. Its flickering light fell on the papers and magazines Judith had left on the end-table beside her chair. He had told her when he accepted the position as director of the Pernicious Anemia Foundation that they could afford to live outside the city, and now she was deep in plans for their home. All evening she had been poring over architect's sketches and color schemes and wall hangings.

Wrapping his bathrobe tightly about him, Richard flung himself into a chair and stared at the little flames in the fireplace. For months, as he watched the plans for the Foundation taking form, he had been growing more and more restless, and tonight he was insanely unhappy. He saw himself imprisoned in the director's office, dictating letters, interviewing salesmen, bargaining for supplies, hiring and discharging employees, and with his whole soul he loathed the prospect. He remembered, these days, with new sympathy, gentle little Dr. Hastings' nostalgic regret at being out of active research. And yet ... Judith was happy and it was his duty to keep her happy. A man had the right to sacrifice his own ease and comfort if he liked, but it was something else to rob his wife of the things she wanted most in all the world.

Sometimes that winter and spring Richard had felt he could stand this uncertainty no longer. More than once he had been on the verge of resigning from the Anemia Foundation and on one occasion he had even written out a formal declination. But he had not actually resigned, partly because Judith was so openly pleased with their prospects and partly because it was not his way to take his hand from the plow once he had started a furrow.

Finally, just as they were beginning to excavate for the new building of the Foundation, he fell ill with a septic throat infection that kept him in bed for two weeks and left him tired and languid. When he did not recuperate as promptly as he should, Lanister insisted on loaning him and Judith this cottage of his in the rolling border country between Pennsylvania and New Jersey. They had been here almost three weeks and until forty-eight hours ago Richard had felt quite sure he was gradually overcoming his physical weakness and getting the better of the restlessness that had dogged him for so many months.

But, two days before, a letter had come from St. Bartholomew's Institute in Scotland to precipitate mental conflict more violent than ever. St. Bartholomew's was a small research foundation whose director believed that medical investigation ought not to be a laboratory affair but should be combined with the study of clinical disease in patients. Because the liver treatment for pernicious anemia was so conspicuous an example of this type of research, he invited Richard to join the St. Bartholomew staff, although he confessed that the Institute's meager resources prevented his offering a stipend of more than two hundred dollars a month. To be sure, the letter went on to state, there was in addition a monthly allowance of twenty five dollars for secretarial assistance, but even with that the total income would be, not six thousand a year or more, but twenty-seven hundred less their passage to Scotland.

When he thought of this, Richard felt he dared not consider accepting the offer. How could he ask Judith to give up her plans and share the uncertainty of this appointment in Scotland? And yet he did not see how he could bear to refuse it. Leukemia attracted him now just as pernicious anemia had done six years before; it too was a disease of the blood that, like pernicious anemia, was always ultimately fatal. To be back in a laboratory, at a microscope, peering at blood smears, coaxing patients to do as he wished, edging every day a little farther into the unknown—how could he turn away from that to sit in an office and write letters and talk to salesmen and tell men in search of work that there was nothing available? How could he? And yet, if he went to Scotland, he would be robbing Judith of the home she wanted and of the security his salary as director of the Anemia Foundation would bring.

Swaying now toward this decision, now toward that, he sat before the fire while the soft-toned clock on the mantel struck two and three and four. His mind was a stream of pictures and faces. There was Montagu, aloof and unhuman. He would not hesitate to sacrifice anyone or anything for the advancement of scientific knowledge. Montagu was never petty: he simply saw that, compared with research, comfort and happiness meant nothing. Then there was Fergusson: suspicious but shrewd, he would never let such an opportunity slip through his fingers for fear it might go to a rival. And Lanister, with his dark eyes and sardonic face, would vote for staying with the Anemia Foundation; more than once he had said there was no point in making oneself a martyr, because it was never necessary. And level-headed Jim Thornton would agree with Lanister: "Why can't you study leukemia here as well as in Scotland? We worked out the pernicious anemia problem here."

Cameron recognized the force of all these arguments but when he had pondered each of them he found himself still possessed by a burning desire to go to St. Bartholomew's which he could not quench. When daylight sifted into the room he was as undecided as ever and his restlessness drove him to dress and go outdoors.

Lanister's cottage was a low, white, shingled house, set close to the ground; behind it was a garden and in front a lawn dotted with trees and flower-beds. In the three weeks he and Judith had been here, Richard had come to love the place. He had been born on a farm, he had never quite lost his instinct for the soil, every spring he longed to get his hands into the ground. He fumbled in the pockets of his old tweed coat for his pipe and tobacco and, having drawn in a mouthful of fragrant smoke, walked along the winding path, between borders of small whitewashed stones, toward the front gate. He leaned against the gatepost and looked about him; that flower bed needed weeding, he must attend to it today.

Then his troubled gray eyes turned toward the little white house behind its screen of trees. Something about it made him think of the squat, yellow cottage in Custer where he had hung up his sign in 1914. Little houses tempted him, he often looked at them wistfully. They stood for stability. But this impulse to seek security clashed with that other instinct of his to search out the unknown and—until now—security had always lost. How was it possible to want to go to Scotland and at the same time want to stay here, with Judith?

Perplexed by his inconsistency, Richard paced up and down the path. He must answer the letter from St. Bartholomew's before night, he must make known his intention to leave the Anemia Foundation at once—if he had such intention.

At the gate he swung on his heel and faced back toward the east. The sky was deep, translucent blue; the scattered clouds were rose-colored; the rising sun above the wooded hills was blazing, molten gold. Beauty spoke to something deep within him. He remembered he had thought Sandy sometimes ran from things it would have been better to face. Was he, too, going to run away from something he was afraid would be unpleasant? Was he too weak to accept poverty for himself and Judith, or too weak to face the duties of a director? Which was it? If he stayed in Northdevon, could he somehow temper the conduct of the Anemia Foundation with sufficient human kindness to keep it from falling into the narrowness of so many research institutes? These questions he must answer for himself.

"I always think better when I'm at work," he muttered to himself, grinning a little. And, having relit the half-burned tobacco in his pipe, he went for a hoe and garden trowel and fell upon the flower-bed that needed weeding.

Here, at seven o'clock, a messenger boy from the village found him. An early morning telegram did not surprise Richard: several had come during the last three weeks, all of them about details of the Anemia Foundation. Carelessly he tore open the envelope, then—having read the first sentence—he scrambled to his feet and straightened out the flimsy sheet of yellow paper in his hands.

Dr. Richard Cameron,
Sweetwater, New Jersey.

Cable today announces Hestvik prize in medicine for this year divided between you and Jim Thornton. Stop. Cash value approximates forty-six thousand dollars. Stop. Come into town tomorrow. Stop. Two years' leave of absence from Anemia Foundation can be arranged for work growing out of this award. Stop. Have concealed your whereabouts but reporters will soon smell you out. Stop. Congratulations.

Ralph M. Lanister.

As fast as his artificial foot would permit, Richard ran toward the house. On the porch he paused to catch his breath and run a hand over his tousled hair. Then he pushed open the door.

"Judy! Where are you, Judy! How long will it take you to get ready to go to Scotland?"

The End

CPSIA information can be obtained
at www.ICGtesting.com
Printed in the USA
BVHW042045051122
651243BV00029B/445